Doubting
Abbey

Doubting Abbey

SAMANTHA TONGE

CARINA™

This edition is published by arrangement with Harlequin Books S.A. CARINA is a trademark of Harlequin Enterprises Limited, used under licence.

Published in Great Britain 2015
by CARINA, an imprint of Harlequin (UK) Limited,
Eton House, 18-24 Paradise Road,
Richmond, Surrey, TW9 1SR

© 2013 Samantha Tonge

ISBN 978-0-263-91807-6

98-0915

Harlequin (UK) Limited's policy is to use papers that are natural, renewable and recyclable products and made from wood grown in sustainable forests. The logging and manufacturing processes conform to the legal environmental regulations of the country of origin.

Printed and bound by
CPI Group (UK) Ltd, Croydon, CR0 4YY

Samantha Tonge lives in Cheshire with her lovely family and two cats who think they are dogs. Along with writing, her days are spent swimming, willing cakes to rise and avoiding housework. A love of fiction developed as a child, when she was known for reading Enid Blyton books in the bath. A desire to write bubbled away in the background whilst she pursued other careers, including a fun stint working at the EuroDisney theme park. Formally trained as a linguist, Samantha now likes nothing more than holing herself up in the spare room, in front of the keyboard. Writing romantic comedy novels and short stories for women's magazines is her passion.

www.doubtingabbey.blogspot.co.uk
www.samanthatonge.co.uk

Huge thanks to Lucy Gilmour and the Carina UK team for this opportunity and their enthusiasm. Same to my agent, Kate Nash, for all her hard work. Thanks to those writing friends who have unconditionally supported my journey to publication, in particular Caroline Green and Emma Darwin. I couldn't have done it either, without the rest of the WriteWords crew, including Jon Gritton with his technical know-how. Plus I've appreciated input into my writing career from Shirley Blair at *The People's Friend*.

LORD EDWARD'S E-DIARY

Welcome to this blog. Your visit is appreciated. May I introduce myself—I am Lord Edward, the son of the Earl of Croxley. Our home, Applebridge Hall, is in the final of the *Million Dollar Mansion* competition. For regular updates of our progress, please do grace this blog with your presence.

Monday 27th August

7p.m. Good evening, readers. Finally I write my first entry. Do bear with me, as I am new to blogging, which I see as a modern twist on my ancestors' habit of keeping journals. The programme-makers insist you will be interested in my thoughts on the competition, so I shall attempt to bring honesty and some perspective to this diary.

Honest thought number one? Chaos has descended. The film crews arrived again today—cue a refresher course on camera and sound procedures. A national tabloid interviewed Father. To my irritation, the photographer suggested we both wore monocles and borrowed a cluster of the Queen's corgis. Regardless of the fact I don't know Her Majesty, my response equalled 'over my dead body'.

Some perspective? I await a phone call from my, um, dear cousin, Abigail Croxley who, I'm sure, will confirm her intention to join us imminently. How we intend to beat the other finalist, the Baron of Marwick Castle, is still top secret. However, here is an exclusive clue: my cousin's cooking knowledge will be an instrumental part of our tactics. I am very much looking forward to seeing her.

Best bit of today? Right now, sitting by myself in our tranquil library.

Worst? Gaynor, the director, handing me a DVD of *Pride and Prejudice*, along with a frilly white shirt and breeches. I made it quite clear that I am a down-to-earth gentleman who will *never*, under any circumstances, resemble some sort of romantic hero like Mr Darcy.

CHAPTER 1

Abbey was born to sophistication, whereas I was more Barbara than Buckingham Palace Windsor. The two of us had just got back from a goodbye lunch with our Pizza Parlour colleagues, and were standing in front of the bathroom mirror. Having toasted each of our redundancies, I felt a bit tiddly, but still sharp enough to realize this idea was bonkers.

'Look, Abbey, I don't know what's behind this plan, but seriously...' I smiled '...wise up. I could never trick people into thinking I was you, a member of the aristocracy. Ask me to mimic a...a pop star or footballer's wife, then I'd give it a shot, but even then I dunno if I could live a lie for very long.' With a grin, I shrugged. 'Run this idea past me again.' Perhaps I'd misheard.

Abbey's bottom lip quivered. 'It's...um, no joke, Gemma—please, pretend to be me. Just for two weeks.' Her cheeks flushed. 'Who else could I trust with such a mission?'

My jaw dropped. 'Are you out of your mind? You know I'd flog all my make-up and fave shoes on eBay if it meant helping you get out of a scrape... But this? Abbey, mate...' My eyes narrowed for a second. 'Marcus next door hasn't given you one of his funny-smelling cigarettes has he?'

'Goodness, no!' Abbey's face broke into a smile. 'Honestly, I quite understand your apprehension, but...'

She fiddled with the waistband of her skinny white trousers. 'It'd only be for a fortnight and it is in a good cause.' She took my hands and squeezed them. 'Oh, please, Gemma. You're the only person in the world who can pull this off. Remember when Laurence, the son of one of Mummy's friends, stayed over a few weeks ago?'

Ooh, yeah. Hotter than Dad's chilli con carne, he was, in that white scarf and tux.

'He caught you fresh-faced in the morning,' she said, 'and insisted we looked terribly alike. If you dyed your brunette hair blonde, he joked we could pass as sisters, what with the same shape nose and blue eyes.'

'He must have still had his beer goggles—or champers shades—on.' I let my hands drop from her grip and looked down at my skimpy skirt, the streak of fake tan and high-heeled shoes. 'Mind you…' I giggled '…remember my first day at work?'

Abbey leant towards me and joined in the laughter. My chest glowed, glad to have cheered her up—but then it *was* funny, me being mistaken for her. Several members of staff had thought that Abbey—who already worked there—had suffered some sort of identity crisis and undergone a chavvy makeover. Or, in their opinion, make*under*. I should have been insulted at their relief when she'd turned up looking her usual sophisticated self.

'Even the regular customers were fooled.' I turned to the bathroom mirror for a moment. Personally, I couldn't see a strong resemblance but time had taught me that the world at large occasionally considered us each other's doppelgänger.

Abbey's grey-haired aunt came in, picked up a bottle of cleanser and passed it to me. 'Do hurry up, Gemma—we only have ten days to complete your transformation.'

A bubble of laughter tickled the inside of my chest. Really? I mean, *really*? This wasn't a wind-up? To humour them, I removed the make-up from half of my face. Minus one false eyelash and a cheek of bronzer, I resembled an unsymmetrical Picasso portrait.

I leant towards Abbey and whispered, 'Come on, spill—tell me what this is really about and what *she*'s actually doing here.'

'*She* has a name,' said the old dear, who clearly had bionic hearing and a strict dinner lady stare.

'How rude of me not to introduce my aunt formally,' said Abbey with a sheepish smile at the old dear. 'Gemma, this is Lady Constance Woodfold, my mother's sister—she used to run her own finishing school.'

'I'm sure you'll look delightful without all that bronzer, Gemma,' said Lady C (posh titles were too long to say in full, unless you were Lady Gaga). 'Surely your mother would prefer to see your skin au naturel?'

'No idea. She um…' I cleared my throat '…Mum got ill when I was little and…'

Lady C's cheeks tinged pink. 'Do accept my apologies. Of course. Abigail told me of her demise.' Her wrinkled face softened. 'Was there no female relative on hand during your formative years?'

I almost chuckled. Didn't people only speak like that on old BBC news reels?

'Auntie Jan's cool. If it wasn't for her, I'd know nothing about clothes and make-up. People always mistook me for a boy, as a kid. When I hit the teen years, she intervened and even bought my first chicken fillets.'

'She's a proficient cook?' said Lady C, brow furrowed.

I grinned. 'They're the inedible kind that you stick down your bra, to up the cup size.'

Lady C pursed her lips. 'Those fake appendages must disappear, along with your heavy eye-liner. Then we can concentrate on the more important things you need to learn, like the art of good conversation and table manners.'

Huh? What *was* all this about?

The old woman glanced at Abbey. 'Does Gemma not know yet that your Uncle James is in the final of *Million Dollar Mansion*?'

'*Whaaat*?' I almost choked on the word. 'Your dad's brother? The one who inherited the family home— Apple…?'

'Applebridge Hall?' said Abbey. 'Yes. That's him.'

'Amaaaaaazin'! I saw a clip of that programme! Castles and Tudor mansions and all sorts competing against each other to win a million dollars to set their place up as… what did they call it? *A going concern*… The dosh is up for grabs from some American billionaire obsessed with *Downton Abbey*. But how…? What…?'

'All you need to know at this stage, dear,' said Lady C, 'is that Abigail is expected to help out with some catering project—no doubt serving cream teas in some shop they've probably constructed within a converted part of the estate. With its exciting armoury and dungeons, the Earl believes the opposition, Marwick Castle, could win. The Croxleys have owned Applebridge Hall since the sixteenth century, so must build on its strength of history, tradition and… family values.' She stood up straighter. 'Abbey is unable to go. That's where you come in.'

'Me? On the telly?' Wow. So it wasn't a joke. I bit my thumbnail. 'Much as I love reality shows, the last thing I'd want is to be on screen. It's bad enough in real life, worrying about spots and bad hair days, let alone in front of the whole nation.'

'But people won't know it's you,' said Abbey. 'Not even my uncle, who hasn't seen me since I was nine, when he and Daddy had words. My parents will be away on a cruise and my friends don't watch such programmes. Even if they do, more than once, people have mistaken us for each other. It's a foolproof plan.'

'What about Rupert?' I said.

'I've discussed the matter with him,' said Abbey. 'You know my little brother—he's jolly loyal and won't say a word. He understands my reasons—and, by the way, thinks you'll do a wonderful job.'

'Didn't your uncle ask for him to help as well?'

'Yes, but Daddy said no way, what with his final year at university coming up. Rupe's already left for Cambridge early. You know him—never happier than when his head is stuck in some book about the history of art.'

I stared at her. What had happened to my honest flatmate, who was straighter than hair squeezed through ceramic stylers; as upright as a sentry box guard? Although she had a point and, apart from lush Laurence, no one had seen me without make-up, for years—even boyfriends, as I lazily went to bed with my slap on. 'But why would your dad want you to help, if he and his brother haven't spoken for so long?'

'You should have seen Daddy when he asked me—he blew his nose and pretended it was hay fever...' Abbey's voice cracked. 'I suspect he desperately wants to end the estrangement.'

'So why can't you take part?'

Subtly made-up eyes all droopy, Abbey sighed. 'It's a long story.'

I squeezed her arm. Bezzie mates we were, even without much in common, apart from loving novels and Scrabble. A lump formed in my throat. Abbey had never been one to veer from responsibilities, so the reason she couldn't help her family out had to be a mega-serious one.

'You... aren't ill, are you?' I said, eyes watering, trying to imagine life without my best bud. Who would listen to me wittering on about the latest lad I fancied? Who'd give me the best hugs at moments of true crisis, like last week when I missed out on getting those designer platform boots in the sales?

'It's Zak... He wants me to travel to Africa with him immediately. The orphanage he helped build there last year in Rwanda is in turmoil. It's overflowing after more beastly violence. There are hundreds of children orphaned or who've lost their parents. Time is of the essence.'

'But why you?'

Abbey shrugged. 'In pockets of the community they speak French, which I'm still almost fluent in, thanks to my finishing school days. I also took a course in childcare. Zak says I'd be a useful member of the team, seeing as I have catering skills as well.'

'Sounds dangerous to me,' I said.

'The organization Zak works for is very well run.'

'But... but doesn't Zak understand that sometimes family has to come first?'

Abbey raised an eyebrow. 'Under these circumstances?'

I sighed. 'No. You're right. Most dads would be chuffed that their daughter was keen to do such charitable work.'

'And anyway...' oh, no—Abbey's voice wavered again '...Zak already thinks I put him second—like last month when he did that sponsored marathon. I couldn't support him because Daddy insisted I accompany him instead, on that trip to France to source new cheeses...'

I nodded. As a catering magnate, Abbey's dad was keen for her to join him in the business. Out of his two children, she was the one interested in cooking. However, it was obvious that the trip had been an excuse. He didn't think minimum wage Zak was good enough for his daughter.

Abbey threw her hands into the air. 'If I go to Africa, Daddy will be forever estranged from his brother—yet, if I don't, Zak might decide his future doesn't include me.'

'Look, Gemma, dear…' Lady C straightened her navy blazer. 'Why don't you and I go for a walk and get to know each other? My niece says you were up for promotion at work—that you were quick to learn and showed initiative. We might both be surprised at how easily you could learn our aristocratic code of conduct. Why don't you pay your parents a visit, Abigail, and find out some more details about this competition?'

Abbey looked at me.

'Guess it's only a walk,' I said and smiled, hoping to see her eyes regain their usual twinkle.

'Right,' said Lady C and smoothed down her grey bob as Abbey left the bathroom. 'You should change before we go out. One's make-up and outfit should look modest and effortless.'

Surely the aim of looking good was to show you'd gone to a lot of trouble?

With a shrug, I went into my bedroom and browsed through my wardrobe. Little did Lady C know that sometimes I'd dress up in Abbey's new outfits. My flatmate never minded—said it was a good way of seeing what they looked like on her. KMid (translated: Kate Middleton, now the Duchess of Cornwall) was her fashion hero and, I had to admit, some of her jeans with blazers looked awesome. Also, we both liked our future queen's knee-high suede boots, high nude shoes and GORGE long layered hair. Plus Abbey had recently bought some amazin' blusher, supposedly favoured by Kate's sister, Pippa.

Minutes later, I emerged in old jeans, a T-shirt and my only flat pair of sandals.

'Well, that's a slight improvement,' said Lady C, who was waiting in the open-plan lounge. 'If you agree to this proposition, tomorrow we'll go through Abigail's clothes. You're roughly the same size and I brought my sewing kit with me.'

Ooh, that would be a plus—perhaps I'd get to wear some of those sparkly evening dresses Abbey owned. One awesome long silver gown was a copy of something KMid had recently worn to a charity ball, following the birth of cute Prince George.

I shook myself. Get a grip, Gemma, this was a ridiculous plan. How could a few glitzy frocks make up for spending every nerve-racking second of two weeks waiting for someone to see through my disguise?

'Now...' Lady C put on a bright smile '...how about removing the rest of that bronzer?'

I took a deep breath and went back into the bathroom. Five minutes later, just as I was taking off the second eyelash, Lady C joined me.

'Goodness me! The likeness between you and Abigail is quite extraordinary—before me stands a glowing young woman with a flawless complexion and eyes as blue as periwinkles.'

I shrugged and tried to familiarize myself with the bare face staring back at me from the mirror, which I usually only caught fleetingly in the morning. It was like the younger tomboy me who'd watch footie and climb trees to keep up with her brothers.

'Auntie Jan wouldn't approve.' I shook my head. 'This goes against everything she taught me. Without Mum, growing up, at least I had her to point me in the right direction.'

Lady C suddenly suffered a coughing fit. I clapped her on the back and eventually she managed a half-smile. Despite her stern words, with her crinkly eyes and lavender smell, Lady C seemed like the kind of aunt the younger me had longed for. Auntie Jan was more like a fun friend who gave mega hugs but never wanted to let go, as if they were more for her.

'Right, let's go for that stroll,' she said and we headed back to the lounge.

'But what if I bump into a mate, looking like this?' I said. Not that there was much chance of that—Abbey's flat was in one of the posher parts of London. And I know it was superficial, worrying about make-up, but the more natural look just wasn't my thing. Even pets looked better pimped up, in my opinion, like dogs with cute bows and sparkly jackets.

'True friends don't care about appearances, Gemma,' she said and picked up her Margaret Thatcher handbag. 'What counts is your integrity, honesty and kindness.'

Yeah, right. Tell that to the women's magazines, who filled their pages with tips on dieting and how to look younger.

We left the flat and entered the lift. Lady C didn't seem so small now that I'd removed my stilettos. As we exited the building, I squinted in the sunshine, feeling like I was in a bad dream where you wander down the street and suddenly realize you're naked.

'Shoulders back, dear,' said Abbey's aunt. 'Chin not too high or low and stomach pulled in. Don't walk too fast or slow, or appear aimless—a lady always knows where she is going. These quick tips on deportment will have to do for this excursion. What you'll need is several hours balancing a book on your head.'

'That only happens in the movies, right?' I grinned.

She arched one eyebrow, then, as we passed a hairdressing salon, tested my ability to hold what she called 'a suitably civilized conversation'. We started with the weather.

'Um…hasn't the sunshine been lovely lately,' I said. 'Aren't you mega hot in those tights and that blazer? After all, we're still in August.'

Lady C almost choked. 'Don't ever mention something so personal and, whilst I think about it, also avoid religion and politics and gossip—'

'But…'

'No interrupting either. Remember people's names, compliment them, don't raise your voice or ever show emotion.'

Whoa! At this rate, I'd need to take notes.

'Keep yourself informed, Gemma. Read the papers,' she said as I stopped to look through the window of my favourite cake shop. 'Let's see what you know about this year's news…'

Reluctantly, I left the yummy chocolate éclairs and we continued along the pavement.

'Do you remember what happened with Jordan?' said Lady C.

'Mega disappointing, wasn't it, when she didn't get back with Peter André?'

Her brow wrinkled deeper than usual as we turned a corner. 'No, Jordan's in the Middle East; it's a place, not a person. Let's try something closer to home… The Double Dip.'

'That new ride at Alton Towers?' I said as the cheeky street cleaner pushed his trolley past and gave me polite look instead of his usual leer.

'I was talking about the recession. Don't you ever read the papers?' Lady C let out a sigh as I led her off the main road and through a small park. 'Failing current affairs, ask people questions about themselves, but nothing too probing.'

Easy. 'So, did you really own a finishing school when you were mega younger?'

Lady C glanced sideways at me and her eyes narrowed. 'Never allude to someone's age. But yes, it was my own business.'

'Amazin'!' I said, remembering her advice to compliment people.

'Amazin*ggggggg*,' she said and veered to avoid some nettles. 'Or "wonderful" would be better. Don't say "mega", try, "awfully" and, instead of "wow", how about "goodness"?'

I opened my mouth. Then shut it. Goodbye spontaneity.

'What a thoroughly delightful place,' said Lady C as two children ran past with nets and buckets. 'A pied wagtail and nuthatch…Well, I never.'

Clearly, she was some kind of birdwatching buff. Perspiring now, I spotted an ice cream van. Comfort food might help me forget my nude look.

'How about a choc ice?' I said.

'Goodness, no. It's highly impolite to eat on the go.'

Instead, we walked onto a bridge. I picked up a twig and threw it into the stream below.

'Now it's my turn for some questions,' said Lady C. 'What do you do for a living?'

'I am—was—a waitress at Pizza Parlour. We've all just been given the boot.'

Lady C raised an eyebrow.

'Oops, sorry! I mean, *made redundant*.' I coughed. 'Such jolly bad luck but I'm sure, um, another job opportunity will arise soon.'

Lady C's mouth upturned. 'Good, although there's just one problem—remember you are Abbey now. Don't talk about your own life.'

'Okay… I was a head chef at Pizza Parlour and, having gained experience out in the real world, will now join Daddy's company, Croxley Catering. This will offer me a super career.' Abbey used words like 'super'. Plus 'terribly'. And 'silly sausage'. Lady C beamed and I felt all fuzzy inside, like when Dad gave me the thumbs-up for explaining the offside rule.

'But what about you, Gemma?' she said softly. 'Tell me about your aspirations.'

I picked up another twig and lobbed it into the current. 'Dunno—never thought about it really. Would love to be able to cook like Abbey, but, well… As long as I earn enough to pay the bills and have a good time, I'm doing okay.'

'There must be more than that, dear. Self-esteem and self-ambition make a lady. Always aim high; consider the long plan. That's the trouble with young girls nowadays— there's too much living for the moment.' She stared at me. 'You've got a real chance to turn your life around, here, Gemma.'

I couldn't help snorting. 'What, in a fortnight?'

'Life has a habit of throwing opportunities our way.' She smiled. 'Who knows what will happen?'

I shrugged and glanced at an oldish woman, further along the stream, who'd stopped to lean on her walking stick. A young teenager approached her and—oh my God!—shoved her to one side, grabbed her handbag and scarpered.

People all around did nothing and acted as if it had happened in their blind spot. Uh oh. Heart racing… I was having one of my adrenaline rushes that made me do something bonkers.

'Oi!' I shouted and within seconds my legs were carrying me after him. The teenager jumped over some bushes and headed into a forested area at the end of the stream. Just as I caught up, he tripped and fell. Swearing, he got to his feet.

'Hand it over!' I said.

'Gonna make me, bitch?'

Er… yeah. I lunged forward. Years of wrestling my brothers, Ryan and Tom, had stood me in good stead for dealing with over-friendly blokes and now thieves. Except his eyes looked glazed and with an unexpected strength he pushed me off. I grabbed onto the handbag before tumbling onto a log. A male voice shouted behind me and the teenager swore again before running away.

'You okay?'

I turned around to see—wow, a total hunk with an athletic build, all wrapped up in a sharp suit. He was pushing forty but flirty eyes never aged. He pulled me to my feet and, with no short skirt or cleavage to distract him, gazed right into my understated face. I held my breath. The hunk didn't flinch or gasp in horror. In fact, he smiled and carefully examined my forehead.

'Bit of a graze, there,' he said and lifted up one trouser leg several inches to reveal a bandage. 'Sprained my knee yesterday. If it wasn't for that, I'd have nailed that young bast… basket case.'

Blimey—he hadn't wanted to swear in front of me.

Fingers curled gently around my elbow, he guided me out of the trees. Lady C and the handbag's owner were waiting by the edge of the stream.

'Oh, thanks so much,' said the woman. 'I'm so grateful. Let me reward you.'

Yes, please! But I caught Lady C's eye. No doubt accepting a fiver for my trouble would be the height of bad manners.

'No, it was my, um, pleasure,' I said and rubbed my arm.

The hot guy shook his head. 'I'll ring the police. I bet that thug wasn't expecting to be collared by such a charming young lady. Really, well done,' he said.

Gemma Goodwin, charming, without her boob enhancers and bronzer? My face broke into a grin as Lady C steered me towards a nearby bench, moved a discarded magazine and we sat down. I bit my thumbnail.

'Mega unladylike, wasn't it—me running like that, shouting "oi!" I just couldn't stand by and watch that bug…that loser steal someone's handbag. I'd do it again.'

'Jolly glad to hear it. You seem to have this idea that minding one's manners and dressing modestly equates with being, well, something of a lily-livered wimp.' Lady C pulled a leaf out of my hair. 'Whereas ladies display strength of character, they are fair and charitable.' She beamed. 'Quite simply, I was impressed.'

'You, um, aren't disappointed?'

Her eyes sparkled. 'Gemma, my dear, I'm beginning to understand why you and Abigail are such good friends. With a new hair colour and clothes, you could be in with a real chance of pulling this off. I used to run intensive etiquette courses and might just be able to teach you everything you need in the next ten days until the final. Tonight we'll start with table manners. I brought some of the more adventurous foods you might encounter, like asparagus, mussels and quail eggs.'

Urgh! She'd better teach me the etiquette for throwing up.

I picked up the magazine. It was a TV guide for next week. Oh my God! *Million Dollar Mansion* was advertised on the front. I flicked through and came to a full page photo of the Earl of Croxley, a slim, grey-bearded man with a pipe, in a tweed suit. Lord Edward, his son, looked a moody so-and-so, as if the camera was his worst enemy. Yet I could forgive his Victor Meldrew expression because of those tousled honey curls and broad shoulders. *Phwoaar!*

On the opposite page were the other finalists. With dyed black hair greased back and an expensive suit, the divorced Baron of Marwick was in his sixties and looked like his middle name was Smug. His son, Harry Gainsworth, wore a flash tie and mega gold watch. Their family had owned Marwick Castle for less than a century. Both held glasses of champagne and in their interviews called the Earl of Croxley a 'boring old fart'.

Whereas the Croxleys… Once more I gazed at the photo of Applebridge Hall. My eye caught tatty gardens and crumbling brickwork—talk about shabby chic. I read the Earl's warm tales about his grandparents and Elizabethan ancestors—it must be hard for him, all that history suddenly at risk. But could little old me really help save the Croxleys' mansion?

'Shame, isn't it, that Abbey's dad and the Earl aren't on talking terms—that Abbey and Rupert aren't in touch with their cousin,' I said.

'It is, dear. I believe Edward made some attempt to contact them when he was…ooh, almost twenty. Abigail and Rupert were still at junior school. He sent them cards and the occasional book. But Richard never passed them on.'

'That stinks! Does Abbey know?'

'Yes. Richard told the children it was for the best. That they were too young to understand the reasons for the estrangement and what was really going on. The cards eventually stopped.'

Blimey. This was hardcore falling out, not to let the kids at least have contact. Without warning, I sneezed and sniffed loudly.

Lady C tutted and passed me her dainty lace handkerchief.

'See?' I said. 'We could change my appearance—even with my own style and hair colour, I've been mistaken for your niece. But everything else about me is wrong. I talk while I eat and, thanks to Uncle Pete, I know more about brick-laying than cross-stitch or croquet.'

'Ladies aren't stuck in the nineteenth century, my dear,' said Lady Constance. 'Expert knowledge in any area is admirable.'

At that moment the National Anthem blared out from her handbag. That was some ringtone. Lady C took out her phone.

'Hello, Abigail… Pardon? School? Oh, dear. Oh dearie, dearie me. No—don't mention that. Ah, and there's something else…?' A pained expression deepened her wrinkles. 'Yes, quite. What a shame. Leave it with me. Speak later, poppet…' She ended the call.

'Bad news?' I said.

Lady C stared at me for a few seconds. 'Abigail misunderstood the start date of the final. Filming actually begins on September the first.'

'This Saturday?' I squeaked. 'That only gives us four days! And wasn't there something else—about a school?'

Lady C's shoulders sagged. 'That's irrelevant now, seeing as your transformation is quite impossible. Poor Abigail. You were her only chance.'

Uh oh—another adrenaline rush as my conscience pricked. Months ago, Abbey had taken me in, after I left Dad's so that he could turn my bedroom into a nursery for his new girlfriend's twins. Truth be told, I still owed her big time. My heart raced, meaning I was about to do something stupid… Urgh—like deceiving people and pretending to be posh. An uncomfortable twinge pinched my stomach. Yet just one look at Lady C reminded me just how important this was to Abbey. And if you couldn't step out of your comfort zone to help mates, then I reckoned it was what Abbey would call 'a pretty poor show'.

'What the hell,' I heard my sing-song voice say. 'Let's give it our best shot. Applebridge Hall, here I come!'

If anyone could imitate my best bud, it was me.

LORD EDWARD'S E-DIARY

Monday 27th August

'Comments'

10.30p.m. After several pleasant hours of reading, here in my beloved library, I've just bobbed back online to close down the laptop. How extraordinary that already several people have commented—for that I thank you.

Drunkwriter, your poem was…thought-provoking. *Historybuff*, Applebridge Hall was indeed built almost five hundred years ago—by the first Earl of Croxley, who fought against the Spanish Armada. *EtonMess*, close as cousin Abigail and myself are, I, um, don't profess to know *any* of her personal measurements. Nor whether she prefers tights to stockings… For details regarding her appearance, you must wait to see her on the show. Which reminds me of terrific news, blog-readers—she just rang, to confirm her arrival this Saturday.

CHAPTER 2

Ever wondered how it might feel to go on one of those makeover shows where they revamp your look for The Big Reveal? Well, take it from me, you're torn between dying to peek and fearing you won't recognize the reflection at all. Especially when you quite liked the former you—I would miss my rub-in tan and Dairy Milk hair.

I glanced at my packed suitcase as I waited for the *Million Dollar Mansion* car to drive me the hour's journey to Applebridge Hall. Lady C had pinned up my newly dyed, strawberry-blonde hair. The nail polish was clear, the chicken fillets gone and the make-up toned down. Nor did my outfit show legs or cleavage.

I hadn't needed as much help from Lady C as I'd expected, appearance-wise. After all, I'd lived with Abbey for months now and knew just how much mascara she liked to apply to her lashes (think more wiry daddy-long-legs and less furry tarantula).

Lady C yawned and pointed towards Abbey's full-length mirror. We'd hardly slept for the last four days. It was like suffering from an almighty hangover.

'Time to take a look, dear,' she said.

I tiptoed forward. 'Shiitt!'

'Gemma! After everything we've practised this week. How terribly disappointing that you still use that ghastly word.'

'What? Oh…Sorry.' I giggled. 'But it's wicked! I *do* look just like Abbey.' Apart from my cuddlier tum and freckles. I swivelled from side to side, eyeing the knee-length navy skirt and red polo shirt. I wore KMid high nude shoes and gold stud earrings and a little silk red scarf around my neck… There was a definite classy air hostess vibe going on!

'Now, you'll have men fighting to open doors for you.'

I shrugged. 'Why should they? Guys, girls, we're all equals.'

'You think that's how men treated you, in your old clothes?' She smiled and shook her head. 'Right, you've got my mobile phone number, dear. Don't hesitate to ring if you need me. Now, remember, cutlery…'

'Work from the outside in…' I said and gave a big yawn, remembering to cover my mouth.

'And alcohol?'

'Don't clink glasses or get drunk.'

Carrying my suitcase, I left Abbey's bedroom and followed Lady C into the lounge.

'Pity Abbey couldn't drop by to see me off,' I said. 'She wouldn't believe what I look like now.'

'Yes, it's unfortunate she had to take her parents to the airport this morning.'

'At least we spoke on the phone briefly last night. She couldn't stop talking about her trip.' I glanced sideways at Lady C. 'In fact, I didn't have time to ask her what she said to you on the phone, when we were in the park—about a school. Seeing as you can't remember.'

Lady C blushed. 'Oh, er, never mind. Right, let's see… If you are expected to help in say a coffee shop,' she said, changing the subject, 'don't hesitate to contact me if you're expected to bake. I have files of recipes.'

I opened the flat's front door. Roses in her cheeks, Lady C gave me a quick hug.

'The best of British, dear. Now remember, most importantly...'

'The three Ms: Modesty, Manners and no Men.' For some reason my eyes tingled. 'Do you, um, think we've done enough? In such a short time?'

'Hard work can achieve great things, Gemma, and I've been incredibly impressed by your commitment. As long as you don't dunk your bread in soup or chew your hair or—'

'Interrupt people?' I, um, interrupted.

We both smiled and I made my way to the lift.

Right. Get into character, Gemma. This could, in the words of Abbey, be *super fun*! Little old me was going to see how the other half lived. I'd ring bells for coffee, eat off silver and servants would have to avoid eye contact and bow. For two whole weeks I wouldn't have to clean or iron. At the most I'd serve cream teas to the The Little People (previously me!) who, in awe of the Croxley name, would hang on my every word. Although Lady C kept hinting that I might be expected to bake, I was sure the local shops would sell scones and the like—I could just raid their supplies.

As the lift approached the ground floor, I chuckled at the idea of me ordering people around. What was I like? Living like that would be the pits. Hopefully the servants (just saying that word felt wrong) would be like family and I could still make myself Cup-a-Soups and Pot Noodles. The real challenge would be resisting the temptation to tell them who I really was. I took a deep breath. Stiff upper lip, as Lady C would say.

As for servants and bells... well, from what the Earl had told Abbey's dad, Applebridge Hall had suffered from years of financial problems. Entering this competition was a last drastic measure. For getting to the final, the Earl had already won twenty-five thousand pounds, to put into motion plans for how the place would eventually start earning its own keep. I'd said that was a mega amount of money. Abbey soon put me right.

'Oh, no, Gemma,' she'd insisted. 'That's nothing, in terms of running a mansion. Maintenance costs for one year would see that gone—and that's without repairing the roof or completing the rewiring. Then there's damp, rising gardening costs and, as for the internal renovations... Tapestries and ceilings need refreshing and apparently Uncle's desperate to reupholster much of the furniture. Metres and metres of brickwork should be re-pointed...'

Still, I couldn't wait to see the place and strode out into the sunshine.

'Yoo-hoo!' called a voice. 'Abigail Croxley?'

I looked at my watch again.

'Miss Croxley?'

Eek! That was me. I shook myself to attention and looked up. A skinny woman with red hair, carrying a clipboard, waved from next to a big shiny black car, parked up by the side of the road. Chin not too high or low, shoulders back, I strolled over.

'How do you do?' I said in a controlled voice, and held out my hand.

'Oh, erm, good, thanks.' She grinned and grasped my fingers, pumping them up and down. 'I'm Roxy—the production assistant. We spoke on the phone yesterday.'

Stomach twisting, I nodded. What if, face-to-face, my pretend accent sounded weird? But then, after all this time living with Abbey, I stood as good a chance as anyone of mimicking a posh voice.

'We'd better get a move on,' she continued, speaking at top-speed. 'The TV crews at Applebridge Hall are on standby. My boss, Gaynor, the director, hates it if people are late. Footage of your arrival will have to be edited, ready for screening on tomorrow's Sunday night show.' She grinned. 'Welcome aboard the roller coaster that is *Million Dollar Mansion*!'

She lugged my case over to the car boot. I'd never met anyone who spoke so fast. A chauffeur in a smart cap and suit got out and opened the door for me. The only time I'd seen anyone dressed like that was at a mate's hen night, but trusted (nay, prayed!) this old codger wouldn't perform a striptease.

While Roxy got in around the other side, I concentrated hard to get into the car just right. The rules were… legs first, knees closed at all times… Phew. Job done. No knickers flashed.

The door closed behind me. I looked to my left and smiled at Roxy. She ended a phone call as the chauffeur loaded my luggage, got in and we pulled away.

'When was the last time you visited Applebridge Hall?' she asked warmly, while scribbling notes.

'Only last year,' I said, chest feeling all tight. I wasn't used to telling such bare-faced lies and in my mind frantically went over what Lady C called my 'remit'—a mega fancy word for the task I've been given, namely pretending to be one of a happy Croxley clan. In an email to Abbey, Lord Edward said she should act as if the family often met up. All members of staff would play along, as the future of Applebridge Hall—and their jobs—depended on it.

'Recently, I've been terribly busy in catering and am so looking forward to taking time out to visit my uncle again.

I'd be interested to know the arrangements for when I arrive,' I continued, articulating every word as if I was the Speaking Clock.

'Quite a, erm, character, isn't he, the Earl?' she said and glanced sideways at me.

Really? I was dying to probe her further but another of Lady C's rules was never to appear over-familiar.

'Although Lord Edward's not half-bad.' She winked. 'Definite eye-candy for the girls.'

'I wouldn't know about that,' I said stiffly. Uncomfortable as it was, good old English reserve was useful if stuck for words.

Roxy rummaged in her jeans pocket and pulled out some fruit pastilles. She held out the packet. 'I never have time to eat these days—fancy sharing my breakfast?'

'That's very kind, but no, thank you,' I said, remembering what Lady C said about never eating on the go. On the other hand, I didn't want to offend her…

'What a, um, charming bracelet,' I said and pointed to her wrist.

'Oh, ta.' She grinned. 'My fiancé gave it to me.'

'Fiancé? Oh, of course, I didn't see the ring.' It was no Elizabeth Taylor rock, but, nevertheless, a mega diamond to me. 'Amaaaaazin',' I cooed. Oops. I caught Roxy's eye. Her lip twitched. We giggled and then quickly I recovered my stuffy act. 'My flatmate… that's um, one of her words,' I said. 'Occasionally, I pick up these things.'

Roxy examined her wedding finger. 'My boyfriend proposed in New York. Although I don't suppose this compares to the huge pendants and tiaras you've grown up with.'

'The, um, setting is utterly exquisite,' I said. 'It's a ring I'd be proud to wear.'

Roxy eyes crinkled at the corners. She held up her clipboard and flicked through the paperwork quick-smart. 'The arrangements, let's see… Late morning arrival—greetings with family and staff. Then you'll have a little private time before, at one o'clock, your uncle and cousin make a special announcement.'

'What about?' I said.

'The business idea they've come up with, to save Applebridge Hall. Lord Edward has been hinting about it on his blog.' She grinned. 'Gaynor had to work on him for ages before he'd agree to spill his thoughts and feelings on-line. But, to be fair, he's gone for it with gusto and is determined it'll attract more fans and contribute to Applebridge Hall's success.'

Ah, yes—Edward's e-diary. Last night Lady C and I had taken a peek. His tone sounded a bit old-fashioned but, to my surprise, he seemed mega friendly towards the blog-readers.

'And this announcement…?' I said airily.

Roxy's eyes twinkled. 'Don't you know anything about it?'

'No. Cousin Edward, he, um, wanted it to be a surprise.' Better not mention the coffee shop, seeing as other people didn't know yet.

She shrugged. 'Even the crew and I don't know for sure. We've only just returned to the properties, since the preliminary rounds.' Roxy consulted her clipboard again. 'Tonight, at seven, you'll be having dinner…' She shot me a look. 'Look, can I give you a tip, Abigail? Woman to woman?'

'Do call me Abbey,' I said and squished back into the comfy seat. Thank God these media types didn't stand on ceremony. In fact, so far, so bloomin' good. My false accent hadn't been rumbled. This speaking malarkey was manageable as long as I gave it more Toff than *TOWIE*.

'Abbey—you seem pretty down-to-earth. If you really want your family to win...' She threw her hands into the air. 'For God's sake, sex things up!'

'I beg your pardon?' I said in my best plummy voice. Ooh, it was hard not to laugh, but Abbey would have certainly cringed at the S word. Not that she was a prude, but once I'd read out a chapter of *Fifty Shades of Grey*— her eyes bulged so much, I thought she was going to croak and search for a lily pad.

'No offence meant,' she said and shoved another pastille in her mouth. 'It's just that word's out that the Baron of Marwick has something wild planned for this evening. In contrast to your uncle, whose idea of an entertaining Saturday night is sharing good food with friends... That's fine for an earl pushing eighty, but your average reality show viewer wants arguments, intrigue or, even better, nudity.'

'Yes, last year's *Big Brother* was jolly good,' I said. 'Um, so my flatmate told me.'

'She's right—viewing figures topped ten million. One of the housemates got pregnant and the police had to break in and stop a brawl.'

I put on a shocked voice. 'How dreadful.'

Roxy stopped chewing for a moment. 'As you probably know, your uncle is a bit camera-shy. But, to stand any chance of winning, he's got to wake up to the fact that *Million Dollar Mansion* is more than a posh version of *Come Dine With Me*. Marwick Castle is a strong contender—the Baron is media savvy and doesn't much care what he has to do to pull in votes.' Roxy took out another sweet. 'To be honest, the production team was amazed Applebridge Hall got this far, and can only put it down to your hunky cousin appealing to female viewers.' She cleared her throat. 'Not that you heard any of this from me.'

'You can trust me,' I said, concentrating now. 'Thanks awfully, Roxy. I'll do what I can. Your input's appreciated.'

As we turned off the motorway and stopped at traffic lights, she consulted her watch. 'We'll be there before you know it, so here are a few tips. Try to act natural in front of the cameras—as if us TV folk are invisible. There's me and the director, Gaynor, various camera operators and sound guys, some set up in the house. Others will follow you Croxleys around the estate doing your daily business. Just consider us part of the scenery, the fittings and fixtures— discreet, unthreatening.' Roxy gave a wide smile. 'There's nothing to worry about. And you look fab—those shoes are to die for…' Her smile broadened. 'The viewers are going to love you.'

My stomach relaxed. Perhaps I'd been worrying about nothing, I thought, as we overtook a tractor on the dual carriageway and I took in the quaint countryside.

'How many episodes will be broadcast each week?' I asked eventually.

'Three—Tuesday, Thursday and Sunday, at eight p.m. sharp, with the Live Final—a special Saturday show, on the fifteenth, two weeks from today. Cameramen have spent the last five days at both locations, filming a fresh load of stock shots—you know, house exteriors, the grounds…' Roxy smiled. 'Don't be nervous, Abbey. I can tell that you're really photogenic.'

If only my appearance was the main concern, now. The mega hard part would be keeping my act up from sunrise to sunset, with all those TV people around.

Roxy texted madly on her phone for a while until, about twenty minutes later, a car cut in front of us, just as we turned into a road welcoming us to Applebridge. The chauffeur braked and Roxy's clipboard fell on the floor. I collected up the papers as the driver sped up once more.

'Thanks,' mouthed Roxy, who was now on the phone to Gaynor. I gazed out of the window again. Wow. What a tiny village. At a first glance, there was nothing in Applebridge, apart from a post office, corner shop and pub called The Green Acorn—although the place was famous for staging a rock festival on some of the Earl's land every summer. According to Lady C, that was at least one source of income for Abbey's uncle.

I swallowed hard. Not long now to meeting my flatmate's posh relatives and potentially being discovered, on camera, as a fraud. To distract myself, I glanced at Roxy's papers and a list of everyone who'd be filmed at Applebridge Hall. With lots of exclamation marks, the names had been divided into two categories: 'Above' and 'Below' stairs.

I gazed at a photo of sharp-eyed Kathleen, the Scottish cook and housekeeper, and the estate manager, Mr Thompson, with a Sherlock Holmes style hat and hunting gun. Then there was a woman in her thirties, wearing cords and a T-shirt—that was Jean, apparently, the head-gardener. She looked nice. Mmm—her assistant, unshaven Nick, was about the same age as me. Sexy eyes! Not that I'd be able to get to know him well. Imagine the scandal if he and I really hit it off.

Roxy ended her call as the car turned into a drive longer than the street I'd grown up on. We drove past rows of little trees, bearing plump red apples, shinier than Snow White poisoned ones—when we were small, my brothers and I would have had heaps of fun playing hide and seek amongst them. Downhill to the right, as the orchards fell behind us, was a pond with tall grasses and bulrushes on the nearside. Even the ducks were a fancy type, with purple chests and red bills.

My throat felt funny. I felt sick. How could I ever have thought this would work? What if the Croxleys saw straight through me? Perhaps they'd laugh at my choice of words or sneer at the way I walked. Or perhaps they'd be over-the-top friendly and I'd feel even worse about fooling them. Either way, I didn't belong here. Urgh! Deep breaths. Focus, Gemma. You can do this. Think of the positives—it's lush; what an amazin' place to be a gardener.

Mmm, yes, talking of gardeners and that photo of Nick, with his short dark hair and eyes, all twinkly...

Oh My God! Forget the nerves for a moment—I'd just thought of an awesome way to sex up Applebridge Hall! That's what Roxy said I needed to do, right? It was my duty. Sorry, Lady C, but I'd have to ignore the last of the three Ms: 'No Men'. To beat Marwick Castle, the Croxleys had to keep the viewers glued to their seats and now I had a wicked plan!

Oblivious to the scene ahead, as the car slowed, I worked hard to suppress a chuckle. Above and below stairs...The answer to winning was obvious. The nation had to believe that the Earl's well-to-do niece and the gardener's assistant were having a forbidden secret affair!

LORD EDWARD'S E-DIARY

Saturday 1st September

11.30a.m. Today is going to be jolly busy and I've just been informed that my cousin's car has pulled into the drive, so quickly… First of all, thank you to everyone who is already 'following' this blog. The TV company has linked us to their website and several local stations have kindly spread word of this diary. Do please connect us to other social sites—no doubt many of you belong to Facebook.

Right, on now with the business of the day—I hereby formally announce the beginning of the competition. Let me use this domain to officially throw down the gauntlet to the opposition: Baron Marwick, if you are reading this, I declare our very determined intention to win *Million Dollar Mansion*. In the tradition of the Croxleys' duelling ancestors, we challenge you to beat our family's honourable loyalty and values. Or, as a more modern opponent might say: Game on!

Just to add, I've done my research and apparently blogs thrive with plenty of interaction. So what about answering this poser question?

How do you think we have invested our semi-final winnings, in order to defeat Marwick Castle? On…

Machinery to produce our very own 'Croxley Cider'?

Transforming part of the mansion into kitchens, for the 'Applebridge Food Academy'?

Converting the old stables into the 'Croxley Coffee Shop'?

I shall attempt to bob on here later to view responses and briefly comment. On a speedy lighter note, may I respond to *bustyfanDownton*: no, I don't dye my hair, nor can I acquire Prince Harry's phone number—apologies.

CHAPTER 3

Don't call the police, Uncle... I mean, Earl...There's a good reason I'm pretending to be your niece. Mr Thompson, put down that gun!

I took a deep breath. There was no point practising in my head what I'd say if found out. Go, girl! You can carry this off.

I looked out of the window as the car ground to a halt. My brow relaxed. Talk about picture perfect. Clearly I'd snuffed it and this was some heavenly palace or, Mary Poppins style, I had jumped into some painting of old England. Looming before me was the mega grand Applebridge Hall.

'Don't know how anyone gets used to living in a place like this,' said Roxy.

'Me neither,' I mumbled, eyes transfixed. Although my older brother Ryan's gaff was a former stately home—he was staying there at, um, Her Majesty's Pleasure! Mega stupid he'd been, crashing into a parked car while texting.

Wow. Applebridge Hall was huge. Mahoosive. Bigger than Hogwarts. My home for the next week had gardens ten times the size of the sports grounds at my old high school. I fanned myself with Roxy's clipboard, in anticipation of stepping out of the air-conditioned car and into the sticky end-of-the-summer heat. The mansion stood three storeys high and triangular gables (I knew that word from builder Uncle Pete) lined the top, where parts of the roof came forward. Where each one peaked, twisted ornamental bits rose into the air like mini totem poles. I'd seen similar ones in the book on Elizabethan architecture that Lady C had given me to speed-read.

'Remember,' said Roxy. 'Big smile as soon as the car door opens. Cameras will be rolling.'

I think I nodded in reply. Not sure. I was still gawping. Although, this close, you could see why the Earl needed those million dollars. The building was made from reddish-brown stone wall and needed a mega good clean. Mouldy patches covered large areas—lichen, I think. Slate roof tiles had slipped out of position and several of the chimneys were missing chunks of stonework.

Yet, despite the crumbling brick and odd cracked window, it was pretty impressive, from the outside at least. Green ivy sprawled across the front and around the window frames. There was a protruding arched entrance in the middle, either side of which the building stretched sideways for the length of four window bays. At each end, Applebridge Hall extended forward so that, from the air, the building looked like a capital E. A tribute, perhaps, to the seventeenth century Queen Elizabeth, in which case it was just as well English letters didn't look like Arabic or Chinese.

'Ready?' said Roxy.

I swallowed. 'What's Charlie Chingo like?' A washed-up eighties pop star, with his trademark quiff and *Blues Brothers* suit, he'd reinvented himself as a chat show host and was presenting the show.

'A total diamond.' Roxy grinned. 'On screen he behaves like a carefree teenager, but no one works harder—he often hovers around our outside broadcast van, helping edit footage for the next show.'

I nodded and stared at the mansion's many windows. Vertical bars divided them into panes. It would take forever to make them all sparkle. Good thing all I had to do for this fortnight was serve cream teas.

The chauffeur opened my door and, thighs together, I slid out. In front of the car was a three-tiered fountain, overgrown with green slime and moss. Across the lawns, birds chirped and the sound of tinkling water filled the air. A line of people gathered at the entrance. Enough of admiring the estate—it was time to kick off this charade.

The cameraman and sound guy hovered like sprinters waiting for the off. Lord Edward stood in front, looking pretty lush (eek, mustn't think that, he was supposed to be my cousin). His eyes were fixed on me. Members of staff were just behind him, with the old Earl. Nearby, hovered a tall woman with a shiny Jessie J bob, black-rimmed glasses and clipboard.

'That's Gaynor, the director,' Roxy whispered.

Ooh, look at me, *taking directions*, eat your heart out, Hollywood. I was in the ideal reality show, where the real me wouldn't be recognized and I didn't have to eat kangaroo bottom or witchetty grubs. Deep breaths as I almost hyperventilated when Charlie Chingo appeared.

'Come, Chat with the Chingo!' said Charlie and led me towards Lord Edward and his dad.

How could the TV presenter wear a jacket? The forecasters had been right about an Indian summer. Hopefully, I looked around for a tray of refreshing drinks to celebrate my arrival.

'Welcome, Miss Abigail Croxley, to *Million Dollar Mansion*! How ya feeling? Nervous? Excited? Thrilled to be back at the ancestral pile?' Charlie turned to the camera. 'This is the Earl of Croxley's niece, the dishy daughter of his younger brother, catering magnate, The Honourable Richard Croxley.' Charlie raised his eyebrows up and down whilst I tried mega hard not to stare at a furry microphone held above our heads. 'So tell us, Abigail—you must just lurrrve visiting your uncle and cousin. How does it feel to be back in the bosom of your heritage?'

'Indeed, it is, um, an enormous pleasure to return,' I declared. Before my makeover, a friendly man like him would have winked at the word 'bosom' and stared at my chest. Instead, Charlie lifted my hand to his lips and gave it a kiss. The Earl stepped forward and took his pipe out of his mouth. He wore tweed trousers, a checked shirt and tweed waistcoat like in that magazine in the park. Wow. Here was a living and breathing member of the aristocracy. The only group of people I belonged to was the Facebook Primark fan club.

'Welcome to Applebridge Hall, Abigail,' he said gruffly.

A whiff of tobacco reminded me of visits to the pub when I was little, watching Dad play darts and fighting Tom and Ryan for the last pork scratching or peanut.

'Um, hello,' I muttered, feeling like FRAUD was my middle name.

'Speak up, girl,' he said.

'How nice to see you again, Uncle. I do hope you are well. Mummy and Daddy send their lo—' better not overdo it '—their good wishes.' Before I knew it, I'd planted a kiss on the old man's bristly beard.

He grunted, lifted his pipe and inhaled, then about-turned and headed into the house. Oh, dear—but surely a friendly kiss was the right move for meeting a relative? I smiled at Edward, wondering how many female viewers would swap places with me right at this moment. Not that I'd risk getting close enough to kiss his cheek—it would look so wrong, if his supposed cousin couldn't stop herself from stroking his tousled honey hair.

My mind went blank as he approached me. If only I'd paid more attention to Lady C's every word. Should I call him by his full title? What was short for Edward? Ted? Was that too casual?

'Hello, Teddy,' I stuttered. Crap! How did that nickname slip out? His cheeks flashed red before he held out his hand and squeezed my fingers a little too tight. 'I mean... I do hope you are well. The estate looks marvellous.'

'Pleasant journey, cousin?' he said, still studying my face. It was weird. He kind of had the same nose as Abbey.

'Very, um, nice, thank you,' I said, squirming under his intense gaze. He had the tiniest green specks in his blue eyes... Ahem. Right. Concentrate. Now, what did Lady C say about conversation? Talk about the weather...

'No blinding blizzards or black ice, if that's what you mean,' I said, my voice giving a little wobble.

'Hardly,' he replied dryly. 'We're only just in September.'

Charlie came in between us and put his arms around my shoulder. 'What a family resemblance!' he said. 'Honey hair! Blue eyes! And Teddy! I like it, Lord Edward! You kept that name from us. Let's hope that Abigail—'

'Abbey,' I said, breaking the rule on interrupting.

Charlie grinned. 'Let's hope that *Abbey* reveals more family secrets.'

By now Lord Edward's face had turned an ugly shade of purple. Swiftly, I moved onto the line-up of staff that stood to attention outside the arched entrance.

'Och, it's lovely to meet you again, Miss Croxley,' said Kathleen, the cook. She wore a bright apron and sensible lace-up shoes. Awkwardly, she curtsied. I smiled at her, both of us knowing she'd never previously met the grown-up Abigail Croxley. It didn't feel right, a top cook like her kowtowing to a pizza waitress.

Next were two chambermaids in black dresses and white hats, only hired for my arrival, apparently. Each one curtsied in turn until I came to the estate manager, hunting gun slung over his shoulder. He nodded, looked at his watch and seemed on the verge of leaving before he gazed behind me. I wondered if he'd caught Lord Edward's eye.

'Ahem, welcome back, Miss Croxley,' he said in a voice deeper than Barry White's.

'Thank you, Mr Thompson,' I said, pleased at remembering his name. Then I smiled at the gardener. 'I hope you are keeping well, um, Jean, and look forward to a stroll around the estate with you later.'

'Of course, Miss,' she said. 'We've worked hard on the vegetable patch this year.'

I turned to her assistant, Nick, with his twinkly eyes and David Beckham stubble. Little did he know it, but we were actually going to be red-hot lovers! Not that I felt remotely kissable without my tan.

'How splendid to see you again, Nick,' I murmured, standing upright to make sure the fluffy mike caught every word. 'I did so enjoy the weeks we spent together last year. Our time amongst the flower beds was delightful and you, um, sowed your seeds so well.'

Charlie snorted whilst Nick raised one eyebrow. I held his hand just a bit longer than Lady C would have deemed decent. His shake was firm, and his mouth twitched as if he was trying not to laugh. Nick was going to be a welcome contrast to the stuffiness of the Croxleys.

With a smile, I turned to Charlie. Drama was like my *worst* subject at school and I just hoped my aristocratic character came across as believable. Although a small part of me irrationally hoped to be found out, cos Jean, Nick and Kathleen seemed lovely. If only they could know the truth—but that was never going to happen. Truth, honour and loyalty were obviously important to the traditional Croxleys… I couldn't ever imagine the old Earl being in on my secret and agreeing to fool the nation—not even to save his mansion.

'Looks like Abigail has *very* fond memories of the gardens,' said Charlie with a wink at the camera.

Lord Edward glared at me and rubbed the palm of his hand against the back of his neck.

'And, with that, folks,' said Charlie to the camera, 'may I announce the start of the final. Two weeks from today I shall proudly announce the winner of *Million Dollar Mansion*. You've now met the cast from both here and Marwick Castle. So ready, steady go! Let the battle begin!'

He stood grinning at the camera for several seconds before Gaynor gave him the thumbs-up.

'That's a wrap, darlings,' she said and lit a fag.

Charlie turned to me. 'Good on ya, Abbey, you're a natural in front of the camera. Once you're settled, Bob, the sound operator will fit you up with a lapel mic.' He turned to Edward. 'See you at one then, Lord Edward, for your special announcement. I believe we'll be filming it in the orchards. You and your cousin have just got time to stretch your legs.'

Charlie bowed and headed for Gaynor, taking a notebook out of his pocket. The staff had already gone back indoors. I glanced at Edward.

'Um…pleasant enough man,' I said and jerked my head towards Charlie, hands feeling clammy.

Edward scowled. 'Don't be naïve, cousin. These media types are only after one thing—a cheap story. Watch what you say to them. Now, come, we'll walk to the pond. There's a bench in the shade. I shall fill you in on today's schedule. And it's not Teddy. Or Ted.'

'So what should I call you?'

'Edward is my name, Abigail.'

'As you wish, but please—call me Abbey.'

I followed him down the path to the main drive and we headed across the lawns. Hands in pockets, he sauntered towards the pond.

'Amaaazin',' I murmured, taking in my surroundings. 'ggg,' I added, hoping the end of the word didn't arrive too late.

'Landscaping costs a fortune nowadays,' said Edward. 'Jean was quite a find.'

We skirted the pond and headed for a bench.

'And how long has Nick been in your employment?' I asked. Ooh, listen to me, all formal. I was kind of getting the hang of talking posh, remembering everything Lady C had told me and trying to speak just like Abbey did.

Edward gave me a stare, as if to say: why so interested?

'Don't we all need to get our stories straight?' I stuttered. Looked like he might already suspect something was afoot between me and Nick—I wanted the public to do that, not disapproving Teddy.

Quick. Change the subject. 'Goodness, it's hot.' Without thinking, I kicked off my KMid shoes and headed towards a patch of bulrushes. I dipped a toe in the water, which was so clear it looked good enough to drink. A few small fish darted among the reeds. I plunged in the rest of my foot and squidged the sand on the bottom between my toes, just like I used to when me and Dad went fishing for tiddlers.

Ahhhh—bliss. Perhaps this would stop me feeling as if the midday sun was frazzling my brain. Lady C had offered me her sunhat, but per-lease. Wide-rimmed? Floral? Nothing was going to get me into that. Although perhaps I should have protected my grey cells, cos, aargh! What was I thinking? A lady would never complain about how she was feeling, let alone strip off and paddle in front of someone she didn't know well. In fact, Abbey once had toothache for a whole weekend without telling me. Stoical…that was the word Lady C mentioned. Brave face. Stiff upper lip and all that.

Quickly, I headed back to the bench and slipped on my shoes. The tall grasses hid us from the TV people hovering outside Applebridge Hall. I sat down. Edward gazed at me, a strange expression on his face.

'Apologies,' I muttered. 'I think the sun has gone to my head.'

'Don't stop paddling on my account,' he said, arms folded, the flicker of a smile on his lips.

'So, about this Nick…' I said, ignoring his comment.

'Only just joined us,' replied Edward. 'As you know, Father and I have had to run the estate on a tight budget and only employed a gardening assistant for Jean temporarily, to spruce up the old place for the show. He's a bit young. Lacks experience, but he's all we could get at short notice.'

I bit my thumbnail—oops, better drop that unladylike habit—and admired the scenery while we sat in silence. 'Do you think the Baron is in with a good chance?' I said eventually.

Edward frowned. 'Half glass full, Abbey. We have to believe we can win. One mustn't let the ancestors down.

That's why I'm doing everything I can—like the blog. Whatever it takes…' His shoulders sagged and he stared across the pond, all of a sudden looking older than the Earl. I wanted to hug him. No… random thought. I mean, he really wasn't my type.

'I'd better watch how I behave if you're writing this online diary,' I said and smiled.

'Only if you are worried what people think about you. But yes, I will be doing my best to give a truthful account of what's going on. People may not like my honesty, but I think it's only fair to our supporters to tell it how it is.'

I tried to imagine his position. His home, his whole way of life was at stake. If the Croxleys lost this competition— everything he knew, everything he believed in would disappear.

'I'm sure you won't let anyone down,' I murmured.

Another of those piercing gazes. 'It's…jolly good to have you here, cousin.' Then the brief glimpse of someone actually human disappeared and his voice hardened. 'It doesn't help anyone to get sentimental, though. We have our heritage to protect. Responsibilities to fulfil. Starting with an on-camera dinner at seven. Family friends are joining us—Viscount Hamilton-Brown, his wife and their daughter. Kathleen suggested Nick help her serve the food, for the cameras. We found tailcoats and a butler's jacket in the attic that he can wear. It's formal dress tonight.' He rolled his eyes. '"Larger-than-life" seems to be Gaynor's motto. I believe Mr Thompson shot some rabbits yesterday and, of course, dessert will include apples from the estate.' He cleared his throat and stood up. 'To the orchards. Father and the cameras will be waiting.'

I got to my feet. 'Can you let me in on the secret announcement?'

'Haven't I already explained everything to your father?' He shook his head and strode off.

My mouth fell open. Almost tripping over clumps of grass, I caught him up.

'Hey!'

He stopped and turned around, a bemused look on his face. Oh, dear. I'd raised my voice.

'Um, I mean…' I grabbed some long grass. '*Hay*… this will make excellent hay… And, talking of rabbits, did you know eating hay prevents them from getting fur balls in their stomach? I, um, watch a lot of nature programmes.'

The top button of Edward's shirt had pinged open and I wondered how smooth his chest would feel if I slipped a finger through the gap. With a sigh, I realized I'd have to try a lot harder to get into character.

'Remember, cousin, I'm here to help,' I said, more softly. 'If we are to carry on this pretence that the family is close, despite the Earl having banished Daddy from the estate and…'

'Whoa! Is that what your father told you?' His face screwed up into a frown.

'Um, not exactly,' I said sheepishly.

'Then you should keep your misguided opinions to yourself.'

'But, wait a minute… Edward… The fact is, we haven't seen each other since I was nine. I demand that you keep me informed—Daddy… Daddy's been very busy lately and probably just forgot to tell me about your plans. Remember, I'm here to do you a favour. Applebridge Hall has little to do with my life. This charade is for your benefit alone.' Oops. I hadn't meant to sound that harsh.

His mouth twitched. Was he bemused? Appalled? Spoilt and too used to having his own way?

'Your father's company, Croxley Catering, trades off our family name, doesn't it?' he finally muttered. 'All things considered, helping us is the least you can do.'

Touché. Still, Edward could have shown a little gratitude if we were to get on well over the next two weeks.

'Anyway,' he said, a muscle in his cheek twitching, 'I tried to keep in touch with you, years ago—sent you and Rupert gifts. Yet I never received a reply.'

'Daddy wouldn't let us see them—said we were too young to understand the estrangement.' Thank God Lady C had told me about that.

Edward's brow smoothed out for a minute. 'Really? I mean…' His voice kind of wavered. 'You would have been interested in receiving them?'

I nodded. Abbey had often said what a pity it was she hardly knew Edward or the Earl—growing up, she wished they'd sometimes met up. 'I never forgot about my cousin Edward,' I said. 'And Rupe would have fitted right in here. He's studying history of art and dreams of working for the National Trust one day.'

The strangest look crossed Edward's face and then his brow once again furrowed.

'Let's get going; we'll be late,' he muttered and headed off. Jeez! He was the one who needed a crash course in politeness. I wondered if there was a male noble's version of PMT. The best way to get through the next fortnight was probably going to be to avoid Edward at all costs.

His stupid announcement could wait a few minutes. I'd find myself a welcome drink. No doubt Kathleen had a jug of homemade lemonade or some country punch. However, Lord Edward had other plans.

'This way, old girl,' he called after me as I veered towards Applebridge Hall. 'Do keep up.'

Cheek! He'd call me to 'heel' next.

Wiping perspiration from my forehead, I decided to follow him. No point causing upset on the first day of my stay. The lawns soon gave way to a path lined by brambles and nettles, as we left the overgrown area to the more orderly rows of apple trees. Out of nowhere, Roxy appeared by my side and Charlie, Gaynor and the camera crew came into view. They were set up, halfway down one row. Roxy stopped me for a moment and, before I knew it, had fitted a mic onto the collar of my blouse, threaded the wire underneath and clipped the battery pack onto the belt of my skirt.

'Gaynor wants you to keep this on for the afternoon,' she said, as quickly as ever. 'The crew will follow you around while the Earl gives you a tour of the house. It's a chance for the viewers to see all the rooms again.'

Ahead, Gaynor fitted Edward with the same equipment—except she seemed to take longer, especially threading the wire into place under his shirt, and, to my annoyance, I felt an urge to do the same.

The Earl appeared and headed over to me, puffing on his pipe.

'Lunch will be served after this, Abigail,' he said. 'It will give us the opportunity to exchange news.' There was no smile, no crinkly smiley eyes. He looked as if I was the last person he wanted here.

'Thank you, Uncle,' I said and breathed in the smell of tobacco, glad I'd not said 'ace' or 'ta'. Gaynor positioned me in between him and his son. I swatted away a cloud of tiny fruit flies.

'Big smiles, everyone,' ordered Gaynor, before giving a rusty smoker's cough. 'Abbey, darling, if you could pick one of those apples and hold it in front of you… Fabulous. Right, Charlie, let's roll.'

Charlie gazed into the camera. 'And here we are, folks, once again back at Applebridge Hall. Teddy, here…' Edward bristled '… Teddy has an announcement to make. Over to you, Lord Edward,' he said with a big smile.

The camera panned over to me, Edward and his dad.

'The prize money we won for reaching the final has gone towards extending the kitchens, at the front of the left wing on the ground floor,' said Edward calmly. 'We've built five work-stations to start with, that will enable us to run top-notch cookery classes—residential ones eventually, we hope, that will accommodate ten students at a time.'

The Earl muttered something about not having strangers kipping in his home.

'We already have three locals eager to be the first students,' continued Edward. 'On Mondays, Wednesdays and Fridays the doors shall open to… Applebridge Food Academy.'

'Classy stuff, Teddy,' said Charlie and clapped him on the back 'So, a kind of cookery school. And where does your cousin fit into this plan?'

'With renowned caterer, the Honourable Richard Croxley, as her father,' he said, 'Abbey has culinary talent in her blood. Applebridge Food Academy will be a traditional, family-run affair with her at the helm.'

'A kind of Mansion *Masterchef*,' said Charlie. 'I love it! After all, cooking is the new sex! Viewers love gastronomy programmes. Your cousin could be the next Nigella, perhaps. So, Abbey, Chat with the Chingo—tell me what you think to teaching people how to cook posh nosh.'

Huh? I felt dizzy. They'd got it wrong. I was only here to serve scones in a coffee shop. Waitressing, that was my experience—plus I could nuke food in the microwave, prepare cold snacks and order takeaway. But wait a minute… Cookery *school*? That's what Abbey must have told Lady C about on the phone, that day in the park. The two of them knew!

My mouth went dry, knees weak, heart fast… Me, cook from scratch and instruct other people? Please don't say the future of Applebridge Hall depended on that!

LORD EDWARD'S E-DIARY

Saturday 1st September

'Comments'

3p.m. Good afternoon. Time for a quick appearance whilst my, um, cousin... recuperates after her journey. Naturally, I am pleased to see her. It means…an awful lot. Family is of paramount importance to Father and me. Indeed, it is with amusement and a touch of family pride that I can again observe Abigail's… outspokenness—a true Croxley trait. However, it's her cooking skills which shall be most significant over the next two weeks, and I'm interested to see your comments about this morning's poser question—do keep them coming until you discover the answer in tomorrow evening's programme.

Some of you have even put forward your own entrepreneurial concepts for us to follow. *Knityourownmansion*, I'm intrigued by your idea of producing woollen earmuffs in the shape of apples. *Tiarablogger*, I like the idea of those cider flavours you suggested—although, utterly English as it sounds, I'm not sure about apple, sage and onion.

Time to dash, but *Lovehotnoble*, let me first decline your kind gift proposal. On a purely practical note, I suspect the sequinned trim would chafe in all the wrong places. I do hope my frankness isn't offensive. I…where possible… always aim to tell the truth.

CHAPTER 4

Within minutes of this announcement I had one of my funny turns. Unsteadily, I wavered from side to side, before my body went into spasm. There was no need to call the doctor. I'd suffered this before. The remedy was an afternoon in bed. Otherwise, I might have had to pull out of the show…

Sounded believable, didn't it? And, sure enough, everyone in the orchard fell for my act, which was the only way I could cope with Edward's terrifying announcement about me being some cookery teacher—distraction was the key, before Charlie asked me any awkward questions.

Yet I felt bad, putting on such a performance, which even Edward fell for after I'd writhed for a few seconds in the soil. He and Kathleen whisked me into the house, my eyes half-shut but still managing to goggle at some fancy staircase leading up to the first floor. Once left alone in my bedroom, I turned on my front and groaned into the pillow.

Urgh. Cringe. Blush. Poor Kathleen had seemed mega concerned, deep lines forming around her eyes as she'd tucked me in. But there was no way I could just stand in front of the camera after Edward dropped that bombshell. Gemma Goodwin run some cookery school? No way. After a minute or so, I sat up in bed and opened my eyes.

Forget my planned tour around Applebridge Hall. I needed the rest of the day to phone Lady C. I tugged off my mic. It was dark. Before leaving, Edward had gently pulled thick curtains around the—listen to this—*four-poster* bed. Stifled in the enclosed space, I drew them back.

Wow. The room was amazzzzzzin', with the walls' bottom half wood-panelled and the top painted plain red. In contrast, the ceiling was white and ornate. I bounced up and down for a moment. Talk about *The Princess and the Pea*—I'd never been on such a high mattress. To my left was the door and opposite an en suite. I gazed around at a floral tapestry and an intricately carved fireplace. On the right was one of the huge windows I'd seen from outside.

I picked up a glass of water from the bedside table. Mmm. I needed that.

Right. Time to ring Lady C. I reached for my handbag, which was on a wooden chest at the foot of the bed, next to a bowl of smelly pot pourri. On Lady C's advice, I'd bought a cheap phone and set it up with the name 'Abbey Croxley' for her, as my supposed aunt, to contact me. Plus that meant I had a mobile to use out in the open, around Applebridge Hall. My real phone—my life!—with all of Gemma Goodwin's contacts, was hidden in a pair of socks.

'Please pick up,' I whispered, which she did, within seconds.

'Hello, Gemma,' said Lady C in a small voice.

'You knew! All about Applebridge Food Academy!'

'Now, calm down, dear, you see…'

'And Abbey! How could she not tell me, at least?'

'Abigail only found out that day in the park—her father failed to mention the details previously. He has such faith— quite rightly—in my niece's culinary talents that he didn't think it would be a big deal. Which, of course, it wouldn't, if it was actually her staying at Applebridge Hall…'

'But why didn't she warn me?'

Lady C sighed. 'I, um, might have persuaded her not to—played down the whole "school" bit. I said you'd no doubt have cooks doing the real work… And she was so wrapped up preparing for her African trip…' Another sigh came down the line. 'Frankly, dear, I didn't want you to change your mind. I apologise. That was selfish.'

'But how did you think I'd cope, once here?'

'Well, surely you can cook a bit, dear. I'll help you choose the recipes. We'll keep them simple…'

I shook my head in disbelief. Didn't she know that, nowadays, it wasn't the goal of every young woman to be a domestic goddess? That plenty, like me, considered the microwave a more important invention than the wheel?

'We've got tomorrow to plan the recipes, then?' she said, more firmly. 'Your first class is on Monday?'

I gasped. 'What… No… I mean…You're taking this seriously? But I *can't* cook, let alone teach. We need to think up some excuse, a good reason why I can't possibly do that job.'

'Keep calm and carry on,' was the answer that came down the line. 'Don't arouse suspicion.'

'But I can't—'

'No such word as "can't" in a lady's vocabulary,' she interrupted—naughty! 'I'm sure your culinary knowledge is better than you think.'

'Okay. Test me on a few cookery terms,' I said, determined to prove her wrong.

'Bake blind.'

'With my eyes shut?' I replied.

'Beat eggs,' Lady C ventured.

'That seems mega cruel.'

'Skin a banana?'

'Barbaric!' I declared.

'Follow the recipe,' she said, hopefully.

'Where's it going?'

'Turn on the oven, Gemma?'

'How? Call it hot stuff and flourish a whisk?'

A sigh came down the phone.

'Look, I can scramble eggs and bake a potato,' I said, 'but, honestly, that's about it.'

'Have they suspected you're not Abigail yet?'

'I don't think so…'

'There you go,' said Lady C, voice brighter. 'Things are off to a jolly good start. All we need to do is talk through some simple recipes.'

Which we did, for what felt like hours. The trouble was, I'd never baked a cake and bought pastry ready-made. I got white sauce out of a jar and mistook broccoli for cauliflower. Finally, Lady C gave up and said she'd call me early the following day. Overnight, she'd study her cookery books, determined to find some impressive dishes that looked more complicated than they actually were.

My stomach gurgled loudly. I wasn't used to missing lunch and suddenly craved a kebab with a triple chocolate milkshake. Someone rapped at the door. I smoothed down my polo shirt.

'Enter,' I said, my voice a bit wobbly. Perhaps they'd sussed out my fake collapse.

The door opened. Honey curls appeared and Edward walked in with my suitcase.

'You look better,' he said, a brief flash of relief in his eyes. He put down my luggage. 'No doubt Kathleen will insist you have some of her Scotch broth.'

'Thank you, cousin.' My cheeks burned. 'Um, apologies for before…'

'Let's hope it doesn't happen again. Health problems don't make for good television. The Croxleys are old school. We don't get ill—certainly not in public.'

Huh? For a second, my shame evaporated! 'Thanks for the concern,' I said, unable to hide a strong hint of sarcasm that I'd never heard Abbey use.

'You might mean that when you hear I've persuaded Gaynor to cut that unsavoury scene from tomorrow night's show.'

Was he bonkers? That *was* good telly. 'Um, Teddy…'

He scowled.

'Edward… That's just the sort of footage that *makes* a reality show—according to my lodger, Gemma,' I hastened to add. 'She's a big fan of that genre. From what I can gather, it's the dramatic bits that gain viewers. It's not a serious illness and my, um, medication helps. Don't edit it out on my behalf.'

'I didn't, Abigail. It's to uphold the family reputation.'

'It's Abbey,' I said, meeting his scowl.

'Throughout history, Croxley women have been strong,' he said and rubbed the back of his neck. 'They are stoic in the midst of war, resourceful during economic downturns, uncomplaining in the face of disease…' His voice wavered. 'You only had to see the way my mother carried herself during her last months. It does our image no good to have you drop to the floor because you… you felt out of sorts.'

It could have been some serious brain condition, for all he cared. Yet my fists didn't curl for long as I reminded myself that I had been acting, plus I'd noticed how the mention of his mum made his chin give a teeny wobble.

'You must miss the Countess terribly,' I said. 'When did she…?'

'Die?' His body stiffened. 'I'm sorry that part of our family history has slipped your memory. Or perhaps your father never found it important enough to explain.'

Of course—Abbey would have at least known that. Urgh. Poor bloke. My stomach twisted really tight.

'No… I mean…' I cleared my throat. 'I was just going to ask: *when did she* first receive the diagnosis?' I guessed she'd had the Big C. 'Father didn't give me many details and, as you know…' blagging for my life, here '… with the estrangement between our parents, attending the funeral proved to be, sadly, quite impossible.'

'Granted.' His cheek twitched. 'From start to finish, the cancer took three years to take her from Father and me. Two years next month she's been gone. Mother was only fifty-five.'

A lump rose in my throat as Edward's eyes looked all dull. Wow. How tragic. Nowadays, fifty-five was like the new forty. And if anyone knew what life was like without a mum it was me.

'How old was she when your parents married?' I tucked a loose dyed blonde curl behind my ear. The Earl must have been a right sugar daddy.

'Twenty-three, I think. Father was forty-two.'

We sat in silence for a few seconds, before I rummaged in my handbag.

'My hairbrush—it was in here earlier…' I must have looked a right mess and totally unladylike. With a sigh, I pulled out all the pins, and locks of hair dropped around my face. Lady C would not have been impressed.

'Here,' said Edward in a gruff voice as he approached and slipped an elastic band from his wrist. He sat on the bed, turned me away from him and deftly twisted my hair at either side before tying it all together at the back with the elastic band.

'Um…thank you so much,' I said and turned back to him, wondering why tingles ran up and down my spine.

'I used to do that for Mother,' he said in a quiet voice. 'Especially at the end, when she was bed-bound.' He stood up and cleared his throat. 'Kathleen will be up in a minute. Please be in formal dress and downstairs for seven sharp at the latest. Viscount Hamilton-Brown and his family will be here at six-thirty for drinks.' The door shut behind him.

What an oddball he was—one minute so gentle, the next abrupt and stand-offish.

I leapt off the bed to gaze out of the window. My bedroom was at the back of the house and looked down onto the cutest courtyard with fancy flower pots and intricate metal benches. Jean stood in the ornamental gardens, weeding flower beds. Nick was further away, working in a regimented vegetable patch. To the left was the maze Abbey had mentioned and in the distance was a forested area, just in front of which was… I squinted…grey headstones, fenced off. Aha—the family cemetery.

My eyes headed back to Nick. He looked shorter than Edward, with a stockier build and more cheerful face—less typically attractive than my supposed cousin, but there was a certain charisma, an air of being confident with women.

He called out something to Jean. She laughed and he grinned back. Nick would need a sense of humour if he was going to agree to my plan. How on earth was I going to catch the gardener alone and put forward my mega idea ASAP, i.e. before dinner tonight?

Another knock at the door interrupted my plotting and Kathleen entered with her yummy broth. Weird it was, calling her by her first name while she addressed me as Miss Croxley, but Lady C had drilled into me that etiquette about names and titles was especially important with staff. So, after I'd done my best to convince her I felt fine and there was no need to worry, we talked about the evening's dinner. Like a nanny, Kathleen hovered until I'd cleared the soup bowl and, thanks to her warm down-to-earth chat, tension seeped out of my shoulders and my bedroom began to feel more homely. For the first time I felt I could cope with two weeks living in this building.

After she left, I took a leisurely shower and changed into one of Abbey's smart black dresses. Its round neckline was modest but low enough to show a little shoulder. Freakily, it went down to the ground, covering every inch of my legs, although it had always looked kind of classy on Abbey. At least it had short sleeves, otherwise I might have really fainted from the heat.

I pinned up my hair again and put on Abbey's crystal necklace and matching earrings. I applied a small squirt of perfume and a subtle shade of eyeshadow, just like my best bud would. It was six-fifteen. My mouth felt dry. Ahead of me was a whole evening of pretending to be someone I wasn't. Inhale. Exhale. Feeling calmer, I left my bedroom and headed along a high ceilinged corridor, actually feeling rather grown-up and glamorous. Halfway down the winding mahogany staircase—yay!—I bumped into Nick!

'Miss Croxley,' he said and gave a smile. Flecks of soil covered his T-shirt. 'Nice to see you've recovered,' he said in a concerned voice.

'Thank you. Kathleen's broth has revived me.' I cleared my throat. 'Actually, I was hoping to catch you.'

He raised one eyebrow.

'About earlier,' I said. 'Me pretending that you and I spent time together last year…'

Nick held up the palm of his hand. 'Please, Miss Croxley. I get it. We've all been briefed about how we need to make it look as if you are a regular visitor.'

'It's not just that… Can I be quite frank? May I speak to you in confidence?'

'No problem, Miss.' Nick's eyes twinkled and I couldn't help smiling—which was great. I'd always been won over by blokes who could make me laugh. A good sense of humour beat looks for me every time. I mean, there was only so much a six-pack could do after a crap day at work, whereas a joke…

'Thank you, Nick. It's just that… According to Roxy, Applebridge Hall isn't the favourite to win. She suggested… Please do excuse the phrase…that somehow the Croxley family…forgive me, but, um, *sex things up*.'

His eyes widened.

A bubble of laughter tickled inside my chest. Oh, God—mustn't laugh. In fact, thinking about it, this wasn't funny at all. I was putting myself on the line here—my true identity might well and truly be rumbled. 'I know—it's a terribly crass idea, but I want to do everything possible to help my family. So, I was thinking that, well…' How would he take this? Be offended? Amused? Or suss out straight away that I'm no real aristocrat? '… a secret affair between a Croxley and a member of staff might improve ratings.'

Nick's mouth fell open. 'Are you proposing, Miss, that you and I...?'

My heart raced. 'Exactly. It would be purely for the cameras, of course, and more suggestion than action. It pains me to resort to such tactics, but my family's heritage is at stake.'

I waited, imagining the disdain of Edward if he'd been listening, hoping that I was right in thinking that good-humoured Nick was the opposite of judgemental. The gardener stared for a moment and scratched his unshaven chin, which was kind of sexy and something you'd never find on Lord Clean-cut, Edward.

'The Baron of Marwick sure is tough competition,' said Nick. 'He also announced his plans to win this afternoon. The Castle has been set up to host weekend medieval hen and stag nights, with banquets held in the dungeons. I bet they'll get pretty crazy. During the week, he'll host corporate team-building trips, incorporating archery and shooting. It all sounds…'

I sighed. 'Awfully sexy.' Oops—that wasn't something Abbey would ever say.

'Yeah, but… A Croxley mixing it up with a gardener? Someone who works on the land?' His eyes narrowed. 'You can't possibly be related to Lord Edward if you're suggesting such a thing.'

I swallowed hard. Surely I hadn't misjudged Nick so badly…

'You'd better show me some form of ID, Miss,' he said, 'before I say something to the Earl.'

LORD EDWARD'S E-DIARY

Saturday 1st September

'Comments'

6.15p.m. Thank you, but no, *Lovehotnoble*—rubber trim would probably be equally uncomfortable.

Now, duty calls—I must hurry to greet our guests. Just a quick word to say that Abigail… How long I've waited to see her face. I mean, erm, of course, it's only been months since our last meeting, but nevertheless… To have her here finally… At Applebridge… It's smashing.

Right. Anyway. Really must go. Dinner awaits.

CHAPTER 5

Nick and I couldn't stop laughing. Mega phew! For one minute I really believed he'd seen through my disguise and was after a peek at my passport.

'Desperate times call for desperate measures,' I said eventually. 'But honestly, Nick, I perfectly understand if you think this idea…improper.' After all, laughs aside, this was all an act to me but it was Nick's real life—he could lose his job.

I caught sight of a designer logo on the bottom of his T-shirt and recognized his cologne as an expensive brand I'd once sniffed when out with a boyfriend. Nick struck me as a bit glam for a gardener.

'Consider me in, Miss,' he said.

'You're sure?' I raised my eyebrows, giving him one last chance to back out. Although I could sense that, unlike Edward, a major drive in Nick's life was fun; I reckoned we would really get along.

'One hundred per cent!' he said. 'How do you suggest we get things started?'

'Slowly.' I backed up against the crimson-painted wall, as Nick had leant forward to keep our voices and plans ultra secret. 'Perhaps a look here, a touch there—although, having said that, we only have two weeks.' Footsteps sounded from the bottom of the staircase.

'Better get things moving, then,' whispered Nick. 'A friend of mine knows a Z-list celebrity who trades off winding up photographers that he's having all sorts of affairs. His specialty is this dud kiss—I can show you if you like. We'll need to practice…'

Before I knew it, he'd placed a hand over my mouth and bowed forward to snog his knuckles. But still, it wasn't a bad idea—from behind him it must have looked mega realistic. And Nick did smell good. It was a while since I'd been this close to a man, especially one who had no ulterior motive. With easy-going Nick, it felt kind of comfortable, until…. uh oh! I could hardly breathe now, seeing as he'd taken me by surprise and I'd had no time to fill my lungs with air.

'Unhand her, you scoundrel!' hissed Edward, who'd appeared from downstairs. He climbed the steps towards us, two at a time, appearing even taller than usual. Nick backed off immediately and I gasped for breath.

'What the hell do you think you're doing, man?' Eyes blazing, Edward grabbed the gardener's shoulder. 'Pack your things this instant and leave. I won't have you disrespect my cousin!'

'Look, Edward,' I said, heart thumping, 'let me explain...' Wow, no one had ever rushed to my side to protect me. My brothers and dad thought me well capable of looking after myself—which I was. But still… This mansion must have brought out the damsel in me!

A few minutes later a snarl still crossed Edward's lips as he stared at Nick. 'Tell me that again, cousin. And you'd better hurry up…' He glanced at his watch. 'It's almost six-thirty. Our dinner guests have been shown in and are waiting for us.'

'Nick, um, used to be a dental technician,' I said, repeating the rapidly made-up excuse while trying not to ogle my supposed cousin in his tux. 'One of my teeth was hurting and Nick very kindly agreed to take a look.'

Knights in shining armour were all very well, but jeez, Edward obviously didn't believe in the process of verbal or written warnings before firing staff members. Although it was kind of sweet. My heart still beat madly. I'd always found loyalty to family and friends mega attractive.

I stared from Edward to Nick, who stood like two spitting hyenas. Perhaps they had more in common than I suspected. Yet, heroics aside, I reckoned Edward would be much harder to live with than laid-back, up-for-a-laugh Nick.

'Yep, Miss Croxley's, erm, got an ulcer,' said the gardener and folded his arms. 'Seems like Your Lordship got the wrong end of the stick. So, if you'll excuse me, I must change into my outfit to help out at dinner.' Nick turned to me and winked. 'I'd gargle with salt water, miss,' he said, and disappeared up the stairs.

'Was he bothering you?' said Edward.

'Not at all.' I moved away from the wall and brushed down my dress.

'Stay away from Nick,' said Edward. 'He's a shifty chap.'

'With respect, cousin, who are you to order me around?' Well, Abbey often demonstrated that being a lady wasn't about being a doormat. It was awesome, listening to her on the phone if someone dared call pretending to be our energy company or acting as if they could give her a better mortgage deal.

Edward's eyes narrowed. 'There's something in his expression—a total lack of respect.'

Yeah, well, not everyone's in awe of the aristocracy.

'Right, Abigail, let's go downstairs,' he said, his tone bringing an abrupt end to the incident. 'Viscount Hamilton-

Brown and his family have waited long enough…along with the camera crew and production staff,' he added, a hint of resignation tainting his voice.

I took a deep breath. This dinner party was the first real test of whether I could behave like a lady. If I couldn't get through this evening without embarrassing myself, then there was no point carrying on with the whole charade. We walked down to the ground floor and came to a door at the front right hand side of the house. It seemed strange, Nick going to the top floor to change, but Lady C had explained that, despite the phrase 'upstairs and downstairs', at different points in history it was nothing strange for servants to live 'up in the gods'. In fact she'd crammed a lot of information into a few days, including a summary of European royals—ooh, of all the places to live, glam Monaco was now top of my list.

'That's the Low Drawing Room,' said Edward. 'Perhaps you remember it from your last visit.'

'Cousin—I was only nine.' Without asking, I ducked inside for a moment and spied furniture with carved animal legs—how amazin'! And just look at the mega detailed fireplace and classy chandelier… However, the spooky grandfather clock creeped me out and seemed better suited to the set of a haunted house horror film.

On closer inspection, I could see that the rugs were worn and wall carvings chipped. Plus the tiled floor was cracked, the tapestries faded and one corner of the ceiling showed signs of damp. It was like stepping back in time, what with no telly or computer and no comfy bean bag or gaming chair to chill out on.

'This used to be where the Croxleys received run-of-the-mill guests,' he said. 'VIPs were received upstairs, in the High Drawing Room.'

'Like who?' I said.

'Depends on the era—Military men, politicians, foreign statesmen, people from the world of entertainment... Noël Coward, the playwright, visited my great-grandparents— like him, they adored jazz.'

We left the room and made our way down a dark mahogany-panelled corridor, eventually coming to another door, on the right.

'That leads to the library,' said Edward, 'which is opposite...' we entered a room on the left '...the Drake Diner.'

Wow. It stretched across the back of the house, with patio doors opening onto the cute courtyard. I gawped at the oak panelling all the way up to the ornate ceiling and admired the family coat of arms and gold-framed landscapes... I'd never been in a place like this without a ticket and tour guide. Feeling as out of place as a pop star at the Proms, I fiddled with my watch. Edward glanced sideways.

'You look, um, quite satisfactory, cousin,' he said. 'Come on—let me introduce you to our friends.'

Jeez, Edward was in no danger of overdoing the compliments! But I was beginning to realize that, with him, less was more. And at least he was no different with anyone else. This included the gushing Mrs Viscount—yes, I really did call her that—well, I'd never come across the word, apart from when Dad used to buy these wrapped minty chocolate biscuits. How was I supposed to know it was 'Viscount*ess*'? Edward announced that her brooch was 'an interesting size' and then commented on the Viscount's 'unusual' tie. Yet a large dollop of charm did appear when he talked to their sophisticated daughter, the Honourable Henrietta Hamilton-Brown. Edward admired her brunette hair, swept up into a high bun. He said it looked 'delightful'—then ruined it by chatting to her about the state of the Euro. Borrrrring.

'It's super to meet some of your wider family, James,' said the Viscountess to the Earl as we sat at the long dining table in padded tapestry chairs.

I squished back comfortably and did my best not to stare at the big fluffy mic the sound guy had just manoeuvred over our heads. 'James' sat at one end of the table, in between the Viscount—Ernest, as he insisted I call him—and his wife, Annabel. Next to her was Henrietta, with me and Edward opposite. My Uncle Pete would have loved this table for pasting his wallpaper on. It must have seated, ooh... at least twenty toffs.

I tipped my chair back (a habit I've always had) and smiled across at Annabel. Right, time to have a crack at conversation. I didn't fancy politics or the recession. That left personal stuff and the weather.

'Have you had to travel far this evening?' I asked.

'Only for an hour,' she said. 'The last half of the journey was through such heavenly countryside.'

'We adore visiting here,' said Henrietta and beamed at Edward. 'Tell me, what's the state of apple prices this year? Are they still in the doldrums because of the economic downturn?'

I did my best to look brainy as they discussed, in great detail, when it would be best to bring contract workers into the orchards. Henrietta's comments sounded so eloquent. How delicately she sipped her wine. He even let her straighten his tie. Jeez, she was like some automated Stepford wife!

'And how's the car boot business?' she said.

'Not bad,' said Edward. He caught my eye. 'I rent out the acres of land that stretch to the left, behind the maze.'

'Ah, for that summer rock festival?' I said.

'Yes. Plus several funfairs that tour through here each year.'

'And a bloomin' mess they make as well,' interrupted the Earl, a grimace contorting his jowls.

Edward sighed. 'But needs must, Father. Along with renting out the land for car boot sales, it brings in something of a steady income.'

'Sounds like a lot of work to organise,' I said.

'When it comes to this estate, Edward is terribly industrious.' Henrietta smiled. 'When he inherits, there's no doubt in my mind that he will do his ancestors and the Croxley tradition proud.'

You'd think such a compliment would bring a smile to his face. Instead, Edward loosened his tie and bit his lip, his eyes dulling for a second. However, the moment soon passed and, as the two friends chatted, my ears perked up at the mention of a Lieutenant Robert Mayhew.

'Is that *the* Lieutenant Robert Mayhew?' I said, interrupting their conversation—soz, Lady C, but I couldn't contain my interest. 'My, um… flatmate Gemma calls him "the Forces Pin-up". Didn't he make it back from Afghanistan, despite gun wounds and second degree burns?'

Henrietta smiled. 'Edward went to school with Robert. They are the best of friends.'

'Such a courageous—' read that as gorgeous '—person,' I said, 'returning to that burning vehicle.'

Edward smiled. 'Only a madman like Rob would go back in when he was drenched in fuel. Apart from his helmet, Rob's uniform was in ashes by the time he'd hauled everyone else out.'

'Terribly modest about it all, wasn't he?' I said.

Edward shrugged. 'He says, just like thousands of other troops, he was simply doing his job.'

'He's organized a big charity ball next month,' said Henrietta, 'to raise money for injured soldiers. He'll be pleased to see you there, Edward.'

'It should be a wonderful evening,' said Annabel.

'Damn brave lad,' said the Earl. Ernest grunted his agreement.

'I remember the first time I met him,' said Henrietta. 'It was at your twenty-first birthday party, Edward; do you remember?'

'Rob was home on leave and danced with anything in a skirt. Even Dundee Douglas, who'd put on his kilt.'

'Your mother always thought him a decent chap,' said the Earl to Edward, 'even when he led you astray at school by suggesting you skip school for the cinema. Rosemary wouldn't hear a bad word against him.'

Henrietta put her hand on Edward's. A display of emotion like that, in public, must have meant they were really good friends, or even…? For some reason, an uncomfortable twinge niggled my stomach.

'Poor you, Edward,' she said. 'Those afternoons at the pictures couldn't have possibly been your idea.'

'Son?' The Earl raised his eyebrows. 'All these years poor Robert took the blame?'

Edward grinned and rubbed the back of his neck.

My stomach tingled. A smile on Edward's lips was a rare thing and, for a few seconds, made him look a decade younger. Just then, in tailcoats and a butler's jacket, Nick entered through a door from the left hand side and the pantry, cellars and kitchens. He'd combed his hair over into a greased-down side-parting and winked at me as if to say: 'this geeky look is deliberate'. His hand brushed against mine as he poured my wine. Clearly, he took my Plan Sex-up seriously. Edward stared at me, only turning away when the starter arrived. I swallowed. This was going to be hard—clinically putting on a show, pretending not to care what other people thought about my actions or about me.

'Asparagus?' Henrietta put her napkin on her lap. 'My favourite. Kathleen really is a treasure. I assume she froze these, freshly picked from your garden. What a joy to eat them out of season.'

Phew! Good thing Lady C had taught me how to eat these green monstrosities that looked like witch's fingers. They lay on a bed of lettuce and were sprinkled with chopped red stuff. I picked one up. Euw. There was only meant to be sauce on the ends but these were slippery all over and had obviously been...'

'Marinated,' said Henrietta, daintily cutting them up with a knife and fork. 'Quite lovely.'

'Have you been away on holiday this year, Annabel?' I said, hoping no one saw me quickly wipe my fingers on a napkin.

While she described her mega Caribbean cruise, I dug into my starter, suddenly starving, doing my best to chew with my mouth closed and not talk with it full. My only faux pas (impressive, eh? Lady C even taught me French) was eating the bed of lettuce. Well, how was I to know it was a garnish? Perhaps the rabbit dish would be easier. Certainly it smelt yummy, with gravy-covered chunks of meat, served with mushrooms, roasted cherry tomatoes and baby onions.

'No haggis tonight, then? That's a change,' said Annabel. Eyes twinkling, she glanced at me. 'Kathleen is fiercely proud of her Scottish roots.'

'She is making a special effort to cook English meals for the cameras,' said the Earl. 'No doubt in two weeks it will be back to normal.'

'Whatever that will be,' muttered Edward. He cleared his throat. 'So, tell me, Henrietta, all about this local animal charity you have recently become patron of.'

Carefully I chewed each morsel and, without dribbling, managed to chat to the Viscountess (Mrs Minty Chocolate Biscuit). We swapped opinions about the Royals (K-Mid of course and the awesome Diamond Jubilee celebrations). It couldn't have gone better until I plunged my fork into one of the tiny onions.

I caught its side and the shiny ball flew into the air, at speed, across the table. Shiiit. It landed right on top of Henrietta's head and, like an egg in a nest, settled in her bun. The camera zoomed in. Eerily, everyone stayed silent. No one swore or shrieked. Clearly, they knew Lady C's rule about staying as cool as a cucumber. I glanced at the Earl, who had put down his pipe.

It was no good. If I suppressed the gigantic giggle inside me any longer I'd spontaneously explode. Oh, God… Here it came… A snort escaped my lips. Then, nearby, Nick cracked and that really set me off as I spied his crinkly, watering-with-laughter eyes. For several seconds we were the only ones laughing, until Henrietta's face scrunched up to release a high-pitched giggle. Next, Ernest and Annabel crumbled. Even Edward's face broke into a grin. He removed the onion while Henrietta whispered something to him about not making a fuss. The Earl shook his head.

'I can't apologize enough,' I stuttered. Must control myself in front of the camera.

'Do you play golf, Abigail?' said the Earl. 'Because I suspect you'd be a whizz at landing a hole-in-one.' For the first time since my arrival he smiled at me properly, eyes all shiny.

Nick cleared away the plates and announced pudding would be simple apple pie—cue a massive sigh of relief from me. However, the Hamilton-Browns teased me relentlessly and ducked for cover when I reached for coffee sugar lumps. Even Henrietta kept giving me grins, so perhaps I could forgive her for being perfect and not spilling a drop of gravy on her silk blouse.

'How wonderful that you are heading up the Applebridge Food Academy, Abigail,' said Annabel as she unwrapped an after-dinner mint.

'Please—call me Abbey.' I tipped my chair backwards. 'Yes, it's, um, a challenge, no doubt about that.' One that I'd rather block out, for the moment. Otherwise, the temptation to go on the run would win.

'Our last chance, that's what it is,' muttered the Earl and puffed on his pipe. 'A great deal is hanging on Abigail's expertise.'

No pressure, then.

'Reverend White is attending Monday's first course, as well as a teacher from the high school in town,' continued the Earl. 'Also, my accountant—an enthusiastic woman… We thought just three students was a sensible number for starters.'

Roxy walked past in the background and stopped chewing sweets long enough to pull a face. She was right. I needed to focus. Catapulted onions were hardly sexy. The camera crew had gone into the kitchens to film the staff. This was my chance to find Nick, get him on camera next to me and instigate Plan Sex-up. Deep in thought, I tipped back on my chair again.

There was an ear-splitting crack as the wooden legs collapsed. Ankles over head, I crashed onto my back. Fuck!

I must have flashed my sequinned scarlet thong, having refused, point blank, to borrow Abbey's big pants. This was more Porno than Sex-up.

'Are you all right, Abbey?' asked Henrietta, on her feet. 'Poor you—I bet that hurt. At least the cameras have gone.'

Edward reached my side quicker than a bullet out of Mr Thompson's gun. Gently he sat me up and made sure no bones were broken. Then, straight away, cheeks flushed, he backed off and examined the chair. Nick helped me to my feet.

'The two back legs are completely ruined,' Edward announced after a quick glance at me rubbing my back. 'It's a shame. This is a matching antique set.'

For some reason, my eyes felt all watery. I couldn't help thinking he was more worried about permanent damage to the furniture than me.

'I'm okay,' I mumbled to everyone else. Lady C hadn't prepared me for such a situation and I'd never seen Abbey spreadeagle her legs in the air.

Edward didn't look at me again, cos I was probably some mega embarrassment—one that felt about as small as the flying onion.

'Although my back is, um, a tad sore,' I said, annoyed at the wobble in my voice.

'You've probably bruised it,' said Henrietta, voice still full of concern.

'Do we keep painkillers in the house, Uncle?' My cheeks burnt. I had to get out of here. This bonkers pretence was over. It would be best to quit before I let Abbey down any more. I couldn't even behave like a lady for the length of one fancy dinner.

'Kathleen has a supply in the kitchen,' he said and nodded in that direction. 'Shall I ring for a couple?'

'No, I'll, um, stretch my back and walk the long way around, through the front of the house. Please, everyone, do excuse me. Apologies, once again, for the disturbance.'

Still rubbing my back, I left the dining room and headed along the dark corridor, back past the Low Drawing Room. With a groan, I slumped at the bottom of the staircase. Aarghh! That could not have been more humiliating. Actually, it could—thank God I'd not gone commando to avoid visible panty lines. But then maybe that would have got some reaction out of those po-faced Croxley men. So much for Edward being a knight in shining armour.

With a sigh, I stood up and walked to the other side of the building, past another winding staircase. Edward had told me that here was the newly converted kitchen area installed for the Food Academy and, curiously, I went in. Talk about fancy.

With a sniff, I inspected the white-washed room and its five new workstations, one extra at the front where the teacher (that's me) would demonstrate her skills. They were basic, each with a silver sink, cooker and cutlery, plus cupboards well stocked with pans, sieves and graters. It was the only part of the house I'd seen, so far, that showed no hint of its noble status. A door at the back must have led to the pantry and cellars and real kitchen, where Kathleen cooked for the house. On tiptoe, I let myself in.

Sure enough, Kathleen and Mr Thompson sat at a large table, mugs in front of them, dead pheasants by the estate manager's feet. In front of a rolling camera, they chatted about how self-sufficient the estate was. Elvis Presley music played from an old-fashioned tape cassette machine on one of the units. Whilst huge, this kitchen was much more homely, with pine units, a huge scratched table and cross-stitch pictures on the walls. A whiff of baked pastry and fruit cut through the air. It was dark outside now. Nick had taken off his butler's coat and was downing a glass of water. He winked and joined me at the back of the kitchen, by the dishwasher. The cameraman and sound guy faced our direction but remained focused on Mr Thompson and the cook.

'Perhaps,' he muttered, 'this is an ideal opportunity to do something romantic—we'll get caught in the background of this shot.'

'No, you see... It's all a mistake, me at Applebridge Hall, and I've changed my mi—'

'Shh!' said Nick, eyes a-twinkle, and crept behind me, expensive cologne overpowering the smell of apple pie. He snaked his arms around my waist, before nuzzling my neck. Ooh—spiky unshaven cheeks. I'd always liked the feel of that... Finally, the gardener drew away and winked as he walked back to Kathleen and Mr Thompson. Back to my senses, I hurtled out of the room.

So much for Lady C's Three Ms—Modesty (thong flashed), Manners (rocketing onion) and No Men (unsightly stubble marks on my neck). At this rate I'd leave Abbey's reputation in tatters. It was over. I'd leave Applebridge tonight, before I made an even bigger fool of myself and lost lovely Nick his job. Run, girl, run!

LORD EDWARD'S E-DIARY

Saturday 1st September

'Comments'

11.45p.m. Thank you for your interest today, blog-readers. Here's one last comment from me before hitting the hay. This evening's dinner has not been without incident and, after an hour or so of reflection, I can only conclude that my cousin will bring more to *Million Dollar Mansion* than I ever imagined.

Of course, I knew she would as we, um, are a jolly close family. However, I'd forgotten the more…spontaneous side to her nature. It's reminiscent of my dear mother, who used to say, like sweet apple with pork, like cranberry jelly with turkey, she compensated for the stodgier aspects of my father and me.

However, what has flummoxed me is that an accident occurred tonight—nothing serious—but it surprised me how much I… If anything bad had happened to… Forgive me—the extra glass of port I drank must be responsible for this rambling. It's just that the power of shared DNA has a lot to answer for—nothing else could explain the strength of a new, unexpected feeling…

Knityourownmansion, many thanks—there's no doubt the Earl would very much like to receive a knitted mohair pipe through the post.

Drunkwriter, thank you for gracing us with your presence again, and I'm sure you'll understand why I had to moderate your comment—references to parts of the anatomy aren't for the everyone, however poetic.

Cupcakesrock, you hope that the answer to my poser question is the Croxley Coffee Shop? And *Blogger569*, I like your suggestion of us producing cider with cloves and orange—no doubt it would sell well at Christmas. I hope you both watch tomorrow's show and approve of the poser question's answer.

Right. Good. Done for the day. Sleep well, all.

CHAPTER 6

Ever declared to the world that you're starting a diet, but then eaten three bacon sarnies, one multi-pack of crisps, two pizzas and a family-sized tube of cookies? Then you'll understand why I didn't leave Applebridge Hall last night, despite my, um, dramatic announcement. As I was about to go upstairs, the Earl appeared. In a gruff voice, he asked how I was and patted my shoulder. Apparently, everyone was worried I'd feel too embarrassed to return to the dinner table. Mouth open, I listened as he muttered some story about his trousers falling down at a charity fund-raiser. It was nineteen ninety-five and gave him the push to finally ditch braces. Perhaps these Croxley men did have more running through their veins than stand-offish, cool tradition.

I yawned, having just got up, showered and carefully selected one of Abbey's outfits. It had a definite KMid feel, with the immaculate skinny jeans (okay, a bit of a squeeze on me) and white T-shirt. If I went out later, there was a short grey jacket to go with it, which was okay, but I was already missing wearing black—and especially my face bronzer.

My phone rang. I sat down on the four-poster bed (love saying that) and grabbed my mobile from the bedside table.

'Hiya. Yeah, I'm okay. Dinner? Um…Fine—there were no problems.' Hope Lady C didn't notice my voice suddenly squeak. Even though the truth would worry her, there was clearly no way she'd agree to me leaving the mansion now. So it was best to spare her the gory details of the astronaut onion and dress-above-waist faux pas. 'So have you chosen the menu I should demonstrate tomorrow, in my first lesson?' I grabbed my handbag from the foot of the bed and rummaged inside it. Finally, I pulled out a pen and a scrunched up tissue—that would have to do for writing down the ingredients.

'Right... An apple theme? What a mega idea, what with the orchards! Okay, Apple and English blue cheese salad to start...' I said, scribbling furiously. Yay for ingredients that wouldn't even need cooking! 'Pork and apple stew for the main, okay...' Chucking everything into a pot seemed doable. 'And baked apples for pudding?' Lady C said I should avoid cake or pastry-making for my first session and to say I'd chosen something less challenging, for 'the sake of the students'.

I kept the call brief, worried I might let slip about my kitchen-smooch with Nick. Also, I had a mega busy day ahead—the Earl was giving me an on-camera tour of the top floor late afternoon, then, at eight, we'd all watch the first Sunday episode of *Million Dollar Mansion: the Final*. It was the first opportunity the Croxleys had to see exactly how the smarmy Baron of Marwick had spent his twenty-five thousand quid. And it was my first chance to get a good look at the opposition.

Ingredients list in hand, I headed down to the kitchens to see if I would need to visit a supermarket. Kathleen greeted me with a warm smile. I felt bad tweaking the truth and telling her I was late up due to my back still aching. Despite her motherly protests, I insisted on simply munching an apple for breakfast (I couldn't face the

Croxleys' usual sausage and black pudding). The cook took the piece of tissue and skimmed the items.

'Not bad choices,' she said, 'although I could recommend some hearty Scottish dishes. I mean, if they were good enough for the Queen Mother...' Ten minutes later she was still describing weird-sounding dishes like Skink Soup and Clap shot! I smiled sheepishly. That Queen Mum thing was a random comment. Perhaps even the staff here were posh and she used to know royalty.

With a flourish, she opened the pantry door and seemed pleased with my gasp of amazement.

'We never run out of anything here,' she said and wiggled her generous bosom.

It was as if the Croxleys had their own corner shop, what with the massive bags of flour, tubs of seasoning, rows of cereals, pickles and preserves... The freezers were chockfull of meat they'd bought from local farmers. Kathleen took out some pork and showed me all the fruit and veg I needed. Plus the fridge's selection of cheese was awesome and even included the English blue for my salad, which was apparently Viscount Hamilton-Brown's favourite.

'Right... I'll lunch alone, downstairs with the computer,' I told her as she shut the fridge door. 'I must brush up my knowledge of, um, reality TV shows and how they work.'

'Och, that's true dedication—good on you,' she said, eyes crinkling at the corners.

I smiled back, having bent the truth again. More likely I'd be surfing YouTube clips about the basics of cooking. Part of the twenty-five thousand the Croxleys won had been spent on a long-awaited Internet connection. Although Kathleen tutted at the idea of on-line shopping, proudly declaring that Mr Thompson drove her into town twice a week and that the fishmonger and milkman delivered to the doorstep.

Several hours later, eyes twitching from staring at the screen and the artificial light in the cellars, I leant back in the chair—then immediately leant forward again, not wanting to risk snapping another piece of furniture. The time jumped out at me from the bottom of the screen—eek! Quarter to five already. I logged off and scurried past racks of wine, up the whitewashed stairs and into the kitchen.

'I'd better get upstairs for this tour,' I said to Kathleen who, wooden spoon in hand, was swaying to her Elvis Presley music. I glanced down at my jeans. 'Do you think I should change into something…grander?'

'Och, lassie, you look lovely,' said Kathleen and wiped her hands on her apron. 'I don't think the viewers expect us to look too glamorous.' She pulled a face. 'We'll leave anything tacky like that to that pompous numpty, the Baron of Marwick. Ee, I cannot think of anyone less aristocratic…'

My stomach twinged. Try the real me for starters.

I left the smell of baking biscuits, headed out of the kitchen and towards the staircase. Then I climbed the steps, trying to get my bearings. As I'd found out yesterday, the ground floor housed the Low Drawing Room and library on the right, the Drake Diner in the middle and on the left, the kitchens. On the middle floor were the family dining room and their lounge, known as the Parlour, then family and guest bedrooms and the High Drawing Room.

Panting slightly, I climbed another flight of stairs, right up to the second floor, at the top. This was where my tour would start and was home to something called the Long Gallery, plus the rooms where the staff slept.

'Good afternoon, Abbey,' said the Earl, in his tweed suit. He stood next to Gaynor and Roxy, who chatted to the cameraman. 'I do hope you slept well. Kathleen said you were spending the day preparing for tomorrow.' He sucked on his pipe. 'That's the attitude. Jolly good show, girl. Although I still think this cookery school idea is a load of nonsense...'

I smiled through his smoke and gazed the length of what was a mega wide corridor. In fact, it was more like a room, really, with doors to the staff bedrooms lining one side, on the left, and large windows on the right—the very back of the house. Plus there were a lot of pictures hanging.

'Right, darlings, let's get this show on the road,' said Gaynor in her husky smoker's voice, with a determined flick of her black bob. 'Lord Croxley, if you could remember that this tour is for the viewers as well, that would be fab...'

He pursed his mouth. 'Don't worry—I'll try to make it interesting.'

Roxy managed to smile at me while still chewing the sweet she'd just popped in her mouth and gave the thumbs-up as the Earl started walking.

'I've never cared much for this marble fireplace,' he said gruffly and pointed to a middle section of the long wall, in between two bedrooms. 'Although Trigger, my father's gundog, loved nothing better than to stretch out in front of it, following an afternoon at the shoot—a treat for the old mutt as he was rarely allowed in the house.'

I nodded, adjusting the mic's battery pack clipped onto my jeans, under my t-shirt, that Roxy had quickly helped me fit. Apparently the lapel mics were better if you were walking about.

'So, this is the Long Gallery?' I said—cue the Earl to duly chat about its features. At the far end stood two buckets and there was a slightly musty whiff in the air.

'A couple of the bedrooms up here don't belong to the staff and haven't been entered for years,' muttered the

Earl. I waited for some mysterious reason as to why not but he just carried on walking—Roxy pulled a face and yawned.

Urgh—she was right, this footage would be mind-numbingly boring. Shame, cos I thought this floor was pretty amazin'. The windows were mega, with shelves below them for seats. In between hung portraits of all sorts of people. Impressive chandeliers dangled from the ceiling and gave me a sudden urge to swing on them. I shivered, despite the summer temperature outside, wondering how many thousands of pounds it would cost to install central heating. The Earl was making points about the history of the interior design, which wouldn't grab the attention of your average viewer. Finally, he stopped still in front of a portrait and puffed on his pipe. It was of a middle-aged bloke in a dinner suit, who sat by bookshelves, dark-rimmed glasses perched on his nose. The man's shoulders sagged as if someone had anchored his cuffs into stormy waters.

'Goodness, he looks, um, terribly serious,' I said. 'Who was he, Uncle? Some important politician who knew our ancestors? Or perhaps a film star who visited? He looks as if he could play a believable stern villain.'

The Earl's cheeks flushed. 'That's Papa.'

'Oh…um…' I stuttered.

'Really, Abigail,' he said. 'I'm surprised you don't recognize your grandfather.'

Suddenly desperate to bite my thumbnail, I swallowed hard.

'This was painted just after the Second World War,' he continued. 'I was only eight but remember it like yesterday. Papa didn't budge an inch for hours, when he sat for the artist. Impressive—but then he was made of strong stuff.'

I studied the man's hair, greased above the ears and black. Perhaps the Earl had looked like this as a young man.

'It was painted just after Applebridge Hall returned to our possession. As you know, this place was requisitioned as a home for children during the war. We still lived here as a family, but evacuees from London were billeted with us.'

Abbey hadn't told me that! Wow. Awesome.

'The family struggled to bring it back to its former glory after those little blighters spent six years running riot. In fact, one of the lads caused a fire,' he said, as if talking to no one in particular. 'Dennis Smith was his name. Always up to no good. He swore blind he hadn't been playing with matches, but none of us children believed him as we'd often catch him in the forest with a lit roll-up of paper, pretending to smoke.'

Rolled up paper? As children, my brothers had bought the real McCoy. The ice cream man got done for selling us single fags from his van.

The Earl turned to the camera and raised his eyebrows. 'Perhaps, if he's watching, Dennis would like to confess his crime. But there—stiff upper lip and all that, my family simply had to tolerate the intrusion and damage. If truth be told, Mama enjoyed doing her bit and I made the most of the company. It was for the good of the country. The real villain was Hitler.' He sucked on his pipe. 'After the war, Papa did his best to restore our home to its former glory.'

Blimey, for a man of few words, that was quite a speech. Sweet—he'd clearly adored his dad.

One thing Abbey had mentioned was this grandfather's failed business dealings. He died from a heart attack, mega young—well, if, unlike me, you don't consider being fifty-something totally ancient. Her dad, Richard, was only a teen. In the days following his death, the Earl and his brother must have become close, which made their fall-out all the more random.

'It must have been a shock when he, um, passed on.' Okay, so a lady wasn't supposed to make such personal comments but, for Gawd's sake, how would viewers warm to the Croxleys if they came across as such cardboard cut-out, unemotional aristocratic figures?

'*Epicccc*,' I said as we moved to the next portrait—a woman in a fancy dress, with geisha-white skin and caramel hair swept up. Jewels dangled from her ears and hung around her neck... Crap! Had I really laxed into Gemma mode and actually said 'epic'? 'I mean, um...*a piccccc*ture one could stare at all day. What an extraordinarily good-looking woman.'

'Mama,' he said and his face went all squishy for a second, before he stared at me. 'Once more, you talk as if you've never seen a picture of her.'

I forced a laugh. 'Apologies, Uncle—Grandmother looks quite, um, different from the photos Father has shown me.'

The Earl gazed back at the portrait. 'During inclement weather, when Papa was away on business, she'd smuggle my pony up here and let me ride the length of the Long Gallery. I loved her for that,' he said softly.

'How, um, enchanting.' I glanced at Gaynor,who'd looked up from her clipboard to listen. Roxy had even stopped chewing. Blimey, the Earl had let his gruff mask slip for a minute.

A smile flickered across his face. 'Well, that's what the Long Gallery was sometimes used for—exercise in bad weather. Up and down we'd go. Our indoor constitutional, Mama used to call it—but she always made it seem jolly.'

He scratched his bristly beard and headed for the next picture. It was a couple, smartly dressed on a fancy sofa. The man had on a cravat and a pocket watch hung out of his waistcoat. I glanced sideways at the Earl. A pocket watch dangled from his tweed waistcoat—perhaps it was the same one. The woman was dressed in a vertically striped blouse and broad-brimmed hat. The couple looked happy and fancy-free, eyes twinkly and mouths upturned.

'My great-grandparents,' he said. 'Terribly well-known for their partying. Splendid hosts, according to one and all. The Drake Diner was home to many a ball. In those days the servants slept in the kitchens and pantry. Up here was for guests.'

We moved onto the next frame. 'My grandparents,' he murmured. 'They were also significant players on the social scene. We believe a young Noël Coward stayed here once.'

'Ah, yes, my dear cousin mentioned that,' I said.

'Your father never told you?' he said abruptly.

Roxy and Gaynor glanced at each other and raised their eyebrows.

'But, erm, of course,' the Earl said after a quick glare at me, 'Richard never was much interested in celebrity. But he must have told you about our great-grandfather's party trick? Papa used to creep down and peek at him doing it in the Drake Diner.'

My cheeks flamed. 'Um, yes, he could make, um, coins appear from people's ears…?'

'That wasn't the one I was thinking of,' he said in a measured voice. 'Apparently, drinking out of his wife's shoe was considered a jolly jape. He'd announce to the room that it made the champagne taste absolutely divine.

Papa got into trouble when he was a little boy for trying the same with his bedtime milk.'

Gaynor and Roxy smiled.

As we came to the end of the Long Gallery, on the right hand side of the house, we stood and gazed up at a ginormous gold-framed portrait of a man. Around his neck was an amazin' ruffle, he had a moustache, beard and wore a feathered hat. His expression looked kind of laid-back, as if not a thing could surprise him. Upright and confident, he seemed like the complete opposite of the bespectacled, world-weary-looking Earl's dad.

'The very first Earl of Croxley,' said the old man and straightened his back. 'Elizabeth the First awarded him the estate of Applebridge for his role in defeating the Spanish Armada, in 1588. The Drake Diner was named after his good friend…'

'Sir Francis Drake,' I mumbled. Even I could work that out.

I exchanged glances with Roxy, who was clearly rapt. This tour had turned into a live history lesson. I gazed at the man on the canvas and tried to imagine him on some ship or proudly bowing before the Queen. He must have been one of the celebrities of the day. Mega important. Probably had his pick of the women, ate the finest food without having to worry about paparazzi and Twitter trolls, like today's celebs.

'Did he build Applebridge Hall?' I asked.

'You don't even know that!' he spluttered, yet within seconds obviously remembered that we were supposed to promote this cuddly image of a close family. He forced a chuckle. 'Ah, my scoundrel of a younger brother… Richard was never much of a historian. Yes. His family lived in a small country house on the estate—since knocked down—whilst the architects and builders set to work.'

Footsteps sounded up the stairwell nearest to us. Honey curls appeared.

'Good day, Abbey,' Edward said. 'I trust that, um, your back no longer hurts.'

Blimey. He *was* making an effort for the cameras. 'Good afternoon. Yes, tickety-boo now, thank you,' I replied. It was weird living somewhere so big that a whole day might pass before you bump into the other housemates.

'Father, the first episode of *Million Dollar Mansion*: *the Final* will be on in around an hour,' said Edward. 'Members of staff are congregating in the Parlour. I believe Kathleen has prepared tea and your favourite lemon crumb biscuits for everyone. We could all go over the plans for tomorrow before the beginning of the programme.'

'Aaaaand cut,' said Gaynor and gave a rusty cough. 'No problem, darlings. We can continue the tour tomorrow, Lord Croxley—we'll still have time to edit it for Tuesday's show. And yes, fab work, everyone—those tales made Applebridge Hall come to life; made the whole place less…grey.'

However, the old man wasn't listening.

'Right, young lady…' he hissed to me and unplugged his mic, before doing the same to mine. 'Let's walk back the length of the Gallery and downstairs to the Parlour. On the way, you can explain to me why you know so little about the Croxley ancestors. Let's hope to God that your cookery knowledge is better than your history.'

Crap. I took off my mic and we handed them to the cameraman. Gaynor and Roxy were still staring up at the ginormous portrait. Edward had disappeared, having muttered something about his blog.

'It's as if you're a complete stranger, Abigail,' said the Earl and glared. 'The Richard I used to know loved these old anecdotes. Estrangement or not, I'm sure any daughter of his would be familiar with what her ancestors looked like and, in God's name, know the origins of how this place was built!'

'I... Yes... You see...' I stuttered.

'Well?' he said. 'I'm waiting for what had better be a damn good explanation.'

LORD EDWARD'S E-DIARY

Sunday 2nd September

7p.m. Good evening, blog-readers, I trust you will soon settle down to watch this evening's show. No doubt you shall find footage of yesterday's events, including dinner, entertaining. Of course, it is somewhat edited, especially during these early days, whilst we get used to the cameras. And not everything is caught on film. As I suggested to you last night, cousin Abigail is quite the dark horse—for a lady—and even made Father chuckle. Erm, I've always thought this, *of course*, during our *frequent* rendezvous over the years. It's just that this weekend her more…*casual* aspect seems more pronounced than before.

This is not a criticism, dear cousin, if you are reading my blog. Not unless your behaviour leads to unseemly conduct and damaged property, such as a valuable chair… And, um, do excuse some rambling comments I made on here last night. The family port has had a lot to answer for over the years.

Moving right on, a few words about my day, not assuming it's of any particular interest, but in the name of promoting 'Team Croxley' (the crew's words, not mine) here goes:

I spent hours in Gaynor's company, yet again fending off suggestions to mimic some romantic literary character.

As I've said from the start, I am no Mr Rochester, no Rhett Butler (names I know, thanks to my mother's love of books). Despite my protestations, Gaynor insisted on leading me to the pond and suggested I bathe in my clothes, then wade out, shirt tight, hair dripping…

Honestly? I can't believe viewers would like to see a non-fictional person do that. Humour me, blog-readers— can that sort of thing really be what the viewing public desires? (Note to Gaynor, I believe in transparency, so anything you say to me might appear in this e-diary).

I shall return to this page anon, to keenly read your answers—and ponder your reactions to tonight's footage.

Thank you for your attention.

CHAPTER 7

Shouldn't I be the angry one, dear Uncle, because you didn't know about my terrible childhood accident? For most of my formative years (yes, cool phrase off Lady C) I'd been in a coma. So excuse me if I didn't know all your ancestral anecdotes...

Sigh—I kind of guessed that such an excuse wouldn't stick. Plus I couldn't face making up any more big lies. Who could blame the Earl for being mad? I hadn't even recognized my supposed granddad. So, instead, on the way back along the corridor, past the portraits, I simply mumbled to the Earl about the teenage years being 'difficult'. I explained that most of what my father said went in one of my petulant ears and straight out the other. For some reason—thank goodness—this tickled his humour. From what the Earl remembered, his brother could have broken any Guinness World Record for non-stop waffling.

Just as we headed downstairs to the Parlour, Edward joined us, having quickly updated his blog. I'd read a snitch last night. Talk about conscientious! Clearly he saw it as his duty to reply to almost every comment—which was kind of cute. I couldn't believe he thought me, acting as Abbey, spontaneous. Blimey, he'd have fifty fits if he met the real Gemma! And, as for his rambling, well—bravo

Edward, for trying to convince people that you and I were close and you really cared about my fall. Anyway, then we chatted about the upcoming screening. My stomach twisted a little as I considered important questions, like did the camera really put on ten pounds and would High Definition telly magnify any old acne scars?

We reached the first floor, crossed a long corridor over to the left side of the house and entered the Parlour, which was nothing like I'd expected—much more modern, in fact homely, with Mr Thompson drinking tea on an ottoman-style pouf and Kathleen and Jean chilled on a cosy mustard sofa. Nick sat on the floor, in between their legs. Opposite them was a slimline telly, with a laptop on a desk next to that. The room was well lit, with a real fire as well. Newspapers and magazines were piled up on a low coffee table in the middle of the room, next to a teapot and cups and a plate of yummy-looking biscuits. There was wood-panelling on the bottom half of the walls, the top half painted a warm orangey-red. The Earl sat down in a high-backed terracotta armchair to the right of the telly and was already puffing on his pipe.

The cook got up to pour us tea but Edward shooed her back to her seat.

'You're not on duty Sunday evenings, Kathleen,' he said, while pointing me to the space next to her on the sofa. 'You put your feet up and let me hand around these delightful biscuits.'

The cook nodded her appreciation and untied her floral apron. Nick looked up and winked at me—I smiled, sat down neatly, knees together, hands in my lap, wishing I could get really comfy and tuck my legs under my bum. Edward passed me a cup and rested next to me on the sofa's wide arm, then Kathleen turned down the telly and we chatted about how the weekend had gone—and what the week ahead might have in store. My chest tightened after some chat about tomorrow's unveiling of the Applebridge Food Academy and my first lesson. I really was going to be teaching. There was no backing out now.

Another cup of tea later, Edward was just about to go over some boring health and safety message about lapel mics again when (thank God) Nick jumped up, turned up the telly volume and, from the screen, Charlie's familiar voice shouted out:

'Welcome, folks, to the final two weeks of *Million Dollar Mansion*. Put up your feet and enjoy an hour of swanky scenery, grand game-plans and blue-blooded banter. Head to head, it's Marwick Castle and Applebridge Hall. Meet the families again. Enjoy their Chat with Chingo!'

'Not much different on screen, is he?' murmured Mr Thompson, still in his Sherlock Holmes hat, with his voice as deep as any bass instrument.

'Maybe a bit more orange,' said Jean and caught my gaze. We grinned at each other.

'Super biscuits, Kathleen,' I said in a muffled voice, crumbs of lemon loveliness tumbling from my lips. Crap—should've helped myself to a napkin.

'Och, thank you, Miss, they were nae bother,' she said. 'I'm looking forward to seeing the dishes you make in your cooking classes tomorrow. Applebridge Hall has only seen honest home cooking before, not haute cuisine.'

I gave a nervous giggle, hoping it would be mistaken for ladylike modesty and not ginormous stress. Tonight I would creep down to the cellars and go online to pick up more tips from Nigella and Delia on YouTube. For a few moments I ran through the recipes in my mind. They sounded simple enough. Perhaps I wouldn't let anyone down.

I turned my attention back to the screen. Everyone was watching last night's footage at Marwick Castle—a raucous hen party. Charlie Chingo explained how the Baron had spent his twenty-five thousand on kitting out the dungeons with water, lighting and heat. At first he stood by the entrance, just past the drawbridge, where there was a humongous stuffed grizzly bear. Charlie Chingo then made his way down to the dungeons. Women dressed up in tutus and Playboy ears shrieked with laughter as topless hunks brought food to the banquet table and topped up their wine glasses.

'Classy,' muttered Mr Thompson and wrinkled his nose.

Weapons better suited to any bondage den hung on the walls. A figure stood dressed in full armour. One of the women went to flash her boobs and, just in time, the camera panned away.

The old Earl puffed furiously on his pipe, while Nick had a grin on his face. Jean watched with her mouth open and Kathleen shook her fading red curls. The Baron sure had sexed up his place. As an expert on reality shows, I knew younger viewers would love this footage. Edward's face was deadpan as Charlie Chingo went on to interview the Baron and his son, The Honourable Harry Gainsworth. I sipped my tea, trying to decide whose fake tan was loudest—Charlie's or the Baron's.

'The Castle was built in the eleventh century, old boy,' said the Baron, a grin on his face, his fingers and wrists showing off his clunky gold jewellery. 'It was part of that William the Conqueror's castle building plan. Steeped in history, this place is,' he said and clapped Charlie on the back.

Okay, that all sounded sexy and romantic and from a distance the Castle was awesome, with its mahoosive grey stone walls, turrets and waving flags. A drawbridge crossed the moat and forest surrounded the whole place. Wow. It brought out all those basic instincts—women could fantasize about warriors with six-packs, while men imagined chucking spears and rescuing fair maidens.

'My grandfather was a very successful industrialist,' said the Baron and puffed out his chest. 'And I think our plans for Marwick Castle prove that good business sense runs in the family.'

'Too right, Dad,' said Harry Gainsworth with a smirk, showing off his celebrity whitened teeth. 'Your granddad bought this gaff in the Twenties, didn't he?'

The Baron nodded. 'Just after he was awarded the title of Baron of Marwick in 1920. Then he renamed this place and renovated the Castle. It was a right dump back then.'

The Earl snorted. 'The government outlawed the awarding of titles in 1925. It's an outrage. People should be born to their names, not buy them like a loaf of bread. And if the Baron was so jolly successful, he wouldn't have needed to enter this competition.' He muttered 'pompous arse' under his breath.

The words 'Baron Numpty' escaped Kathleen's lips.

Still Edward said nothing and sat as stiff as one of the headstones in his family cemetery, only leaning forward when the programme moved onto Applebridge Hall. Oh my God! That was me, getting out of the car when I arrived. Or was it? I hardly recognized myself. Without my chicken fillets and tarantula lashes I looked kind of older. And yes, even I could see the resemblance to my flatmate. Plus, hallelujah! My bum wasn't half as big as I expected—my brothers must have lied about that all these years.

The footage moved to the orchard. Oh, no. I hadn't warned Edward that... My cousin smacked his hand down on his knee.

'I instructed Gaynor to edit that out,' he said as the camera zoomed in on me, supposedly convulsing on the soil.

'That's my fault,' I said and cleared my throat. 'Gaynor and I decided it would be best to leave this shot in, after all.'

His lip curled. 'What about self-respect and dignity? I told you that scene wouldn't work.'

'And I told you that, during my stay, I should have a part in the decision-making,' I said quietly.

'Splendid decision,' he sneered. 'You sprawled amongst tree roots, legs akimbo, is a real credit to the family.'

A lump rose in my throat. He was right. But high viewing figures were everything. At least I recognized that.

'The pace of the show has sped up, though,' said Nick and jerked his head towards the screen. It showed Edward sweep me up into his muscular arms. How easily he carried me into the house. I smiled at Nick, appreciative of the support.

'If I may be so bold, My Lord,' Nick went on, 'like it or not, refined cookery lessons won't compete with girls in skimpy outfits dancing on tables among joints of meat.'

'I'd keep your opinions to yourself then, if they are that negative,' said Edward in a measured voice. 'The Croxleys will not throw away their principles. Not for anything.'

'Our ancestors must be turning in their graves,' said the Earl's gruff voice.

Crap. If they were that put out by my collapse, then how would they react to my hug with Nick in the kitchen? My mouth went dry as the show moved onto yesterday's dinner with the Hamilton-Browns. I busied myself by handing around the last of the biscuits.

'Och, will you look at my hair,' said Kathleen, gazing at the telly.

Um, I don't think so—I was too wrapped up in studying my terrible table manners. I'd started my bread before everyone else and—oh my God—I wiped my nose with the back of my hand. Good thing my mobile was off. Any horrified texts from Lady C could wait for a couple of days. Suddenly Nick and Jean guffawed at the flying onion. My hands felt sweaty as the next shot was in the kitchen.

There sat Kathleen, at the pine table, talking with Mr Thompson—I gazed at the background of the shot. You could just make out Nick, sliding his arms around my waist. Or could you? His dark hair kind of merged in with the shadows and the short-sighted viewers might possibly mistake his arms for a really thick belt. As for me, the background light was so bad, you couldn't make out my face. Heart racing, I watched the gardener nuzzle my neck. I hardly dared glance at Edward.

Which was bonkers. I was only here for two weeks. Why did I care about his opinion of me? My throat hurt because I knew the answer—like it or not, Gemma Goodwin, you're starting to care about the Croxleys and their house.

Urgh. Edward had clearly spotted me, his noble cousin, on screen, getting intimate with a servant, because his cheeks flushed maroon and he jumped up, practically tossing his cup onto the tray as the credits rolled. While the rest of us stared at him, jaws open, he picked up the laptop and stormed out of the Parlour, slamming the door shut on his way.

LORD EDWARD'S E-DIARY

Sunday 2nd September

'Comments'

9.10p.m. I've just flipped open my laptop, here in the library. My first thought was to check the blog instead of the news or weather forecast. Gradually I'm understanding why social media is popular—it offers a break from the responsibilities and obligations of the real world. Even though this e-diary is about my life, it lacks the stresses and strains of the genuine thing.

No doubt you are all still digesting tonight's show. Several people, however, have already responded to my earlier question of what viewers really want.

I see that *BustyfanDownton* and *Lovehotnoble*—like Gaynor—are absolutely in favour of men standing in ponds. Erm, please, both of you stop fighting over who would—hypothetically—help me unbutton my shirt to dry off. I'm quite old enough to do that myself. And Mr Darcy I am not. *Knityourownmansion*, many thanks, but I won't need woollen Speedos. No, *EtonMess*, I don't think cousin Abigail will take a dip in the pond wearing a tight T-shirt.

CHAPTER 8

'Awwwwesome,' I said in a loud voice, having finally found Edward downstairs in the library, knocked and gone in. But urgh! What was I thinking, speaking like that? 'I mean, *awwww, some* of my favourite books,' I quickly added.

My mouth fell open at the number of shelves going up, ooh, over six feet high. If you wanted a book from the top, you'd have to use the nearby set of ladders. Unlike the other rooms, the panelling in here was made from a warmer, caramel-coloured wood. Ignoring me, Edward closed his laptop. Lit-up lamps across the room gave it a mega cosy glow. He leant back into the sage-green upholstered chair behind the large wooden desk. Catching my breath after searching for him, I slid a leather-bound book off the shelf. It was by Dickens, Abbey's all time favourite author. Her parents had bought her the complete works, in red leather, all embossed in gold. I lifted the book to my face and sniffed.

'My mother always used to do that,' muttered Edward and stared. 'She believed you could smell a good story.' He gazed into the distance for a second.

My eyes tingled. Stubborn old sausage or not (as Abbey would probably say) it hurt to see him in such a state.

'Look…' I said. 'About what you saw on that programme tonight…the gardener… It appears worse on screen than it was.'

'Really?' he said and looked up.

My mouth went dry. Seems like this *Upstairs Downstairs* love stuff really was a serious business.

'Nick and m…' oops, that should be *Nick and I* '…we wanted to create some entertainment and…'

Edward shook his head. 'That's the least of my worries, you and a member of staff bursting into laughter over an onion. In any event, we all eventually joined in. Just try to remember next time, Abbey, that at Applebridge Hall, *guests* are our friends—not the staff. Of course, Jean, Mr Thompson and Kathleen are very important to Applebridge Hall,' he said gruffly, 'but Gaynor thinks we should present this clichéd image of being distant, upper-crust toffs. She thinks viewers like stereotypes. As a compromise, I've agreed not to appear over-familiar with people on the pay-roll, whilst the cameras are on.'

Huh? He thought I meant me and Nick laughing together when the onion went flying? Looked like he hadn't seen the sexy smooch after all.

I slid the book back. Right. So if he hadn't noticed me getting down and dirty with the help, why did he storm off?

'I know Nick is your own age,' he continued, 'which may be appealing, but please… Try to keep up appearances.'

I bit the inside of my cheeks. Jeez, he made me sound about twelve.

'The ironic thing is,' he said, 'that one of the staff—Kathleen—is the most uppercrust thing about us.'

I raised my eyebrows.

'Her grandmother worked for the Queen Mother when the latter's father, Claude George Bowes-Lyon, inherited the Earldom of Strathmore and Kinghorne.'

Aha, that must be why Kathleen was always mentioning the Queen Mum.

'Lady Elizabeth Bowes-Lyon she was back then, a young girl in the early nineteen-hundreds,' he continued. 'Kathleen's grandmother helped out in the kitchens and passed down the recipes she learnt to her own family.'

Ooh, I wondered what the Queen Mum liked to scoff.

'Mother was very excited when Kathleen mentioned this in her job interview.' Edward gave a wry smile. 'She loved the royal family and was hugely pleased at the thought of us having connections through anyone in the house, even if the link was super tenuous.'

'How long has Kathleen worked here?'

'Over thirty years. She took up the position the year before I was born. Mother and Father weren't long married.'

'She never wanted a family of her own?'

He shrugged. 'There was one gentleman, I believe, but it ended badly—she told Mother all about it.' He stared vacantly at the wall opposite. It was hard to imagine how much someone must miss their mum if they'd actually known them. I missed mine and she was just a distant figure made up from the memories of a toddler.

'Dear Edward, do tell me what upset you tonight,' I said gently, and sat in a wooden chair opposite him.

'Here, take my seat,' he muttered. 'It's more comfortable.'

We swapped. Blimey. Not that I was into being seen as the weaker sex, but no man had ever been quite so concerned for my comfort. Lee, my ex, used to hog the duvet and bagsied the window seat when we flew to Benidorm.

Edward jerked his head towards a portrait, high up on the wall. I recognized the serious man in specs from the picture in the Long Gallery. It was the Earl's 'Papa' as he called him—Edward and Abbey's granddad.

'There are eyes everywhere in this house,' he muttered, 'reminding me of my duty; the responsibility to maintain standards.' He shook his head. '*Million Dollar Mansion*— the whole concept is just so disrespectful to our heritage. Grandfather did his best with his business dealings but, I regret to say, it wasn't enough; we've never really recovered since the war. Father has struggled and finally we've had to do the one thing the old Croxleys would never have considered. The Earl detests me renting out the land for car boot sales and fairs…' His shoulders sagged. 'We're taking money off people to come into our home. "Entering trade" as Father would say. How has it come to this? That's what's upset me. Plus realizing how much the public are going to love the Baron.'

'This family is doing what it has to, Edward.'

'But I know Father feels that he's let our ancestors and the village down. This estate used to provide jobs for life for many families in Applebridge, back in the days when neither the grounds, nor the house ran on a shoestring staff.' Edward bit his lip. 'I'm not stupid. Father might sneer at the Baron of Marwick, but I go on the Internet and see the magazine headlines in the shops. Hen nights, drunkenness, vulgar behaviour in general, with no sight of a moral compass… Rightly or wrongly, that's what the viewers of these shows want. But we Croxleys will never go as far as providing that sort of entertainment.'

I was one of those viewers he talked of. *Big Brother* fisticuffs, *Love Island* drunken flings… It made good telly, didn't it, and it was something to chat about the next day at work? I blushed.

'But Edward—you are being true and honest to yourselves, at least. The Baron is putting on a show.'

'True? Honest?' he muttered and—oh, no!—Edward held his head in his hands. 'If only you knew,' he muttered in a strained voice. 'The continual… If only I could tell one person… My life is just a…' A tortured pain in his eyes, he looked up.

'What is it?' I asked gently. 'Please, let me help.'

He opened his mouth but closed it again. 'Apologies, cousin. Ignore me—it's just sometimes the pressure…'

My eyes felt wet. I'd rather see him all arrogant than torn like this.

Edward got to his feet and paced up and down. 'Can Applebridge Food Academy really compete with medieval banquets?' he said, back to his normal controlled voice. 'Father still isn't happy about the classes eventually becoming residential. It took me long enough to convince him that car boot sales were worth it for the income.' He sighed. 'Over the years, I've had to persuade him to become more pragmatic. I'm always looking for new ideas. We can only host around fourteen events on the land per year without planning permission. If we don't win the competition…'

'As Charlie Chingo pointed out, cookery programmes are all the rage,' I said, noticing for the first time the dark circles under Edward's eyes. Funny. I'd only ever thought about the upside of owning a stately home and never considered it could be a burden that could give you sleepless nights. Croquet on the lawn, cucumber sandwiches, diamonds worn to dinner, that's what I'd imagined—not family expectations, leaky roofs and disastrous debts. 'It'll be all right,' I said softly.

He smiled at me. 'You really think so?'

I nodded.

Edward rubbed the back of his neck and eventually straightened. 'Of course. I'm sure it will. Don't you worry.'

'If you ever want to talk…?'

'That's kind, cousin, but really there's no need.' He was back into formal coping-mode. 'It was an early start today. Mr Thompson had to show me some fencing that's desperate for repair, right at the bottom end of the estate. I'm probably just tired. Do excuse my whining.'

My stomach squeezed. Like it or not, I longed to cheer up this uptight, stubborn… goddamn good-looking noble. Yet I guessed he wouldn't want to watch trashy TV or gorge on chocolate, and probably didn't own a Wii or karaoke machine. I gazed outside for a second. It was dark now.

However, in the dim corner of the room, on a bottom shelf, I spied a flat green box.

'Would you care to join me in a game of Scrabble?' I said. That would at least take his mind off things.

'What—now?' His brow furrowed. 'I should check the weather forecast for tomorrow, and set up more buckets if rain is due.'

'Worried I might beat you?'

'What utter tosh!' His mouth twitched. 'Okay then. You're on.'

I fetched the box and cleared some stationery from the desk. Then I set up the board and grabbed a pen to mark the scores. We both selected our letter tiles. Edward began. 'DECEIT' was his first word. I bit my lip. Was that fate telling me that he'd eventually uncover my true identity?

Forty-five minutes later we were neck and neck. The floorboards creaked outside the door as someone went upstairs to bed. PROFIT, RANK, ACCOUNTS and HUNT were some of his words, but nothing compared to the one which got me my highest score. I remembered it from a previous game with Abbey—MUZJIK, a Russian term for a peasant. Although I doubt Edward was impressed with the rest of my words, which included TIT (the bird, of course) and BUM (sorry, but needs must).

'You aren't allowed that. It's slang for a body part,' Edward had said with a smile.

Victorious, I'd shaken my head. 'Sorry. I checked this once when playing with Ab...my lodger Gemma. It's a proper word that means lazy person or vagrant.'

'She must be quite clever, this Gemma,' he said.

I smiled nervously. 'Um...' What would Abbey say?

'You get on well, living together?'

I smiled. 'People sometimes mistake us for each other and yes, I suppose in several ways we are rather like sisters... Brothers are super, but as well as dear Rupert,' read that as annoying Tom and banged-up Ryan! 'I would have loved a female sibling.'

A curious look crossed Edward's face for a moment and I could have sworn he mumbled, 'Me too'.

Loud chimes cut through the wall from the Low Drawing Room next door—from the spooky-looking grandfather clock. Yikes. Eleven? I'd completely forgotten about Googling Nigella and Delia and there were only...I swallowed hard...ten hours to me playing teacher. Applebridge Food Academy was to open at nine a.m. sharp.

'Would you mind terribly if we picked this game up another time, Edward? I didn't realize it was so late and must go on the computer to check a few things for tomorrow's cookery lessons.'

'Who's worried now?' he said, a twinkle in his eye. 'I'm clearly going to win.'

'I doubt that. Although you do have a decade's knowledge above me. My youth puts me at a disadvantage.'

'I'm not on a Zimmer frame yet!'

'You check weather forecasts,' I said and shook my finger at him. 'No one under forty does that. What next? Discussing arthritic knees? Declaring mobile phones are the downfall of our society?'

We grinned at each other. It was only a board game, but the first indication that stuffy old Edward knew how to have some sort of fun.

I stood up and turned to the door, my gaze falling on the bookshelves to the right. Halfway up was about a one metre length of pastel and pink book spines. I walked over and pulled out a book. It smelt flowery, as if the last person to read it wore a lot of perfume.

'Sophie Kinsella! Marian Keyes!' I said, scanning the shelf. 'I love these books! Um, as well as the classics, of course.'

'They were Mother's. Crime and any sort of romance were her novels of choice.' He jerked his head. 'On the opposite side of the room are my childhood books. We've the whole Beatrix Potter series and I grew up thinking I was Christopher Robin.' He shrugged. 'Borrow books any time you want, cousin. Or read at this desk, if you prefer. Father doesn't much care for the media people and often seeks refuge in here as well.'

'That's very kind,' I said and tried to imagine him as a little boy, with curly blond hair. Serious, he'd have been. I doubted he ever got a detention or less than a grade A.

'So.' He stood up. 'The computer. Will you find your way down to the cellars okay?'

'Yes, thank you.' I sat still and fiddled with my watch.

'What is it?' he said.

Slowly I met his gaze. 'I hope I don't let the family down tomorrow, Edward.' Better warn him—just in case the cooking went pear-shaped.

Abruptly he stood up, as if jolted back to reality by the potential whiff of failure. 'We're relying on you, Abbey. The future of Applebridge Hall is at stake. Remember, strong Croxley women never lose that stiff upper lip. There's a torch in the cupboard to the right of the cellar entrance. You might need it to find your way back to your bedroom if you are the last up and we've switched off the lights. We don't leave them on unless we have to. It's all about cutting costs.' Any warmth in his eyes had now evaporated. 'Until morning, cousin.'

He was right. I had to get a grip and find that stiff upper lip Lady C liked talking about. If Abbey could help war orphans, the least I could do was cook in front of a camera. Still, talk about a lack of sympathy! I could have done with an encouraging hug or, at the very least, a squeeze of the arm as he brushed past me and out of the library. But then Edward wasn't touchy-feely. In fact I couldn't even imagine him cuddling a girlfriend. Like those hunks from *The Vampire Diaries*, he'd probably rather suck them dry first...

Mmm, thinking of sexy vampires, I could imagine kissing Edward's cherry-coloured stubborn lips that not nearly often enough curved into a smile...

Urgh! No. That was mega wrong. I mustn't ponder his snogability if I was to keep up this charade of us being cousins. I shook myself and, with new determination, slipped out of the library and made my way along to the west wing kitchens.

Mr Thompson was still up, sitting at the pine table, gun laid next to a small glass of whisky. He muttered something about trespassers before tilting his hat at me and going outside. I grabbed the torch, switched on the cellar lights and made my way down to the little desk and chair positioned next to rack after rack of wine.

Despite the warm day, I shivered slightly—through cold or fear for tomorrow who could tell. I took a deep breath. How difficult could it be, throwing together a few ingredients? Billions of people did it every day, all around the world.

I pressed the button and the computer sprung to life. I thought about Nick and his kiss and how I only had two weeks to sex up Applebridge Hall. Instead of typing in Nigella or Delia, I typed in Facebook and entered my password. There I was, in my account, under my mum's name, Eleanor Goodwin. Not Gemma, cos this weird ex once cyber-stalked me, sending virtual voodoo dolls.

After a quick search I soon found a fan page for *Million Dollar Mansion*. Uh oh—my heart raced. Here came one of my adrenaline rushes, cue doing something impulsive. On automatic, I joined the group, deciding that the public needed help in spotting the signs of the aristocrat and gardener's mega unsuitable romance. The rumour-mill needed a shove into motion, regardless of what Edward or the Earl might say. I took a deep breath and typed:

Hello all—amazin' final, isn't it? Has anyone noticed the sizzling chemistry between gardener Nick and Abbey, the

Earl's la-di-da niece? I could have sworn they were in the background of that shot in the kitchen tonight. Talk about getting close! When they first met, she reminded him of their time together in the flower beds... Naughty, naughty! Wonder what that was all about? Perhaps we should rename Miss Croxley, Lady Chatterley. Open your eyes, guys. It's obvious. We're in for a scandalous Show-mance!

LORD EDWARD'S E-DIARY

Sunday 2nd September

'Comments'

11.45p.m. It's taken me the best of half an hour to read all your comments regarding tonight's show. Thank you for the feedback, even the, um, many comments about Marwick Castle. *BustyfanDownton*, I'm glad you and *Lovehotnoble* have settled your differences, since you've now decided to root for the other side—or the, erm, 'bloomin' buff' Baron's son as you describe him, aka Harry Gainsworth. Just a word to the wise, Marwick Castle may appear colourful and exotic but, as with people, first impressions don't hold for ever.

Cupcakesrock, sorry to disappoint that we aren't, in fact, opening a coffee shop. But, yes, I'll certainly suggest to my cousin that she themes one lesson around how to cook biscuits, brownies and banana bars.

Drunkwriter, thank you for penning another poem, this time with only a single swear word. It's, um, encouraging to know you're a fan of Applebridge Hall, despite not believing that we'll win the show. In fact, I deemed one verse particularly crude and you accuse me of deleting it for its favourable Marwick Castle slant.

What tosh! I fear nothing from our hedonistic opponents and as proof shall post your words, with asterisks suitably inserted. Apologies to all those who may be offended and, out of respect for my cousin Abigail, first thing tomorrow it shall be removed.

A noble female fainting in the orchard
Won't compare with debauched hen nights,
Flying onions ain't much better,
Whereas lobbed medieval spears win the fight.
Watching your Ps and Qs
Frankly does in my head,
To win or not to win? If that's the question,
You're well and truly f**cked, Ted.

Quickly moving on, you have now all heard the news of Applebridge Food Academy. Tomorrow my cousin shall hold her first lesson. Tonight she and I played Scrabble. It was…nice, relaxing, a distraction from the difficulties of the day. I…I wish she could visit Applebridge more often.

Abigail may not have been wearing Playboy ears and I certainly didn't get drunk and dance with a stuffed grizzly bear. But we talked and got reacquainted because, everything else aside, family is what matters. And, as this programme progresses, I hope you'll all see past the surface and eventually feel a modicum of the…the fondness I have for Applebridge Hall—a wonderful home and historical site.

Goodnight, all.

CHAPTER 9

Miss Abigail Croxley was murdered in the kitchen with the corkscrew by one of three suspects—Reverend White, Professor Parker or Miss Diamond.

Well, honestly—is it just me, or didn't my first three students sound exactly like Cluedo characters? Plus they stood a mega good chance of killing my—or at least Abbey's—reputation, if this first cookery lesson was no good and their dishes turned out rubbish. I stared around the whitewashed room. At this moment, fending off some assassin seemed preferable to cooking in front of the nation.

'Is that the last of the ingredients, Miss?' said Kathleen as she entered the room from her back kitchen. She carried a box of apples, still covered with dew. 'I sent Nick out early to the orchards.'

I nodded, breathing in the smell of bleach as, despite Kathleen's protests that she could do it, I'd given the work stations a quick clean. I'd also double-checked the items the three students would need.

Despite protesting that I was after the natural look, at that moment Roxy darted forward and brushed on a last bit of rouge. Apparently I looked 'peaky'. To be honest, dog-rough would have been a more accurate description— the price for staying up until four in the morning. After

Facebook, I logged onto YouTube and must have watched Delia break eggs, fry meat and chop vegetables a billion times.

After giving my arm an encouraging pat, Roxy left the room, muttering something about going to collect Charlie Chingo and the students.

'So, um, which is your preferred way of making a salad dressing, Kathleen?' I asked innocently, picking her brains at the very last minute. 'Lemon juice, sugar, oil, mustard… Do you shake, whisk or stir before tossing?'

'Och, I don't bother with that Continental nonsense,' she said. 'Oily lettuce? Nae, you can't beat a solid mayonnaise. If it's good enough for the Queen Mother… At Applebridge Hall we still like a good old-fashioned salad cream.' She stared at me. 'Are you suffering a wee bit from nerves? How about a dram of something strong before the cameras roll?'

Tempting as that was… 'No, Kathleen. I'm fine. Thank you for being so terribly supportive. I just hope I don't drop my knife or cut my finger when I'm chopping the blue cheese or peeling those apples for baking.'

She raised her eyebrows. 'Forgive me, Miss, but, as I'm sure you know, the blue cheese is to be crumbled and apples are baked in their skins.'

'Of course. I was just speaking generally. Everyone knows that. Baked apples without their skins… Ha, ha, ha,' I said in a bright voice, cheeks hot as she stared.

Kathleen smoothed down her floral apron. 'I still remember the last time you visited, all those years ago when you were nine.' She stepped forward and peered into my face. 'The prettiest pine specks you had in those blue eyes.'

Now she mentioned it, Abbey's eyes did have a greenish tint, just like Edward's—it must be a Croxley thing.

'You seem to have outgrown them.' Her eyes crinkled. 'Remember how your mother let you make cakes with me in the kitchen, whilst "the grown-ups" discussed business in the Parlour?'

'Um, how could I forget?' I thought back to the clips I'd seen of Delia baking. 'Breaking the eggs and folding in flour, what fun fairy cakes are,' I said with a grin.

Kathleen's brow furrowed. 'Nae, Miss—we made Scottish oatcakes, which don't contain egg… Och, it was a long time ago.' She stared again for a moment. 'Will you be needing anything else?'

'No. Thank you.' Eek, please go away before I make any other mistakes.

Gaynor swanned in and skirted the room, black bob swinging side to side, the smell of fags clinging to her like a bezzie mate.

'You won't have a personal mic, Miss Croxley,' she said. 'The sound man will follow you around with a boom—that equipment is better for picking up cooking noises. Frying, sizzling… It all adds to the atmosphere of the show, darling.'

I glanced at my watch. Half past eight. Apparently Gaynor had just briefed the Reverend, professor and accountant, who were still having their make-up done in one of the guest bedrooms. Good. Time to read through the recipes once more, which I'd typed up, decorated with an apple motif and printed out.

Right. Brave face. Nigella and Delia hadn't spent years training in professional kitchens before they found success. How difficult could it be? I'd always wanted to learn more about cooking and here I was—except, talk about being thrown in at the deep end, I was doing it first by actually teaching!

A hand touched my arm. Hmm, that expensive cologne—Nick must have crept in from behind. Roxy hissed something to the cameraman and I felt sure she muttered the word 'Facebook'—the online rumour-mill had clearly sprung to life. Without having to look, I knew the camera was now panned on me and Nick and a sound guy hovered nearby.

'Just wanted to wish you luck,' he said and squeezed my hand.

Aw, he was really getting into our role-play.

'How thoughtful.' I shook my hair back and licked my lips in what I hoped was a seductive move. Nick wore a polo shirt, open at the neck, and he gave a lopsided grin. I could see the attraction of staff to uptight nobility—especially unshaven, slightly reckless ones who smirked at authority. Let's face it, Nick was a risk-taker who could lose his job over our pretend romance, yet still he agreed to play along. Me likey!

'It's kind of you to come, Nick,' I said in a loud voice. 'I, um, asked Kathleen to send you in so that I could thank you for picking such delicious apples. I'm sure they will contribute to the success of this morning's session.'

'Nothing but the best for you, Miss,' he said in a husky voice. 'I'm good at plucking anything that's firm, round, fragrant…'

Nick winked and sauntered out of the room. Okay, so I cringed a little, but we hadn't got time to be subtle.

Right, enough acting up for the camera—must focus now on the job ahead. The pork stew took one hour to bake, so would be prepared first…

Chatter interrupted my thoughts. I looked up as Roxy came into the kitchens, followed by Charlie Chingo and the three Cluedo suspects…*students*, I mean: a man in a black cassock with a warm smile, a smart woman in high shoes and an emo guy—the professor—in dark trousers, a loose shirt and glasses hanging around his pale neck.

The students and I did what Lady C would call 'exchanging pleasantries', which I was getting good at now—particularly concerning the weather. While today was sunny, the air was fresher, so not too hot for baking, we all agreed. Boring, I know—but a great topic if the only thing you had in common with people was that you breathed and pee'd.

Then I quizzed them about their cooking experience…

'Isn't puff pastry a challenge?' said the Reverend. 'I finally gave it a go last week.'

'How do you stop your soufflés sinking?' asked Miss Diamond.

'It took me years to master hollandaise sauce,' muttered the professor.

Yikes! It became clear that they saw the Academy as a place they could perfect their already pretty good know-how. If Applebridge Hall won the show, the Croxleys would need to hire a proper chef. Mind you, if today was a success and a pizza waitress could blag her way through the job, maybe not.

The clock hands turned to nine and I stood to attention behind my work-station. Like a soldier from the trenches, I faced the enemy head-on. Okay, so it was a bit insulting to compare my situation to a battlefield, but here I was, amongst people whose language and culture was as alien to me as that of the Zulus or Spartans.

My stomach twisted. Gaynor said there would be no stopping and starting; she reckoned viewers wanted to see things as they really were, not lots of takes edited together to look immaculate.

'Three, two, one, let's roll,' said Gaynor and nodded at Charlie, who'd been standing next to me, practising his intro.

'Hello there, folks!' he said and gave the camera a cheesy grin. 'Thanks for joining us on *Million Dollar Mansion: the Final*. Today's the big day—the opening of Applebridge Food Academy. Watch Miss Croxley attempt to whisk, beat and knead her way to the prize money.' He smiled at me. 'Chat with the Chingo, Abbey! How are you feeling?'

'Um, awfully excited,' I said. 'This is a day I shall never forget. It makes me incredibly proud to be heading up the business that might save my family's estate.'

'I believe there is an apple theme to today's show? That rocks! How spot on, to use homegrown produce, what with the recession.'

'Precisely. Plus, the, um, Croxleys' apples are some of the tastiest in England. I'm confident they will make every one of today's dishes a winner.'

Each student waited by their work-station wearing a white apron with an apple motif in the top right corner. Hands perspiring, I discreetly wiped them on the back of my linen trousers. Edward slipped into the room from the back kitchen. Gaynor smiled at him and put a finger to her lips. He folded his arms—no thumbs-up for me, no mouthing 'Best of British'. I was on my own. Oh God— pass the smelling salts!

Charlie beamed. 'I hereby declare the Applebridge Food Academy officially open.' He patted me on the back. 'Spatulas at the ready!'

'Good morning, ladies and gentlemen,' I stuttered. 'Reverend White, Miss Diamond, Professor Parker, it is my great pleasure to welcome you here as my first students.' I picked up a glass of water and sipped. What if I accidentally swore or insulted a student and, under pressure, came over all Gordon Ramsay? Please, God, don't let me inadvertently call them Reverend Willy, Professor Piss and Miss Dickhead.

'As you've heard, students, Applebridge Hall's orchards produce splendid fruit,' I instead said. 'For our starter, we shall prepare Apple and English Blue Cheese Salad, with Pork and Apple Stew to follow. Mouthwatering Baked Apples with Ginger and Honey complete our menu. Please study the handouts in front of you.'

Air in…air out…in…out… Croxley women… Strong… Glass half-full… Stiff upper lip.

'We shall start the stew first, as it takes the longest to bake,' I said in strangulated tones.

The students crowded around my work-station as I arranged my ingredients. Roxy caught my eye and swished her finger side to side across her face in the shape of a semi-circle. She had a point. I probably looked mega terrified—must smile.

'First of all,' I said, battling the waver in my voice, 'chop up the onion, press the garlic, cube the meat and fry that in the flour.' Hands trembling, I measured out the herbs and poured out the red wine, thinking perhaps Kathleen was right about taking a wee dram. However, every few seconds I glanced at my recipe to check the procedures—so far, so good. My stomach relaxed a little as I finally sent the students back to their places and then paraded around the room, hands clasped behind my back, Prince Charles style.

'Jolly good.' I smiled at Miss Dick—Miss *Diamond*, as she pressed her garlic.

'Brown that pork a tad more,' I said to Reverend White.

'Excellent chopping skills.' Encouragingly, I nodded at emo-guy.

'And into the oven for one hour,' I eventually announced to them all.

This was all too easy—maybe I could become a great chef like Abbey, after all!

'Shouldn't you have added the apple?' asked Miss Diamond.

Urgh—I'd spoken too soon. My cheeks flamed. 'Um, of course—but Applebridge's variety is not the hardest and we don't want them to lose their texture by being over-cooked. Add them halfway through.' Wow—quick thinking or what!

Next, I showed them the salad, which was easy-peasy, apart from the dressing, which I'd leave until the last minute—mainly because I still hadn't decided whether to shake, whisk or stir.

'Finally, the baked apples—with ginger and honey, an old family favourite.' I glanced up. Edward had gone. Hopefully, that meant I was doing a good job.

'I've been making baked apples since I was a child,' muttered Miss Diamond and shook her head.

'That may well be but, in my opinion, this is an underrated dish,' I said. 'It takes great skill to cook it just so, um, the flesh melts in the mouth. In fact it was once served to me as a dessert when I visited the German royals.'

Emo-guy's brow furrowed. Crap. Of course. I bet Germany didn't have a monarchy.

'That's what they call their most talented pop family,' I said with a smile. 'Franz, um, Strudel and his wife. They're a bit like the Osbournes. We were working on a charity project together. He knows my brother.'

Great recovery! Although it concerned me how lies tripped off my tongue. As a child, Dad warned me that, sooner or later, porkies always tripped people up.

My demonstration finally over, I chilled as they made their desserts. Not a bad morning, all in all—apart from me nicking my finger on the peeler and taking ages to chop the onion. Top chefs always took their time, I'd explained, warming to my theme—apparently it was a little-known secret that the frantic slicing you saw on TV bruised vegetables and ruined the flavour.

Inwardly I chuckled, waiting for the onslaught I'd probably get from real-life chefs on Twitter. Yet it would all be good publicity and who could argue with me when these dishes turned out fab? Humming quietly after a quick interview update with Charlie on everyone's progress, I took my stew out of the oven.

Except that 'fab' wasn't exactly the word that escaped my lips. Instead I almost mumbled a different F-word. The gravy and meat had totally dried out. All the students' stews were the same. Urgh! Why had I ordered them not to bother leaving the pots' lids on? Ah, yes—it was cos know-it-all Miss Diamond disagreed, which made me even more determined to stick to my guns.

As for the baked apples, I paid the price again for thinking I knew better. The recipe had suggested a moderate heat for twenty minutes. But apples are as hard as tennis balls, aren't they, so I'd tweaked the recipe, changing the oven temperature to the highest possible. The result? Forget tennis—these were black snooker balls.

Thank God for the Apple and Blue Cheese salad that at least looked half-decent. We all picked up forks.

'As any good chef knows,' I said, 'it's not presentation but flavour that's king.' Perhaps there was a tiny chance that, despite appearances, the menu would taste amaaazin'.

We all dug into our salads. I coughed. My throat itched. Suddenly, it burst into flames. Miss Diamond gasped and grabbed her glass of water. The two men spluttered.

Eyes watering, I re-checked the recipe. One tablespoon of dried mustard in the vinaigrette? Even easy-going Reverend White had questioned that. Okay, so I'd upped it from one teaspoon, but I'd never seen mustard power before—it was weaker than the ready-made stuff you buy in jars, right? Or, rather, wrong.

'This lesson is a joke, Miss Croxley,' muttered Miss Diamond. 'No offence to Lord Croxley, but I've paid good money for this and my ten-year-old niece cooks better than this.'

'Perhaps the stew will be better,' said Reverend White, as tears pricked my eyes. Cautiously, I took a mouthful. It parched the mouth and the apple cubes felt as hard as dice.

Miss Diamond pulled off her apron. 'I'm not even going to try that ridiculous-looking dessert. Call yourself a chef?'

Emo-guy nodded. 'Sorry, Miss Croxley. You must be having an off day.'

'If you just let me explain,' I said, willing tears not to fall. 'It's these new ovens... Perhaps I should have checked the equipment.'

Reverend White shook his head and tutted. 'Honesty is a virtue, young lady, unlike pointing the finger at innocent people—or objects.'

Miss Diamond tossed off her apron and stalked out. The Reverend followed her lead. At least he folded his and smiled at me before striding past the cameras. Then, without catching my eye, emo-guy skulked out last. I stared at Gaynor, who looked a little bit too pleased. Roxy gave me a sheepish smile. I suppose it at least made good telly—even though I'd let down Lady C, Abbey… everyone.

Muttering something about a headache, I hurtled out of the room to the front of the house and past the students, who were chatting in the entrance corridor. Ignoring Miss Diamond's calls for a refund, I rushed past the Earl and Edward, who were just outside the open main doors by the fountain. Lowering my gaze, I speed-walked around to the back of the house, towards the perfect place to hide—the maze.

Talk about embarrassing. Yet I couldn't help a small smile as I remembered Miss Diamond's bulging eyes when she saw the burnt baked apples. I charged into the avenues of bushes. Straggly bits caught my blouse but I carried on, running now, around corners, into dead-ends… Panting, I finally ended up in a circle of the hedge surrounding a rosebush in a big pot. This little area was turfed. It must be the middle.

I collapsed onto the grass, breathing in woody smells as I bent up my knees and covered my face with my hands. Could it have gone any worse? No. Had I ruined Abbey's reputation? Yes. Would I be the laughing stock of the nation tomorrow night? No doubt.

I sniffed loudly. At least I gave it my best shot. And, without that dressing, the salad was probably pretty good. What's more, I'd enjoyed it, this being the first time I'd ever prepared a three-course meal. But perhaps learning how to cook was more difficult than I'd ever thought.

Dust flew up towards my face as footsteps stopped right by me. Breathing heavily, someone sat down. My heart sank as I looked up.

'Apologies, cousin,' I said. 'If it's down to me, there's no way we'll win this show.'

'Roxy filled me in.' His mouth twitched. 'I know I keep saying that Croxley women are made of strong stuff, but it doesn't mean they can stomach generous portions of mustard and charcoaled apple.'

'You aren't…disappointed?'

His eyes twinkled.

'What did Uncle say?'

'I don't know,' said Edward. 'He was too busy trying to placate Miss Diamond, who's threatening to take us to court.'

'How dare she! I mean…' Cool as a cucumber, remember. 'Goodness. On what grounds?'

He grinned.

'Ha, ha. Very funny joke.' Spurts of warmth tickled the inside of my chest and I grinned back.

'Secretly, I think Father is pleased that the Academy's first day wasn't a roaring success. Sometimes he can be a stubborn old fool.' Edward rubbed the back of his neck. 'You were nervous. There was little time to prepare. Father and I expected a lot from you. Perhaps… I never thought I'd say this, but we should get in a chef, just for Wednesday. Until you find your feet. They won't be family, but…' He shrugged and, even though my head told me to agree with him—aarghh!—unfortunately, I gave a different reply.

'Not on your nelly. Wednesday will be different. My, um, aunt—Lady Constance Woodfold—she believes that, with a courageous spirit and correct frame of mind, a true lady can achieve anything. Today has been a temporary glitch.'

'Really? Well, that's an admirable attitude.'

We looked at each other. He opened his mouth as if to say something but then closed it and stood up. At that moment, Kathleen appeared, carrying two glasses of that fancy red drink with cucumber and strawberries in.

'A wee Pimms sorts out any nerves,' she said.

I smiled at her, those spurts of warmth in my chest glowing stronger.

'Not for me, Kathleen,' said Edward. 'Whilst she's here, Miss Diamond wants to have a look at the books. You take my drink. I'm sure my cousin could do with the company.'

'Erm... If you're sure—but His Lordship will be expecting lunch.'

'Leave him to me,' said Edward and disappeared.

'Yes, do join me, Kathleen,' I said. 'Those drinks look gorgeous.'

She inspected the grass before sitting next to me, then passed me a drink. Just in time, I remembered not to rudely clink glasses.

Kathleen stared at my fingernails. Crap. Without realizing it, I must have bitten my thumbnail.

'My hands are in a terrible state after that cooking,' I said, and forced a laugh.

She sucked in her cheeks, shook her head and then stared me straight in the eyes.

'Miss, can I tell you something?' she said in a low voice, and leant forward.

'Of course.' Ooh, interesting... What could this be?

'Your father—the Honourable Richard Croxley... Little Dickie, that's how he was known at Applebridge Hall. Well, Lucy Dearing worked here before me as cook, and always had a soft spot for him. Lovely lady, she is. It was thanks to her that I got an interview with the Earl's wife, the Countess. Lucy's husband regularly travelled to Scotland on business and knew my father well. When Lucy got pregnant, they decided they could afford for her to be a full-time mum. Through her husband, Lucy heard I was looking for a secure position and the canny lass put in a good word for me, down here.'

I nodded, wondering what she was going to tell me, hoping it was juicy enough to boost ratings. I could slip it into a conversation, next time I had my mic on.

'Well, I met her just before I started. Och, such a kind nature. Just so fond of little Dickie. I don't think His Lordship knows this, but your Da still sends her a Christmas card every year.'

Was that it? I gave a quiet sigh. It was hardly like announcing she knew the whereabouts of Lord Lucan.

'On in years now, Lucy is, but we still speak on the phone every Hogmanay. Do you know what she told me this year?'

Aha! I held my breath.

'Little Dickie always personalized his cards with a word or two about his family. Lucy felt this time he seemed more reflective than in years past. He talked about Applebridge Hall and everything he missed. He even mentioned your visit here, all those years ago.'

'How sweet.'

Her eyes narrowed. 'Aye. According to your Da, only last Christmas you reminisced about the oatcakes made in my kitchen—and yet this morning you could have sworn they were fairy cakes.'

The Pimms almost choked me now.

'Eyes don't lose specks of colour, lassie,' she said, 'and no lady I know ever bites her nails. You can't cook for toffee and you give that young Nick, who's on the staff, the glad eye… Nae, something's not right. The game's over. Tell me who you are this instant and what you've done with the real Abigail Croxley. It's obvious you're an imposter!'

LORD EDWARD'S E-DIARY

Monday 3rd September

2.30p.m. Ahead of tomorrow night's show, let me give you an exclusive insight into today's first cookery lesson. Most appropriately, Abigail chose an apple-themed menu. Perhaps, blog-readers, you'd share with me your favourite dish using that fruit? Mine is good old-fashioned apple crumble served with piping-hot custard.

I digress—back to this morning… As is often the case at the beginning of any project, not everything went to plan. My mother always said I expected a lot of myself *and* other people—which today has been proven true. Therefore, I stood back, took stock and realized Father and I had given my cousin little time to prepare. Onwards and upwards. In her view, this is a solitary hiccup that has already been suppressed.

Forgive me now for talking of money, but I've promised to be honest with you… I've just finished going through the books with our accountant. Apparently, we can manage financially until the end of the month—no longer. Only yesterday, a good friend, the Duke of Missfield, rang to wish us luck and said he didn't mind if I shared his story. Last year he and his family moved out of their Tudor mansion as it had fallen into such a state of disrepair.

The wiring was dangerous and it suffered from dry rot. Rather than sell off estate valuables, such as ornaments and paintings, to survive, he took a tremendously difficult decision. The estate now belongs to the National Trust. The Duke lives in a two-bedroom flat and sells car insurance.

A tale which—I hope—dispels some myths about aristocrats. We may live in impressive grounds but, from our point of view, we are mere caretakers. Whilst Applebridge Hall is my home, it really belongs to our ancestors, centuries of visitors and the nation. Baron Marwick might call us snobs but, in all honesty, our needs are simple: preserving jobs; maintaining art; protecting history.

Right. Enough chat for now. Off to inspect the orchards and reports of crumbling plaster in the Long Gallery.

CHAPTER 10

'No! Not the police!' I shouted, heart thumping, and chased Kathleen through the maze.

Her Scottish lilt carried over the top of the hedge on my right. 'If you won't tell me the truth, lassie, perhaps I'll fetch Mr Thompson and his gun instead.'

'This is all a terrible mistake,' I called and turned the corner. Urgh. If only Kathleen had stayed put and given me time to create a cover story. Or, even better—if only I could tell her the truth. Instead, after several probing questions, she'd snorted at my poor answers, huffed and puffed to her feet and disappeared.

'Think of the family name,' I called. 'Your accusations will certainly lose us the competition. The, um, only hope we have is to endear ourselves to the nation with our strong family values…'

I stopped running. What was the point? My secret was out. All decorum lost now, I slumped to the ground. 'Shit.'

'That unladylike word is further evidence that your blood is no bluer than mine.' Kathleen had appeared out of nowhere. 'One last wee chance—who are you? Where is the real Abigail?'

I scrambled up. 'Please, Kathleen. Just trust me.'

'Och! Famous last words! You're talking to the woman who scrutinizes every bill, receipt and bank statement that comes her way with a magnifying glass.' She sighed. 'You leave me no choice. No doubt Constable Jenkins can get to the bottom of this.'

I bit my lip, a small pocket of relief swelling in my chest. While coming clean was a risk, I could at last stop deceiving one person. 'Okay—but if I tell you the truth... Not a word to anyone else.'

'I can't promise that. The Croxleys might be in danger.'

'The only thing they're in danger of is losing the competition. I'm here to help them win all that dosh.' There was no point in speaking like a lady now. I lowered my voice. 'Look, let's go into the kitchen. I'm mega thirsty. I'll tell you everything over one of your nice cups of tea.'

Kathleen crossed her arms under her bosom and wiggled side to side for a moment. 'Okay—but I want honest talking, or else there'll be trouble.'

I followed her out of the maze and we hurried into Applebridge Hall.

'There's your tea,' she said ten minutes later and sat down opposite me at the kitchen pine table. For once, she hadn't switched on her Elvis music. 'Now... Spill.'

'What, the drink?' I smiled.

'This is nae joke.'

'Agreed. Look, I've hated fooling you all but, the thing is... Abbey—my flatmate—asked me to replace her. After I dyed my hair blonde, removed my false eyelashes and let the fake tan wear off, we kind of look alike.'

Kathleen stirred her strong tea, eyes fixed on my face, and eventually let out a low whistle. 'But why? I know His Lordship and Abigail's da have had their differences, but this is about saving the building that has been home to their family for, och, generations. Does that mean nothing to your flatmate? I've only met her briefly, all those years ago, but she seemed a generous, kind-hearted sort.'

'She is! But her boyfriend, Zak…'

'Och aye… I should have known a man would be involved.'

'But it's more than that—they both headed urgently to Rwanda. Newly orphaned children need them there.'

Her face softened. 'So, it was you or nothing. Does anyone else know?'

'Only her aunt—Lady Constance Woodfold. She taught me about deportment and manners. Until the last minute, we assumed I'd be running some coffee shop—not a high-falutin' cookery academy.'

'Lady Woodfold's reputation precedes her. I've heard of her finishing school.' Kathleen leant back in her chair. 'Tell me… Do you know *anything* about food preparation?'

'Um… I make a mean cheese and pickle sandwich.' Legs apart, I slumped back in my chair. It was a relief, just for a moment, not to have to worry about how modest I looked or whether my voice sounded syrup-smooth. And mega to feel the sense of guilt slipping away as I finally told Kathleen real things about me—Gemma Goodwin.

'Did your mam never teach you the basics?'

I shrugged. 'She died when I was little. Dad's not a bad cook, but I guess he didn't always have time to play Jamie Oliver.'

Kathleen's lined face smoothed out further and she ran a hand through her silver-red curls. 'What's your real name?'

'Gemma—Gemma Goodwin.'

She swilled a mouthful of tea around her mouth and swallowed, before shaking her head.

'I am doing this as a favour,' I blurted out. 'I could leave here at any moment, if I wanted.'

'Go on, then.'

'No! I promised Abbey. And…I get it; I understand why winning the show is so important.'

Kathleen pursed her lips, but her eyes crinkled at the corners and looked warmer than before. She looked at her watch.

'His Lordship will be waiting for his very late lunch,' she said finally and put down her cup. 'Will you be eating with him, Miss?'

I clapped my hands. 'You mean it? You won't reveal my true identity? Wow! Thanks, Kathleen! I'll do my mega best to win that million dollars!'

'To leave now would just bring scandal to the house. Och, but if you jeopardise their chances of happiness in any way…' She shook a teaspoon at me as if it were a sword.

'I promise to be on my best behaviour!'

'You'll need my help if Wednesday's cookery lesson is to go ahead. Today's was shambolic, but you don't strike me as the kind of girl to give up at the first sign of trouble.'

'That would be amaaaazin', Kathleen. We could practise a few dishes tomorrow afternoon.'

'All day, more like,' she said. 'I saw what you did to those apples.' Her eyes crinkled again. Then she got up, fetched a loaf from the bread bin and took butter and corned beef out of the fridge.

'What about a Scottish theme?' I said.

She snorted. 'Flattery will get you nowhere.'

'No, I'm serious,' I said. 'The history of your grandmother working for the Queen Mum would go down a treat—the public love all that stuff. We could decorate the room with thistles and you could tell Charlie Chingo your stories about the young Elizabeth Bowes-Lyon.'

'You know about that?' Kathleen stopped buttering bread. 'Perhaps my grandmother's life might interest viewers. I've got a bundle of tartan tea cloths, somewhere that we could put out.'

'There must be some simple Scottish recipes I could manage.'

Kathleen put down her knife. 'Hmm…The Queen Mother loved her fish. I know from my grandmother's stories that Herring in Oatmeal was one of her favourites. It's easy enough, although I'm assuming you've never learnt how to de-bone?'

I shook my head.

'Best avoided then… How about apple-stuffed pheasant breasts…? Us Scots like our game.'

'What, like tossing the caber?'

'No, lassie—I mean game as in hunted birds.'

'Really?' I said innocently.

Kathleen gave me a grin. 'It's an infallible recipe, Gemma, and will look fine with a prune sauce. Served with simple mashed potato, it'll appear as good as anything on those fancy cookery programmes. Thanks to Mr Thompson, we always have plenty of pheasants. We could start early tomorrow. Aye. Wonders can be achieved with a bit of hard work. I can freeze our practice batches. We've got bacon and breadcrumbs… All you'll need to nip into town for are prunes.'

I pulled a face. 'It sounds mega complicated. Can't I just deep fry pizzas and Mars bars. They are Scottish meals, right?'

She folded her arms. 'Despite what the papers say, not all Scots live off chocolate and lard. Meat and two veg—you can't go wrong with that. This pheasant dish is straightforward and doesn't require a whole range of skills.'

'What about a starter?'

Kathleen snorted. 'After yesterday's disaster, stick to two courses. It's said the Queen Mother loved a Bloody Bull. How about that cocktail to start, instead?'

My brow furrowed.

'As it happens, Noël Coward, who supposedly visited here once, invented the drink—it's a Bloody Mary, with beef consommé added in. Canny red colour. I saw it in a magazine once.'

'Like tartan, that'll fit in with the colour scheme.' I grinned. 'I'll insist that they drink it whilst cooking. We'll all be in a good mood then.'

'Cranachan for pudding,' she continued. 'That's traditional with its honey, Scotch whisky, double cream and raspberries. The most challenging part is toasting the oatmeal topping and I've lots of fruit in the freezer from our garden's summer harvest. As a dessert, it'll look as pretty as that Henrietta Hamilton-Brown.'

'You think she's pretty?' I asked, my voice suddenly all squeaky.

Kathleen's eyes narrowed and she studied my face for a moment. 'Indeed. I feel a marriage coming on soon. It's only a matter of time before a man snaps up that girl.'

My stomach twisted a little and I wasn't sure why.

'Lord Edward… Do you think I should tell him who I really am?' I said.

Kathleen shook her head vigorously. 'Nae—that would be a huge mistake. Your cousin can't bear dishonesty. He's…come across deception before in his life and despises lies and…and… having to lie with a vengeance.'

Ooh, that sounded intriguing, but Kathleen shot me a cutting stare which clearly meant 'don't ask any questions'.

'Reveal your true identity to no one,' she ordered. 'Especially that young Nick.'

I shrugged. 'He's been very helpful since I got here.' Hmm, better not tell her about Plan Sex-up.

'Huh. Ideas above his station, he's got.' She straightened her apron. 'So. Tomorrow morning. In here. Seven o'clock sharp.'

'Seven?'

She raised one eyebrow.

'I mean, wicked—thanks very much.' I got to my feet and gave her a quick hug.

'Och, there's no need for that, dearie,' she said, cheeks tinged pink. 'Right, go and join the men in the Parlour.'

'I might stroll around the garden first to clear my head.' I needed to get back into character before I spoke to His Lordship—or, rather, Uncle—and Edward.

I left through the back door. Jean was digging in the vegetable patch and waved. Straight ahead, to the left of the maze, Nick sat on top of one of those big lawnmowers. It was shiny red and apparently another investment the Croxleys had made with the twenty-five thousand pounds. Further in the distance were the little cemetery and the forest. The grass all around looked as green as the best astroturf. I breathed in. Was there any better smell than a cut lawn?

If I was a crap cook, I owed it to everyone to give this sex-up Applebridge Hall plan my best shot. Awkwardly, I made my way over to Nick, court shoes rubbing, the small heels sinking into the turf. While not as hot as yesterday, it was still sunny, although there was an autumnal breeze.

'Good day,' I said.

'That it is, Miss,' he said and removed a long blade of grass from between his lips. 'I heard about the baked apples,' he said and grinned. 'Roxy said you'd certainly helped liven up tomorrow night's show.'

'My, um, nerves overcame me, I'm afraid to say.'

Nick jumped down from the lawnmower and put an arm around me. 'You did your best.' He glanced towards the house. 'They're filming, by the way, so…' Nick pulled me close.

I turned around. Cameraman at her side, Roxy hovered by the main entrance. She turned away as soon as she noticed me gaze in her direction. Ooh, the gossip-mongers must have been in full swing on Facebook. I'd have to take a look tonight.

'If only we could create some really interesting footage,' I said and stepped away. It was nice, being close to Nick— comfortable. Relaxed. Yet I didn't want our supposed relationship to look too obvious on screen. There had to be some doubt, so that Abbey's reputation could be defended.

'Like what?'

'Something visual. For example… I don't know, think of the really romantic scenes from movies—ones your, um, girlfriends might have watched. It might give us some ideas.'

'How about that Darcy guy walking out of a pond?' he said and stepped away to brush grass clippings off his shirt.

'Hmm. *Pride and Prejudice* is a bit of a cliché for a stately home. *An Officer and a Gentleman* is awfully romantic when Richard Gere, in uniform, sweeps that woman up into his arms.' I clapped my hands (oops, shouldn't show too much excitement for a lady). 'That's it! We should enact scenes from certain films.' Duh! I should have come up with that idea before, when reading Edward's blog. Gaynor had suggested that he came over all Mr Darcy and bathe, fully dressed, in the pond, hadn't she? Of course, he'd said absolutely not—so Nick and I could make up for his lack of adventure! It'd be fun—an occasional break from the continual pressure of pretending to be someone else.

'Very funny,' he said.

'No, I'm not joking! It's a super idea. What other slushy scenes can you think of?'

'My last girlfriend insisted we see romantic vampire movies.'

'The *Twilight* series? Yes! My, um, lodger, Gem, is obsessed with that. Although it might be too much if you stalked me with fangs and red eye contacts.'

'I can just imagine Mr Thompson as some old werewolf,' said Nick.

We smiled at each other.

'Then there's *Titanic*… Don't laugh, Nick. I'm serious. This would jolly well liven things up.'

Nick shook his head. 'Okay…Yeah, *Titanic* might work—what with the class divide, you'd make a perfect elegant Rose, me pretending to be the working-class geezer, Jack.'

'It's a quite lovely scene when they are both up on the ship's bow, arms outstretched, his hands around her waist. But how could one recreate that?' I strained to control the bubble in my voice. This could be mega fun.

My eye caught the lawnmower. No. That was a bonkers idea. I was meant to be a lady, now. But still… Uh oh. Arenaline rush. My heart raced. I was going to do something stupid.

Five minutes later, Nick burst out laughing again after I'd told him of my plan. 'It's certainly visual. But perhaps a little dangerous?' he stuttered.

'I'm game if you are,' I said. Okay, I admit maybe I was getting carried away. 'Or haven't you got the nerve?' There was something irresistible about his cheeky face that urged me to dare him on.

He snorted and wiped away a tear of laughter.

'And, in a roundabout way, I am your employer, so I could pull rank, be beastly and, say, threaten you with losing your job.'

'Looks like I haven't got much choice, then.' Nick grinned.

'Super! Now, please, drive the lawnmower up the hill, past the cemetery, before I change my mind. And Nick?'

He nodded.

'I, um, know it's an awfully unorthodox plan. I do so appreciate your help. After this morning's debacle with the pork stew, I have ground to make up. So, thank you very much. I wouldn't normally behave in such a vulgar manner, of course, but this is not the time for me to be reserved. My family's future is at stake.'

'I'm at your service, Miss. Any time.' Nick bowed his head and the breeze caught his aftershave.

'Is that your jumper on the ground?' I asked and pointed to a heap of green material.

He nodded. 'Today there's a nip in the air.'

'Let me wear it,' I said. 'Just to keep the viewers guessing a little—let's not make it one hundred per cent clear that it's me.'

Nick winked, passed me the jumper and climbed up onto the lawnmower's seat.

I put it on and gazed back to the house, before following him on foot. Roxy and the cameraman were still there, no doubt kicking themselves that I wasn't wearing a personal mic. Nick drove right past the cemetery, near to the forest and higher ground, before turning the lawnmower around. I clambered onto the ship—ahem, I mean, machine—in front of him, feet on the foot rests, facing Applebridge Hall down below. With the sprawling ivy and decorative chimney stacks, to anyone else it would just look impressive. Yet I was beginning to see it as a home—kind of cute and welcoming. Nick's arms slipped around me from behind and his fingers grasped the wheel. Standing tall, I closed my eyes for a second to imagine old-fashioned cruise ships and icebergs.

'Now or never,' I muttered and opened my eyes as Nick turned on the engine.

'You're sure about this, Miss?' he said.

'Yes.' No. But what choice did I have? My job here was to help the Croxleys win.

Kate Winslet style, I stretched out my arms, trying to remember what her character, Rose, said to Jack at this point. The ship's helm—I mean lawnmower—moved forward and, within seconds, hurtled down the hill.

Whee! Past the cemetery, air whizzing into my mouth, arms still crucifix style. As we passed the maze, I gulped a large mouthful of air. The mower jolted up and down. Hey, hey, heeeeeeey! Good thing my old chicken fillets weren't stuffed down my bra—by the time we reached the bottom they'd have moved to form shoulder pads. Roxy pointed in our direction. This was fab, like some fairground ride! Then *Titanic* Rose's words finally popped into my head—they were something like...

'Look at me fly!'

Which, all of a sudden, exactly described my move.

Despite Nick struggling to keep me steady by clamping my waist tightly between his arms, the mower hit something and, at speed, veered sharply to one side. With a scream, I rocketed through the air and crash-landed onto the turf.

LORD EDWARD'S E-DIARY

Monday 3rd September

'Comments'

6p.m. I thought reading about your favourite apple dishes before I went to dinner might whet my appetite. And you have not disappointed me—thanks to everyone who commented.

Historybuff, I didn't know the apple was probably the oldest cultivated fruit and has featured heavily in worldwide mythology. So, China grows the most? I don't think Applebridge can compete with their rate of production! I agree with you, it takes a lot to beat the natural fruit. You like green? Red are my variety of choice. I even eat the core, which used to make my mother's toes curl. She insisted the seeds would give me appendicitis.

Knityourownmansion, mmm, toffee apples too are delicious. They remind me of autumn nights as a boy, and Kathleen helping me persuade Mr Thompson to try apple-bobbing. *Blogger569*, I like the sound of apple brandy on pancakes.

And *Cupcakesrock*, of course, who could forget scrumptious American Caramel Apple Betty? I didn't realize you'd just moved over from the States. Thank you for telling your family about the show. It must be terrific to be one of five brothers and sisters. How super that they are following our progress online. In answer to their questions, no, I don't have a valet. We don't eat cucumber sandwiches. Nor does Abigail say she must 'powder her nose' if she wishes to use the lavatory.

CHAPTER 11

Listen, micro-light yoga… It's a new craze. Hold the crucifix position while travelling at speed.

Look, I'm a white witch. Nick was helping me cast a complicated good luck spell over Applebridge Hall. Jeopardizing one's life on a lawnmower was all part of sealing the charm.

Okay. Hands up. It was a selfless suicide mission. We can't compete with the Baron of Marwick's booze-fuelled banquets, so what could be more dramatic than the death of two young people, to attract viewers?

I sighed and leant back into the sofa. It was Tuesday night. Everyone was in the Parlour to watch the next episode of *Million Dollar Mansion*. I still hadn't thought of how I was going to explain my *Titanic* behaviour. To be honest, I couldn't really explain it myself. It hadn't even looked romantic. What on earth had come over me?

Roxy and the cameraman had rushed over, not even stopping to carry over their equipment.

'What did we hit—an iceberg?' I'd muttered, glad to see my only injuries were a grazed knee and elbow. Finally, Nick managed to tame the mower and bring it to a halt. Forget *Driller Killer*, Manic Mower would make an ace horror film. Luckily, Jean hadn't actually seen what had happened or he really could have been fired for such reckless driving.

'Wowsers,' Roxy had said with a giggle as the dumbstruck cameraman helped me to my feet.

'You, um, like that Kate Winslet movie then,' she said. 'Wouldn't it have been safer to recapture this scene on one of the many cruises I'm sure you must go on?' Once again, she dissolved into giggles. 'It was so cool. Who would have thought that Miss Abigail Croxley, I mean… That was real rock 'n' roll!' Roxy gazed at my knee, a worried look on her face. 'Um, are you sure you're okay, Abbey? That was quite a fall.'

My chest had tightened as the now familiar guilt took hold. If only I could tell her the truth and say: 'I'm not bonkers. You don't need to worry about me. This is all part of a plan to win.'

'I'm fine. Thank you. It was, um, an accident. I stood on the lawnmower to thoroughly enjoy the estate's views and the engine suddenly sprang to life. There was little Nick could do. I, um, stretched out my arms to provide some sort of balance…' I cleared my throat. 'I assume it goes without saying that neither of you will mention this to anyone or on the Internet…' I raised my eyebrows. 'And if you must show the footage, please edit out the ending, which is close up.'

Reluctantly, Roxy and the cameraman nodded. Then I made my excuses and, despite the initial aches and pains, headed back inside to my four-poster bed for a lie-down.

Thank God I didn't sleep on the top floor, like the staff, along the Long Gallery—I couldn't have coped with all those relatives in the portraits glaring at me for risking their reputation. Fingers crossed they understood that I was fighting the good fight for their sakes.

Later in the afternoon, the Earl and I finished off our tour of Applebridge Hall. I tried to find the words to warn him about my bonkers antics, but it was impossible.

'You've practised your cooking today, Abigail?' said the Earl gruffly, seated in his usual high-backed chair. Tonight he'd spurned tea and Kathleen's yummy chocolate-dipped shortbread for a glass of brandy and, of course, his pipe. 'Miss Diamond rang me today, once again ranting about yesterday's cooking.' He put down his drink and chuckled. 'That's quite an achievement you pulled off, ruffling her feathers. Normally she's jolly calm about everything.'

'Kathleen's helping me to, um, conquer my nerves before tomorrow's lesson,' I said. 'She's a real treasure.'

The Earl nodded. 'My wife used to call her that.'

Kathleen blushed. 'This shortbread was the Countess's favourite biscuit.'

'Along with your Dundee cake,' said Edward and offered the cook another cup of tea.

'Hmm, and you make a mean whisky fudge,' added Mr Thompson.

'Here we go, at last,' said Nick, glancing at the screen as the theme music to our show played. He took off his iPod, just as his phone rang. Edward glared at him and he switched off his mobile.

I sat on my hands. Hopefully, no one in the room would realize that it was me on the lawnmower with Nick. The Marwick Castle footage came first, featuring a corporate team-building trip, now that the weekend's hen party posse had left—cue professionals dressed in combat gear doing paintballing, fencing, archery and shooting.

'Now tell me, Baron,' said Charlie Chingo, from the screen. 'Since broadcasting that hen party in your dungeons on Saturday, I believe you've had a lot of business enquiries?'

The Baron clapped Charlie across the back, cheeks bulging more than ever.

'Och, he's a smug so-and-so,' muttered Kathleen.

The Baron looked straight into the camera. 'What's not to like?' he boomed. 'All you guys and gals out there, come to Marwick Castle for the time of your life. It's the recession—everyday life is tough. You deserve to treat yourselves to a day or two of opulence. Feasts with tables of meat joints, breads, fresh fruit and pickles and cheese... Beer on tap and wine in huge goblets... Hunky waiters and waitresses whose sole aim is to treat you like kings and queens. During the day play paintball in the forest or learn how to shoot clay pigeons. There's no class system at Marwick Castle. Dosh is the only thing you need here to enjoy pursuits normally reserved for the stuffy aristocracy.'

'What a berk.' Edward clenched his fists. 'I didn't realize we were watching the adverts.'

'There'll be an accident before you know it,' said Mr Thompson. 'Rifles are a serious business, not to be handled in between pints of beer.'

'Silly bugger, that Baron chap,' said the old Earl. 'He'll soon destroy anything worth preserving about that castle.'

'Your son, Harry, has some wild party games up his sleeve, I believe,' said Charlie Chingo's voice.

While the Baron talked, louder than a town crier, the camera panned the large room the interview was being held in. A variety of swords hung from the grey stone walls. There were stuffed animals, plus coats of arms.

'I wasn't sure whether to show you these,' said Jean to everyone, cheeks red as she passed around a handful of celebrity magazines. 'They came out today,' she said.

'I was in the corner shop and saw the Honourable Harry Gainsworth's face stare out from every cover.'

'I seem to remember he was a popular lad in the qualifying heats,' said Kathleen. 'Canny face.'

Hmm. He had a mega popular fan page on Facebook. I'd been on the computer today and taken a peek at how much people were chatting about me and Nick. Plus I'd bobbed onto Edward's blog. It almost read as if he was enjoying writing his e-diary and chatting to some pretty weird strangers.

Edward snorted as he turned to a photo of the Baron's son in nothing but a crown and pair of designer Y-fronts. With his fake tan, white teeth and playboy good looks, I could see why he was their 'Torso of the Week'.

'Oh my God… um, goodness,' I said, reading an article. 'Next weekend this Harry is inviting his new celebrity friends to the Castle for a party. How do we compete with that?'

'Who's going?' said Nick.

'Dodgy Dirk, the lead singer from, um, some new rock band.' I fought to keep the excitement out of my voice. Hot or what? If I wasn't stuck here, I'd deffo watch the show anyway, to drool over Dirk in paintballing overalls and gorging on lush food. 'Also several cast members from one of the soaps.'

'A publication called *Top Shelf Totty* contacted me to do a photo shoot,' said Edward, cheeks flushed.

'Really! How aw…' awesome! '…*aw*ful,' I said. 'Although it would have been terribly good publicity.'

'You think so, cousin? Me, wearing nothing but an apple in front of…'

My eyes widened. Kathleen and Jean giggled. Mr Thompson shook his head with disapproval. The old Earl tutted loudly.

'This house was awarded to my family for their efforts protecting this country,' said the old man and stood up. 'Four hundred years later, is this what it's come to? My son, a grown man, stripping down, butt naked, in front of the nation?' He headed for the door. 'I can't watch any more of this tosh. I'll be downstairs, in the library.'

We sat in silence until the door clicked shut, itself sounding like an ancestral tut.

'Sorry, My Lord,' said Jean. 'I didn't mean those magazines to upset His Lordship.'

Edward offered her another biscuit. 'Nonsense, Jean. Father has a strong constitution. It's best that he knows exactly what's going on and what it takes to win this competition. I'm sure he'll watch the rest of this on catch up. If nothing else, he very much enjoys seeing the panoramic shots of our estate.'

I glanced sideways as Edward sat back down on the sofa, shoulders sagged. He was staring vacantly at the floor's worn rug.

'Charlie Chingo's just been splatted with red paint,' said Nick with a snigger. We looked at the screen. Marwick Castle's antics really were mega good telly. Poor Edward's shoulders sagged further. The programme cut to commercials and we flicked through the magazines again.

'And just when we thought things couldn't get worse,' I muttered as Charlie Chingo came back on screen and introduced my cookery lesson from yesterday. The camera focused on Nick as he'd squeezed my hand just before the lesson had started, to wish me luck. Next to me, on the sofa, Edward's body stiffened.

'Um, thank you once again, Nick,' I said to the room, 'for hurrying upstairs to fetch one of my homeopathic calming pastilles and discreetly putting it in my palm. I couldn't have got through the morning without it.' Despite my innocent tones, Kathleen gave me a funny look.

The footage moved on to my demonstration and a bubble of laughter inflated in my chest. Oh, come on! Well, it was funny, me trying to work out how to use that garlic press. At first I'd thought it was a tin opener. As for Miss Diamond's face when the smell of burning apples filled the air... Look at me shaking my dressing like a manic cocktail maker doing the Macarena!

'Tell me when it's over,' I mumbled, not daring to watch any more. It was so baaad, I felt an irrational urge to giggle.

'Now, Miss, don't you fret,' said Kathleen. 'Nerves were understandable and you've practised so hard today—that oatmeal was toasted to perfection. I'm sure tomorrow's filming will run seamlessly.'

'Yeah, that pheasant you cooked today smelt wicked.' Nick gave the thumbs-up.

Kathleen let me eat a bowl of your Cranachan.' Jean smiled. 'It tasted divine.'

'I can second that,' said Mr Thompson's deep voice. He tilted his Sherlock Holmes hat.

'Thank you all for being so terribly kind.' My cheeks felt hot.

'The Bloody Bull I tried before dinner tonight tasted very decent, cousin,' added Edward.

I poured everyone another cup of tea and went to the loo, hoping the *Titanic* scene would be over before I got back. I was riding high on their compliments and didn't want to come back down to earth. However, no such luck. I walked into the Parlour and my mouth went dry. As I sat back down, Nick and I were on screen, at the top of the hill, just as I clambered onto the tractor. In the jumper and at a distance,

to your average viewer, I didn't think it would be obvious
that it was me. However, I'd texted Lady C that afternoon to
warn her; said she may not approve of tonight's show, but for
her to trust that everything I did was part of a game-plan to
win the contest. Without reading, I deleted all the messages
she'd already left and then turned off my mobile.

I swallowed hard. On screen I'd just adopted the crucifix
pose. I lifted my teacup to my lips, then up in front of my
eyes. Jean giggled. Kathleen snorted. I put down my cup.
Fuck—I looked ridiculous.

'Who on earth is that lassie?' said Kathleen.

Edward jumped to his feet and glared at Nick, who
smirked for Britain. Tears of laughter streamed down
Jean's cheeks.

'This is hilarious,' she spluttered.

The words 'Look at me fly' resounded around the
Parlour.

Kathleen shook her head. Jean dabbed her eyes. Mr
Thompson leant right forward, to the telly, when that
footage suddenly ended.

Eyes ablaze, Edward faced me. 'Did you take leave of
your senses, Abbey? As for you, Nick, good God, man—
did you not consider the dangers?'

'It wasn't m…' I began.

Edward snorted. Sigh—there was no fooling him

'I insisted that he do it,' I muttered. There was no point
trying to convince Edward that it was an accident and that
the lawnmower had a life of its own.

'Good God, woman, why? Not only could you have
destroyed hundreds of pounds' worth of machinery, we
could have ended up in court if Nick was injured.'

'And, of course, Abbey might have been hurt,' said Nick.
'I'm sure you were also concerned for your cousin.'

'Get out of here,' said Edward to him and scowled. 'Before I... Go on, leave. Everyone else... Mr Thompson, Kathleen and Jean—I wish to speak to Abbey. Alone.'

'Abbey?' said Nick to me.

Without looking, I could feel Edward glower.

Mr Thompson put a hand on Nick's shoulder and patted it. They all got up and, as they left, Edward grabbed the remote from the Earl's chair and flicked off the programme. He paced around the room.

'Look, I'm sorry, Edward, but—'

'Surely you aren't going to attempt to justify such behaviour? You...' His voice wavered. 'You could have killed yourself. And what did you hope to achieve? I can't imagine any other lady I know, like...like Henrietta, for example, conducting herself in such a manner.'

Why did he have to bring *her* into this? My stomach squeezed. But then, he did have a point. The more I thought about it, the more I couldn't come up with a suitable excuse. It hadn't looked remotely lovey-dovey. But boy, had I enjoyed the freedom. I'd found it hard to control my behaviour and speech every single minute of the day since my arrival on Saturday. It had been a bloomin' relief to do something wild and wacky.

'And with *him*... The gardener...' Edward couldn't even say his name.

'I never had you down for a snob,' I said and thought back to one of Lady C's many lectures. 'I was always brought up to believe that...that a position of privilege was an honour and that no lady—or gentleman—considered themselves above any other person.'

'I don't.'

'Then why do you always sneer at him? If that's not snootiness, I don't know what is.'

'Clearly, in four days, you've nailed my personality,' he said stiffly.

We stared at each other for a moment.

'Look, if it was me, I would never have agreed to such a daredevil plan,' he said.

'So, he should have refused, even though I'd threatened to fire him?' Well, okay, Nick knew I was joking, but still, technically I'd ordered him to drive that mower or join the dole queue.

'You did *what*?' Edward shook his head. 'But yes, you could have been seriously injured or... or worse...' His voice petered out to a whisper. 'I would have lost my job, to protect you.'

Ooh... Why was my stomach tingling?

'I mean... you're my cousin—family,' he said in a firmer voice and sat back down. 'Although that's hard to believe at the moment—such a let-down. What ludicrous behaviour.'

'Nothing wrong with a bit of fun and I don't think, with Nick's jumper on, every viewer will believe it was me,' I said, eyes tingling. A lump rose in my throat. Despite all my good intentions, I just seemed to be making things worse for the Croxleys. 'Look, the sun had gone to my head—it was a momentary lapse of judgement...'

'How self-indulgent,' he muttered. 'Fun?'

'Yes. You do know what that is, right?' I said, my voice shaking. 'Or perhaps not. I mean, I've been here, what, four days, and hardly seen you smile. Pleasure is not a crime. Nick and I...'

'Are young and foolish.'

My lips pursed.

'You're hardly geriatric,' I said, 'yet act as if you belong to the time of dinosaurs.'

A muscle flickered in his cheek.

'Apologies if I don't live up to your expectations,' I said in a measured voice, 'but I refuse to discard my sense of humour—even to save Applebridge Hall.'

Edward folded his arms. 'I don't think you understand the seriousness of our situation. If we don't win this competition, that's it—Father and I are homeless. Jean, Mr Thompson, Kathleen; they all lose their jobs. The cemetery where Mother and other relatives are buried...' His voice cracked. 'We will probably have to move the bodies, as God knows who will buy this land and what they will do with it. Even worse than that, four hundred years of our ancestors' sweat and tears will have come to absolutely nothing... History will be lost. Stories of visitors disappear for ever. And all because of a bit of fun?'

'So it's all my fault if we lose?'

'You've done little to help so far, what with your inadequate cookery class and childish, impulsive behaviour. Within minutes of arriving you collapsed.' His eyes flashed. 'Perhaps you should never have come.'

Impulsive? Oh dear. Lady C would not be impressed. But then, impulsive was the real me, Gemma, all over. Inwardly, I sighed. What if my sex-up plan backfired? What if the Croxleys became a laughing stock and the likelihood of the public voting for them was now smaller than ever? Calling me self-indulgent, however, was a step too far. I'd given up two weeks of my life to save his bacon.

'I was thrown to the lions, Monday morning,' I said in a quiet voice, 'having never taught cookery to anyone, let alone in front of rolling cameras. On Sunday, I stayed up practically all night, trying to pick up presenting tips from well-known TV chefs on the Internet. I may not have fought against the Spanish Armada, or wined and dined famous playwrights—but in my own way I'm doing my bit.

Maybe I should leave if I don't meet your impossibly high standards of what it means to be a thoroughbred Croxley.'

'A thoroughbred Croxley?' He gave a bitter laugh.

'What is so funny?'

He pursed his lips, as if afraid of what words might tumble out.

'Fine!' he said eventually. 'Leave if you must.'

My stomach squeezed.

'Applebridge Hall has managed without you all these years.'

'So you really believe I'm no help at all?' I said and got to my feet.

'Go on—abandon ship.'

I was tempted to explain that's precisely what I'd done in my imagination, by falling off that lawnmower, but my throat hurt too much to make a joke.

'Abandon ship?' I stumbled to the door. 'Point me to the plank, then, Cousin. I'll happily jump.'

LORD EDWARD'S E-DIARY

Tuesday 4th September

9.30p.m. Apologies for this late posting—it's been a busy—in fact, exhausting day. This morning I was caught up in an interview with the local press. Then Charlie Chingo questioned me, in the High Drawing Room, about my childhood and education—'last resort filler footage', in his words. It's a good thing I've got a thick skin. After lunch, *Top Shelf Totty* magazine contacted me to request a quite unsuitable photo shoot, featuring my naked silhouette, a long gun and two apples. Naturally, I declined. The Croxleys won't be joining the celebrity circus. But I'd be open to sensible offers from *Country Life* or the *BBC History Magazine*—on the understanding that the only photos of unclothed figures came from our various pieces of art depicting nudity.

No doubt, blog-readers, you've just seen tonight's show. If nothing else, I hope the, erm, bizarre lawnmower incident gets you talking. I suspect, as *Million Dollar Mansion* progresses, you'll realize that our family is not much different from that of Joe Bloggs: a mixture of different elements with no obvious properties in common. Yet, one would hope, when it matters, they bond together, strength fused to act as one—despite previous fireworks or unexpected sporadic behaviour.

In fact, truth be told, tonight I've behaved in a fiery way myself. Talking of which, the truth is very important to me, friends, even if…sometimes in life…duty prevents one from being totally transparent. Imagine that—having to betray the very principles that are core to your beliefs in order to protect somebody… something else…

But please, excuse the low spirits. Today I've experienced feelings that are unfamiliar and it's knocked me off balance. The new strong sense of caring for someone… The depth of my concern must be due to that DNA bond I spoke of before. Mother Nature must have a way of hard-wiring relatives together, regardless of whether they've spent every day of every year together, or not.

Ahem. I've indulged my long-winded thoughts enough. Sleep well, friends. Until tomorrow.

CHAPTER 12

'Let me buy you a drink, love,' leered a man at the bar.

Not difficult to guess, is it, that I'd changed out of my Abbey disguise? Head all over the place after my argument with Edward, not only did I hurry out of the Parlour—I got changed and practically ran to the Green Acorn, the local pub. The further I got from Applebridge Hall, the more my upset turned to anger.

Okay—it was hard times for Edward, but how much criticism could a girl take? Do your best; that's what counts most, my dad always says.

'Pear cider, if you've got it, mate,' I said to the barman and breathed in the lush smell of hops, thrilled that he hadn't looked at me twice. Without anyone suspecting that I might be Abbey, I could release my inner Gemma. 'And a packet of cheese and onion crisps. Plus a KitKat. Ta.' Mmm, comfort food that I could just shove in without worrying about which fork or knife to use or whether I'd got crumbs around my mouth.

Cos I needed comforting. Perhaps Edward really wanted me gone. Well, tough. I wasn't leaving. Whether he liked it or not, the Croxleys needed me and my 'childish, impulsive behaviour'.

With a yawn, I went to rub my eyes but remembered, just in time, that I'd got my false eyelashes on. Without telling anyone—in other words, Lady C—I'd smuggled a handful of my own 'Gemma' clothes into my suitcase. Having left Edward, I'd gone straight to my bedroom and—yes, you've guessed it—adrenaline rushed through my veins and a sudden urge to become me again overpowered all rational thinking.

I'd pulled on my shortest skirt and tightest top (ignoring bleeps from my phone—a disapproving Lady C, no doubt). Then I slapped on a mega generous helping of make-up, dusted on bronzer and squished two chicken fillets into my bra cup. As for my demure blonde locks, I sprayed them with a wash-in-wash-out red hair colour I'd brought with me on a whim, and wore a headband topped by a big black bow.

I gazed around the pub, having admired the cute thatched roof and window boxes on the way inside. It was small, with round mahogany tables and gardeny green walls. On the floor, in the corner, was a dog's bowl. Laughter and chat almost blocked out the strum of a guitar, played by some guy sitting by a brick fireplace.

'Cheers!' I said to the barman and handed over a ten pound note. What a bloomin' relief not to have to say 'Thank you so much'. In fact, now I was the real me again, everything—eating, drinking, talking—went at a much quicker pace.

I approached a table occupied by some old fogey and his pint. It was the only seat left. A couple of weeks ago, there's no way I'd have shared a table with a stranger old enough to be my granddad. But, since I'd been trained by Lady C, something weird had happened. Politeness had made me more…open-minded and aware of other people's needs. Perhaps he was just a lonely old gent instead of a potentially creepy pervert. I gave a tentative smile and asked if it was okay to sit down, hoping once again that I would be unrecognizable from the posh gal on the local reality show.

'Certainly, miss,' he said and stared at me for a long moment while my stomach went into knots. Perhaps I hadn't put enough bronzer on to disguise my, um, aristocratic disguise... Urgh, this was becoming mega confusing! Folds of skin hung over his eyes and, from those mega wrinkles, I could tell he clearly loved a fag. The old man wore a striped shirt with a cravat and smart navy trousers. 'I'm afraid I'm staying for a while, though,' he said eventually. 'Or are you on your own?'

'Yeah, it's only me.' My stomach relaxed. Looked like he hadn't rumbled me. I sighed. 'Ever felt the need just to get out?'

'Certainly—like when the wife watches soaps back to back,' he said, and chuckled. 'Although I can't complain... There's usually a decent hot chocolate waiting for me on my return.'

I stared into my cider bottle. If only I could stay in this cosy pub for the rest of the next fortnight. No doubt, tomorrow, Edward would give me the silent treatment. Then there was the Scottish cookery class ahead of me... I gave another sigh.

'I'm Bill,' said the old man. 'Bill Cochrane.'

'Gemma Goodwin,' I said, having to stop myself from going into Abbey mode and add on: 'What a pleasure to meet you—hasn't the weather been delightful today?'

'Forgive me, Gemma,' he said, 'but is everything all right?'

'Just tired, I guess. I've done a mega amount of cooking today.'

'I don't recognize you from around here.'

'No... Um... I'm doing some work at Applebridge Hall—helping out in the kitchens and with housework.'

'Ah, how is my old friend, Lord Croxley? What with this competition, it's a while since he's invited me over for a drink to discuss local farming matters.'

'You know him?'

Bill sipped his pint. 'We go back a long way.'

I raised my eyebrows.

'My earliest memories are from the war,' he said. 'Lord Croxley was only eight when it ended. I was nine. Mother used to take me up there to play with the evacuees, whilst she helped change beds and cook dinners.' He shook his head. 'Those kids would have loved that escapade on tonight's show with the lawnmower. My wife spilt her cup of coffee. And, as for that disastrous cookery class...' He guffawed. 'That Miss Croxley seems like a bit of a loose cannon.'

If only he knew! And today, with those disastrous dishes, she'd truly fired blanks!

'Have you kept in touch with the evacuees, Bill?' I sat more upright.

'No. Damn shame that I haven't. In fact, the last time Lord Croxley and I had a brew together, he mentioned this boy called Jonny Jackson. We both had vague memories of the three of us getting lost in the maze...' He sighed. 'It would be great to meet up—see what he and the others made of their lives after such a tough start. There was this older girl, Linda... I remember she was great with the other kids when they missed their mums. Linda Sloggit. We kept in touch for a few years, like penfriends. I think she became a midwife in Manchester.'

Wow. My eyes widened. An amaaaazin' idea had pinged into my head. Emotional reunions were telly gold. What if some of the old evacuees came to Applebridge Hall, having not seen each other for over fifty years? That would be awesome! Plus, could just possibly compete with the celebrity party at Marwick Castle this weekend. While Bill chatted to a nearby couple, I tugged open my handbag, rummaged around inside and found a pen.

Crap—no paper. A beer mat would do. I scribbled down the names: Bill Cochrane, Jonny Jackson and Linda Sloggit.

'Any other memories of the evacuees, Bill?' I said when he turned back to his pint. 'It's, um, fascinating hearing stories from the war.'

He leant back in his chair. 'Odd time, Gemma, it was. Bloody awful memories, some of them, like one of the lads finding out his dad had been blown up.'

Blimey. Imagine that.

'Another lad suffered like hell because his father got injured on purpose, to get sent home.' Bill sipped his beer. 'And I'll never forget the looks on the children's faces when I first turned up with my mum. They were dead brave, trying not to show how much they missed theirs, especially if they had younger siblings who looked to them to stay strong. But then there were good times as well. Gerry Green was an all round good egg and got the kids through it with his jokes. He even made Matron laugh—apart from when he put worms in her bed and swapped the contents of the salt and pepper shakers around.'

I grinned. This Gerry Green sounded just like my brothers.

'Years later, I saw his name in the paper. He was trying to make a living as a stand-up comedian and had done okay on the holiday-camp circuit… And then there was Dennis Smith and the fire…'

Ah, yes. I remembered the Earl talking about him. I nodded encouragingly.

'The morning room was burnt out—it used to be behind the library on the ground floor, at the back of the house. It was a bad do. The family lost treasured possessions—some musical instruments, including the piano and well-loved portraits. Fortunately, everything important in the library was saved, apart from a few first editions. When rebuilding, they did away with the morning room altogether. The fire caused enormous damage to the Drake Diner as well. After the war, the Croxleys put all their efforts into restoring that room—to the detriment of other projects, they later decided, like the roof.'

A bell rang. 'Last orders, folks,' called the barman.

I stuffed the beer mat in my handbag. Gerry Green, Jonny Jackson... I could Google these names tonight and see if they or their relatives were on Facebook. Once I'd run the idea of a reunion past the Earl and Edward, I had... Eek! Only three days to arrange everything. I'd have to lay it on thick about how important this reunion could be for Applebridge Hall. If nothing else, this whole war thing might distract everyone from me and the lawnmower.

'Evening, Bill,' said a man in his, ooh, early sixties. He carried a bright-eyed Jack Russell.

'Todd. How's the accountancy business these days?' Bill shook his hand. 'This is Gemma. She's helping out at Applebridge Hall. Pull over your chair, son. Gemma, this is Todd Raynor. He works with Miss Diamond, Lord Croxley's accountant, who—'

'I know who she is,' I said and tried hard not to pull a face.

Bill chuckled. 'A tad abrupt, isn't she?'

Todd sat in between me and Bill, the Jack Russell—unimaginatively called Jack—on his lap.

'We were just discussing the war years,' said Bill. 'Your mum taught the evacuees, didn't she?' He turned to me. 'Todd's mum lives in Wisteria Cottage—you might have seen it next to the post office. She's won awards for her gardens. Pushing ninety she is, but still as quick-witted as ever.'

Todd tickled Jack's ears. 'She taught them English and Maths. Several are still in touch with her, after all these years'

'Really?' Bill leant forward and, despite Jack's growl, he placed a hand on Todd's arm. 'How come I never knew that? Is she in contact with Jonny Jackson?'

My eyes went all tingly. The memories clearly meant so much to Bill. Right—Mrs Raynor. Wisteria Cottage. I would have to visit her tomorrow and somehow convince her to give me her list of contacts.

Drinks finished, we said our goodbyes and I walked—okay, ran, heart racing, back to Applebridge Hall which, in the dark, looked mega spooky. Todd had offered to walk me home, but I insisted I'd be okay. I couldn't risk Jack barking and waking everyone up.

All the lights were out and, without the familiar orange city glow, I had only the moon and the fountain's tinkle to guide me to the front entrance. By the time I reached the end of the drive, my chest heaved and I was perspiring like one of those unfit middle-aged dads you see out running, thinking they look cool in their designer trainers.

Talking of feet, my little toes cramped in agony and I slipped out of my mega impractical high heels. A random noise caught my attention from the pond on the right—aw, a croaking frog. Hoping I wouldn't trip over some unseen molehill or rock, I stole over to the water and sat down by the edge. I gazed around the estate, just able to pick out the forest and orchards. Even though the Indian summer temperature had dipped today, it was still warm and I had a sudden urge for a swim.

No one would know—only the little tiddlers darting around on the bottom. Stupid idea, I know, but uh oh, adrenaline rush, and, before I realized it, mega fast I'd stripped down to my bra and knickers. I pulled out my chicken fillets and slid them into my high heeled shoes. Slowly, I entered the water. Wow. Talk about refreshing.

Weed tickled my feet as I pushed forward and water rose up over my thighs, my waist, then my boobs… Mmm. This was lush, despite the smell of dirty fishtanks. I tied up my hair with my headband. The last thing I wanted was to tint the pond with red dye. A random cloud covered the moon for a moment, and for, ooh, it must have been twenty minutes, I floated. Bliss.

Urgh! Was that a rustling behind me? I jerked my head up.

'Who's there?' I hissed and swam into the bulrushes. Crap!

LORD EDWARD'S E-DIARY

Tuesday 4th September

'Comments'

11.30p.m. Just bobbed back to say that after two hours in the library in the company of Ernest Hemingway, my problems are almost back in perspective. Like one of my mother's favourite white wines from more affluent times, I feel pleasantly chilled—nay, nearly fully revived. Enough to return to this e-diary and properly consider your many reactions to tonight's show, which seems to have been a source of immense amusement.

Tiarablogger, if that, um, was my cousin, then I agree, perhaps she failed to learn about lawnmowers at finishing school. *Jobsworth*, welcome to my blog and yes, we have taken out all the insurance policies we need to. *EtonMess*, how, erm, supportive to say you'd eat anything Abigail cooked as long as she wore high heeled shoes. Oh, and *Knityourownmansion*, that was quick work: today my father received the knitted mohair pipe in the post. I'm sure he's very grateful. Glittery pink was, erm, an inspiring colour to choose.

But… Wait a minute… What's that? Out of the library's side window I can see… Surely not? Excuse me, blog-readers, I must investigate—it would seem someone is bathing in our pond…

CHAPTER 13

Phew! The dark must have spooked me. No one was there. Still, I couldn't enjoy my swim and after ten more minutes was about to get out, when... Oh, crap! Now I heard heavy breathing. Again, I darted into the bulrushes.

'Who, um, is there?' I said once more.

'Shouldn't I be asking who *you* are?' replied a familiar voice. The silhouette of a head covered in curls came into view. 'Trespassing is a crime,' said Edward, and caught his breath. 'This isn't a municipal swimming pool.'

As if they were curtains, I pulled the bulrushes apart.

'Isn't it cold in there?' he asked.

'How long have you been perving?'

'Don't flatter yourself,' he scoffed, ever the charmer. 'I've just this minute arrived—having been in the library.'

As I swam out into the open water, he sat down, next to my pile of clothes.

'Look, um, I got lost and ended up on your estate. It was so hot and the pond looked mega inviting,' I said. 'Just let me get out and I'll be gone.'

Edward stared at me through the darkness and I turned away. Thank God I'd not gone underwater as my false eyelashes and make-up would have come off. The moon shone more brightly as the cloud moved and I couldn't resist squinting back up at him.

'Why are you here, really?' he asked. 'No one just stumbles their way onto this estate.'

I bit my lip. 'Um… Look… If you must know, I'm a fan of *Million Dollar Mansion* and wanted to see the place for myself.'

Edward snorted. 'You've only got to read the papers to know that we're hardly the favourite. A real fan of the show would break into Marwick Castle.'

Urgh, this was what was so attractively infuriating about my supposed cousin! He was intelligent, difficult to fool and, for a la-di-da toff, refreshingly outspoken.

'What about, um, your fans on the blog?' I said. 'I bet they'd like to see the place in person.'

'But you aren't one of them, right?' He stood up. 'I'm calling the police. You've clearly got some agenda.'

'No! All right… Look…I'm Gemma.' Phew. There, I'd said it. And it was great to be honest.

He shrugged.

'Abbey's lodger. I saw tonight's show and knew she'd be upset. I, um, got my brother, Tom, to drop me off on his motorbike.' Okay, some white lies were necessary. 'I only live forty minutes away. He's picking me up at, er, one a.m.'

'Gemma? My cousin has mentioned you. So, she's still here?' Through the shadows, his face kind of brightened and my chest glowed. Perhaps, after all, he didn't think me as Abbey was a joke.

'The last time we spoke, she announced her departure.' His mouth drooped at the corners and… Oh my God. I had this sudden urge to kiss it hard! The sudden flashes of his vulnerable side were…were… My pulse raced. Hot, hot, hot!

'Abbey's got sticking power all right,' I said. Although I wasn't going to let him off the hook completely—let him stew for a while and actually think about what a tough week Abbey, in other words *I*, had suffered.

'She's mortified about the cookery lesson—and dog tired,' I continued airily. 'It's been a *knackering* week for her. If it was me, I'd jack the whole thing in. She was falling asleep when I left, so I decided to look around.'

Edward grunted as a shiver ran down my spine.

'Urgh! Must swim, otherwise I'll freeze my tits off.'

His mouth upturned.

'Why don't you come on in?' I said—as a joke. I mean, *as if*. The words spontaneous and Edward didn't go together.

'Are you mad?' he replied.

'It's only a bit of fun.'

His shrugged. 'According to Abbey, I don't know what that is.'

'Then prove her wrong.' I splashed his trousers. Yay, this was great, not having to be on my best behaviour.

He gasped. 'We're not at nursery school. Look. Don't you think you should get dry?' He looked at his watch. 'It's already gone midnight.'

I soaked him again.

'Now look here, young lady…'

'Whoa!' I said. 'Less of the young. Who are you, my dad? Or perhaps you're just scared of the titchy tiddlers swimming around?'

He folded his arms.

'You'll get just as wet standing on the bank,' I said and hit the water with my palm, to increase the splash.

He stared at me for a moment, studying my features… I swallowed hard. Would he accept that I wasn't the same person as his supposed mad cousin who'd sailed down a hill on a lawnmower?

Clearly, yes, because, seconds later, he pulled his shirt over his head. Mmm. Broad smooth chest… Nicely toned tum… I cleared my throat and tried to look interested in some weed floating on the pond's surface, dying to look again as the thumpety-thump of my heart sped up. It was like that famous *Pride and Prejudice* scene played backwards, him walking *into* the water. Phew! Get a grip, Gemma.

'It's a good twenty years since I've swum in here,' he said, head now bobbing next to mine. His eyes narrowed. 'Cousin Abbey was right.'

I raised my eyebrows.

'She said people think you two look alike…' He squinted in the dark. 'There's a definite similarity.' With that, he swam to the other side.

Phew. So far so good—ta very much, dim moonlight. He came back my way and gave a big splash.

'Think I owe you that,' he said.

I stuck out my tongue and we floated in silence for a moment.

'It's awesome here,' I said softly, as an owl hooted from the forest. 'All this space… green…quiet...'

Edward continued floating on his back.

'Did you hear me?' I asked.

By way of an answer, he lurched and grabbed my leg.

'Aarghh! What are you doing?' I said, in between gasps of laughter.

'That got you. Who's scared now?'

With a giggle, I pulled away and crawled out onto the bank, goose bumps pricking up on my skin—my cue to try and act sensible and get dressed again. About to ask him to avert his eyes, I noticed that he'd already turned away. Quickly I stuffed my chicken fillets into my bra, pulled on my skirt and top and picked up my bag and high heels.

'Beat you to the top of the hill behind the house, by those gravestones,' I said.

'That's one long run,' he said. 'And I need to get my clothes on first.'

'My legs are shorter than yours. It's only fair that I have a few seconds' advantage. Come on! It'll be a mega way to get dry.'

I started running, past Applebridge Hall and the vegetable garden at the back. By the time I reached the maze I was exhausted, but God, this was good. I felt as free as one of those birds the Earl spied on through binoculars, even though my thighs killed as the hill got steeper.

'Here I come,' said a deep voice behind me. 'Give up; you don't stand a chance.'

'Not on your life,' I hollered but he passed me, glancing sideways with a grin, shirt unbuttoned. As he reached the cemetery first, Edward punched the air and collapsed to the ground. Blimey. He almost looked human! Seconds later, I lay down next to him on the grass.

'I don't know how…but…you must have…cheated…' I gasped, spreadeagled on my back.

He chuckled. 'Aw—no one likes a sore loser.'

A few minutes later we both sat up and he pulled a green blob of weed out of my hair.

'Warm enough?' he asked. 'Borrow my shirt to cover up. You might get cold on the way home.'

What a considerate offer. It made me feel all fuzzy inside. ''S okay—but thanks, all the same.' I nodded towards the cemetery. 'So… All the Croxleys are buried there?'

He rubbed the back of his neck, his hair in tight wet curls. 'Yes. My mother most recently.'

'Sorry. I didn't mean to… Abbey mentioned that you'd lost your mum a couple of years ago. That can't have been easy.'

Edward picked a handful of grass and let the blades tumble back to the ground.

'I miss mine,' I mumbled.

'How long…?'

'She died when I was little, but I still have vague memories. Her perfume. Her bonkers laugh.'

'And there's me feeling sorry for myself when I knew mine for almost thirty years.'

I shrugged. 'It's just different, I guess. I don't have constant memories to bring back the pain, like watching her fave TV show without her, or cooking one of her meals. Although, now and then I do something and get a sixth sense that she would approve.'

'Like what?'

'Usually something wild and wacky.' That *Titanic* episode, for example. 'Dad's pet name for her used to be flibbertigibbet. She was nothing like him—a huge fan of seafood—exotic for Dad means trying a different brand of sausage. She was also into amateur dramatics. Dad's mega proud of photos of her in costume.' I bit my thumbnail. 'According to Dad, she used to call me her little Gem… What was, um, your mum like?'

'Patient,' he said. 'The best listener. And…'

'What?'

'Nothing—just being sentimental.'

'Promise I won't tell anyone,' I murmured.

Through the darkness, he stared at me for a moment. 'She gave tremendous hugs. Even when I'd grown up, she always sensed when things weren't going well. With her arms around me, I felt invincible, as if any problem could be solved.' He shrugged.

'She sounds like a wonderful woman.' Wow. Was this really the same strait-laced, po-faced guy I'd argued with a few hours ago? I slipped my arm around his shoulder and squeezed tight. A bolt of electricity went through me and I pursed my lips together to contain a gasp. I hadn't felt that physical reaction with a guy for... for... Perhaps never.

'Thanks,' he said.

'What for?' I said, feeling my body flush.

'Tonight. It has been fun—I needed that.' A strange look crossed Edward's face, as if he didn't quite believe what he'd just said.

'Hard day?'

'I got into an argument and...' Edward sighed. 'Probably said things I shouldn't have.' He got to his feet. 'Race you back? It's almost one.'

'Sure... And, um, Edward, would you mind not mentioning seeing me to anyone—including Abbey? She's mega proud and wouldn't want people to think she was finding it difficult to cope.' And I'd lose my head if Edward had conversations with me, pretending to be Abbey, about Gemma, who I really was and... Urgh! You get the picture.

'Of course. Right. I'll see you to your brother's motorbike,' he said. 'Where, exactly, is he waiting? It's quite a walk back to the gates.'

My chest felt all fuzzy again—of course, gentleman Edward would want to do that. However, I had to keep up the pretence of leaving the estate. Somehow I'd have to hide until he gave up on finding me and assumed I'd met Tom and got my lift home.

'Um... ' I pretended to rummage in my handbag. 'Oh, no! I've lost my purse. Would you mind having a look by the pond while I check around here? I'll meet you there.'

He charged off and I waited a couple of minutes before sprinting away from him, around the back of the house.

LORD EDWARD'S E-DIARY

Tuesday 4th September

'Comments'

Gone midnight. Strictly speaking, we're now on Wednesday 5th, and I should start a new thread. However, I'll comment on this post—for some reason, oddly, I don't feel like doing things precisely by the book! Not whilst the night breeze still chills my lungs and I sense a glow in my cheeks... Erm, so yes, I am back, blog-readers, and many thanks for all your concern.

As it turned out, the intruder meant no harm and the day has enjoyed an unexpectedly good end. In fact she said... You see, we... Oh. I can't think straight. It's time to retire to my bed and mull over this evening's... I mean, the day's events. They have sent me on quite a roller coaster ride because tonight, by the pond... It was most welcome... And surprisingly... Apologies. I ramble.

No doubt I shall be more like my usual self tomorrow. Goodnight to you all. And, erm, no, *Lovehotnoble*, no one else has ever told me I have really kissable lips.

CHAPTER 14

'Och, get off me, girl or I'll report you for assault.'

I grinned at Kathleen. The Scottish cookery lesson had just finished and as soon as Gaynor said 'Cut!' I'd raced (in a ladylike way, of course, which meant swishy power-walking) into the back kitchen, closed the door behind me and threw my arms around the squat Scot's neck and waltzed her around to the background Elvis song.

'No chance!' I said and gave her another big kiss, before stepping away.

'Control yourself, lassie,' she hissed, but couldn't hide the shine in her eyes. Cheeks ruddier than ever, she smoothed down her grey-red hair. 'I take it everything went to plan?'

'Oh, Kathleen, it was wicked. At first, I was a bit worried, changing the schedule, but no one suspected and the pupils didn't mind.' We'd moved the lesson to the afternoon. I'd just needed a bit more practice this morning. So instead of starting at nine o'clock, it was at three. I looked at my watch. Blimey! Already dinner-time!

Without delay, I needed to tell the Earl and Edward about my evacuee reunion plan. Although when I say 'without delay' I actually mean 'after a much-needed cup of tea'.

'Phew—I'm knackered. Mega parched,' I said, never one for being subtle.

'Shh! People might come in at any minute.' Kathleen jerked her head to the window. 'I'm sure someone just walked past. If you're not going to speak like a lady, at least keep your voice down.'

I gazed outside. Dark clouds hung threateningly over the horizon.

'I suppose you deserve a drink then, lassie.' Kathleen filled the kettle. 'So, nothing burned, or tasted disgusting?'

'Nope! Reverend White returned—he reckoned I deserved another chance. Two lovely ladies from the church joined him and came over all giggly after downing their Bloody Bulls. I can't believe I actually put together that pheasant main course and pudding. My hands were shaking, but mega posh they looked and, more importantly, they tasted awesome.'

'Did the prune sauce go shiny? How about the mash— lumpy or smooth?'

I undid my hair bobble and took a cup of tea from Kathleen. 'As smooth as a Botoxed bottom. My demonstration dishes were ace. Reverend White patted my shoulder before he left and said I'd done well to conquer my nerves this time. He called me a talented chef!' I snorted. '*Me*? And it's all down to you.'

'Aye, well… No need for any more grand shows of emotion.'

We smiled at each other and I restrained myself from giving her another hug.

'I mean it, Kathleen—thanks for ever. I've always wanted to learn proper cookery stuff… Anyway, how did your interview with Chingo go? Any interesting questions about your gran working for the Queen Mum's family?'

'Och, the usual probing—Charlie trying to find out about her early boyfriends and parties. Of course, I revealed nothing. That Gaynor woman seemed happy enough with my stories about the young Elizabeth Bowes-Lyon's family life, holidays and society dinners.'

'Love your kilt,' I said.

'Thank you, lassie. You don't look so bad, yourself.'

I gazed down at Abbey's sleeveless polka-dot dress—too sweet and girly, but, I had to agree, so well tailored that it made even me look sophisticated. Despite the cloud outside, I'd dressed as coolly as possible in case the kitchens got hot. With a yawn, I ran my fingers through my hair. Kathleen reached out to touch it.

'Those locks look a wee bit dry today. Would you like me to make up a batch of my famous goose-fat conditioner?'

Ick! 'It's, um, all right, ta,' I said and drained my cup, not letting slip about the real me being out and about last night and the red hair dye. The packet said 'wash-in, wash-out'—I'd missed the bit saying 'lasts for ten shampoos'. Consequently, I'd been up practically all night, scrubbing my scalp. The shower looked like it had been in that knife scene from *Psycho*, with all the red stains.

'Why don't you go to the Parlour?' said Kathleen. 'Their Lordships are waiting there for sandwiches—tonight's just a light tea. But, if you're lucky, I'll bring in some of my shortbread and Dundee cake.'

'Not getting carried away with the Scottish theme, are we?' I grinned. 'Don't tell me—you've made haggis and thistle sandwiches?'

'Och, be gone with you, now. Tell the men all about your victory.' She folded her arms snugly under her bosom. 'Tomorrow we'll plan the menu for your next lesson on Friday.'

I nodded vigorously.

Twenty minutes later, I sat on the sofa in the Parlour with Edward, his laptop lying between us. I chewed a yummy ham sandwich, dying to grin at him, Gemma-style, and, in the fun spirit of last night, challenge him to a food fight. Unsurprisingly, he didn't say sorry for accusing me (Abbey) for 'abandoning ship' last night. Clearly, we weren't going to have it out—how typically English.

In fact, Edward's head seemed elsewhere and he barely grunted when I announced my success. *Sigh*. The laid-back man I'd got to know in the pond had well and truly disappeared. Perhaps it was an illusion and I'd imagined it. Edward was probably still sulking about the lawnmower argument. I bit my lip. Ah, well. No use moping. As Auntie Jan would say, 'Time to turn the page.'

'Congratulations, Abigail,' said the Earl gruffly and wiped his mouth with a napkin. He sat in his usual high-backed chair. 'You know I'm not a huge fan of this Food Academy nonsense, but I admire your tenacity. I hear that today you've done a jolly good job.'

'It was, um, very enjoyable,' I said and glanced at Edward. Since I'd entered the room, he'd been reading the same page of the newspaper. Clearly, his mind was on something—or someone—else. Henrietta, perhaps? Or just the competition?

'Mother would have been impressed,' he said eventually. '*MasterChef* was one of her favourite programmes. According to Gaynor, the food looked very professional.'

Perhaps that was his olive branch.

'Rosemary was a splendid cook,' muttered the Earl. 'Anyway, old girl, you certainly redeemed yourself with Reverend White. Silly old bugger was over the moon.' He puffed on his pipe and we sat in silence for a few minutes.

Eventually the Earl nodded at Edward and raised his eyebrows. 'Go on, son,' he said. 'Say what needs saying.'

Edward put down the paper and rubbed the back of his neck. 'Father and I would like to discuss something with you, Abbey. It's rather delicate. If Mother were here, it would be her remit to take you to one side. But now it is just me and Father, so…' He cleared his throat. 'A problem has come to our attention. Not that the TV people would see it as such—or thousands of fans on-line. I consider it my duty to keep up with commentary about *Million Dollar Mansion*, so I briefly browsed Facebook and Twitter late last night, after signing off from my blog.'

A nervous twitch tickled my stomach. Had my Facebook comment provoked chat about a possible upstairs downstairs showmance? I still hadn't found time to check yet.

'How is the Baron of Marwick doing?' I asked innocently.

The Earl snorted. 'Last night he hosted another drunken banquet for some executive types. They ended up trying on armour. One chappie blacked out in the full regalia and it took two firemen to cut him free.'

Urgh—more great telly from the opponents, then.

Edward cleared his throat. 'Abbey—have you seen the film *Titanic*?'

My cheeks felt hot. 'Yes.'

He exchanged looks with his dad. 'After the incident with the lawnmower, we suspected it might be a favourite of yours—so did precisely twenty thousand fans on a new page set up on Facebook who are all discussing whether the woman on the lawnmower was actually Abigail Croxley.'

Result!

'Do you know what the page is called?'

I shook my head.

'*Nick and Abbey—the new Jack and Rose*,' continued Edward. 'There is speculation by some fans on the Internet that you and Jean's assistant are…excuse me for voicing this…*having an affair*.'

'Goodness. That's ludicrous as, no doubt, you guessed,' I said casually and, hand shaking very slightly, poured myself another cup of tea. 'Nick and I simply get on and, as for the lawnmower… He slid his arms around my waist to prevent me slipping off. Sunshine doesn't always agree with me and goes to my head, as I told you last night, Edward, and the whole incident was, I can seen now… misjudged.'

'You must be careful, cousin; on camera much can be misunderstood. People also believe you two were, erm, intimate together in the kitchen on Sunday night.' Edward shook his head. 'We want Applebridge Hall to be popular, but not at the cost of dignity. Remember, innocent situations can easily be misconstrued on film.'

I rolled my eyes. 'Quite, dear cousin, and the Internet is full of conspiracy theories—last week some poor soul swore they saw Michael Jackson teaching Marilyn Monroe how to moon-walk. I do, um, hope you haven't confronted poor Nick about these unfounded claims.'

He shrugged. 'Father insisted I speak to you first.'

'Apologies for any embarrassment that my behaviour might have caused, but I trust I don't need to assure you that there is nothing untoward going on. In future, I shall take more care over how my actions might appear on screen.'

'Make sure you do, Abigail,' said the Earl. 'What would your father say about the nation pondering such things? I doubt even *he* is that liberal.'

Understatement, or what? Abbey's dad clearly had a problem with good-hearted professional volunteer Zak—he'd go even madder at the idea of his daughter dating a cocky gardener. And Lady C had carried on texting me this morning about last night's programme. I'd only read one, reminding me indignantly of the three Ms (Modesty, Manners and no Men).

'Always remember, Abigail,' said the Earl, 'affairs of the heart—or fun—must never lead our heads. We are Croxleys. Family, duty, standards… All of that comes first. Generations of our family have made huge sacrifices to ensure the continuity of our good reputation.'

'And extra care is required,' said Edward in measured tones, 'when we are on screen and playing up to our aristocratic image to win votes. You know what Gaynor believes—stick with stereotype; present an image of believing we are above everyone else.'

Not hard for you then, was my automatic response, yet, after last night, well—he had swum in the bulrushes with a pizza waitress! Plus he was getting quite chummy with his blog-readers.

'Although reality viewers love a good romance.' I gave a nervous giggle. 'Um, according to my lodger, Gemma.'

Edward's mouth upturned before he went back to his newspaper—was that a smile or a smirk? Maybe, in the light of day, he'd decided that Abbey's lodger was completely bonkers?

'Perhaps I should ask Henrietta if she has any suitable male friends for you, then,' he said.

'No, thank you.' I picked up a piece of shortbread, remembering to hold a plate underneath. 'I'm, um, far too busy here for hearts and flowers. Now, if I may change the

186 Doubting Abbey

subject… Uncle, you talked of sacrifices. Remember when Applebridge Hall homed evacuees?'

Pipe in his mouth, he grunted.

'I've come up with a plan to compete with the Baron of Marwick's celebrity high jinks. It will involve an enormous amount of work, but I—we—have a few days and the Internet to get organised.' I took a deep breath. 'I'm not a fan of reality shows myself, of course, but I have it on good authority…'

'From Gemma, no doubt,' said Edward, without looking up from his newspaper.

'… that reunions go down well,' I said, ignoring him. 'Out and, um, about in the village, I've got to know a few facts about Applebridge Hall during the war. A lady who taught the children lives in Wisteria Cottage, by the post office, doesn't she?'

The old Earl straightened in his chair and put down his pipe. 'Mrs Raynor? Todd's mother? Yes, indeed she does.'

'Oh, is that her name?' I asked innocently. 'Apparently, some evacuees still write to her.'

'Well, I never.' The Earl rubbed his beard.

I clasped my hands. 'Why don't we organize a reunion lunch for Saturday? I'm sure I could trace enough people online.'

'The evacuees? Here again? After all this time?' The Earl gasped. 'How…? What…?'

'And remind them of a brutal time when they were separated from their parents?' said Edward and shook his head.

'What do you think, Uncle?' I asked. 'Surely your memories of that period aren't *all* sad?'

'No, but it was jolly easy for me as I stayed in my own home.'

'But the youngsters must have had good times as well?'

For a moment the Earl stared vacantly into space. 'Us children just got on with our daily lives, I suppose' he said eventually. 'One lad was a real joker. Now, what was he called…?'

'Ooh, um, Bobby, Bert; what about Giles or Gerry…?' I said innocently.

'That was it!' said the Earl. 'Gerry Green. Clever guess! And I got to know a terrific little chap called Jonny Jackson. He'd save his carrot fudge for the young'uns who cried at night because they missed their mums.' The Earl's eyes shone. 'Yes, well, perhaps this reunion is a good idea—unlike that damned Food Academy.'

'That Academy will earn us money, Father,' said Edward.

'Only if we win the prize to get it up and running,' I said. 'And, in my opinion, to win that show we need to provide the viewers with something more…emotional than the Baron's celebrities and inebriated guests. Why don't I visit this Mrs Raynor, Uncle, and search on the Internet for any names you remember? Perhaps there's a friend in the village who could help jolt memories,' I said, more innocently than ever.

'Bill,' said the Earl without hesitating.

Yay! This was going to plan. Although I couldn't quite give a beaming, warmth-in-the-eyes smile. It was scary how easy it was to manipulate people. Now I understood how Auntie Jan had been two-timed and deceived by her last boyfriend. If you had no conscience and lies tripped off your tongue, it was easy to dupe anyone.

Problem was, I *did* have a conscience and it was pulling me apart. On the one hand, I was mega excited about my success at being Abbey—on the other, I'd have done anything to be honest about who I really was.

'What about the unused bedrooms upstairs where the evacuees used to sleep?' I said. 'Would they hold written records?'

'That's irrelevant,' said Edward, 'as it would be quite impossible to organize this in just three days.'

Talk about negative! However, he had put his newspaper down.

'Half-glass full, cousin, isn't that what you always say?' I stared him in the face. 'Without a doubt, it's an enormous challenge, but if we emphasize to everyone we ring how important their participation is for the future of Applebridge Hall... I assume close friendships were formed here, Uncle, despite it being a time of great upheaval? That's got to be worth something.'

'All these years later?' said Edward.

'And why not, son?' said the Earl. 'Just because we've lost touch doesn't mean those years counted for nothing.'

'Let's be honest,' I said, and smiled sheepishly. 'Even though today went well, it's going take more than my cooking to get the public vote.'

'Yes, I suspect today's successful plum sauce won't be quite as entertaining as that mustard dressing.' Edward half-smiled. 'I suppose I might be able to persuade Gaynor to put on speedy cars to pick up guests—if she agrees that a reunion lunch will boost ratings.'

The Earl rubbed his hands together. Aw—his face had lit up.

'Mr Thompson can drive me into the village first thing tomorrow,' said the old man. 'Let me visit Bill. Together, we can call on Mrs Raynor. That will leave you time to go on your computer, Abigail, and use those online engines, or whatever they are, to find out information.' He cleared his throat. 'Well done, girl. All things considered, it's a splendid idea.'

I beamed. 'Edward—perhaps you could help me sort through the bedrooms that used to be dormitories. We might find interesting memorabilia.' I put down my plate. 'Kathleen and I could organize a Second World War themed meal.'

'Back in those days, Cook was ingenious,' said the Earl, 'and could rustle up pretty decent meals from practically nothing. Often, I'd slip down to the kitchens and she'd let me help. Of course, with the vegetable gardens and orchards, here, we were luckier than most. She'd make a savoury carrot pudding, I seem to remember, with breadcrumbs and minced onion.' The Earl gazed into space for a moment. 'Mmm, plus a vegetable roll—she made the pastry out of mashed potato and served it with a cheese sauce. Damn decent, it was. Then there was this whipped pudding made from grated apple and…condensed milk, that was it—she'd add orange juice instead of sugar, which was rationed. And, of course, she was always baking apples…'

'I don't think I'll risk cooking those again,' I said in a small voice.

Both men caught my eye and we all laughed. This was mega—us three sharing a joke, for a fleeting second just like a proper family.

'In fact, you sound quite knowledgeable, Uncle. Perhaps you should run Friday's cookery lesson.'

'Now that would have made my Rosemary laugh,' muttered the Earl and picked up his pipe.

'Nowadays, Father can't even make a decent cup of tea,' said Edward. 'Clearly he's forgotten his skills from the war. One day last year, Kathleen fell ill. We insisted she go to bed early and said we'd cook for ourselves.' He grinned. 'Only my father could burn soup.'

The Earl's eyes crinkled at the corners.

'Richard was always good with his hands, Abigail,' said the Earl. 'It was no surprise when he went into catering.'

Edward rubbed the back of his neck. 'We ought to swap mobile phone numbers, Abbey. This project will involve a mammoth amount of organization and we might need to contact each other at a moment's notice.'

I nodded. Good thing Lady C had made me bring that mobile under the name of Abbey Croxley.

At that moment a knock on the Parlour door disturbed us. Kathleen came in.

'Um, Miss Croxley, you have a visitor.'

Huh?

'Thank you,' I said and left the room as Edward picked up his laptop. 'Who is it?' I hissed as we hurried downstairs, past the entrance and along to the Low Drawing Room. With her fingers, outside the door, Kathleen formed the letter C. Charlie? But why so formal? With a shrug, I stepped forward and pushed open the door.

Oh my God.

There to greet me was a grey bob and shiny pearls. My visitor was Lady Constance Woodfold—Lady C— complete with umbrella, a small suitcase and her fierce dinner lady stare.

LORD EDWARD'S E-DIARY

Wednesday 5ᵗʰ September

6.30p.m. Just when I don't think my cousin can surprise me again, she succeeds. As a consequence, I think you will all be very interested in tomorrow's show. A clue? Just let me say, 'World War Two'. In fact, why don't I ask you another poser question? This weekend, Applebridge Hall will host which of the following three events?

A cookery demonstration, based around foods from the Second World War?

A reunion lunch for evacuees who stayed here almost seventy years ago?

An historical day, revealing the life of my grandparents, where the Croxleys and staff must dress in vintage clothes from the 1940s?

As for this morning's cookery show, if you hope to see burnt or undercooked fare again, in the words of our Scottish cook, you'll be 'scunnered', (Googling that word will reveal whether, this time, Abigail got control of her nerves).

My day has been spent chasing up payments for the last car boot sale we hosted, and surveying the estate. After last night's shenanigans, normal service has resumed and I am indeed feeling more myself. Despite *Million Dollar*

Mansion, daily maintenance of the Hall and gardens must go on. Mr Thompson showed me cracked windows, a diseased tree and some mysterious red water in the pond.

However, a brief respite from my duties came in the form of a call from the editor of an online historical magazine. As a result, I shall be writing an article on what it means to be an aristocrat nowadays. Thankfully, it's a serious publication and won't expect tales of trips to the Maldives or Cristal champagne parties.

Right, apparently now Father and I have a visitor to greet...

CHAPTER 15

'You have five minutes to explain yourself, young lady, before I tell the Earl everything; before you reduce my niece's reputation to tatters,' said Lady C, straight after Kathleen had left and shut the door.

Not caring about my varnish, for a moment I bit my thumbnail as Lady C put down her umbrella and suitcase.

'Gemma? I am waiting. Or shall I ask that charming Scottish woman to show me to the Earl?'

'What are *you* doing here?' I said, all polite tones forgotten.

Lady C's brow wrinkled deeper. 'Initially, when staying with friends in the area, I thought you might need extra clothes and packed some to drop off. However, you haven't responded to my calls and, in light of recent footage, I deemed it necessary to hear any possible justification for your reckless behaviour. Have you forgotten everything I taught you?'

I shrugged sheepishly. ''Course not. But what about winning the show? As I said in my texts—everything you've seen is part of a game-plan. You've got to trust me. And if you reveal my true identity, everything will fall apart and the two Croxley brothers will never bury the hatchet.'

'But you've portrayed Abigail as someone more suited to living with that dreadful, over-the-top Baron and his son.' She folded her arms. 'What have you got to say for yourself?'

I swallowed. 'Um, isn't this room amaaaazin'? Look at that chandelier and the tapestries. As for the carved furniture legs and mantelpiece…'

'Don't change the subject,' said Lady C in clipped tones. 'What happened to the three Ms?' She sighed. 'At least you have kept appearances up, literally, by sticking to my rules about make-up and clothes.' Shaking her head, Lady C sat down on an embroidered chair. I collapsed into the one next to her.

'Look, it's been mega hard, keeping up this act twenty-four seven. Have I really done that badly?' I said.

'The lawnmower episode…' Lady C shuddered.

I had to admire her, really, for sticking to her principles. So far she hadn't raised her voice or sworn—not so much as a flicker of emotion.

'Such a lack of decorum and, as for that young chap, Nick…' Lady C eyed me beadily. 'Camera footage and Internet rumours would suggest something untoward is going on.'

'Online nonsense; it's nothing and not everyone believes it was Abigail Croxley…' I cleared my throat and pointed to a framed landscape. 'See this? It was drawn centuries ago and shows the estate before the Hall was built, and—' Oh, dear, fierce dinner lady stare—distraction not working. My stomach twisted. I could tell poor Lady C was upset. 'Look—Nick is just a mate. We're friends.'

'No. With friends you have common interests. Remember, you are Abbey and, as far as I know, my niece knows little about gardening or…or maintaining ponds. Equally, I suspect this Nick has little knowledge about dinner etiquette or how to chat to a countess…'

'Nor does Zak.'

'And it's because of Abigail's relationship with him that we're in this mess.' Lady C's eyes softened. 'Gemma, dear, I'm a romantic at heart and have nothing against two people—from any background—falling in love. But you are here to promote a certain image. Please—if you have feelings for this gardener, at least conceal them until the end of the fortnight.'

'I don't fancy him.'

'Then why—?'

I walked over to another portrait and pointed. It was of the first Earl of Croxley, a whip in his hand, standing next to a horse. 'Elizabeth the First awarded this estate to the Croxleys for this man's bravery in fighting against the Spanish Armada. My—Abbey's—uncle is so proud and, like every heir since, has tried to maintain this place's standards.' My voice wavered. 'I'm only a pizza caff waitress. My family isn't famous. In fact, my brother's in the nick. But I feel…it's kind of down to me to save the Croxleys' future and I'll do whatever it takes. Don't you think Abbey would want that?'

'So what exactly is it you're doing?' said Lady C, a puzzled look on her face.

'Roxy, the production assistant, told me that Applebridge Hall was trailing behind the Baron's place. She suggested…ahem…sexing things up.' I coughed. 'No doubt you've read *Lady Chatterley's Lover…* What could intrigue the British public more than a suspected love affair between two people of a different class? Not that class seems a big issue nowadays but, I dunno—with shows like *Downton Abbey* on everyone's minds…'

Lady C's mouth fell open.

'Nick kindly agreed to help me,' I continued, 'although he doesn't know who I really am.'

'But…'

I wouldn't tell her about Kathleen knowing my true identity because right at this moment Lady C looked as if she might faint.

'This is getting complicated,' she said, 'and, eventually, lies always out. Oh, dear. Can't you just let this *thing* between you and this Nick fizzle out? I can help you think of another way to make the show more interesting.'

'How? By demonstrating…I don't know…your elocution and deportment skills?'

'That's not a bad idea,' said Lady C.

'No! The only way to boost ratings is to add intrigue. As for the dishonesty…' My eyes widened. 'Surely you understand? I'm just taking things a step further; it's still all part of the same charade—that *you* got involved with, right at the beginning. Why did you agree to help Abbey deceive everyone in the first place if you're finding it so hard now?'

Lady C's cheeks tinged pink, matching her pastel rose blouse. 'Neither Abbey nor I relish misleading people, but I understand my niece's plight. You see…My parents were terribly strict and…'

My eyebrows raised.

'I became fond of a young man in my twenties. He worked in a shoe shop. Papa didn't approve and forbade us from courting. I cried for weeks.' Her voice broke. 'In private, of course—in public, one must never let one's dignity slip.'

'That must have been hard,' I said, feeling bad now for asking. I leant over and squeezed her arm.

'I never met anyone else quite like John and instead dedicated my life to the finishing school,' continued Lady C. 'That was rewarding in its own way, but if Abigail is anything like me, spinsterhood… It can get very lonely. So, if I can help resolve this situation with Zachary…'

A lump formed in my throat. Her eyes were all shiny.

At that moment the door opened and the Earl and Edward came in, followed by the cameraman, the soundman, Gaynor and Roxy. The director flicked her Jessie J bob. I removed my hand from Lady C's arm.

'Visitors—fab, darlings!' said Gaynor, smelling of smoke as usual. The cameraman positioned some lights. Outside, the sky was becoming increasingly dark. 'Kathleen has made tea for you all to enjoy. This is unexpected footage we can edit into tomorrow night's show. Is this a relative of yours, Miss Croxley?'

'Um, yes. Excuse my manners,' I said and stood up with Lady C. 'Allow me to introduce my dear aunt, Lady Constance Woodfold. Auntie—this is Gaynor, the director and her assistant, Roxy. And please meet Lord Croxley and his son, Lord Edward.' Urgh. I should have probably introduced the titled before the TV crew.

Roxy sidled up and brushed a strand of hair out of my face. 'Make it interesting,' she whispered. 'Marwick Castle is hosting a murder mystery banquet tonight for the corporate guests. You'll have to work hard to beat that.'

While Lady C shook everyone's hands, I winked.

'How lovely to meet you, Lord Croxley,' she said in a honeyed voice, revealing none of her previous inner turmoil. 'Please forgive my unexpected arrival, but I was staying in the area and thought I would call in to see my niece before returning home tonight. I do hope I haven't inconvenienced you.'

'Not at all,' said the Earl gruffly.

'It's a pleasure to meet more of the family,' said Edward in his usual unemotional voice.

That had been the great thing about last night, by the pond—he'd shouted, laughed, pitched his tones high and low… For the first time his voice had sounded alive.

We all sat down, the Earl and Lady C together on a ruby-red sofa, facing the front window. There was a polite silence. Roxy looked at me and rolled her eyes. Okay—must liven things up.

'I, um, was just about to tell my aunt details of my plan to…'

Her eyebrows shot up in horror and I suppressed a giggle. Maybe she thought I was going to come clean about my fake romance with Nick. Okay, I shouldn't really find that funny.

'… about my plan to organize a very special reunion on Saturday.' I smiled at Lady C. 'Applebridge Hall was home to evacuees during the war and we intend to bring them together after almost seventy years apart.'

Blimey. That made Roxy stop chewing her gum and Gaynor looked up from her notes.

'What a truly wonderful idea,' said Lady C. 'My family is still in touch with the girl who came to stay with us in autumn 1940, just at the beginning of the Blitz. Vera Watkins. She's about six years older than me. I was only five when the war ended, so I don't remember her early years with us—but she had a lovely voice. I'll never forget how she always used to sing her mother's favourite song, "The Lambeth Walk".'

'Did her parents survive?' asked the Earl as the sound guy adjusted the boom.

'Ironically, she lost her mother in the bombing and her father returned from the war without a scratch—not of the physical kind, anyway. Vera grew up to marry a plumber, had three children and now lives in Wales. Until she developed arthritis, I used to meet up with her every few years in Oxford Street, for shopping and lunch. Have you kept in touch with any of the children who stayed here, Lord Croxley?'

The Earl shook his head. 'Would be good to meet some of the old chaps again, though—to see how they've spent the intervening years. For several Christmases, some sent Mama cards. One family even visited. The mother wanted to thank us, in person, for looking after their son. Alfie, I seem to recall he was called.'

'It must have felt rather odd, sharing your home with strangers,' I said.

'What, like now?' said the Earl and gave a wry smile. He fiddled with his pocket watch. 'It never crossed my mind to complain, as Mama drilled into us that Dickie and I were very fortunate living how and where we did. I remember sitting in lessons with the children, Mrs Raynor reading *Huckleberry Finn*. We'd all moan about our "pudding basin" haircuts and go picking wild blackberries on the outskirts of the forest in autumn. One had to get on with life and, for us youngsters, it could be immense fun. Sorry things they were, on arrival, though, the children—labelled like parcels and carrying gas masks.'

Yay! Gaynor and Roxy were still rapt. War stories were a far cry from Marwick Castle's tacky flashes of boobs. Maybe, just maybe, this reunion would give Applebridge Hall's chances a much-needed boost.

Lady C nodded. 'Vera says now that she spent many a night, those first few months, crying herself to sleep. It still brings tears to her eyes if we talk about the moment she waved goodbye to her mother at Waterloo Station. In fact my mother used to well up when she recalled the look of apprehension on little Vera's face when the Billeting Officer dropped her off at our house.' She looked into the distance. 'In our village, the girls had an easier time of it, though—there was a lot of rivalry between the local lads and evacuee boys. Then there was Vera's cousin, sent to a family who stole his rations and fed him on nothing but bread and water...' She cleared her throat. 'However, I suspect children who stayed here will have pleasant memories. Remember dried eggs, Lord Croxley?'

'How could I forget?' He smiled. 'Perhaps, Lady Woodfold...Would you care to stay to dinner?'

'How exceptionally kind of you,' she said, 'but, I, um, wouldn't want to impose...'

'Stuff and nonsense,' he said. 'In fact, why don't you stay for a few days? We converted the nursery next to Abigail's room into a guest room many years ago. There's still the big rocking horse in there, but it has a pleasant view of the orchards. And I'm sure we'll need all the help we can get, arranging this reunion. Edward, please ask Kathleen to prepare the room.'

Edward's jaw dropped. Mine, too. As a rule, I'm sure the Earl didn't like unexpected, unfamiliar guests.

'Of course, Father.' Edward stood up, just as Kathleen walked in with more tea. 'But, first things first—Abbey wanted me to show her the bedrooms upstairs that used to belong to the children. We haven't searched through all that gubbins for years. If this reunion is to take place, we need to crack on.'

Suddenly, Lady C jumped to her feet and almost headed the boom—she had a lot to learn about filming a reality show.

'Goodness me!' she said. 'Is that a common yellowthroat I saw on the fountain outside? What a treat.'

The Earl stood up beside her. 'Well, I bless! You recognize a yellowthroat? Bravo! So few people nowadays take an interest in our country's immensely varied birdlife. As you probably know, that species is a rarity. We must go out with my binoculars some time and...'

With a nod at Roxy, Edward and I exited the room, leaving Kathleen to serve tea to Abbey's excited uncle and aunt.

'Hold on!' called Gaynor, fag already in her lips. She sidled up to us. 'A bang-on concept this reunion is, Lord Edward—well done.'

'Actually, it was my cousin's idea,' he said, and ran a hand through his honey curls, but the director wasn't listening.

'Mics, Roxy!' she hissed at her assistant, who'd just appeared by her side.

Roxy rummaged in a bag she was carrying.

'We'll send the cameraman up when he's finished filming your father,' Gaynor said to Edward, still ignoring me. 'Delving into the past, the evacuees' dorms... I'm sure you'll agree that's just too good to miss.'

Taking her time as usual, with her hands on his chest, the director fitted Edward up with his mic while Roxy put on mine. Then Edward and I climbed the staircase, up to the Long Gallery. I hadn't been there since the Earl gave me a tour. The buckets placed to catch raindrops were still empty, thanks to the warm spell.

Edward stopped outside a bedroom, opposite the portrait of the glamorous couple known for partying—the Earl's great-grandparents—while I thought about Lady C. She must have been mega chuffed to land an invite to hang around for a few days, and keep an eye on me and Nick. Edward pointed to his battery pack, clipped onto his waist, and pulled out the mic lead. I followed suit.

'No need for them to hear our every word,' he muttered, 'until the cameraman arrives.'

I nodded and glanced out of a window on the other side and gazed down at the maze. Talk of the devil—Nick was working late, busy shaping it with an electric trimmer, no doubt hoping to avoid the imminent rain. The little avenues looked sharper and more defined. No doubt Croxley kids had played hide and seek in it over the centuries. He stood up and stretched and I smiled at the sight of his cheeky face. Yes, the gardener was a relief from the stodgy Croxleys but…I swallowed hard. How I'd felt with my arm around Edward… Who could make sense of that?

I turned back around and followed Edward into the bedroom. He'd switched on the light, which was just a glaring bulb with no lampshade.

'It looks as if no one has touched this room since the war,' I said.

Edward shrugged. 'They haven't really—only once when we had the whole of this top floor rewired.'

The room was big and full of clutter, with dismantled shelves against the walls and nuts and bolts scattered across the floor. It smelt of books that had been left in the loft too long. On each side were two pairs of bunk beds, so eight children had slept here. Cardboard boxes were stacked against the beds and on them. I crouched down and lifted the lid of one. On top of a pile of toys was a doll wearing a dusty bonnet and stained dress.

'Look at this,' I said, voice all mushy, and held it up. 'Talk about antique. With those choochy cheeks and rosebud lips, its face is quite beautiful.' I lifted up a knitted toy. 'Hey, Teddy, this looks like a teddy!'

But there was no humour in Edward's eyes or even a scowl for me using his pet name. He simply stared, before heading for the door.

'Back in a minute. I'm just getting the laptop. It might be good to search online and familiarize myself with background knowledge about wartime evacuees, so that I can show some genuine knowledge on screen.'

'Ever the honest, conscientious one, aren't you,' I said in a teasing voice, probably sounding more Gemma than Abbey.

He stared at me for a moment and his eyes narrowed. 'Whenever possible. Someone has to be. In fact you can drop the pretence. Don't you think I've guessed your little secret?'

My mouth went dry.

'It's become clear, since Lady Constance has arrived. Perhaps, when I return, you'll do the right thing and come clean.'

He left me in the room, my heart racing.

LORD EDWARD'S E-DIARY

Wednesday 5ᵗʰ September

Comments

7.30p.m. I've just bobbed back to the Parlour to pick up my laptop and noticed some responses already to my poser question. Thank you, all, for your continued participation.

Cupcakesrock, so, you think we're hosting a demonstration of Second World War meals? How interesting that your grandmother used to make carrot cakes during the war called Beady Buns—because they helped people see during blackouts.

Historybuff, I agree, a reunion of the evacuees, incorporating subsequent personal stories, would be a fascinating social documentation of life in post-war Britain.

bustyfanDownton, nice to see you back, even if it is just to tell us we don't stand a chance against Marwick Castle—unless we scrub all current ideas and declare Applebridge Hall a naturist destination. Hmm. I have a rather awkward image in my head now, thanks to your suggestion of us playing naked Twister...

CHAPTER 16

'So?' said Edward, now finally back from the Parlour.

'Um…'

'For goodness' sake, woman!'

At least he no longer considered me some juvenile little girl.

'I've worked it out! Lady Constance is taking you home. No doubt you're still upset after I suggested you abandon ship.'

I breathed a sigh of relief. Wow. For a while there, I thought my disguise had been rumbled.

'Are you still determined to see the worst in me, Edward?' I said eventually. 'To doubt my convictions, my abilities, my every move…? What about that half-glass full?'

'So, Lady Constance just *happened* to be in the area?'

'Yes,' I said firmly, although it was rather a coincidence.

We gazed into each other's eyes for a moment. His shoulders relaxed.

'Okay. Fair enough. Apologies, then, Abbey. Although, if you ever felt… I'd understand your departure, if you weren't happy or found this reality show experience difficult to endure. Only this morning, on the phone, Henrietta pointed out how much of a challenge this fortnight must be for you. Father and I aren't always the, erm, easiest people to live with.'

'You don't say?' My mouth upturned. 'Look—you aren't on your own any more, Edward. I'm here to help you and Uncle—to see this thing through.'

His eyes crinkled at the corners and in that moment I longed to wrap my arms round him; to see another glimpse of the carefree Edward who'd swum with me last night in the pond.

'You and Henrietta are good friends, aren't you?' I asked.

'Henry's a special lady,' he murmured.

For some reason my stomach went into a Sheepshank—or Overhand Bow (I'd learnt about knots from Dad). Edward was clearly mega fond of her.

'Look, I'm fine. This week has been stressful, but I'm a fighter,' I said. 'You don't need to worry about me.'

'Then perhaps your aunt has called by because *she's* worried and doesn't trust us to look after you.'

'More likely she doesn't trust me to do a good job,' I mumbled.

His brow relaxed. 'Well, you *do* do—a good job.'

'Do-bee, do-bee, do,' I said without thinking.

We exchanged glances and laughed. Fuzzy feeling inside again. Nope. He's supposed to be my cousin. Musn't dream of a snog.

'Edward, don't you think there's a chance…I mean surely it's possible that our fathers will make up? I don't know the full details of why they haven't talked for so long, but perhaps me contributing towards this programme, perhaps us pulling together will—'

'Don't raise your hopes, Abbey. Father's feelings were very hurt. The rift… It could have destroyed our family name. Perhaps it's better things stay as they are.'

I raised my eyebrows. 'You know what happened between them?'

'I've already said too much. Someone's coming.' His eyes dulled. In other words, subject closed.

The door creaked open and, as the cameraman entered, we both plugged our mics back in. Extra lighting set up, the room looked twice the size. Just as we were about to start filming, the Earl appeared.

'Kathleen is sorting out your aunt's room, Abigail,' he said. 'How delightful Lady Constance is. Tomorrow I shall take her on a stroll to spot the birds that frequent our estate.'

'Good idea, Father,' said Edward. 'Although I doubt many wildlife boffins watch *Million Dollar Mansion*.'

'Pah! I'm not spending every minute of this fortnight doing things to please this blasted show.'

'Did, um, Roxy fix you up with a mic, Uncle?' I asked innocently.

He, Edward and I looked at each other and grinned.

The cameraman chuckled. 'Don't worry, folks. I'll get that bit edited out.'

'I haven't been in this room for years.' The Earl sat down on one of the beds and lit his pipe. The cameraman gave us the thumbs-up. While Edward sifted through a cardboard box full of paperwork, I carried on discovering toys.

'Look at this!' I held up another knitted toy—aw, what a cute elephant.

'Damn me, I'd forgotten about Mrs Trimble,' said the Earl. 'She'd make us soft toys, using old jumpers for wool, rags for stuffing and mismatched buttons for eyes. Factories only made weapons during the war—anything else had to be made at home.'

'What about this?' I said, and with two hands lifted out a clockwork train set.

'We were lucky to keep that,' said the Earl. 'I used to have a big collection of metal soldiers I shared with the boys, but eventually Mama gave them up to be melted down for the war effort. Most of the toys we had were handmade. Our butler, Mr Carter, was a whiz with a saw, chisel and mallet. There should be some wooden zoo animals in there.' The Earl scratched his beard. 'And a farm, if I remember rightly.'

After rummaging in the box for a few minutes, sure enough, I pulled out a zebra, penguin and lion. Something clattered in the bottom and I pulled out a handful of marbles.

'We'd roll them along the Long Gallery. Jolly good fun, it was, although Matron wasn't impressed. She always said someone would trip over them and break their neck. Gerry Green did sprain his ankle once.' The Earl chuckled. 'We had to play covertly, after that.'

'What about these…?' I lifted out a folder of paper dolls and a shower of dust fell over my blouse. 'Plus Snakes & Ladders!' I pulled out a box.

'Us boys made our own fun a lot of the time,' said the Earl, 'like hide and seek in the maze or digging for worms. But my old family games and the ones made by Mr Carter were a godsend during inclement months.'

Digging for worms? Ooh, that brought back memories of me growing up with my brothers. No Barbie dolls for me. Action Men were cool, as was our favourite game, ninjas versus aliens.

'Have you managed to find a register, Edward?' I said.

A mound of papers now littered the bed.

'Yes—although if we're really holding this lunch on Saturday, it won't give us much time to trace the girls who've married and changed their surnames. There's a tremendous amount to look through—medical papers and school work…

'Roxy must be used to doing research,' I said. 'No doubt she could help.' The knitted elephant lay on its back amongst the paper dolls and seemed to stare at me. How many homesick children had clutched that to their chest at night, all those years ago? I shook myself. Edward wouldn't approve of soppiness.

The Earl moved to the wall behind the headboards of the beds.

'They're still there,' he muttered.

'What's that?' I got up and gave a loud sneeze, from all the dust.

'See these marks. Some of the children used to scratch the number of days they stayed here into the wall.'

I went over. My eyes tingled. At the end of one huge set of scratches was a big smiley face and the words 'Going Home'.

I opened up another box to find a pile of ration books and gas masks.

'Once we know who is coming—' if anyone, fingers crossed '—we could present them with all their paperwork. I'll clean up these toys,' I said.

The Earl nodded and picked up a yo-yo that I'd put on a bed.

'I could never master this,' he said. 'Jonny Jackson showed me again and again.' He gazed at it for a few moments before giving it an unsuccessful go.

'Let's get cracking, then,' said Edward and unplugged his mic. The Earl and I did the same, as the cameraman put down his equipment.

'I, um, just need some fresh air,' I said, wondering if Nick was still trimming the maze. 'Then I'll check on my aunt before going online to search for names. Shall I use the computer in the cellar whilst you use the laptop, Edward?'

'Whatever you prefer, cousin,' he said.

'I'll visit Bill in the morning,' said the Earl.

'Let's meet tomorrow, a couple of hours before the next episode of *Million Dollar Mansion*, to see how far we've all got,' suggested Edward. 'I'll pick Roxy's brains and see if she can speed up the research process.'

'Super idea,' I said.

With a swing in my step, I headed downstairs. This was wicked! Although there was no point getting carried away—we still had one more week, after the reunion, to go. Things might fall flat, so, despite Lady C's disapproval, I had to find a way for me and Nick to give the cameras a bit more reality show gold.

I legged it out of the main entrance and immediately my skin came up in goose bumps. It was mega cool now. I looked at my watch. It had already gone nine o'clock. In the dusk, by the fountain, Roxy chewed gum and talked non-stop with Gaynor, at her usual breakneck speed.

'Get the cameraman,' said the director, fag hanging out of her mouth. 'This brewing storm could provide some excellent moody shots. They'll make the perfect backdrop to edit in if any dramas take place. Take some of the pond first, and then the cemetery, plus a panoramic view from the back of the house.'

They stopped chatting as I walked past. Slowing my pace, I made sure they saw me primp my loose hair as if I wanted to look my best. Then I headed around to the back and Nick, who stood next to a wheelbarrow.

'You've done a splendid job on the maze,' I said. 'But it's almost dark. Don't you think you should stop? What about dinner?'

On cue, my stomach grumbled and we laughed.

'Um, Nick… after the lawnmower debacle…'

'Have you been on the Internet? Seen the fallout on Facebook? How have the family reacted?' Nick's top lip curled. 'I didn't want to leave you alone with your cousin last night.'

I smiled. 'It's nothing I can't handle. Naturally, I've played down our, um, relationship. Still, it's perfectly understandable if you don't wish to—'

'Bring it on!' Then he stared at me for quite a long moment.

'Anything, um wrong, Nick? Have I smudged my mascara?'

'Sorry! It's just… You're not at all what I'd expect of a lady—no offence. You're so easy to talk to, whereas your cousin…'

'He's under a lot of pressure at the moment,' I said with a shrug.

'Sure. But with him I'm always very aware that I live in a one-bedroom flat and he owns a mansion. You could be the girl next door.' He grinned. 'Well, almost—bet you've been to university and…'

'No. Catering college,' I said, remembering Abbey's history. 'But not straight away. I went to finishing school first.' Eek, please don't let him ask me exactly where. All I knew was that it was somewhere in Switzerland, where they spoke French. Hence Zak wanting her immediate help in Africa…

'Really? People still do that? Although, for someone in your position, it's probably a good idea.' He looked sideways at me. 'So what did you learn?'

After Lady C's training, this was easy to answer.

'The art of good conversation. Deportment. Etiquette.'

'You studied in England?'

'No…' I cleared my throat. 'Switzerland. I speak fluent French.'

'Cool. I've been there. Whereabouts?'

Crap. Think hard. The only Swiss city I knew, thanks to a pub quiz, was the capital.

'Um, Bern,' I mumbled.

He gazed at me. 'Ah, you learnt your French there…'

'Um, *oui, bien sur!*' I said quickly and smiled. Good thing I'd done GCSE French. 'By talking to the locals every day and, um, watching the regional telly, all of us girls soon picked it up.'

He took a moment to reply and then eventually nodded. 'I never went to college. My dad's a gardener. I learnt my trade off him. Always fancied myself as a bit of an actor, though,' he said with a wink. 'So yeah, I'm up for performing any more classic movie scenes.'

I touched his arm, which felt warm and comfortable, but there wasn't a hint of the electricity I'd felt with Edward. 'That's very decent of you, considering how angry my cousin was.'

'I don't scare easily, Miss.' He jerked his head towards the pond. 'Fancy keeping me company? Mr Thompson mentioned that the water looked a bit red this morning. I wondered if a fox had killed one of the ducks and left it behind. I'd like to check it before the rain starts. We should just be able to see in this twilight.'

Ahem. It was nothing to do with me. My crimson hair couldn't have possibly dyed that pond, considering the mega number of shampoo washes it took to finally get that coloured stuff out.

Nick put down his trimmers and, aware of the cameraman setting up behind us for the so-called moody shots, we headed around the side of the house, towards the pond. With all his equipment, the poor guy couldn't follow quickly and by the time he appeared we were already at the edge of the water, hidden behind the bulrushes and long grass.

The occasional fat drop of rain now fell into the pond. As the waves rippled I recalled my swim from last night, and the water's fresh silkiness.

'There's one classic romance movie scene that I'll never forget,' I said with a dreamy sigh.

'What's that?' said Nick and leant forward, presumably looking for dead ducks.

'*Dirty Dancing*—the lake scene where they are both in the water and Johnny lifts Baby above his head.'

'Ah, yes. I've watched that with several girlfriends.'

I grinned. 'What a stir it would cause if we attempted that.'

He pulled a face.

'What's the matter? Aren't you strong enough?' I teased as rain fell steadily now. A faraway rumble of thunder spurred on my daredevil instinct. 'It's not as if anyone would see us clearly in this half-light and we are partially hidden by plants.' Uh oh. Surge of adrenaline. 'In fact, the more I think about it, Nick, the less wacky the idea seems.'

'Are you serious?' He straightened up. 'But your clothes…?'

'This outfit is exceptionally lightweight. Just think of the buzz we'd create on the social media sites. If our tribute to *Titanic* got people talking, this would take their breath away. The camera's view won't be crystal-clear. I'll simply deny everything.'

'But how will you get back into the house? Your dripping wet dress might be a giveaway.'

'I can blame the rain.' My eyes widened. 'Do say you'll be a sport, Nick.' This might be one of the last chances I had to do something really outrageous, now that Lady C was around.

Nick chuckled and took off his light blue raincoat, which I put on, partly to disguise myself again. He duly stripped off his shirt, his skin surprisingly pale for someone who'd always worked outdoors. My pulse sped as I thought back to Edward's naked torso…

With a shake, I squinted towards the Hall. The cameraman had set up there and his equipment happened to be pointing right our way. I took a deep breath and, unusually for me, considered how undignified my behaviour might look. After the lawnmower incident, I felt a little uncomfortable doing something else wacky, dressed up as my flatmate.

'Quick,' I said and waded in, screwing up my nose at the fish tank smell. The sooner this was over, the sooner my doubts would disappear. Nick plunged straight under the water. Seconds later, he came up spluttering.

'Jeez! That's freezing!' he hissed and placed his hands around my hips. 'Right, here goes, Miss. Jump after three. One, two, three…'

I bent my knees and sprang into the air as high as I could—about ten centimetres, as it turned out. I fell forward onto his chest. We both sunk under the water and came up laughing.

'I hope that isn't blood in this water,' he said and spat out a mouthful. 'Let's try again.' We got into position. 'Right, again, Miss, one, two, three…'

This time I jumped higher and he managed to hold me above his chest for a few seconds, above the long grass.

The rain poured heavier and felt warm, compared to the pond. Rumbles of thunder got louder. Or was that my stomach again?

'Almost there,' he gasped. 'I reckon we'll get the perfect position this time. It's our last chance. The sun's almost gone and then the cameraman might pack up his stuff.'

Blimey. He'd need mega strong biceps. I was no flyweight. Certainly no size eight 'Baby' from the original film. One, two, three… I jumped for my life and he lifted me higher than before.

Yay! Like a sequinned dancer on one of those ice-skating shows, I finally stretched out, skirt edging above my thighs, me star-shaped above his head. Talk about fun! However, I did feel kind of clumsy and, in truth, probably looked more like some deranged skydiver. Poor Lady C would have a fit and everything she'd taught me about decorum suddenly pierced my conscience.

At least the deed was done and we could now hurry back to the house. But… aarggh! What was that? A distant deep voice shouted and I fell into the water.

'Don't move, you ruffians, or I'll shoot you to smithereens!' shouted Mr Thompson.

'Shit!' hissed Nick as I surfaced. 'Excuse my language, Miss, but get the fuck out of this water… Now!'

Nick scrambled onto the bank and held out a hand. Once I was out, we grabbed our shoes and ran as fast as we could around the back of the house.

'Don't move!' hollered Mr Thompson, coming from… I wasn't quite sure. 'My finger's on the trigger.'

Oh, no. What if Mr Thompson caught us? Edward and the Earl would never forgive me. Out of nerves, I gave a low giggle.

'It's not funny,' hissed Nick. 'One thing that old codger can't abide is trespassers.'

'No. Sorry. Of course,' I said, in between breaths. 'Why don't we split up? That might confuse him.'

'Good idea,' said Nick. 'I'll go to the front of the house and perhaps lead him down the drive, towards the orchards—that way, you can slip in via the back entrance to the kitchens.'

'Okay. Thank you so much, Nick,' I said, rain pelting into my face as I spoke. I peeled off Nick's raincoat and gave it to him before he dashed off. A flash of lightning lit up the grounds and helped me navigate the vegetable garden.

Where should I go until Mr Thompson was well and truly distracted? Of course—the newly trimmed maze. In I hurtled, following the small avenues that twisted and turned. Finally, I sank to the ground. My body trembled. Despite all the running, I felt mega cold now. But I'd had to remove Nick's coat, which had bits of weed sticking to it—evidence that I'd been up to no good.

I squinted at my watch but it was too dark to make out the time. A twig snapped. What if Nick's plan of creating a diversion had failed? Thunder rumbled just as a voice—not a mega deep one like Mr Thompson's—muffled by the weather, said, 'Who's there?'

I stood up and tiptoed to the end of the avenue I was in—it was all clear. Slowly, I edged along the hedges, searching for a way out.

'You can't hide,' shouted the voice.

Oh God. Maybe some psycho had stumbled onto the estate or… Thunder clapped. Did vampires really exist? Please, no. Even the human-friendly *Twilight* hunks might find my sizeable muffin top hard to resist. Deep breaths.

Get a grip, girl. Lightning lit up the way for a few seconds and I rushed to and fro, determined to escape. Oh my God! A gunshot fired in the distance. Another twig snapped near me and heavy footsteps plodded my way. I backed into a dead end and screamed. A strong pair of hands had grabbed me from behind.

LORD EDWARD'S E-DIARY

Wednesday 5th September

'Comments'

11.45p.m. A quick goodnight before I change out of soaking clothes. Earlier, Mr Thompson alerted me to the presence of intruders in the gardens. Promptly I joined him in his hunt for the culprits. Take heed, prospective trespassers, his gun is loaded, lethal and lightning-quick. Indeed, tonight, harm was done. A price has been paid for his vigilance.

CHAPTER 17

'What an absolute hero—you saved my life last night, Edward,' I said.

He was pacing up and down in the Parlour, ahead of the Thursday night episode of *Million Dollar Mansion.*' From near the front window, Lady C tutted. With the Earl, she'd been admiring an oil painting of a pheasant.

'Do explain once more, Abbey, how you got lost in the maze, clothes soaking, unprepared, without an umbrella…?' Cue fierce dinner lady stare.

I'd decided not to tell Lady C any more about my sex-up plan with Nick. It would only stress her out and the less people that knew, the better.

'The maze has claimed many victims over the years,' said Edward and smiled. 'My cousin could have been in there all night—like Mr Barden.'

The old Earl chuckled.

'He was a business associate of my father,' continued Edward. 'After a glass of red wine too many, he wandered into the maze. We didn't hear his calls for help until after breakfast the following morning.'

'Indeed, I was a silly sausage, Auntie,' I said. 'After an afternoon in the hot kitchen and dusty evacuees' room upstairs, I needed some fresh air. Once outside, unable to, um, resist a challenge, I entered the maze, convinced

I'd find my way out. I should have kept an eye on the approaching inclement weather. Thank goodness Edward found me and led the way out.'

'It's a jolly good thing Mr Thompson didn't spot you,' said the Earl as he crossed the room and sat down in his terracotta chair. 'Nothing or no one gets in his way when he's tracking intruders with his shotgun.'

'But he, um, still hasn't found any, has he?' I asked as Lady C joined me on the mustard sofa.

The Earl snorted. 'No. Damn lucky so far, those blighters have been. Mr Thompson's hearing is super-human. That man could shoot a rabbit dead with both eyes closed, if he had to.'

Lady C looked at 'James' and smiled.

'He swore he almost caught some youngsters by the pond, last night,' the Earl continued. 'In fact, he spotted one, hiding behind the fountain. Fortunately for them, his shot just missed. Instead, it hit the water feature, which now has a chunk missing.'

Fortunately for Nick, more like. Relief had surged through my veins this morning when I found out it was the fountain and not Nick that had been damaged.

I cleared my throat. 'Right, well, we've got two hours until the staff join us to watch the programme.' I bit into a yummy teacake, making sure my chewing was dainty. In between bites, I wiped my fingers on a napkin, before picking up an A4 pad and pen. 'Please excuse me for eating and writing at the same time… Saturday looms and, as Edward suggested yesterday, now is a good time to take stock of how much progress we have all made in organizing the reunion.'

'Would you like me to pour, James?' Lady C said to the Earl and pointed to the teapot.

'Thank you, Constance,' he said and her cheeks tinged pink.

Aw—first name terms already. Perhaps Abbey's aunt and uncle might add a more genuine dimension to the sexing— or at least romancing—up of Applebridge Hall's footage.

'Cousin, did you ask Gaynor if the TV company would put on cars to pick up guests?' I said.

'Of course. She said "no problem".'

No surprise there. Her hots for Edward were so steaming, she'd have probably agreed to put on private jets.

'I also sorted the medical notes and ration books into alphabetical order,' he said and stood still, for a second, near the fireplace. 'I came across a diary left behind by a Norman Barker, and a bundle of school reports. With Kathleen's help, I cleaned the bedroom and the toys. She found sheets to make up the beds, to give viewers a better idea of how it used to look.'

'What about the other dorms?' I asked.

'Not much in them,' said Edward.

The Earl sucked on an empty pipe. 'Mr Thompson drove me to see Bill Cochrane this morning and the two of us called on Mrs Raynor. Jolly thrilled she was, with the whole idea.' He leant down, opened a leather briefcase and slid out a sheet of floral paper. 'Here is a list Mrs Raynor made, of people she is still in contact with. She didn't think they'd mind her passing on their details to our family. Apparently, despite the war, they still remember Applebridge warmly. The list used to be much longer but, due to one reason or another, has diminished over the years. Her writing's a bit spidery now, but still legible.'

I took it from him. Wow. Twenty or so names... '*Wiiiiiiicked!*'

Lady C glared at me.

'I mean… *Weeeee could* start ringing them straight away.'

'What success have you had?' said Edward and smiled. Just lately, I'd noticed what nice teeth he had. And, although his clothes were far from trendy, I was coming around to the idea that he could slip into a potato sack and make it look, well…kind of…lush. I shook myself. As if he'd be interested in the real me, without a posh accent and titled background—Gemma Goodwin was no Henrietta Hamilton-Brown.

'Any luck tracking down people on the Internet?' Edward asked.

I nodded. 'Linda Sloggit was easy to find because of her unusual surname. Of course, the fact that she's never got married helped tremendously. I searched on Facebook and found a woman in her twenties with an aunt called that, who used to be a midwife. It had to be her.'

'Good Lord,' muttered the Earl.

'The niece got back to me more or less straight away and said she'd just spoken to her aunt and passed the message on.' I beamed. 'Believe it or not, she is the first of three guests to have already confirmed.

'Excellent,' said the Earl, hanging on my every word.

'On the phone, Linda sounds like a lovely lady,' I said. 'Despite the late notice, she's cancelling her bowling and declared she couldn't wait to see Applebridge Hall once more. As regards timings, I took an executive decision and asked her to arrive at twelve on Saturday. That gives people the whole morning to get here, if they're close enough to travel on the day. Others will probably stay somewhere nearby, the night before. They could all have drinks whilst looking at items we found in the dorm, before a lateish lunch.'

'That sounds like a decent plan,' said Edward.

'Linda rang again, having contacted two other evacuees she'd corresponded with over the years—her good friend Cynthia Williams. plus her young brother, Albert. Apparently, they were due to lunch with relatives on Saturday, but have been watching *Million Dollar Mansion* and said they wouldn't miss a reunion for the world.'

'Bertie Williams,' muttered the Earl and shook his head. 'I'd forgotten him. He taught me how to head a football. What about Jonny Jackson?'

'Well, Uncle, I tried Facebook and a corporate networking website without success, but it doesn't matter as I've just noticed his number's on Mrs Raynor's list. And there's hopeful news about Gerry Green...'

'The old rascal's still around?' The Earl sat more upright.

'Absolutely. He's still doing the routine he was quite well-known for in the sixties and seventies—now in British Legion and Conservative clubs. It's called the Gerry Green Gag Show. I found an advertisement for one of his shows in North London at the end of this month. So I rang the premises—they were awfully helpful and promised to pass my message and phone number onto him right away.'

'He always did like to keep busy,' muttered the Earl, whose cup of tea hadn't been touched.

I turned to Lady C. 'Auntie? I believe you and Kathleen looked into the possibility of a Second World War themed lunch?'

'Yes, dear—after James took me on a delightful walk around the estate with a pair of binoculars, once he'd returned from seeing Mrs Raynor. We were lucky enough to spot woodpeckers, warblers and a jay in the forest. As for the Mandarin Ducks by the pond...'

Enthusiastically, I nodded as if this all made complete sense. Mandarin Duck? Perhaps Satsuma Seahorses and Tangerine Toads existed as well.

'Constance insisted we hurry back to the house, though,' said the Earl gruffly. 'To help with the weekend plans. It is very decent of your aunt to help out, considering she is our guest.'

'It's the least I can do,' she said, 'and Kathleen came up with some excellent ideas. We thought lentil soup to start…'

The Earl pulled a face. 'I'd never eaten lentils before the war and haven't since.'

'… and then the famous Woolton Pie for the main,' said Lady C.

'Good Lord, that brings back memories,' said the Earl. 'Named after the Minister for Food, wasn't it? Our cook could work miracles with Potato Pete and Doctor Carrot.'

Lady C let out a girlish giggle. 'I haven't heard those terms for years.'

'So what's in this pie?' I asked.

'Vegetables,' said Lady C, 'and a gravy made from Marmite and rolled oats. The pastry lid is made from potato and, if you were particularly lucky, one would grate cheese on top.'

Ick. What a shame I'd probably be joining the guests for lunch.

'And dessert?' I asked.

'Apple jelly, followed by eggless jam sponge with the coffee.'

Even worse! It was hardly chocolate brownies with ice cream and fudge sauce.

I drained my cup of tea and reached for the phone on the low coffee table. It was one of those old-fashioned ones where the receiver was horizontal and it had a rotary dial instead of touch buttons.

'Shall I start to work my way through this list, then?' I said, once again looking at the floral sheet of paper.

'Give me half of the names,' said Edward. 'I'll phone from the library. The sooner we can contact these people, the better. And we've a bit of extra time now, before we watch tonight's show, as it's been moved to a later slot at nine o'clock.'

I raised my eyebrows as I folded the sheet of paper and tore it neatly in half.

'There's been several complaints about the content of the Marwick Castle footage, so the programme had to move to after the watershed.' Edward shrugged and took his half of the list from me. 'Gaynor's pretty happy as they'll now be able to broadcast any unsuitable scenes that were previously edited out—starting tonight. She said something about nudity at the Castle, and a drunken brawl.'

'How terrible,' I muttered.

'Indeed, Abbey,' said Lady C. 'It's disgraceful, putting viewing figures before moral standards.'

'No, I mean how terrible for us,' I said. 'Reality show viewers love those risqué scenes. The Baron and his estate will be more popular than ever because of this.'

'Bill said The Green Acorn has installed a television,' said the Earl, 'so that regulars can watch it together in there.'

If only I could become invisible and sit with the locals to get their take on how entertaining Marwick Castle really was... I sat more upright. Of course! Like the other night, all I needed to do was dress as myself. Then I'd find out whether Applebridge Hall was losing the votes of the loyal villagers.

'The most risqué footage of ours tonight is probably shots of those intruders Thompson saw messing about in the pond, during that storm last night,' said Edward.

'Really?' I squeaked. 'And no one's still got any idea who they were?'

'None whatsoever,' he said. 'Must have been cold in that water.' The hint of a smile crossed his lips.

Could he be thinking about me, Gemma, and our time in the pond the other night? Was it too far-fetched to think he'd like to see the real me again?

Jeez, this was mega mad…crazy. I'd only known Edward a few days. All these feelings that were starting to surface… Perhaps I had Stockholm Syndrome—where a girl's kidnapped and falls in love with the bloke keeping her captive. Except Edward wasn't holding me prisoner; I was here by my own free will, and we were so mismatched it was bonkers to even mention the word 'love'.

Yummy teacake finished, I needed to get down to The Green Acorn ASAP. 'Well, if you don't mind, I might head to the computer in the cellar and go through this list of names. If I don't come back at nine to watch the show, perhaps someone could fill me in on how it went, tomorrow.' And, please God, let none of them recognize me as the intruder, legs akimbo above the pond.

Lady C stared at me for a moment and then patted my arm. 'You're a good girl, doing your best to help.' She cleared her throat. 'I mean, apparently yesterday's Scottish cookery class was a great success—Kathleen, erm, told me how much you'd practised.'

We exchanged looks and, for the first time since her arrival, she gave me a mega warm smile. At last I was finally doing something right. Perhaps I really would save the day for Abbey. In fact, on my way out of the Parlour,

Edward earnestly whispered, 'Best of British with the phone calls.' His breath tickled my neck and the hairs there stood on end. My stomach knotted slightly—lying to him was the pits. But how could I come clean about my identity after Kathleen saying that the one thing Edward hated in life was deception?

I bolted to my nearby bedroom. Boobs, lashes, gloss, bronzer... I had no time to lose in dressing up as me and slinking out to the pub. Phone calls to people on that list would have to wait until first thing tomorrow morning, no doubt after another night of washing red dye out of my hair.

In my favourite short black dress with a snug-style denim coat and high shoes, I crept down the staircase and past the kitchens, keeping an eye out for Mr Thompson. With a sigh of relief, I made it past the orchards and to the bottom of the drive in one piece. Speed-walking now, I soon reached The Green Acorn. A couple of smokers sat outside on wooden benches, just in front of the pretty window boxes filled with orange and yellow flowers. I shivered and reckoned the Indian summer was over, despite smudges of candy-pink sun against the evening sky—ooh, listen to me, all poetic.

With a deep breath, I went into the pub, which was a lot noisier than the last time I was there. In fact I could hardly get to the bar for bodies—people of all ages, from toddlers in prams to pensioners older than the Earl. Free, once again, from my duty to behave like a lady, I craftily pushed my way to the bar. Mmm, a mouthful of pear cider and the crunch of pork scratchings—what more could a girl want? Apart from a chair—but there was little chance of that, so I hovered by a coat stand, to the right of a mega TV that had been set up on a high table.

I swigged (yep, unladylike me 'swigged'—yay!) my cider. By the looks of it, I'd missed just the first few minutes of the show as my cookery class was underway. Blimey. Would I ever get used to seeing myself in such classy clothes? Yet it was strange—my Gemma outfits weren't as comfortable now. The chicken fillets seemed a bit silly and the false eyelashes itched. Most of my tops and bottoms were tight and my shoes squeezed my toes. Whereas Abbey's stuff, some of it quickly altered by Lady C, just fitted to a tee and seemed to show off a shape I'd never thought I had. Perhaps that's why my flatmate was always banging on about the importance of good tailoring.

'Bit of a prat, that Chingo bloke,' muttered the young guy next to me, in an old man's flat cap. Even weirder, considering we were indoors, he hid behind huge shades and had a blinding iceberg-white smile. 'You've watched all the series?' he said.

'Um, yeah. Us villagers owe Applebridge Hall a bit of loyalty, right?'

The man sneered. 'We ain't in Jurassic times, you know, when locals bowed before the Lord of the Manor. As for cookery lessons? Borrrrrrring—although that Abbey bird's all right. Bit up herself but, after a couple of drinks, I bet there's a vamp inside.'

Vamp? What *would* Lady C say? I stuck the cider bottle in my mouth to suppress a chuckle. For some reason, he made me want to laugh.

'What do you make of that Baron chap?' he asked and pulled his cap further down. 'Now a castle… That's the sort of building that deserves to win this show.'

I shrugged. 'Dunno—his family haven't lived there very long.'

'Who cares? Dungeons, banquets, swords... What's Applebridge Hall got to offer, apart from a stupid maze and apples?'

'You're not from the village?' I said in a low voice, as everyone quietened down and listened to one of Kathleen's Queen Mum stories.

'No,' he said eventually, after Kathleen's voice had stopped. He grinned. 'How did you guess?'

'Well done, Miss Croxley!' shouted someone as Charlie Chingo was now on the telly, congratulating 'Abbey' on a successful cookery class.

'Those pheasant breasts look a darned sight better than Monday's stew!' called another voice.

Titters filled the pub—but I stood taller, as if I'd been awarded an OBE. The banter was mega friendly and when the on-screen me bowed to the camera, people in the pub whistled and clapped.

'Hey, Tim,' shouted someone to the landlord, 'how about free Bloody Bulls all round?'

The cheers subsided as Charlie Chingo interviewed Edward and his dad about the planned reunion. The weirdo next to me listened intently. Perhaps stuff to do with the war would interest him more.

'I remember some of those children,' said an elderly woman from the back. 'My father used to deliver groceries to the estate and would take me with him to play with the girls and boys there. I wonder if I'll recognize them.'

'What, sixty-odd years later, Mabel?' said a wrinkled man next to her. 'At our age, we don't know ourselves in the mirror, let alone anyone else.'

Laughter rippled around the room.

The footage now cut to the storm and me in the pond. A group of youngsters in the pub snorted with laughter as my legs appeared above the bulrushes. Phew. Thanks to the twilight, no one could work out it was me and Nick.

'Reminds me of that scene in *Dirty Dancing*,' said a girl leaning on the bar and texting into her phone.

Bingo! I nearly cheered!

'Bloody hooligans,' said the landlord and shook his head. 'Think I'll get some extra cameras set up outside. All sorts of nutters might turn up if the Earl wins this show.'

So the locals thought we were really in with a chance? Now Charlie was talking to the Baron. A few jeers came from the far side of the pub.

'Good. The Castle. It's about time we had some proper entertainment,' muttered the man next to me and straightened up.

I put my empty bottle down on a nearby table. It was the Murder Mystery night at the Castle that Roxy had warned me about. The room went silent. In fact it was so quiet for the next fifteen minutes, apart from the odd 'ooh' or 'aah', that I could hear a dog drink from the pub's water bowl.

Crap. People were mega rapt, trying to work out which of the corporate team was the murderer. When it was finally revealed as a bleach-blonde PA, the girl who'd cleverly identified my *Dirty Dancing* scene clapped her hands. Apparently most people had already guessed that, on Twitter.

The footage cut to the banquet and, apart from the occasional elderly tut from the back of the room about 'vulgar low-cut tops', excited chatter filled the pub. When a corporate director slipped over after too much beer, young men near the screen clinked beer jugs and reminisced about their last big night out. Then humorous cries of disgust rose into the air when the blonde PA dashed outside the Castle to throw up. Awestruck gasps followed this as the camera focused on the banquet nosh. OMG. Even I ogled the enormous chunks of cheese, juicy fat grapes, mahoosive meat joints and lush-looking pickles. Yum.

A small sigh escaped my lips. Marwick Castle still led the way; anyone could tell that. Whether people disapproved of the Baron's drunken events or not, it made compelling viewing. Even the disapproving old biddies at the back had left their drinks untouched since the Murder Mystery event began.

'You want a drink?' said the man in the flat cap, after consulting his huge twinkly gold watch. He grinned at me and I stared again at those super-white teeth. Even the fair hair sticking out from the grotty flat cap looked a little too blond. His appearance just didn't add up, like the modern sunglasses against the creased boring shirt. As if he'd just read my mind, he took off the shades and winked. My mouth fell open. Of course. Why hadn't I spotted this before? But it didn't make sense…

'You're the Baron's son,' I hissed. 'The Honourable Harry Gainsworth.'

'Pleasure to meet you, babe.'

A bubble of laughter tickled my chest at the thought of us both sitting here incognito, neither of us seeing through each other's disguise. It was like some freaky parallel universe.

'What the…?' I stuttered. 'Why are you here?'

'Free country, ain't it? I was just passing and…'

'*Really?*'

'Okay, you aren't stupid, darling, I can see that. If you must know, I'm sussing out the so-called support for the opposition. Nothing to worry about, by the looks of it, though…' He smirked. 'Even the locals preferred our part of the show.'

'They seemed very interested in the evacuees' reunion,' I said airily.

Harry yawned. 'What, a bunch of old fogies talking about sad times without Ma and Pa? Like that's going to make great viewing.'

Uh oh. Adrenaline rush—that feeling I got when I was going to do something stupid… Like grab the nearest beer and tip it over this jerk's head. Shame the nearest drink was only an inch of orange juice.

He looked me up and down. 'Nice outfit,' he said. 'What's a doll like you doing in this dump?' He smiled. 'My car's outside. Why don't you let me take you for a drink in a place with real class?'

I smiled politely. 'No, thanks.'

'Right. I get it, babe. You're one of the few locals loyal to Applebridge Hall. And that's a good thing. But having a glass of plonk with me isn't a crime. I mean, there's not some local court in this one-eyed village that's going to hang you for treachery, right?'

Guess it might be interesting to get to know the Croxleys' adversaries.

'I suppose one drink wouldn't hurt,' I said. 'Okay. You're on.'

'Atta-girl! Come on, let's get out of here.' He snaked his arm around my waist, holding me just a bit too tight—unless I'd simply become all prim and prudish, spending so much time as elegant Abigail. As soon as we were outside, he pulled off the flat cap and threw it to the ground. Harry took out his mobile, selected a number and pressed dial.

'Hey, Pops,' he said into the phone as we strolled along the pavement. 'Job done. Put the champagne on ice. Even the locals here think we're the dogs' bollocks. Those boring old farts at Applebridge Hall don't stand a chance. The million-dollar prize is in the bag, no probs! Get the party going! I'll be there in an hour, with a new friend.'

Huh? 'We're going to the Castle?'

Harry grinned.

'What better way to win you over to our side, babe? Follow me. You're about to have the night of your life!'

LORD EDWARD'S E-DIARY

Thursday 6th September

10.20p.m. Good evening, I hope you enjoyed tonight's show and appreciated the news that on Saturday we are hosting…an evacuee reunion lunch. I know that *Historybuff*, at least, will be delighted. The idea has, indeed, ignited Father's enthusiasm. The amount of work necessary to arrange this get-together is not for the weak-hearted, although I have already contacted one former evacuee, who happily accepted the invitation. Plus my cousin has impressed me with her ability to apply herself when necessary. As you saw tonight, nerves now under control, yesterday's cookery lesson was exemplary.

It's hard to explain, but today, for the first time in weeks—months, even—I feel positive. Thanks to Abigail's input, the weight of preserving Applebridge Hall's future is…less oppressive. I'm beginning to appreciate that her ideas and gusto are refreshing. And I'm sure her friends, such as her, erm, lodger, would be equally inspiring. Plus funny, easy-going and spontaneous…

Abigail has made me realize that, without Mother's light touch around here, Father and I have become as stale and musty as an antique book from our library. We needed dusting off and that's what she's achieving. The arrival of Lady Constance Woodfold has also raised my father's spirits.

What's more, Abigail's aunt helped me think of another poser question: she used to run a finishing school—if there was one thing about yourselves you could improve, what would it be?

CHAPTER 18

Quick! Put your foot down, Harry, the drawbridge is rising. If those zombies catch up, we won't escape alive. Hurry! Any slower, we'll miss and go crashing down into the moat...

Okay. There was no zombie apocalypse, but boy, Marwick Castle really was the stuff of fantasies. As we turned into a long drive, it came into view at the top of a hill.

My heart raced and I came over all romantic and medieval. *Me wench, Harry...* I would have liked to say *warrior soldier* but, with his groomed appearance and designer clothes, his look was about as rugged as a soft deep-pile carpet. When we'd reached his car, an old Jag with—get this—blacked-out windows, he'd torn off his old top, opened the boot and changed into a mega sharp slate-coloured silk shirt. Several squirts of aftershave later, he was ready for the off. His shoes shone and trousers were neatly pressed. Harry was no rough and ready knight.

'Home Sweet Home, babe,' he said when we reached the top of the hill and followed a road to the left, along which several cars were haphazardly parked. Eventually Harry pulled up in front a double garage. What a relief. I couldn't take a minute more of his name-dropping and tales of celebrity life. Having his photo appear in the gossip mags had clearly gone to his head. Although, secretly, I was in awe of the stars coming to his party this coming Saturday night, including an actor from my favourite TV soap, a footballer and *Big Brother* contestant, plus an agent, who apparently reckoned Harry had a big future ahead of him. Cue 'Macho from Marwick'—yep, Harry had already been told to think up a name for his own scent.

We walked up to the Castle, which didn't look quite so mahoosive in real life. But still, with outdoor lights illuminating the turrets, it impressed me. Lights flickered from the small windows and dance music pulsated through the night air. We crossed the drawbridge and I looked down into the moat.

'Wow. That's a mad fall.' I gazed at inky black waves. 'In olden times, it must have put off loads of intruders trying to cross over the top.'

'It wasn't really for that, babe. Moats were to stop people tunnelling underneath.' He rolled his eyes. 'We had to learn all sorts of stuff for this gig, to try and look as if we give a monkey's about our so-called heritage.'

'So you don't know which battles were fought here?'

'Yeah, the biggest one of all time, between Pops and Ma, before their divorce.' He grinned and took out a key to open the huge solid oak inner door. 'We're not history boffins. My great-granddad bought this gaff cos it was the biggest place he could find. Size was everything, to him,' he said and puffed out his chest. 'Right. Champers. Burgers. You up for good times, babe?'

I gawped. We'd passed through the doorway and stood in the entrance, which looked onto an open square courtyard. I bent down and brushed my fingers over the golf-green perfect grass. Oh my God, it was—

Harry smirked. 'Astroturf. It's much more practical when we have one of our famous barbecues out here.'

In the middle of this fake lawn was some sort of well. People in trendy clothes milled to and fro. The grey stone castle, surrounding the courtyard, went up two storeys high. In each corner was a turreted tower. To the right of where I stood was an open oak door, leading to the Castle's ground floor rooms. To my left was another door and the humungous stuffed grizzly bear.

Doors also opened onto the courtyard from all four sides of the Castle. For a moment, I stood in awe. Harry gave a self-satisfied smile.

'Nothing compares to this at that poxy Hall in Applebridge, does it, babe? Am I right or am I right?'

I gazed up at one of the towers and a flag waving in the night sky. It made me think of Henry VIII's poor wives locked up. Or Rapunzel. After all the dyeing and washing, my hair wouldn't support an adventurous ant, let alone an ambitious admirer.

Dreamily, I stared across the lawn, where a couple smooched. For some reason an image of Edward, dressed as Robin Hood, popped into my mind, on horseback charging across the drawbridge to steal a million dollars, bow and arrow on his back…

It was different thinking about him, out of my Abbey disguise. For a start, the word 'cousin' didn't pop into my head. Imagining him rescuing me from a tower, his strong arms hauling me onto the back of a horse, didn't feel so… *wrong*.

'Hiya, Harry, darling,' said a blonde staggering past. That was the PA from the Murder Mystery episode. Girl after girl in short skirts came into view. Some sprawled on the courtyard, holding brightly coloured cocktails, their even gaudier thongs on view.

'Fancy a drink, babe?' Harry asked me, after patting the PA on the bum.

'The name's Gemma,' I said and cringed, especially after a week with the Croxleys, who were the opposite of touchy-feely.

'Yeah. Okay, Sienna.'

'No, Gemma.'

'Whatever. Here, follow me to the bar.' He waved to a brunette, who wiped her mouth after vomiting down the well. 'This is the life,' he said. 'Admit it, you ain't seen nothing like this at Croxleys' mansion.'

Hmm… Impressive as the building was, the scene before me was like a Friday night out on the town. All that was missing was the shouts of bouncers and wails of ambulance sirens. So I was tempted to reply 'no, thank fuck I haven't' but I felt uncomfortable just thinking the F-word. Blimey, this pretending to be a Lady malarkey was affecting me more than I'd thought.

'Any chance of a tour, Harry?' I said. 'The outside of the Castle's pretty cool, but perhaps your rooms don't match the Earl's amazin' interior.'

'You've seen inside Lord Croxley's gaff?'

My cheeks flamed. 'Um, yes. A friend works there and showed me around.'

'Ooh. Any goss? I hear that Lady Abigail is a real eccentric bird. And that Edward's head is stuck right up his—'

'No. Nothing. Soz,' I said through gritted teeth, which was weird—I was hopping-mad that he'd insulted Edward. It must have been cos Abbey's cousin really felt like family, now. Yeah, that was it. There was no other explanation for my passionate loyalty.

He shrugged. 'What do you want to see? Take my word for it, by the end of the evening you'll have changed your mind and decided to vote for us.'

'Allow me, son,' boomed a voice. By the grizzly bear stood the tall Baron, with slicked back dyed black hair, in smart trousers and a shirt open almost to his generous waist. He wore a chunky gold necklace and matching bracelet. With bloodshot eyes, he came over and clapped Harry on the back.

'Okay, Pops.' Harry grinned at me. 'Hope you can keep up with the old boy, Sienna—he's a party animal.'

'Grrrrrr!' roared the Baron, all lion-like, thinking he was oh-so-funny.

'Um…hi,' I said.

The Baron bowed. 'Nice to meet you.' He lifted my hand to his lips. Ick. What a slimy kiss.

At least I had my mobile on me and could ring for a taxi if I wanted to leave. I couldn't decide which phone to bring, so just brought my cheap Abbey Croxley one which fitted more snugly into my denim jacket's pocket. I half-smiled at the Baron. What a red nose. What ruddy cheeks. His eyes bulged as he stared at my boobs—aka chicken fillets. I looked down. Urgh! Talk about paying the price for getting dressed in a rush. I'd just squished them in and, instead of them lying flat, they'd bunched up and made my breasts look as if I'd borrowed one of Madonna's conical bras.

'How about the dungeons first, then, little lady?' he said, eyes still on stalks. 'That'll give you a chance to see the bit of the Castle most featured on the telly.'

'That would be epic,' I said and pulled down my teensy dress as I followed him through the door on the right. In my Abbey disguise, there's no way he would have ogled me up and down like that. Euw. He was old enough to be my granddad.

We walked down a dark stone staircase at the front of the Castle and entered the banqueting room that I'd seen on the telly. Scraps of bread, meat and grapes littered the table. In the corner was a spit. I picked up a chunky brown stoneware goblet. There were matching bowls and plates.

'That crockery's the business, isn't it?' said the Baron, words slurring a little. He passed me one of two opened beer bottles that he'd fetched from a nearby fridge, hidden by a hessian cloth. 'We got them from an online company that hires out gear for medieval parties.'

I guessed they couldn't be originals from almost a millennium ago, but still felt disappointed that they'd just been ordered off the Internet. I twisted the top off my beer bottle and then walked over to a full suit of armour. Awesome. How on earth did soldiers breathe in that lot, let alone fight? On tiptoe, I stroked the head of a stuffed stag, mounted on the stone wall. The room was dark and dingy and, by the feel of it, only heated for paying guests. I shivered. The Baron took down a shiny sword from the wall.

'Here,' he said, still talking to my chest, and passed me the weapon. 'It's the real McCoy, all right—feel how heavy that is.'

I ran my finger along the smooth blade and admired the gold handle, with silver twisted around. The Baron took it back and I dodged the blade as he clumsily swiped it from side to side.

'In the old days, I'd have protected a lass like you easy-peasy with this,' he said in a loud voice. Panting, he put it back on the wall and then took down a catapult. 'The more unusual weapons, like this, we ordered from some American guy who can make anything out of plastic. You see that axe, the hammer and those shields? Cheap replicas. The dogs' bollocks, aren't they? You'd never know, unless you looked close. That twenty-five grand from the last round of *Million Dollar Mansion* sure goes a long way when buying tat.'

'What else did you get?'

'Medieval junk to pimp up the other rooms. After talking to the TV folk, I realized the public love that sort of stuff.'

'Weren't the rooms styled like that before?'

The Baron swigged his beer and sat down on one of the high-backed wooden chairs. 'Nah. My family's made up of practical, modern people. That's where those stuffy Croxleys are going wrong. I could do up a whole room with what they'll spend on restoring one sofa. I'm proud of that. It's why I think we deserve to win. Pimp up the whole Castle and more people than ever can stay here for the weekend. It doesn't have to be one hundred per cent authentic. I mean, who wants to sleep in a room lit and heated by a frigging candle?'

'I'm sure the Croxleys aren't that bad!'

The Baron snorted. 'Yeah, well, they can't compete with me offering loads of fun, in comfort. It's not like the original Castle ain't still standing.'

But only the shell of it. Where's its soul gone?

Where's its soul gone…? Jeez—that sounded like something Lady C might say. This time a week or two ago I'd have thought a fun place like Marwick Castle should win the money, no argument.

He put down his beer. 'I'm making history accessible to the general public—unlike that jumped-up twerp, the Earl. I'm not wasting money on genuine articles that cost a bomb and will only be appreciated by intellectual toffs, and I don't care who knows it.'

'But you should see the family portraits at Applebridge—somehow they make the place more...alive.'

'How? Those people are all dead? Sure, I've got photos up here of my grandparents and an aunt who's snuffed it, but then I actually met them in the flesh. I've no interest in boring visitors with portraits of relatives I never even knew.' The Baron shook his head. 'Nah. What I offer people is a bit of the spectacular.'

'What would you spend the million on, then?' I asked and sat down at the other side of the table.

He winked. 'I like that—a girl with half a brain who asks a lot of questions and has got knockers to die for.'

My mouth fell open. Really? Did he really just say that?

'I'd spend that million on a bloody good time.' The Baron grinned. 'For a start, the second floor needs doing up. Since Grandpops bought this place in the Twenties, we've never quite been able to make it habitable—too many square metres of dry rot and crumbling stonework. Heating alone would cost a packet, then there's the plumbing, as well as various Health and Safety issues...'

It sounded like the place had similar problems to Applebridge Hall.

He belched and patted his chest. 'Me and Harry, we've got big plans for this place—bedrooms with en suites, an indoor spa and a long games room for indoor archery when the weather's crap. I want Marwick Castle to become one of the best hen and stag night destinations in the world.' With his sleeve, the Baron wiped beads of sweat from his brow. 'A kind of cross between a theme park and Olympic village, that's how I see it. Whereas a cookery school...?' He sneered. 'That's hardly innovative; hardly ambitious.'

From what I'd already seen, Marwick Castle was going to end up more like the Playboy Mansion. I could just picture the Baron in a silk dressing gown, like Hugh Hefner, with surgically enhanced castle-mates stroking his turrets.

'But what about its history?' I said. 'Its tradition? Is there any art or books from over the years? What about special architectural features?'

Now he looked at me as if my questions had gone too far. And I could see his point. Suddenly I was sounding kind of stodgy. I mean, his plan was fun—and clever and he was clearly passionate about it. The Castle would easily pay for itself. He and Harry would have a ball. The Baron guffawed.

'Curious little thing, aren't you?' he said. 'Tradition?' He ran a hand over his slicked back hair. 'Why bother? No Tom, Dick or Harry who visits is going to be any the wiser if a shield is plastic or not. Even if I spouted out dreary old facts, your average visitor would have forgotten them before they'd crossed the moat on their way back to their little lives. Marwick Castle ain't about boring your visitors to death with statistics and dates—it's about forgetting your real life. Who wants to know about medieval war strategies or how people in those days made their clothes and grub? Going on the slash, down in the dungeons, after a day pretending you're a soldier or member of the SAS, that's what it should all be about.'

He leaned across the table. 'Hanging out in this castle can be fun. Booze, bread and bedrooms…It's about going back to basics. It's about fulfilling people's most primeval fantasies.' He grinned. 'And, as I'm sure even the Earl will agree, it's mainly about earning dosh. Winning this competition will take my family's aims and achievements to a whole new level.'

'Do you know anything about the people who lived here before your family?'

'The TV company did a bit of research—mentioned something about an industrialist and a distant relative of Henry VIII.'

'That's exciting!'

'Is it?' The Baron stood up and wavered on his feet. 'There's a picture of William the Conqueror in the Throne Room—I guess you might like to see that.'

'Throne room? That sounds posh,' I said.

He beamed. 'Yeah. One thing I'll give my ex-wife—she thought up some glamorous names for the rooms once my dad died and she wanted to put her own stamp on the place. The Throne Room is where we hold dinners—it's the main reception area and home to our collection of stuffed animals. Then there's the Gold Room—our family lounge—and the Nightery where we play music on a jukebox. It's got a dance floor and bar. Talking of which, come on, little lady, let's get you a proper drink—the Marwick Cocktail. Thursday night, the cameras aren't around, so it's our turn to let our hair down before weekend guests turn up tomorrow.'

We went back upstairs and through the door leading to the right, his arm tightly around my shoulders, as if I was helping him keep upright. Apparently, family bedrooms were at the far end, opposite the entrance, and the left side of the castle housed the kitchens, Throne Room and the 'Chophouse'.

'That's where the family eat. Brill name, right?' boomed the Baron as we entered the Nightery. Bodies sprawled over sofas and a disco ball lit up the room. Harry danced with the blonde PA. They both held bright blue cocktails, cherries and pineapple threatening to fall out with every sway of their hips. Timber beams crossed the ceiling and lances and helmets were attached to the whitewashed walls.

'Here, get a few of these down that pretty little neck,' said the Baron and passed me one of the fancy drinks. He knocked back a short and put down the glass.

'Yo, boss,' said a man in his twenties, behind the bar. 'The cellar is running low. We've plenty of beer and wine for tomorrow night but if your celebrity guests want cocktails at the weekend, we're almost out of vodka, tequila and gin.'

The Baron tugged a crisp white hanky out of his shirt pocket and dabbed his face.

'Do you want me to get Harry to sort it?' asked the man.

We all looked across the room at the Baron's son, who sat on a leather (probably faux) armchair, being given a lap dance by several girls wearing nothing much more than bodices and heels.

'Nah, Mike, I'll sort it. Just…give me a tick. We'll… do a proper stock-take,' he said, words slurring even more now. He lifted my hand to his mouth again and gave it another slobbery kiss. 'Don't move,' he whispered. 'I'll be back before you know it. Make yourself comfortable. My bedroom's the one with the mirror on the ceiling. And if you hunt around, you'll be sure to find a whip and pair of handcuffs.'

With a belch, the Baron smiled and staggered away. Seconds later, my phone vibrated. I took it out from the pocket of my short denim coat. It was a text message from Edward. Oh my God. He wanted to join me in the cellar with his laptop, so that we could brainstorm further ideas for the evacuee lunch! I wasn't even in the cellar, let alone in Applebridge. How on earth was I going to stop him discovering that 'Abbey' had disappeared?

LORD EDWARD'S E-DIARY

Thursday 6th September

'Comments'

11.30p.m. What a response to tonight's show—thank you all, for your comments. I'll briefly reply whilst waiting for a text from my cousin. *Knityourownmansion*, no, I hadn't heard of Second World War 'Bundles for Britain'. How kind of American women to knit clothes and post them to British soldiers. Goodness, *Historybuff*, were nearly two million children really evacuated? *Blogger 569*, I agree, your great-aunt had an intolerable experience. Father told of a similar story, where one of the evacuee's friends was sent to live with shopkeepers who fed him nothing but their out-of-date stock.

As for Lady Constance's poser question: no doubt I could improve myself by mastering the art of conversation. I've never been one for polite chit-chat. Mother used to tut and say it was of vital importance—that meaningless talk about the weather put people at ease and represented the first steps to getting to know someone. Whereas Father has always thought 'mindless prattle' is 'pure poppycock'.

Drunkwriter, just a suggestion, drinking less alcohol might enhance your deportment. *EtonMess*, agreed, not, erm, gawping at a woman's 'm*l*ns' (I've edited your fruity word) would undoubtedly constitute improving your manners.

Ah, a text reply. Excuse me, for a while, kind blog-readers—but do keep the comments coming.

CHAPTER 19

Writing lies in a text seemed even worse than speaking false stuff. I replied to Edward not to go to the cellar, cos I was tired and had already gone to bed—but would get up ridiculously early to keep going through Mrs Raynor's list.

Phone away, I then left my drink at the bar and headed out into the courtyard and straight over to a door opposite. I entered the Throne Room. A man was slumped under a window in there, smoking something that smelt a bit dodgy. He tried to focus but gave up and sang some reggae music, before shutting his eyes again.

I gazed around the room and couldn't resist a chuckle. Despite the name, I hadn't believed there would actually be a throne. It stood at the far end, on a podium, at the top of red-carpeted stairs. A gold and orange curtain hung behind it, from the ceiling. The throne was high-backed and upholstered, unlike the rest of the chairs along the dining table that stretched the length of the room.

A massive wooden shield bearing a coat of arms was at the other end, near a door presumably leading to the Chophouse. Tapestries of flowers and fruit and vegetables decorated the walls. I went up to one. It looked brand new and I lifted up the bottom to see a very modern white label. It said 'Made in China'.

'No medieval weaver wove that,' said a familiar quick voice.

I swung around to a flash of red hair and gum-chewing mouth, at the top of a floral green dress. What was Roxy doing here?

'Um, hi,' I squeaked, mouth suddenly dry. Would she recognize the shape of my face or eyes? 'Mega good party, isn't it? You're a friend of the Baron's?'

'Not really.' Roxy walked past me and towards the podium. She went up the red-carpeted steps and sat in the throne.

'Won't he mind?' I said, squeak gone, pulse back to its usual rhythm. Phew.

Roxy looked at me and chuckled.

'No. The Baron's a cool dude,' said Roxy. 'It's open house as far as he's concerned.

'Yeah, he's a pretty chilled guy,' I said, 'and doesn't hide the fact that most of this stuff hasn't been in the Castle longer than a few months.'

'Why should he?' She shrugged. 'He's not born and bred aristocrat or serious renovator or historian. I think that's why the public warm to him—he doesn't pretend to be someone he isn't.'

They wouldn't warm much to Gemma Goodwin, then.

She stood up and smiled. 'I'm Roxy. Part of the *Million Dollar Mansion* crew—the director's assistant. I mainly work at Applebridge Hall but sometimes assist the team here.'

'I'm Gemma. Love your dress.' It was strange to see Roxy out of jeans and a T-shirt, and not carrying a clipboard or running around to fulfil Gaynor's every need. 'So, um, aren't you supposed to remain objective? Should you really be here, out of hours?'

Roxy sat down at the long table and yawned, before speaking at her usual top speed. 'What, because I'm at one of his parties, the Baron's my favourite to win? No, I'm here for the free booze and he's an okay bloke if you can get past his outdated flirting. Harry's pretty harmless too.' Roxy offered me some gum and I shook my head. 'They're both very confident of their brand and concept,' she continued.

'Are they right to feel so optimistic?'

Roxy stopped chewing for a moment. 'Presumably you've seen the show?'

I nodded.

'Then as a viewer, tell me what you think.'

'Marwick Castle has…a mega appeal. The fun factor—I'll give it that. But, like with the hare and tortoise, I reckon Applebridge Hall might overtake them in the popularity stakes over the next week.'

'You actually believe the Earl is in with a chance?'

I raised my eyebrows. 'Do you?'

Roxy shrugged. 'On paper, the Baron should win hands down… But…I don't know. There's something about the Croxleys… When I visit this castle it feels just like a hotel but at Applebridge Hall, it's like…I've just walked into my parents' pad. There's an atmosphere there of… family… care… trust—or something.' She grinned. 'Do I sound like a complete wuss?'

A lump swelled in my throat. She'd just put into words exactly how I felt.

Roxy gazed around the room. 'I guess it all depends on whether that atmosphere transmits itself across to the audience at home.' She took out her car keys. 'Right. Time for bed. Busy day tomorrow. You're friends with Harry?'

'Not really. I just met him in a pub. What's, um, Lord Edward Croxley really like, then?' I asked innocently.

'Even hotter in the flesh, but impossibly hard to talk to. He doesn't do chit-chat, rarely smiles, is arrogant, uptight—yet chivalrous and polite.' She winked. 'I wonder if he's such a gentleman between the sheets... Miss Croxley's nice, though,' she added.

'At least her cooking went better yesterday.' I grinned.

'She's a real sport and a lot easier to talk to than her cousin. There's a Facebook group obsessed with her high-jinks on the lawnmower. Did you see tonight's show?' Roxy's eyes twinkled. 'I still can't make up my mind as to whether there's something going on between her and the gardener or not. Her Facebook fans are convinced they're the *Dirty Dancing* intruders.'

Yay! Another mission accomplished. Nick and I would have to plan our next movie tribute, although I already had a thousand things to do tomorrow, and would have to get up mega early to ring those names on my half of Mrs Raynor's list...

Eek. Better get back and start washing out red hair dye.

'Are you travelling back to the village?' I asked. 'Is there any chance you could drop me off? I'm not in the party mood any more...'

'Sure thing—but have you had a look around?'

I shook my head.

'Gemma, this is too good an opportunity to miss. The Baron won't mind—let me give you a quick tour!'

I followed her out of the Throne Room and through the Chophouse (what an awesome indoor barbecue and chocolate fountain). We passed along a corridor, with doors opening to various bedrooms. The majority were unlocked as most of the corporate guests had left. We peeked in a couple. Sheets were strewn everywhere. There was a lot of work to be done before the weekend party guests arrived tomorrow night. Each was identically kitted out with crossed swords (plastic, no doubt) above the headboards and tapestries of unicorns. Then we came to a door with a dagger mounted in the middle.

'This is the Baron's,' said Roxy.

We pushed open the heavy door and went in. Sure enough, above the bed was the huge mirror he'd boasted about. The bed sheets were gold and folded down over a burgundy blanket which matched lush pillows. Ornamental black iron light fittings were decked around the room and opposite the bed was a huge wall hanging of soldiers on horseback. Two animal skins lay on the wooden floor.

'Even I know that zebras and lions didn't roam Medieval England,' I said and giggled.

'Fancy a quick scoot up one of the towers?' said Roxy.

'You bet!'

I followed her along to the end of the corridor, past two more bedrooms, and she pulled open an oak door to the left. Wow. The tower was bigger than I expected, with stone stairs going up in circles, the small windows simply paned. Out of breath, we climbed past a door opening onto the first floor until we were right at the top and came out into the night air. I ran across to look out through one of the turrets at the back of the castle.

'Is that a digger?' I said and squinted, through the darkness, at a vehicle at the foot of the hill.

'Sure is. The Baron didn't have enough of the twenty-five grand left to finish the job—he's hoping to build a go-karting track.' She looked at her watch. 'Come on. Let's go.'

We returned to the courtyard and picked our way across, avoiding drunken guests crashed out on the floor. The Baron stood at the bar. Harry gyrated across to us.

'Surely you ain't leaving already, girls?'

'I, um, have got to get up early for work,' I said, 'but thanks for the invitation.'

'So, babe, have we won you over? Can I count on your vote?'

'Let's see what next week brings,' I said.

Harry smirked. 'I can tell you there'll be no surprises from Applebridge Hall, just more of the same: like apples, old-fashioned tweed clothes and wacky relatives on lawnmowers; like moody Lords who think they are better than everyone else; like estate managers in stupid hats and cooks with the weirdest accent.'

'Ciao, Harry,' said Roxy brightly, while I took some deep breaths. 'Good luck with the party on Saturday.'

He kissed her cheek. 'Cheers, doll—no luck needed, though. Not with my new celebrity mates. Just hope you don't die of boredom at that war fogies' reunion thing.' He gave us the thumbs-up and headed back to a brunette who was calling his name.

'Arsehole,' I muttered under my breath as we crossed the drawbridge and headed for the road leading to the double garage.

Roxy chuckled. We got into her red Mini and chatted about other reality shows all the way back to Applebridge.

'Where would you like me to drop you?' asked Roxy as we eventually drove into the village. We'd just finished a heated discussion about whether Channel Five had done a good job of reinventing *Big Brother*.

'By The Green Acorn is great, ta,' I said.

Roxy pulled up. 'You're sure I can't take you to your front door? It's two o'clock in the morning.'

'This is Applebridge,' I said and smiled. 'Not inner city London.'

She yawned. 'Point taken. Okay. Wicked meeting you. Hope you enjoy the rest of the series.'

I closed the car door behind me and waved as she drove off.

Ten minutes later, I entered through the Hall's gates. An autumn chill now hung in the air and I buttoned up my denim coat. Spooked by the hoot of an owl, I looked over my shoulder, convinced footsteps were following me across the grass. A blister nagged my heel as I passed the orchards. Near one of the trees, I bent over to take off my stilettos. As I straightened up a click sounded behind my back.

'Don't move or I'll shoot,' bellowed a deep voice.

Crap. I swung around and stared down the barrel of a shotgun. As fast as I could, I ran away. A gunshot rang out. With a scream, I fell to the ground.

LORD EDWARD'S E-DIARY

Friday 7th September

Awfully early in the morning. In fact, it's around 2.15a.m. I'm absolutely done in, having spent time in the old evacuees' dorm once more, up in the Long Gallery. Cousin Abbey was too tired to help, but is getting up early to continue our efforts. Now I must retire to my room, so do forgive this very short post.

Lovehotnoble, you gave an interesting reply to the poser question. I'm not sure the kind of 'improvement' Lady Constance had in mind involved breast implants and your lips being injected with fat from your, erm, posterior.

Excuse me a minute... What was that...? I've just heard something that sounds remarkably like a gunshot.

CHAPTER 20

Like a gun dog proud of its catch, Mr Thompson hovered by my side. Eventually running footsteps approached. Ouch. My leg hurt. Maybe trying to escape had been a mega bad idea but, out of my Abbey disguise, I had no power over the estate manager. Plus I didn't really think he'd shoot me down like a rabbit or pheasant.

'Don't move,' he ordered, voice deeper than ever.

'I can't help shaking,' I said and spat out crumbs of soil.

'Thompson! What on earth were you thinking?' Within seconds, Edward was on the ground by my side. Gently, he turned me over. I sat up and rubbed my knee.

'I'm okay…' I muttered. 'It's just a graze. I tripped over a stone. The bullet missed.'

Edward helped me to my feet and I slipped my stilettos back on. He tilted my chin to the moonlight, eyes full of concern.

'Are you sure, Gemma?' he asked. 'You aren't hurt anywhere else?' He brushed some soil off my cheek.

'You know this…this juvenile?' stuttered Mr Thompson. He squinted through the darkness and lowered his gun.

'This woman is a friend of my cousin's,' Edward said, eyes ablaze. 'But good God, man, even if she was built like a bodybuilder and carrying a swag bag, you should never have aimed and fired.'

'Especially as my back was turned,' I muttered. 'How cowardly is that?'

Mr Thompson shuffled his feet. 'I only shot into the air. Sick of these intruders, I am, My Lord. They're taking us for mugs.'

Edward shook his head. 'Go to bed and leave this to me—and count your blessings this didn't end more badly. You could have ended up in jail.'

Lips pursed, Mr Thompson slung his gun over his shoulder and headed up the drive to Applebridge Hall.

'He won't mention me to anyone, will he?' I said. Lady C would go mad if she thought I'd risked blowing my cover. 'Abbey's, um, got enough on her plate without worrying about me getting shot at.'

'I'll have a word with him in the morning.' Edward stared at my knee. 'You're trembling. That gunshot must have been quite a shock. Come inside for a drink. It'll calm you down.'

'I'm fine,' I said, but Edward already had an arm around my shoulder and started guiding me back to the house, as I limped.

'Everyone else is in bed,' he said. 'It's gone two a.m. What are you doing out here at this time?'

'Um… My brother was passing this way again tonight. He got a two-week night-shift contract stacking shelves in a supermarket a few miles on from here. Tom offered to drop me off if I wanted to see Abbey once more, and pick me up on his way back, at sunrise. So I, um, texted her to see if she'd like me to visit. I've been helping her ring some of the evacuees on that list. Then she was tired so we hit the sack, but I couldn't sleep. I just fancied a walk and then…'

'Won't you be tired for work tomorrow?'

'I've recently lost my job,' I said, glad not to be lying for once.

He squeezed my shoulder and warmth surged through my veins. 'Come on. A hot chocolate will restore your spirits.'

'Could I meet you by that bench at the pond?' I said. 'It's a beautiful night. I could do with a bit of peace—my ears are still ringing, thanks to that bullet.'

'Okay. Somewhere Kathleen's got a flask...'

'Mr Thompson's gone in, right? Or do I need to carry a white flag?'

Edward smiled. 'He's not a bad man—just a creature of routine. All the filming... it's stressed him out.'

I knew that, really. Despite his gruff manner and this evening's murder attempt, the estate manager had grown on me.

'See you there in ten minutes, then,' said Edward. 'I'll bring something to clean up that knee.'

'Don't worry—I'll just wash it in the pond.'

He looked at me for a second, as if I were a puppy that had just performed the cutest trick. Then he disappeared inside the main entrance. Still limping a little, I reached the bulrushes, bent over and splashed water onto my knee. Graze cleaned, I pushed through the longer grass to the bench and sat down. Mmm. Quiet. What a difference to the hustle and bustle of the Castle. I breathed in the woody smells with a tinge of fish tank pond—much nicer than the whiff of vomit at the Baron's place.

'I wondered if I might find you swimming again.' A grin on his face, Edward appeared by my side. He passed me a thick anorak. 'Take this. Autumn is well and truly on its way.' He sat down and poured two cups of hot chocolate out of a flask and then unwrapped slices of Kathleen's

Dundee cake. In silence we watched the occasional frog jump as moonlight caught the surface of the pond.

'That was good,' I said and swallowed the last mouthful, wiping my mouth on the borrowed coat's sleeve. 'That Kathleen's a mega cook.'

'Abbey's pretty decent in the kitchen as well.'

Good thing I'd swallowed my cake, otherwise I might have choked at that compliment!

'What will you do once she's left?' I asked. 'Who will take over the Applebridge Food Academy if you win?'

Edward threw some crumbs into the pond and tiddlers bobbed up to the surface for a midnight feast.

'I think that's what you'd call the Elephant in the Room…' He sighed. 'It's jolly hard discussing these things with Father. With a million dollars, we'd be able to hire a top calibre chef who'd be happy to take the job on once we'd finished the refurbishment of the guest bedrooms, properly kitted out the kitchen and added more work-stations. But he still loathes the idea of strangers living in our home.' Edward drained his cup.

'With all that dosh, you wouldn't have to make the decision straight away,' I said.

'True—we could postpone it for a while, but I have to think long-term. I don't want Applebridge Hall to be in the same precarious position ten or twenty years from now. When Father inevitably passes on there will be death duties to pay and… Well… A million dollars must be invested very wisely. I don't want to pass the responsibility I carry down to another generation…' For a second deep lines cut across his forehead. 'We also want to employ more locals from the village again, like in the old days. There's a lot to think about.' He shrugged. 'It's a pity Abbey never mentions staying, to work here in some capacity.'

'Really?' My mouth fell open. 'I mean…You get on that well?'

He glanced sideways at me. 'As far as I'm concerned, yes. And she's had some great ideas. It's… It's tremendous having my cousin around, after all this time. Even if we don't win, she'd be an asset. I'm afraid the stiff upper lip faltered tonight and I wrote on my blog about…feelings… and praised Abigail.'

Wow. I must take a gander.

His cheeks flushed. 'There's something about the virtual world that makes it somehow easier to offload…' He grinned. 'And being around you, Gemma. That's what I like—your honesty. Forthrightness.'

I grinned back. 'You're pretty forthright yourself, from what Abbey says.'

The humour dropped from his face. 'Oh, Gemma… If only you knew… Sometimes I wish I could be a lot more upfront…'

Huh? What did he mean by that? I linked my free arm through his. 'Abbey, um, talks mega fondly of you, too,' I said. 'It's just… About the future…Your two families don't exactly get on well.'

'We're all so stubborn, that's the problem.' He smiled. 'Abbey included—she's a Croxley woman, all right. Absolutely determined, yet with that feminine edge that stops her just short of behaving like… Well, like trigger-happy Thompson.'

'I'm glad you find it funny—he nearly killed me!' My heart raced. Edward liked me—well, in my disguise as Abbey. I'd done it—passed the test. Edward believed I was a true member of his aristocratic family.

'Anything I can do to help tonight?' I said. 'My brother won't be here for a couple of hours. Abbey mentioned some ration books and toys… Do you need help sorting stuff out?'

'No, thanks.' He yawned.

'Oh… Sorry, Edward, I should have thought—you must be knackered. Not everyone's a nightbird like me.'

Inside, I felt as if a balloon had just been popped and deflated down to a shred of plastic. If I'd been sophisticated Henrietta, I bet he'd have jumped at the chance to spend a night together in the library, arranging the evacuee lunch. 'I'll go back to Abbey's room and crash out for a couple of hours.'

'No, don't… Come with me, Gemma, up to the forest at the top of the hill. The fencing behind it keeps getting broken. Mr Thompson suspects the usual vandals or perhaps fans of the show. I said I'd check it out—which would be less, erm, fun, on my own.'

Yay! He enjoys my company, after all! I stood up and, still arm in arm, we headed around to the back of the house, chatting about all sorts of stuff. He attended private school, I went to a comprehensive. Edward learnt Latin and enjoyed a study trip to China. I took a BTEC in hospitality and visited Alton Towers. I described my job at Pizza Parlour. Edward confessed that he'd never eaten so much as one Margherita. As for ordering delivery pizza by phone, he just didn't get the concept.

When was the last time I'd had a conversation with a man that didn't revolve around asking if I'd like a cider or beer? Yet, what was I doing? I shouldn't eke this evening out; tomorrow was a huuuuge day, as far as organizing the reunion was concerned. Lots to do, plus an early start after a night of washing out hair dye and dawn was already on its way…

Reluctantly, I let go, dragging my feet behind him. I caught up, just as Edward reached the cemetery, pretending I'd just received a text.

'My brother's finishing early,' I said. 'I'll have to go to the gates in twenty minutes.'

'Oh.' He stopped still and gazed at me through the moonlight, shadows under his eyes suddenly pronounced.

'But I've still got time for a quick look at that fence,' I said brightly and linked arms with him again as tree roots and stones made walking through the forest bonkers in my stilettos. Finally, we reached the fencing at the back and, sure enough, there was a gaping hole, surrounded by fag butts and beer bottles.

'Mr Thompson hates litter,' said Edward. 'By the look of it, this is just kids messing about. One summer we found a couple of tents here. Another year they built a tree house.'

'Doesn't it bother you?'

He shrugged. 'They're only enjoying themselves. You know, Mr Thompson used to play hide and seek with me in these woods when I was a lad. Great tracking skills, that man. He always found me.' He sighed. 'Who'd have thought one day I'd be having words with him for doing what he does best?'

'What, stalking innocent people and taking a pop?'

He half-smiled. 'Mr Thompson would do anything to protect this estate.'

Just like Edward.

Suddenly I longed to rub my cheek against his tousled honey curls. And, as if on cue, here was one of my adrenaline rushes—I had to do something about that little boy lost look on his face, which for a split second said 'If only I was ten again.'

'Tig!' I said and smacked him on the chest, before running as fast as I could amongst the trees. 'Catch me if you caaaannn.'

'For God's sake, Gemma,' he called after me, 'you'll trip over again.'

'Come on,' I yelled back and dodged behind a tree, my knee feeling fine now and the blister forgotten. Chest heaving, I stood statue-still. Footsteps came and nearby twigs snapped. I held my breath.

'If you insist!' said a familiar voice and a hand came around from behind the tree.

'Aarghh!' I screamed, yet felt all tingly as he tickled my neck.

I dodged around to the other side of the trunk. Edward chuckled and looked back to make sure I was following him as he ran. Faster I sprinted, to the left and then to the right, around trees, skirting bushes, jumping over tree roots, praying Edward would stick to the moonlit areas so that I didn't tumble over a boulder and land in a pile of mud.

I ran into a clearing and stopped still, chest heaving up and down, wishing now that I wasn't wearing the mega thick, sauna-hot coat. Edward had disappeared. I turned my head. What a giveaway! Someone sneezed from the left. I tiptoed across a grassy area and peered over a large bush.

'This is too easy. Tig!' I said and ruffled his hair.

He roared and with a scream I ran back the way I'd come. Laughing, I could hardly breathe and lost my way. Where on earth was I now? Heading for the broken fencing or towards the cemetery at the front? I lay flat on the ground behind some tall grass.

'Aarggh!' I screamed as someone grabbed me under the arms. I turned and glared at Edward. 'You scared me!' I shouted and jumped up.

'Your...face,' he stuttered and wiped away tears from his eyes.

I giggled. 'Beautiful as ever, I hope, even if mega surprised.'

He stopped laughing and stared at me, his familiar serious expression back in place. 'Yes. Yes, it is. Don't ever change, Gemma. Never alter who you are.'

Before I knew it, his arms had slipped behind my back and pulled me towards his chest. Like popping candy, teeny-tiny tingly feelings burst in my stomach. On tiptoe, I wrapped my arms around his neck and instantly forgot about the competition and why I was here... Eyes closed tight, heart beating in nanoseconds, I lost myself against his tender lips.

'Edward...' I mumbled eventually. 'Gotta go...' Gotta breathe... Gotta get my head around this.

Lord Edward Croxley and me kissing? It was mad. Mental. Totally random. How could that irritating, uncommunicative, unreadable, mega frustrating man be the one for me?

He stood back, eyes crinkled at the corners, then grabbed my hands and squeezed them almost tighter than I could bear.

'Come back, again, Gem,' he murmured. 'Tomorrow. Do me the great honour of meeting me by the pond at midnight.'

LORD EDWARD'S E-DIARY

Friday 7th September

'Comments'

3.30a.m. In case any of you are insomniacs and still awake, just a word of reassurance—the gunshot, fired in defence of the estate, was into the sky and hurt no one.

I can hardly breathe or think due to... How did...? Yet she's so... Erm, do ignore me—I'm incoherent, due to fatigue.

Goodnight. Sleep well, friends! I've a feeling this is going to be a damn decent day!

CHAPTER 21

Bed at four. Up at six. Wash hair once. Relive that kiss.
Consult Mrs Raynor's list. Choose which evacuees to ring
first. Wash hair again. Remember the feel of my lips on his.
Make some excuse not to go to breakfast. Picture Edward
laughing so hard in the forest he couldn't speak. Wish I
could once again feel his arms hold me tight. Wash hair
once more. Explain to Lady C that I had, um, slept badly,
and would lunch in my room. Recall popping candy feeling
in stomach. After a few more washes, finally dry hair…

How typical it was that the one morning of my life I
would have liked to moon around dreaming of romance
I had a mega long list of stuff to complete. There'd been
no time, last night, to make sense of what had happened
with Edward. Having waited for what seemed like ages
outside, until I thought he'd hit the sack, I'd gone inside in
a state of shock. On automatic, I'd crept into my bedroom
and plugged in the laptop which I'd found in the Parlour.
Edward must have left it there, after he finally went to bed.

Logged in, I first read Edward's blog and felt all warm
and fuzzy inside at the nice things he said about his cousin
(that's me!). Then I scooted over to Facebook and nearly
collapsed! There were over four hundred—four hundred!—
comments about the *Dirty Dancing* scene. An argument
had broken out over whether the intruders were Nick and

me. At the moment the majority decided that there's no way an aristocrat would live out some fantasy of skinny-dipping with Patrick Swayze.

Now the only problem was to maintain that momentum with—brainwave, or what?—a competition! Before going to bed, I set out the details on-line. Now, several hours later, having just got dressed into cotton trousers and a beige top, I sat on the bed, picked up the laptop and logged in again to see the reaction.

Wow. There were already one hundred replies and nearly two thousand 'Likes'. Under my Facebook name of Eleanor Goodwin, this was what I'd written:

Hey everyone! Seeing as some of us are convinced that the mystery couple is really Miss Abigail Croxley and Nick, let's make Million Dollar Mansion *interactive as they might read this page. Obviously, their kicks come from re-enacting famous romantic movie clips. So let's get this Showmance on the road and vote for the scene us viewers want next. Choose from the following three:*

Ghost—*the scene at the potter's wheel, where Patrick Swayze sits behind Demi Moore and helps her mould the clay.*

Bridget Jones *when she runs out in the snow in her underwear to find Colin Firth. (it's not winter, yet, but I'm sure Abigail Croxley could improvise).*

Or, finally, just a good old-fashioned snog like Rhett Butler and Scarlett O'Hara in Gone with the Wind.

Let's see if Nick and Miss Croxley take up our challenge and re-create the film of our choice.

I swallowed. In daylight, maybe this wasn't such a good idea. If they chose *Bridget Jones*, it would be hard to explain Abbey running around outside in her birthday suit. I scanned down the votes and let out a sigh of relief.

The clay-turning scene from *Ghost* was winning hands-down. Someone rapped on my door and I wiped my mouth, having just eaten a ham sandwich that Kathleen had kindly brought in. It was two o'clock and, even though I'd been madly ringing evacuees for a while, it was time to officially resurface.

'Enter,' I said and readjusted the pillows behind my back. Edward came in.

'Are you all right, cousin?' His eyes sparkled and there was an uncharacteristically cheerful ring to his voice.

'I, um, didn't sleep well.' Earnestly, I inspected my nails, having quickly revarnished them so that Lady C wouldn't think my standards were slipping.

'It's a good thing we cancelled the cookery lessons today as we've so much to prepare for the reunion tomorrow,' he said. 'Have you worked your way through your half of Mrs Raynor's list? May I?'

I nodded as he sat down at the end of the bed. Glad to avoid his eye in case I winked or lunged forward for an awesome snog, I picked up a piece of paper from my bedside table.

'So, cousin, have you contacted your half?' I said. It seemed stranger than ever now, putting on my posh accent with him. It felt worse, as if the deception ran deeper than before. I had everything crossed that if the charade ever came out he'd understand. 'I've had a certain degree of success,' I continued. 'Four people can definitely attend. One wasn't sure as his arthritis is bad. Another politely declined and one poor chap had recently died. Two others were wrong numbers and one didn't answer.'

'Jolly good work,' said Edward with a broad smile. 'Father is delighted as I rang Jonny Jackson and he's game to come on the show. Two others are definites. Two more had other engagements they couldn't cancel.'

I scribbled on a piece of paper.

'Right, so that's three acceptances from your list,' I said, 'four from mine, then Bill Cochrane, Linda Sloggit, Cynthia and Bertie Williams and Mrs Raynor… Oh, yes, and guess what? Gerry Green got back to me and was very keen to accept the invitation. So that's thirteen guests… I also struck lucky with one of the names on that school register you found. One man set up his own bathroom fitting company and it is still run under his name, a Norman Barker…'

'The one who left that diary?' said Edward.

'Yes. He lives in Wales now, but is actually on holiday not far from here. Every September, he stays at his nephew's caravan park once the school holidays are over. Mr Barker said he'd be thrilled to attend.'

'So that's fourteen in total,' said Edward and rolled up his shirtsleeves. Scratches covered his arms. Tig in a forest at night clearly had hidden dangers. I pointed at them.

'What on earth happened?' I suppressed a smile.

Edward looked sheepishly at his arms.

Oh, dear. I was forgetting myself and shouldn't have mentioned something so personal—unless he was embarrassed about the kiss last night. Was he looking at me, dressed as sophisticated Abbey, and wondering whether he had lost his senses, snogging an unemployed waitress?

'Apologies, Edward—that was rude of me to ask.'

'It's okay, cousin,' he said. 'I was just checking on the fencing in the forest last night. An enormous amount of prickly bushes grow there.' He stood up. 'By the way, to appease Gaynor as we cancelled today's cookery school, Father and I hoped you could show off your skills to the nation once more and rustle up dinner for guests tonight.

The Hamilton-Browns are visiting again so, with your aunt, there'll be seven of us.'

'Oh, um, of course, it's just…'

'Problem?'

'Aren't we setting up the Drake Diner tonight, for the reunion—you know, with the display of old documents and toys?'

'We've got all morning tomorrow, until twelve. Plus I had a word with Jean and she'll pick and arrange flowers.'

I glanced at my watch. 'Right. Lots to do. I'd better get cracking.'

We walked downstairs together, me wishing our fingers were intertwined.

'Until later then, Edward,' I said.

He grunted and headed outside. I made my way to the kitchen.

'Kathleen!' I groaned and flung my arms around her. 'Help me think up an amazin' menu and please cook it for the Hamilton-Browns tonight. I'll be your bezzie mate for ever!'

Kathleen unwrapped my arms, stepped back and looked over my shoulder. I turned around. Lady C stood behind me, in the back doorway.

'Oh, Aunt… How lovely to see you. Kathleen was, um, upset about something. I was just offering my sympathies.'

Lady C's mouth upturned.

'Och, Gemma. No need to pretend,' said Kathleen. 'Lady Constance soon worked out that I was in on your secret.'

Lady C walked over to the table and sat down. I joined her. Kathleen smoothed down her apron.

'Soz I didn't tell you—it was just in case you worried.' I smiled nervously at Lady C. 'But, after that first cookery class, I really needed some support and Kathleen's been mega.'

Lady C nodded. 'It's been a very sensible decision. Kathleen and I got to know each other better whilst researching this Woolton pie for tomorrow. I'm sure the three of us will make a very good team.'

'You're a brave lassie, young Gemma,' said Kathleen. 'Lady Constance and I agree on that. So we'll both do our best to help you with anything, until the show ends.' She pursed her lips. 'Although Abigail's aunt told me about your madcap plan with Nick, which explains a lot—but I don't trust him. You need to watch your back.'

'Yes, you're probably right…' I said, trying to play things down. And I was dying to tell them both about my eye-opening trip to Marwick Castle, but fearing what might happen if Lady C had an unknown heart condition.

'As for tonight's dinner,' said Lady C, 'James mentioned it to me this morning and…'

'Ooh, *James*,' I said without thinking. Her cheeks tinged pink, while Kathleen and I giggled.

'The Earl is a lovely gentleman,' said Lady C and tucked a loose strand of grey hair behind her ear. 'His ornithological knowledge is impressive.'

'Well, you've certainly put a bounce in his step, m'lady,' said Kathleen. 'This morning he sang like a bird whilst taking a shower.'

I giggled again and Lady C folded her arms.

'Please may we get back to the subject in hand—tonight's dinner? Unless you can manage it by yourself, Gemma…'

'No… No… Please—I won't interrupt again.' I grinned.

And I didn't—not while she'd described the cold buffet supper she and Kathleen would secretly prepare on my behalf. Lady C said that the weather was still warm so a dinner like that would be 'perfectly acceptable'. I would set it up inside and we'd all eat on the patio.

So while those dear ladies chopped and mixed and baked their way through the afternoon, while humming to Kathleen's favourite Elvis CD, I finalised details with Gaynor about pick-up details for tomorrow's guests. Then, eventually, I went back to my bedroom and made some last minute phone calls, like double-checking that Bill Cochrane could still pick up old Mrs Raynor tomorrow. Then there was just time for a quick bath and change before the Hamilton-Browns arrived at six-thirty.

I wore a knee-length navy blue sleeveless dress with classy sequins lining the round neck. My hair brushed up into a bun and pearls in place, I really felt the part.

'Good evening, Abigail,' said the Earl, as I walked into the Drake Diner. He and Lady C were admiring the cold supper.

'Damn good effort you've put in,' said the Earl. 'Those slices of ham and beef look very appetising. And is that a mackerel and tomato tart? How did you know that was my favourite?'

Modestly, I shrugged. Good old Kathleen. Mmm, the cheeses and pâté looked tasty. As did the bowlfuls of salad and what looked like home-made coleslaw.

'I, um, made the bread myself, of course,' I said and pointed to a seeded brown uncut loaf.

'My niece is an excellent baker,' said Lady C and gave me a small smile.

I small-smiled back, knowing she found the lying as difficult as me—especially to her new friend, *James*. With a yawn (hand over mouth, of course), I suddenly felt tired, what with the late nights and strain of keeping up my daytime pretence. It was a good thing ladies wore make-up as, without it, at the moment I had deep rings under my eyes and new lines on my forehead.

'Is that your famous, erm, home-made trout pâté?' she asked.

'Um, yes.' We exchanged glances. At least now I knew what I was supposed to have cooked. But trout? Ick. Just give me a jar of supermarket sandwich paste any day of the week. I gazed at an amazin' fruit pavlova with shortbread on the side.

'Of course, I didn't have much time to prepare pudding,' I said, 'so Kathleen kindly helped me out and, um, baked the biscuits.'

'Kathleen is a wonderful cook,' said a pleasant voice. It was the Viscountess, as Edward and the Hamilton-Browns walked in. She smiled at Lady C. 'You are Abigail's aunt, I believe? I've heard so much about you.'

'Annabel, this is Lady Constance Woodfold,' said the Earl, a bit flustered. 'Constance, please let me introduce the Viscount and Viscountess Hamilton-Brown—Ernest and Annabel—and their charming daughter, Henrietta.'

'It's a pleasure to meet you,' said Henrietta and then turned to me. 'The food really does look scrumptious, Abbey. It's probably one of the last days of the year we'll be able to enjoy supper on the patio.'

'Thank you,' I said, guilt pinching as I accepted the credit.

'What a delightful dress, Henrietta,' said Lady C. 'Edward often talks of you.'

Did he really? I shook myself. So what? I was the one he'd kissed.

'James tells me you and your husband share a love of birdwatching,' Lady C said to Annabel. 'On my first day here, I was absolutely thrilled to spot a common yellowthroat.'

Annabel nodded. 'Several visited last year and we wondered if they were nesting in the forest. James really must bring you over to the Manor. Jarvis, our gardener, has spent two years planting out a special area to attract the best of Britain's wild birds.'

And they were off—the oldies moved outside, chatting furiously about nuts, berries and nesting material. The room went quiet as the cameraman followed them outside and I was left with Edward and Henrietta.

'I'm not sure bird talk is going to compete with Marwick Castle's celebrity guests,' I muttered. 'According to Roxy, they arrive this evening before tomorrow's party.' Oops. I sounded very negative. How unladylike. 'Apologies, Henrietta,' I said. 'Forgive me. I shouldn't bother you with such issues.'

Edward put a hand on his friend's shoulder. Wow! In polite company, that was outrageous physical contact!

'Don't apologise, cousin,' he said. 'I have discussed all of this with Henry. In any event...' He cleared his throat.

'Later on this evening,' said Henrietta, 'we have an announcement that will liven up the proceedings.'

I didn't like the way they exchanged looks, her eyes all chandelier sparkly.

'Do tell,' I said and fixed a smile on my face as my heartbeat increased.

Kathleen appeared at that moment, with a tray bearing six glasses and a jug of Pimms.

With a sigh, I followed Henrietta and Edward outside. 'The food looks mega,' I whispered to Kathleen. 'Thanks for everything.'

She squeezed my arm and left. I offered to pour the drinks.

'Have you chosen a dress yet, for that Lieutenant Robert Mayhew's charity ball?' I asked Henrietta as I finally sat down, booze poured and conversation flowing.

'Ooh, yes—from a wonderful boutique not many people know about, in the city. I must take you there some time.'

'Boutique' sounded posh. 'Bargain basement' were words I normally used when clothes shopping.

Edward's mouth twitched. 'As usual, I imagine Rob will dance with practically every lady between eighteen and eighty.'

Henrietta giggled. 'It's such a shame that, after all these years, you still abhor dancing.' She shook her head at me. 'Even at his twenty-first, Edward was quite rude to the queue of girls begging to partner him on the dance floor.'

Leaving Henrietta to reminisce, I relaxed back into the wicker chair and gazed towards the vegetable garden and up towards the forest. Last night's popping candy inside me had gone decidedly flat as she and Edward laughed together. Discreetly, I sipped my Pimms until, before I knew it, my glass was empty—listening to everyone's plummy accents and tales of their fancy lives made me feel more than ever that I didn't belong here.

'I don't know about anyone else,' said the Earl, 'but those sausage rolls are calling. Ladies, please help yourselves to some cold supper.'

'That tart looks absolutely delicious, Abbey,' said Henrietta. She linked arms with me as we headed for the table. 'I was in awe of your cookery lesson on Wednesday. Those pheasant breasts looked divine. Please say you'll give me a personal lesson. I found the recipe rather quick to follow on the television.'

Green eyes all smiley, she gave a small laugh. It was no good. Even jealousy couldn't stop me liking the woman.

'Of course,' I said and glanced sideways to see an unusually chatty Edward talking to Roxy. She clapped her hands together and jumped up and down. I had a bad feeling about this special announcement.

Four slices of Cheddar, two portions of tart and three chunks of yummy bread with pâté later, I felt no better—so much for comfort eating. It was just as well the cameraman had taken a break from filming. Although it had brightened up my evening watching poor Lady C's eyes bulge as a bit of the real me crept in and I kept stuffing myself with the goodies!

As the sun sank towards the horizon, we moved inside. I struggled to keep my yawns subtle. Out of nowhere, Gaynor appeared. An extra lighting man came in. Roxy paced up and down. Edward took Henrietta's hand and muttered the word...*engagement.*

Ernest clapped Edward on the back. Girlishly, Annabel whispered something to Lady C, who gasped before—get this—*offering her congratulations.*

'Uncle?' I said weakly, 'what's going on?'

He puffed on his pipe and consulted his pocket watch. 'Well, it's not really my place to say—wait a few more minutes and you'll find out, live on TV.' He smiled. 'Hopefully, something that will boost our popularity.'

Roxy muttered the word 'ring' and both Edward and Henrietta gazed at each other.

I felt giddy. And sick. More tired than ever and frowning, no doubt increasing those lines on my forehead. A lump rose in my throat and fortunately blocked the release of what Lady C would call 'a very unpleasant word'.

Last night… That kiss… How could I have been so stupid? As if a member of the aristocracy would see me as anything more than a passing fancy. I curled my fists. His loss—wouldn't want anything to do with such a snob anyway. But this was the twenty-first century, for God's sake. Commoner KMid was good enough for the future King of England—what *was* Edward's problem?

'Not long now, Henry,' Edward muttered and patted her arm.

My eyes tingled, which must be because I was knackered and definitely not to do with being used by some aristocratic bastard. But…poor, good-natured Henrietta. How could Edward cheat on someone so pretty and classy? There was no way I could stay to watch this farcical announcement without blurting out that he'd recently snogged another woman. Honestly… And there was me guilt-tripping about *my* deception.

Mumbling that I felt unwell, I rushed out of the Drake Diner and almost collided with someone. To avoid saying hello, I lowered my head, catching sight of polished shoes and pressed trousers. As quickly as possible, I made my way upstairs and into my bedroom. Deep breaths. In and out. I tugged out my hair pins and shook my hair loose.

Four-poster bed, tapestries, furniture with fancy carved feet… What was I doing here? The Croxleys and Hamilton-Browns of this world might as well have come from another planet. I pulled my dress over my head and yanked my suitcase out from under the bed. I flipped it open and grabbed a short skirt and skimpy top, chicken fillets, bronzer and red hairspray. Great. I was me again. Er, not so great when, minutes later, someone rapped on the door.

'Cousin, are you all right?' said Edward's voice. 'There'll be a special announcement in about fifteen minutes. May I come in? I could do with picking up the laptop, to use later, before I go to bed—if that suits you.'

Eek! I lay motionless.

The door handle turned and Edward entered the bedroom.

'Do you always come in without an invitation?' I snapped and sat up.

'Gemma…' Sunshine trickled into his voice. 'It's you… How…? Weren't we meeting by the pond at midnight?'

I jumped off the bed and stood in front of him, arms folded. 'Have you no shame? I thought you were a cold fish, but this… What about Henrietta? Don't her feelings matter?'

His brow furrowed.

'Don't plead ignorance. Abbey's just told me—before, um, she had to rush to the bathroom.'

'Told you what? And why are you here so early?'

'I didn't leave. My, um, brother was offered an extra shift at the supermarket, so he stayed over, on a colleague's sofa. Abbey put me up last night and said I could chill out here all day and help her with some phone calls.' I glared at him. 'Anyway, don't change the subject. Did you know about this announcement last night?'

'Why does that matter?' He stepped forward and gently unfolded my arms. 'Tell me—what's wrong. How can I help ease your distress?'

'You're unbelievable! Despite what happened between us, you're about to announce your engagement.'

'I am?' His mouth twitched. 'Gemma, there's been some kind of misunderstanding.'

'It's not funny,' I said, hardly stopping for breath. 'What are you hoping for, one quick shag with a commoner before you commit to noble blood?'

His cheeks flushed.

'Oh, soz,' I said, 'shouldn't a lady speak like that?'

'I don't care how you speak,' he muttered. 'What concerns me more is that you won't even listen to my explanation.'

'Your excuse, more like.' My voice wobbled. 'Just go. Leave me alone.'

'Gemma, you've got it wrong. Henry and I...'

I swung around. 'Just a bit of fun, wasn't I?'

He grabbed my hands. 'Fun? Yes. Thank God. It's a long time since I've felt so carefree. Gemma, you have no idea... Until you came along, my life, it was like...a silent movie. But it's as if you've added a soundtrack and a whole new dimension.'

'Stop it,' I said. 'You're a disgrace to the Croxley name. Where's your sense of loyalty?'

'But...'

'I know your sort, Edward,' I said, trying to control that wobble. 'Gentleman by name or not, you're only interested in me for one thing. I mean, surely Henrietta must have the fun factor as well?'

'She has...' he said, 'but for some reason doesn't bring it out in me. Not like you do, Gemma... Henry has always been... a good friend. My parents...Father, he's known Ernest and Annabel for almost thirty years—'

'Oh, poor you,' I said. 'Now you're trying to make your relationship with her sound like some crappy arranged marriage. She's a mega girl ...from, um, what Abbey says. Yet, like lots of blokes, you just want to keep your options open.'

The light faded in his eyes. 'No point defending myself, then,' he said in a measured voice. 'You've already made up your mind about my intentions.'

I bit my thumbnail, willing my chin not to tremble.

'Don't worry.' He picked up the laptop and went to the doorway. 'This…what was it?…*cold fish* won't bother you again. I do apologise, Gemma. I thought… You and me… The pond… Tig…' He swallowed. 'Perhaps talking movies aren't the great invention people thought them to be. Perhaps silence is… safer.'

LORD EDWARD'S E-DIARY

Friday 7ᵗʰ September

'Comments'

11.55p.m. Forget what I said about today being damned decent. In fact, I'm wondering whether I should bore you further with my thoughts. Blogging brings to mind words 'heart' and 'sleeve'. Maybe the programme-makers were wrong about this e-diary and, for everyone's sake, this should be my last entry.

CHAPTER 22

'Took your time to get up this morning, didn't you, cousin?' Edward scowled. I'd just walked into the Drake Diner. It was almost eleven. In one hour, the first evacuees would arrive.

'Forgive me,' I said with a sneer. 'I assume you haven't spoken to my aunt yet? She would have told you that I was ill last night, and needed time to recover.'

The cameraman picked up his equipment to film us, but I glared at him and, mega fast, he changed his mind. For the first time in days, I felt no guilt at lying to that cheating scoundrel, my supposed cousin. Anyway, I had felt ill—physically sick to my stomach. And dog-tired, as if the intense days of late had suddenly caught up with me. Shortly after he'd left last night, Lady C had hurried up to my room. I delayed her entry by pretending to need the loo and quickly took off my Gemma clothes as she had no idea I'd brought them with me. Also, I wrapped my red hair in a turban of towel. When I finally allowed her in, she took one look at me and tucked me straight into bed without a word, which suited me fine. However, I didn't sleep well and ended up having some random dream, where Edward turned out to be a cockney barrow boy in disguise.

I glanced at the trestle tables, near to where Edward stood. Toys from the evacuees' rooms were spread out, next to piles of ration books and various paperwork.

'You've done a good job,' I muttered, despite myself. 'By the way, Norman Barker telephoned to say he's bringing along another evacuee friend—somebody Smith, I believe.'

Edward nodded.

'Abbey, darling, how are you feeling?' Lady C swept into the room. 'That cream trouser suits you to a tee. You looked truly dreadful last night—as white as the meringue on Kathleen's pavlova dessert. Did you manage the scrambled eggs that dear woman brought up? They always sort out a gyppy tummy.'

'Thank you, Aunt. Yes. It was very thoughtful of her.'

'So…' Lady C smiled '…I assume you've heard the exciting news.'

Edward's shoulders tensed up. Deep breath. Mustn't show any emotion when she announces the engagement.

Lady C's face lit up. 'Henrietta is getting married!'

'How wonderful,' I said in a flat voice, trying to act all dignified as I knew Abbey would in such a situation.

'Don't you want to know who to?' Lady C sat down at the dining table, already set with silver cutlery and fancy napkins. 'To Edward—'

My heart sank. Now it was confirmed.

'To Edward's friend,' she said. 'Robert Mayhew.'

'Par… Pardon?'

'You know—the dashing lieutenant chap.'

Mouth dry, knees like jelly, I sat down next to her.

'He was here last night, Abbey. Such a pity you missed him. He arrived shortly after you left the room.'

Of course—the polished shoes and pressed trousers I'd caught a glimpse of.

'Little as Robert likes his newfound celebrity, he suggested announcing the engagement on air, to boost Applebridge's Hall's popularity,' said Lady C.

'He is a good friend indeed,' said Edward, eyes flashing in my direction. 'Henry insisted she and Robert owed me this favour because I introduced them to each other all those years ago.'

My head swirled. Crap. Double crap. How could I have doubted reliable Edward? His loyalty to the ancestors and the family home should have told me he'd never cheat. I'd read into his relationship with Henrietta what I was frightened of seeing, not what was really there. A feeling of nausea rose at the back of my throat. Tears filled my eyes. Talk about a roller coaster journey. Now I knew why celebrities often suffered breakdowns on reality TV shows. I bit my lip. How much more of all this could I take?

'And what's more,' continued Abbey's aunt, 'to extend their favour, the couple insist on holding an engagement party here, next Wednesday evening. Robert will organize a raffle for his army charity—Edward, didn't you suggest the prize could be a short stay at Applebridge Hall and lessons at the Food Academy?'

He nodded. 'Gaynor also suggested a competition, linked to the show, for two viewers to win the chance to attend the party.'

'Are you all right, Abbey?' asked Lady C. 'You look terribly pale again, dear.'

I smiled weakly, ignoring Edward's dagger glares. Finally, he looked away as Charlie Chingo entered the room.

'Yo! How ya doing, folks?' Charlie ran a hand through his quiff and stood still for one second as Roxy powdered his nose. 'Everyone ready to *Chat with the Chingo*? I believe the lunch is at one. From twelve, the camera and I will mingle among the guests.'

Gaynor came in with a clipboard.

'Can we speak for a moment, Charlie, darling?' she asked. 'I'd like to run you through the types of questions to ask. We want to see real emotion on the screen—you've got to remind the evacuees how much they missed their parents. Dig deep. If any were treated badly, all the better.'

Now it was her turn for a glare from Edward.

'Not that anyone would have been abused here, of course,' she said brightly and flicked her black bob. 'But perhaps some spent several years elsewhere, before or after their stay at Applebridge Hall. Ask if their dads returned from military duty. Maybe they lost relatives during the bombing.'

'Brutal business, this reality shoe malarkey, isn't it?' said Lady C and shook her head as Charlie disappeared with the director. 'Right, I must find James. Roxy asked me to make sure he was in the Drake Diner by half past eleven.' She stood up and left.

'You must, um, be very pleased for Henrietta and the Lieutenant,' I mumbled to Edward when we were alone.

But he'd closed off from me and simply continued flicking through the ration books on display. Through the patio windows I saw Nick, working in the vegetable garden. He stood up and waved. Discreetly, I waved back.

Okay, Gemma. Get a grip. Forget your huge cock-up with Edward, just for one moment. Forget wanting to jump up and down because Edward isn't actually engaged to somebody else. Concentrate on the bigger picture instead.

Plan Sex-up needed to move forward. Nick and I had a romantic scene to re-enact. What with the reunion dinner and engagement party and Facebook fan page, things were finally coming together. I couldn't lose it now and allow all this love stuff to ruin my week's hard work. If nothing else, I now owed it to Edward, more than ever, to make sure the Hall won the show.

'Do excuse me,' I muttered to no one in particular, and went out through the patio doors just as Roxy appeared and pointed out things on the trestle table she wanted filming to the cameraman. Edward left by the other entrance and muttered something about going to the library for a moment.

Phew. Fresh air. There was nothing like it for clearing the head—well, apart from a Coke and Alka Seltzer.

I gazed around. This was the first mega overcast morning in ages, yet the estate still looked wicked. Not like where I'd grown up, which looked down and out, even on a blistering August day. I walked over to Nick, who was leaning on his hoe.

'Have you heard about the competition on Facebook, Miss Croxley?' he said, a twinkle in his eye.

'Yes. If that doesn't keep the viewers hooked, nothing will,' I said.

'You sound as if you planned it yourself.'

I smiled. 'Um, I wish—it's a really good idea. What's the final result? I've been off-colour and haven't looked. Somehow we have to re-enact the chosen movie scene this afternoon.'

'*Ghost* won, by a long stretch.'

I looked at my watch and then pictured that movie scene in my head. Urgh. I kind of wished now that I'd chosen more conservative film scenes. What a good thing I'd played down the sex-up plan with Lady C—she'd have done everything possible to talk me out of this latest re-enactment. Plus I'd done her a favour; now she was closer to the Earl, it was one less thing for innocent her to lie about. Along with everyone else, she could speculate about who was the Demi Moore to Nick's Patrick Swayze.

My heart fluttered and an adrenaline rush surged through me as a plan popped into my head—wacky as it was—how Nick and I could re-enact that pottery scene right now and get it over with.

'Could you fetch some overalls and a bucket of water and meet me out the front, by the fountain, in five minutes? Cameras are out there as well today, to catch the guests as they arrive. I've got an idea.' The part of me that still recalled Lady C's lessons about modesty just wanted to get this over with now.

He grinned. 'Certainly, Miss.'

I went back inside, past Edward, who looked as if he was only half-listening to Roxy. Chest thumping, I walked to the front of the house. Sure enough, another cameraman was there, taking shots of the drive, waiting for the ex-evacuees to turn up. Charlie and Gaynor smoked outside as she gave the presenter some last-minute instructions. They'd headed back inside by the time I stopped by the fountain and turned around to see where Nick was. I gazed back at the water feature, eyes focusing for a second on the chunk missing, due to gun-slinger Mr Thompson. The whole ornament was filthy with mud and green algae.

'This needs a jolly good clean, don't you think?' I said to Nick as he appeared by my side. 'Thanks for the overalls,' I said and quickly slipped into them.

'Nick… Just set the bucket down there,' I said and pointed towards the fountain's base. 'Right… Think of that scene from *Ghost*,' I whispered.

'Sure,' muttered Nick. 'Who could forget Patrick Swayze, crouching behind Demi Moore whilst she runs her hands up and down that wet, vase-like shaped clay that's spinning around. He puts his hands on hers and…'

'Exactly,' I whispered and jerked my head towards the base of the fountain. 'Don't you think that looks like a vase?'

'You don't mean…?'

'It does need a jolly good clean. First impressions are important and there are, um, a lot of people visiting Applebridge Hall today.'

He gazed at me, mouth open.

'Now or never, Nick,' I said. 'Hopefully, the cameraman will catch a few seconds of footage.' I knelt down on the ground at the bottom of the fountain. Nick brought over the bucket and sat right behind me. He passed me the cloth. I dunked it in the water and started to scrub the column, up and down. My other hand moved at the same time, around the other side of the vase-shaped stonework. Nick moved closer behind me and placed his big fingers on top of mine. They felt surprisingly smooth for a gardener. Subtly, I glanced up. Sure enough, the camera was focused on us.

'Lean in closer,' I whispered. 'Make it look as if you are kissing my neck—hopefully, that will hide my face.'

I dunked the cloth in the bucket again. Torrents of water dripped down the base. Now our arms swapped positions and my hands lay on top of his. Up and down, up and down… Demi Moore eat your heart out…

Except this wasn't as much fun as I'd expected. Damn me getting used to being a Lady. All I could think of was how the Croxleys might react if they saw this. Luckily, our cue to stop quickly came: the sound of a car on the drive.

I glanced at the camera—thank God it now focused on the vehicle. Gaynor would have fired the cameraman if he'd missed the shot of the first evacuee arriving. Nick and I stood up and, heads down, we hurried across to the pond. I crouched behind some bushes and slipped out of the overalls. Well, almost. One foot got stuck and aargghh! No! I fell sideways towards the pond.

LORD EDWARD'S E-DIARY

Saturday 8th September

11.45a.m. Before logging on here, I still wasn't sure whether to carry on with this blog. If I did, this morning's contribution was to be brief and dedicated to last-minute preparations for the imminent lunch. So, I've bobbed into the library, with only minutes to spare until the guests arrive—it has been awfully busy and this is the first moment I've had to myself.

All I can say is…dear blog-readers, instead, I shall dedicate this post to you. Thank you. I am… overwhelmed…Clearly, you sensed that, at the moment, all is not well in my world. Yet there are no prying questions, no sarcastic comments, simply support—(apart from the rather unpleasant contribution from *Internetking*. Thank you for the advice, all—I shall simply remove his comments if he returns in future).

I think what touches me most is that you don't see me as an aristocrat. It doesn't matter whether I'm in line to inherit an estate or who my family is or what I sound like… It's as if the online world has removed all barriers and my loyal blog followers just see me as me—you'll never know just how much that means.

Drunkwriter, you wonder if it is due to a woman. I am sorry your current, frequent inebriation follows a brutal break-up. *Cupcakesrock* is right—perhaps you are better off parted from someone who laughed at your poetry. Maybe you could meet like-minded people at a local writers' club?

Knityourownmansion, so you understand feeling low and downhearted? I'm sure that, like you, many people, post-retirement, feel they have lost their sense of worth. Clearly, knitting has filled a hole in your life. Have you ever considered setting yourself up online and selling your own handcrafted goods?

BusyfanDownton, nice to see you back here (and no, I won't tell Baron Marwick that you've visited my blog). I'm sorry to hear that you are on medication for low self-esteem. Just by supporting me, whilst still wishing the Baron to win, shows what a charitable, kind-hearted person you are.

And *Lovehotnoble*, that's an exceedingly generous offer, but I must decline. Apart from anything else, Mr Thompson could be tempted to shoot if he saw you creeping into my bedroom with sadistic equipment—I don't think he's read *Fifty Shades of Grey*.

CHAPTER 23

Phew. That was close. Nick caught me just in time. My clothes were still as dry as the infamous pork and apple stew I made. A bald man with a wrinkled face and cheeky smile stared right at me as I headed towards the car. I smoothed down my trouser suit and hoped my mascara hadn't run, due to splashes of fountain water. Quickly, I shook hands with the first guest and then dashed in as he stayed to chat with the driver. I flashed an innocent smile at the cameraman as I walked by. It was just before midday when I hurtled into the Drake Diner. The Earl and Lady C were chatting to Edward who, for some reason, looked a little brighter than before. Extra cameramen and boom operators had been brought in for the reunion. Gaynor strode in.

'The first car has just arrived!' she said, while Roxy came over and offered me a mint.

As slow footsteps approached, we all glanced towards the door. The bald man came in. He wore a smart grey suit and held a walking stick.

'Jonny? Jonny Jackson?' said the Earl. 'I'd recognize that mischievous smile anywhere!'

'James...Jimbo!'

The two men shook hands as if they were never going to let go. In fact... Blimey! The Earl actually leant forward and gave him a hug. My eyes tingled. Even Lady C couldn't disapprove of that uncharacteristic show of emotion.

'How are you doing, lad?' said Jonny as they finally drew apart. 'It's great to be back at Applebridge Hall. I can't believe it's been over seventy years since I was last here.'

At that moment another more familiar guest walked in.

'Bill!' said the Earl. 'Here's Jonny!'

'You old rascal!' Bill clapped the guest on the back. 'Good Lord. This is a rum deal—us in this room again, as old codgers! Remember that time we got lost in the maze? Matron blew a gasket when we returned, covered in blood and scratches, having forced ourselves through the hedges.'

'Always leading me astray, you two were,' said Jonny and gave me a wink. He gazed around the dining room. 'I've watched the show. It's been nice to see the old familiar rooms and gardens—reminded me of days spent running through that forest. Do you two remember us stealing ladybirds from the girls and threatening to drown them in the pond?'

The Earl gave a hearty laugh. 'Weren't we horrors?'

Bill chuckled. 'No—soft as putty, more like. We used to secretly release them onto lily pads so that they were all right.'

Light footsteps approached and a sprightly man with dyed brown hair combed over to the side came in. He wore a sharp slate suit and flash stripy tie.

'Well, I never,' muttered the Earl.

'Gerry Green,' said Bill.

'Congratulations, old boy,' said Jonny. 'I've followed your comedy career over the years. You've done all right.'

Gerry shook hands with them all. 'Sod, this, maties,' he said with a guffaw and pulled them all close for a hug.

'Lovely to meet you, Gerry,' I said. 'I'm Abbey, the Earl's niece—we spoke on the telephone.'

'But where are my manners?' said the Earl, eyes sparkling, as he proceeded to introduce everyone. Then the next hour until lunch was served passed in a bit of a blur. Linda Sloggit turned up from Manchester. Everyone chatted and laughed as if the world might end tomorrow. Eventually Charlie Chingo strolled in and worked the room as the rest of the ex-evacuees turned up. Lady C and I cringed at his gruesome questions:

'You must have missed your parents?'

'Any members of your family killed by bombs?'

'No doubt some of your childhood friends weren't so lucky as you, and ended up with abusive families...Could you tell us their tragic story...?'

'Linda? Is that you?' stuttered a short woman with Arctic-white hair and lips surrounded by smoker's wrinkles. 'It's Irene. Irene Cooper.'

Linda held out her arms and, like a little girl, Irene ran towards them. The whole room went quiet for a moment. Even Charlie shut up. After several minutes, the two women stood back from one another.

'You were like the big sister I never had,' said Irene, voice trembling. 'I was only four when I came here and would never have got through it without you. How did we lose touch?'

Linda's eyes glistened. 'We shouldn't have. Looking after others, though… It helped me cope.'

'Remember that knitted elephant?' said Irene. 'You always used to make sure I had it in bed with me at night.'

I fetched it from the trestle table. Irene took the toy from me as if it were the crown jewels.

'Cuddly toys were for wimps,' said Jonny with a wink at Linda. 'So us lads used to say.'

'And marbles were for stinky so-and-sos whose brains could only cope with rolling balls,' retorted Irene and stuck out her tongue.

Chuckles echoed around the room.

'Feels like I'm back in nineteen-forty,' said Gerry. 'Anyone remember the worm in Matron's bed?'

'Yes!' chorused Linda's friends, Cynthia and Bertie Williams.

'She made you clean the patio with a toothbrush,' said Cynthia, a striking woman wearing dangly gold earrings.

'Good, Lord, I'd forgotten that,' muttered Gerry. 'Good times, though, heh? All things considered?'

Grunts of agreement echoed around the room.

'Your mother was an angel, James,' said Bertie. 'Always knew how to cheer me up. She said that Mum would want me and Cynthia to enjoy ourselves—that it didn't mean we had forgotten her.'

Silence filled the room again. Bespectacled eyes stared vacantly for a moment, into the past. I sniffed and Lady C passed me a tissue. Thank God I wasn't wearing my false eyelashes; tears would have unstuck them by now. It was as if the last half a century or so hadn't happened. These old fogies still had such a strong bond. All our hard work, it had paid off—even if this reunion didn't win us the show, it was worth it.

Several of the guests stood at the trestle table, handling the toys as if they were made of the finest porcelain. The hush had the strangest effect on Chingo, who found his voice again, only to ask more respectful questions, like:

'*Tell us what positive effect staying at Applebridge Hall had on your life.*'

'Gave me aspirations,' said Jonny. 'I saw this place and wanted a bit of the high life. Got into banking, I did, and own a nice little holiday villa in Spain now, as well as our four-bed detached.'

'Made me realize how much I cared for people,' said Linda, 'especially children. Without the evacuation, I doubt I'd have become a midwife.'

'Taught me laughter really is the strongest medicine,' said Gerry.

'Made us realize how important family is,' said Cynthia and smiled at her brother, Bertie.

'And, erm, what did it teach you, Lord Croxley?' said Charlie.

'This is fab stuff,' Roxy whispered in my ear, having moved right behind me.

The Earl slipped an arm around Bill's shoulder. He thought for a moment. 'I'm the first to admit that this show, *Million Dollar Mansion*, has been nothing but a damn inconvenience.'

Everyone chuckled.

'My…my son, Edward, has carried a lot of the responsibility for trying to make it a success.' The Earl and Edward exchanged looks. 'He's come up with the ideas. He's liaised with the producers. But lately, since my niece Abigail proposed this reunion…' Blimey! The Earl's eyes shone watery bright. A lump came to my throat. 'It's made me think about the past,' he continued. 'Made me realize, more than ever, that Applebridge Hall is not just mortar and stones.'

Lady C squeezed his arm.

'Damn important memories have been made here,' the Earl said. 'My family has struggled for a long time to bring them back to life. And this reunion, especially now I've seen everyone…it makes me more determined than ever to embrace change, if it means saving our heritage, for future generations to learn about the estate's past.'

I gazed around at puckered chins and a trickle of applause became a huge wave. Eventually, Kathleen's appearance brought an end to the clapping. 'Lunch is ready, Your Lordship,' she announced.

The Earl smiled. 'Please, everyone, take your places at the table.'

When we were all finally sitting, one seat remained empty.

'Norman Barker,' said Edward, as if reading my mind. 'The man whose diary I found.' Ah, yes. The man who was staying at his nephew's caravan park.

I sat next to Lady C, who, in turn, was next to the Earl at the end of the table. On the other side of me was Linda, the midwife. Opposite sat Edward and old Mrs Raynor.

Nick came in, dressed in a tailcoat and the old butler's jacket he'd worn when the Hamilton-Browns came to that fateful dinner where I flicked the onion. He helped Kathleen serve wine from the Earl's cellar. Then the two of them disappeared, no doubt to fetch the starter. I stared at the cutlery and when I looked back up caught Lady C's eye. She smiled at me. I'd come a long way in a week and hadn't even considered picking at my bread roll. Less and less I had to ask myself: what would Abbey do?

Nick and Kathleen returned with bowls of steaming soup.

'Oh, no!' said Gerry. 'Lentils?'

'I haven't eaten them since rationing stopped,' said the Earl.

'We used to call them dead fish eyes, remember, Jimbo?' said Jonny and everyone laughed.

Roxy appeared, followed by two men. Edward stood up.

'Norman Barker?' he said to both of them.

The shorter of the two men held out his hand.

'Norm!' shouted Gerry. 'Still play football like a girl?'

'Watch it, Green,' said the short man and grinned. 'At least I didn't go in a strop every time I lost at marbles.'

Edward cleared his throat and stared at the taller man behind Norman, who wore an expensive-looking suit and the shiniest shoes I'd ever seen. At the end of the table, the Earl's eyes narrowed. Gradually, all the cheery chat came to a halt.

'*Dennis?*' said Bill. 'Dennis Smith, who set fire to the ground floor?'

The man half-smiled. 'Norm and I have kept in contact over the years. I wasn't sure whether to come when he told me about the reunion, but, well, I was a kid back then…' He coughed. 'Thought about it often over the years, I have. Little ruffian I was. Reckoned matches were exciting grown-up things.' He walked over to the Earl and held out his hand. 'I owe you and your family a huge apology.'

The camera zoomed in on him. Gaynor must have been wetting herself at this TV gold.

'It was no way to repay your hospitality,' Dennis continued. 'I never meant to cause so much damage, but I understand if I'm not welcome today.'

The Earl put down his napkin and stood up. He shook Dennis's hand.

'It takes a big man to apologise so wholeheartedly— especially on camera. God knows, we all did stupid things as children.' The Earl's eyes crinkled. 'This reunion wouldn't be the same without you rolling up a piece of paper and secretly smoking it in the forest.'

Everyone laughed and spoons dipped into soup once more.

'So what line of business did you eventually go into, Dennis?' Gerry asked as the unexpected guest and Norman sat down. Edward pulled over an extra chair, to squeeze the arsonist onto the corner of the table. 'Flogging fireplaces?'

Dennis grinned. 'No, I own two restaurants—one in London, another in the South of France which has gained two Michelin stars.'

'That's quite some achievement,' I said.

'Thanks,' he said without looking at me and sipped a glass of wine Nick had just poured. 'Of course, my son keeps an eye on them both now.' He grinned at the Earl. 'I just test out the menu.'

'Perhaps you could assess our new kitchens,' said Edward. 'If we win…any advice on how best to spend the money regarding the Food Academy would be most welcome.'

Dennis beamed. 'My pleasure. The least I can do. In fact…' now he eyed me '…I've watched young Miss Croxley with huge interest.'

Under the table, Lady C patted my hand. Please, no awkward questions about how I marinate meat or make a tomato sauce.

'I'm fascinated, Miss Croxley, by the way you presented those pheasant breasts,' he said. 'Dished up whole like that—not sliced so that the customer can see the mouthwatering inside. And the Cranachan—you served it in what looked like a soup bowl. I would have stacked it into a glass on a stalk, to really show off the contrasting colours of raspberries and oats.'

'I, um, followed Kathleen's advice—she's our Scottish cook,' I said and cleared my throat. 'I aimed to make everything as authentic as possible.'

'And where was it you studied catering?' he said. 'Your chopping and slicing techniques again are… out of the ordinary.'

Bloomin' slow, he really meant.

'My niece attended an extremely well-established college in Surrey after finishing school,' said Lady C sharply.

I glanced around the room, glad that most other people were busily catching up, even though Dennis was talking loudly. Nick stood with the carafe of wine and winked at me.

'It sounds as if you doubt Abbey's credentials,' said Edward and gave a tight-lipped smile. 'You've heard of her father, the Honourable Richard Croxley? He of Croxley Catering?'

I shot Edward a grateful glance.

Dennis nodded. 'A damn fine organisation. And don't get me wrong, I thought Miss Croxley's Scottish session was cracking.'

Kathleen came in and nodded at Nick. He put the wine down on a side-table and the two of them cleared the soup dishes.

'Just ignore Dennis, dear,' Linda said, eyes twinkling. 'It seems like he hasn't changed much, with regard to his manners. Always used to interrupt and be the centre of attention; liked to see intrigue where there wasn't any—didn't you, Dennis?'

Mrs Raynor opposite nodded. 'Accused me of being a spy once, the little scamp did,' she said, 'just because I had a working knowledge of German. He trailed me for a whole day. I cottoned on pretty quick, so took a long detour on the way home that night. He was exhausted by the time I hauled him back to Matron.'

Everyone laughed, including Dennis. Even Edward's mouth twitched. Although he hardly spoke during the Woolton Pie (surprisingly yum) and eggless sponge (as heavy as stale bread). As we sat drinking coffee, I leant back in my chair and gazed around the table. There'd been laughter. A few tears. One friendly argument (Gerry and Jonny both denied stealing some of the wooden zoo animals to take home after the war, despite the Earl's accusations). After another glass or two of wine each, everyone seemed to forget the cameras—cue a few juicy revelations.

Take Gerry, who was three times divorced, and Linda Sloggit—bless, she'd never had a boyfriend! (or, in her words, 'suitor'). Bertie Williams once went bankrupt and Norman had spent time in jail for dangerous driving. In the background, I spotted Gaynor rubbing her hands together, clearly pleased with these confessions. As people dispersed, to flick through the ration books or go upstairs to inspect their old bedroom, Edward headed out of the patio doors. Dennis Smith made a beeline for him. Perhaps he was going to badmouth me. Shame, cos I could have done with some time alone with Edward myself, to try and apologise for giving 'Gemma' the wrong impression about him and Henrietta.

I left the table and followed them outside. They disappeared around the left hand corner of the building. Fanning my face as if I needed fresh air, I hovered by the kitchen's back door. The two men's voices wafted around from the side. It seemed like Dennis had managed to catch up with him.

'Apologies, Lord Edward,' I heard Dennis say. 'I hope you didn't think I was being disrespectful to your cousin earlier. It's just…'

'What?' said Edward's voice.

I leant back against the stone wall and something—a spray of ivy—tickled my ear.

'How well do you really know her?'

My stomach twisted. Here went the roller coaster again.

'I beg your pardon?' said Edward in stilted tones.

'Forgive me if I am speaking out of line, old chap, but I've watched every cookery lesson on the show so far. As someone who cares about what happens to this place, I have to speak my mind. If the future of Applebridge Hall lies on that young woman's shoulders then there is no hope. As an award-winning professional chef, as someone who's taught the art of food preparation and cooking, I can categorically tell you that she has hardly ever set foot in a kitchen.'

LORD EDWARD'S E-DIARY

Saturday 8th September

'Comments'

11.50p.m. Blog-readers, you are in for a treat when watching footage of our reunion lunch. I shan't spoil it too much for you, only to say that our guests were real characters. They talked openly about the ups and downs of their past—which is odd, considering they were brought up to keep schtum, due to the mantra 'Careless Talk Costs Lives'. In fact, Father has only just retired for the evening, having talked non-stop about how today has made an important part of Applebridge's history come alive.

Other than that, the Second World War food was more than passable. Plus a controversial uninvited guest turned up. Controversial due to the past and, it would seem, his, erm, thoughts on the present. Hmm…

Now, I bid you all a jolly goodnight. Thank you once again for the support. Whatever happens from here on, I promise to continue with this blog, right until the end—one week from today.

Oh, and *Knityourownmansion*, I'm pleased you're excited at the idea of setting up your own business. Of course I'll write a review about the mohair pipe if you create a website.

CHAPTER 24

Monday mornings truly were the crappiest time of the week—especially when I had to give a cookery lesson, on camera, in front of Edward's suspicious eyes. Thanks to Dennis Smith, he probably doubted I could even boil an egg. Before trying to get to sleep I'd visited his blog, which hadn't given much away.

I straightened my black skirt and smoothed down my crisp white blouse. It was the waitress look—smart and efficient, to give the impression that I was a professional caterer. I yawned, fuelled mostly by my increasing desire to win this show for the Croxleys and... My heart beat out a sexier rhythm as I thought about Edward.

I shook myself and focused, for a moment, on Charlie Chingo, who stood like an obedient child while Roxy, as usual, powdered his nose. Gaynor chatted to Edward, who just gave her cursory grunts and nods. My cookery students, young mums from the village, explored their work-stations and examined today's ingredients.

Grateful for a moment to myself, I took a deep breath. The theme for today was Traditional British Fare. I'd shared Dennis Smith's overheard thoughts with Lady C and Kathleen, so yesterday they'd spent hours coaching me while I prepared steak and kidney pie and sherry trifle—again and again and again. The shortcrust pastry wasn't as difficult as

I'd imagined, and the pies were teeny-tiny, like the fancy grub served up on *MasterChef*. Handling raw kidneys was the biggest challenge—*ick*—and made me realize I'd be totally useless if there ever was a zombie apocalypse.

At least the trifle was fun and I eventually mastered getting sponges to rise—sort of—and custard to thicken without lumps. I'd never realized how rewarding it was to put a completed dish that tasted good on the table.

Seeing as today's pupils were all women, and alcohol had gone down very well at the last class, first off was girlie cocktail-making so that we could drink our way through the session. The booze of choice? *The English Rose*, a classic mixed drink (apparently), using apricot brandy, vermouth and grenadine. This ladylike tipple was topped with a shoe-shiny maraschino cherry.

Hopefully, I waved at Edward. Talking of zombies, expressionless, he stared back and my heart squeezed tight. In vain, I'd tried to apologise several times about the engagement misunderstanding, but each time he cut me off. He'd still been down in the dumps last night, when we'd all watched the Sunday episode of *Million Dollar Mansion* in the Parlour and cheered our success.

The general opinion was that the Second World War reunion was much better than Marwick Castle's celebrity orgy. Even cool young fans on Facebook got involved and posted war stories their grandparents had told them. They also loved the tribute to *Ghost*'s pottery wheel scene and without my help (or, that is, my Facebook persona Eleanor Goodwin) had set up another vote. Plus, luckily, the jury was still out as to whether it was really Miss Abigail Croxley taking part in these movie re-enactments. One of the 'beastly tabloids'—Lady C's words, not mine; I loved the smaller papers cos you could just look at the pics—

was running a poll and, at the latest count, thirty-nine per cent of viewers thought it really was Abbey cleaning the fountain with Nick.

On the downside, their suggestions for the next one were…eek! Mega racy:

The sexy food feeding scene by the fridge in *Nine and a Half Weeks*.

The naughty interrogation scene from *Basic Instinct* where Sharon Stone uncrosses her knickerless legs.

Numerous scenes from vampire movie series *Twilight*, like where Robert Pattinson breaks the bed or Taylor Lautner strips to the waist.

If it was sexing-up Roxy wanted, that's certainly what she was going to get.

Still not waving back—in fact, arms folded—Edward leant back against the kitchen wall, unaware that the young mums were ogling him. Last night, he'd barely blinked while watching the footage of Nick and, ahem, another person stroking the fountain. Thankfully, Lady C missed that scene as she'd been talking animatedly to Kathleen and the Earl about the vulgarity of the Baron's party. Even I had to agree (along with a surprisingly large number of people on Facebook and Twitter) that Dodgy Dirk the rock star wasn't all that hot. More than once he'd thrown up down the well, peed against the Grizzly Bear and come out of the Baron's bathroom with a mysterious white powder clinging to his moustache.

Online, people were getting bored with the Castle's flashes of boobs and bums. One Facebook comment got a lot of 'likes'—it said stag and hen nights were 'only fun to watch if you were also pissed'.

'Ten minutes to go,' said Roxy, who'd sidled up to me. She opened her mouth and then closed it again. She cleared her throat. 'Abbey, can I just say something?'

Perhaps Edward had mentioned his doubts.

'I think you are fucking fantastic,' she muttered in her usual quick voice.

My eyes widened.

'Excuse my language.' She giggled. 'I never thought Applebridge Hall stood a chance, but the evacuees' reunion was a piece of genius and, as for you and Nick…'

Aw, I loved Roxy, yet, despite feeling all warm and fuzzy inside, I managed to take on an innocent air. 'I beg your pardon?'

'Well, whatever…' said Roxy. 'All I wanted to say was: you Go, Girl. Miss Abigail Croxley rocks.'

'Thank you…' I said. 'I just hope it all…that my presence here pays off.'

She grinned. 'Apparently, the Baron of Marwick was spitting last night after the show aired, and said something about taking his game "up to the next level" to outdo Lieutenant Robert Mayhew's engagement party on Wednesday night. He better come up with something good, because that's basically his last chance. After Thursday night's broadcast, when voting lines open, all that's left is the live final on Saturday.' Roxy stopped to breathe for a moment. 'He won't have much time to change people's opinions by then. So, bravo! You've really managed to turn things around.'

I fiddled with the waistband of my skirt. 'The engagement party idea was nothing to do with me.'

'Yes, but, thanks to you, viewers have a vested interest now in watching the Applebridge Hall footage,' she said at her usual top speed. 'They care a lot more since your, um, high-jinks—intended or not. You're more…human, rather than some old-fashioned figure who could have stepped out of a Jane Austen book. And, as for the moving stories about

the Second World War and old Lord Croxley…' She shook
her head. 'I've just seen him walking towards the pond
with your aunt. Your uncle's really come out of himself.
For the first time, at that reunion, we saw some emotion
from him. At last people can relate to him in some way.'

I nodded. He *had* become a touch more laid-back.

'Then there's been numerous comments online,'
continued Roxy. 'Even one of the broadsheets mentioned
his little speech. How he made no bones about not really
being into the show until this reunion. How he felt
everyone who'd ever lived in the house deserved to have
their tale heard. Your family may be uptight and stuffy
and hopelessly straight, Abbey, but…' she shrugged '…
you've got principles. Whilst the Baron is open about his
motives, there's somehow something more honest about
the Croxleys, and that counts for a lot as far as the British
Public are concerned. It's a certain sincerity—like the
way family friends on the show are genuine. Most of the
Baron's famous guests have known him for a month or two
at the most.'

Honest? I almost laughed out loud. What if Roxy and
the British Public found out the truth about me?

'Positions, darlings,' called Gaynor.

Roxy grinned and slipped a stick of chewing gum into
her mouth.

Charlie Chingo came over to me, on the way winking
at the three young mums. He spoke to me but I couldn't
remember, afterwards, what he said. Then, somehow, I
demonstrated the cocktail. Somehow my pastry didn't
crumble and my trifle actually set. Afterwards, the cookery
session seemed like nothing but a blur. Kneading, frying,
whisking, beating… All I could think of, instead, was how
increasingly important it was that my real identity stayed

secret. Often, now, I'd find my stomach scrunched or hands sweaty… It reminded me of those tense weeks doing GCSEs.

Edward stayed right until the end and then shot off before we could chat. I did my wrapping-up interview with Charlie. After congratulating the young mums, I charged out of the house, perspiration dripping from my forehead.

I needed air, which could smell of the Earl's roses or Jean's fertilizer—who cared, as long as it filled my lungs and slowed my heart and took away the sense of panic I'd felt ever since Roxy spelt out how important I was to the Croxleys winning this show?

I headed for the bench by the pond and sat down, gazing at a multi-coloured bird with a long black tail. Lady C would have known its name.

'Cousin?' Edward emerged from the other bank, behind the bulrushes. 'Nick said you headed this way.' He sat down next to me.

'Did you, um, enjoy the show?' I asked.

'Yes. It was… interesting.'

Nausea rose up at the back of my throat and I held my head in my hands. 'Go on, admit it. After everything Dennis Smith said, you doubt me and my qualifications.'

'Everything he said?'

I looked up. 'Um…I mean at the dining table… It was obvious he thought I'd never trained as a chef.'

Edward snorted. 'You should have heard what he said later on—he tried to convince me you were useless so that I would employ his granddaughter instead.'

'Really?' I hadn't stayed to hear that bit.

Edward rubbed the back of his neck. 'Apparently, she has run his South of France restaurant for five years. She isn't married, has no ties and wants a new challenge outside of the family enterprise. According to Dennis, she'd be perfect to mould the Applebridge Food Academy into a modern, thriving business.' He shrugged. 'I watched your capable performance this morning so that if he pesters me again I'll be able to knock back any of his ridiculous criticisms.'

'Oh… How very loyal. It's appreciated.'

He stood up. 'That's what family is for, Abbey. You've stood by us in these difficult times. It's the least I can do. Oh, yes, Nick...' His nose wrinkled. 'Apparently, you asked to see him earlier, some query about the vegetable garden…'

Did I?

'He asked me to tell you he's there at the moment if you've still got things to discuss.'

'Oh…thanks.' Ah, nice excuse, Nick. We did need to talk about our next strategy. 'Are you returning to the house? Let me walk with you.'

It was a quiet stroll back and I fought the urge to hold his hand. There was no point apologizing again about the engagement mix-up, but now I felt even worse, seeing as he'd stuck up for me. Edward had closed himself off again and had a detached look on his face. He merely grunted when I said goodbye and headed around the back. Jean was nowhere to be seen. Nick passed me a freshly picked strawberry.

'We'd better get practising, Miss,' he said and grinned. 'Guess which scene our Facebook fans have voted for.'

'Not the fridge one from *Nine and A Half Weeks?*'

'Of course, if you don't think it's appropriate…'

My heart sank. 'Fine. This is the final week. One must pull out all of the stops. That's if you are okay with doing it?'

He ran a hand through his thick hair and I caught a whiff of cologne. 'Yeah, of course.'

'Although we must make every effort to keep it classy— we don't want our footage to be as tacky as the Baron's.'

Nick nodded. 'So, how did this morning's cookery class go?'

'I'm reasonably pleased.'

'I couldn't help overhearing what that Dennis Smith said in the dining room, when I was serving him wine,' said Nick and leant on the hoe. 'I'm surprised your uncle didn't throw him out there and then. So you studied catering in Surrey, after your finishing school in Bern? That must have been a bit of a come-down.'

I smiled. 'Not really. Surrey's, um, a delightful part of the country.'

Nick stared at me for a moment, before brushing down his trousers. 'Right, so… You and me and sticky fruit… When do you think we can access the kitchen fridge, Miss, with cameras hanging around but no Kathleen?'

'Good question,' I mumbled. 'On Wednesday the kitchen will be busy all day, due to preparations for the engagement party, so we'll have to find time tomorrow—although Kathleen will still be preparing food in advance…' For one second I wondered whether to tell Kathleen of this latest bonkers plan, but no—safety in numbers. She might tell Lady C, who definitely wouldn't approve.

'Unless we get up extra early,' said Nick. 'I could give a nudge and a wink to the cameraman that you—Miss Croxley—wanted to see me in the kitchen.'

'I'm not sure anyone from the crew will be keen on an early start.'

'But you must realize,' he said softly, 'that they're all aware of the excitement on Facebook. Just one hint from me that I'm meeting a woman secretly is all it will take for a discreetly positioned lens to be waiting.'

I nodded. Perhaps it might be better, though, if I fed Nick. Then, if people found out that the mysterious woman was Abbey, at least they wouldn't be left with a totally undignified image of her mouth stuffed with fruit.

'How about I feed you, unlike in the film, where Mickey Rourke feeds Kim Basinger?'

'Yeah—I don't reckon it matters too much, either way. I really admire you, Miss,' he said and picked up his shovel. 'Not many, um, ladies, would be prepared to put their reputation on the line.' He glanced at me sideways. 'You must really feel a strong connection to Applebridge Hall.'

Aarghh! More compliments! My conscience couldn't take it. 'See you tomorrow then, Nick, in the kitchen, about seven a.m.,' I said weakly. 'Perhaps I'll keep my hooded dressing gown on, so that there's no obvious clues to say that it's me.'

My mood didn't improve all afternoon, whilst discussing the coming party with Kathleen and Lady C. Wednesday's cookery class would involve making canapés for the evening do and Kathleen had insisted she would make the cake tomorrow and put together some fancy fruit bowls (the contents of which would come in handy for the *Nine and a Half Weeks* plan). Apparently, Henrietta insisted on bringing in outside caterers for the buffet, as she knew Applebridge Hall's staff would have their work cut out, just cleaning the place and getting it ready to receive lots of important guests.

At least chatting with my supposed aunt and the cook I could be my real non-aristocratic self, which only increased the urge to rush to my room after dinner and dress as Gemma. I stripped off my Abbey clothes—along with all the lies. Phew. That was better—although, having dressed in my own clothes, put on my make-up and sprayed my red hair, I stared at the chicken fillets. Was I really going to spend the rest of my adult life padding out my bra? Out of habit, I put my hand up my top and slipped them into position.

It was dark outside and rain threatened, but I didn't care. I needed a break from the mansion, otherwise my head would explode. Slowly, I crept downstairs. The Earl and Lady C were laughing together in the Parlour, whereas— less communicative than ever after dinner—Edward was nowhere to be seen and probably in the library.

Once outside, I headed for the back of the building. In spite of my high shoes, I jogged up the hill, the night breeze tickling my cheeks. Bliss—what freedom!

Eventually I collapsed onto the grass near the cemetery and gazed down at the silhouette of Applebridge Hall. I couldn't make out the ivy and lichen-covered walls now, but moonlight illuminated the triangular gables and mini ornamental totem pole bits sticking out of the top. By the looks of it, I'd left my bedroom light on and I also spotted an Edward-like shadow on the ground floor pass by the inside of the library window.

Aarghh! What was that? Footsteps came from behind. Someone grabbed my arm.

'Trespassing, are we?'

I pulled away, stood up and turned around. Phew. For a moment I'd thought it was Mr Thompson with his gun.

'Um, hi…' I said, relieved, but remembering, just in time, to pretend I hadn't a clue who Nick was. 'Soz. I'm, um, a mega fan of the show and didn't think anyone would mind if I took a sneaky look around the estate.'

Nick smirked and looked me up and down, his eyes resting on my chest. At least he was less interested in my face—the only real clue that I was 'Abbey'.

'What's it worth, me not reporting you?' he said with a leer.

Huh? This wasn't the polite Nick I knew, who was helping out Miss Croxley. I folded my arms.

'Look, I'll go now. No harm done,' I said, still baffled. What was up with him?

'Really? How am I to know you haven't vandalized, say, the pond?' He winked. 'Keep me company for a while. You look like a girl who likes to have fun. In fact, yeah, nice skirt,' he added.

Suddenly it felt very short. Oh my God—it looked like I wasn't the only one putting on an act in Applebridge Hall. Clearly, away from the aristocratic life, Nick was an absolute jerk. A wave of anger cascaded through my chest. Just because my clothes were less conservative, he thought he could treat me with less respect?

I hurried away down the hill. He followed and eventually cornered me by the pond edge.

'Come on,' he said and stepped closer. 'Let's enjoy ourselves. I could tell you anything you want about stuck-up Edward or bonkers Mr Thompson, who's mental, always worrying about hooligans… I was just checking the forest for him. You'd be in a lot of trouble if I handed you over. He's got a gun and no sense of humour.' Nick slipped a hand around my waist, pulled me close and then, urgh— patted me on the bum.

'Hands off!' I said, cheeks burning as I pushed him away. My mouth went dry. Up until now, when I was dressed as Abbey, Nick had seemed like a mega nice guy. 'What kind of a girl do you take me for?'

'I think that's obvious.' He sniggered and stepped forward again.

I looked around in the dark. Suddenly the estate seemed very secluded.

'No need to play hard to get,' he scoffed.

'Shut up!' muttered a voice. Edward appeared out of the darkness.

'My Lord…I found this young woman trespassing,' said Nick. 'I was, uh, just escorting her off the premises.'

'Get out of my sight,' said Edward to him and scowled. 'Good thing I was taking an evening stroll, because I won't have anyone on this estate treated with disrespect, whether they are invited or not.'

'But—'

'Now!' snapped Edward. 'Do as you're told, man, if you want to keep your job.'

Nick's top lip curled, along with his fist. He glared at me before sauntering back to the house.

'Thanks,' I said, heart still thumping, and straightened my skirt, 'but I was managing just fine.'

'What are you doing here?' he said. 'Visiting Abbey again?'

Our eyes met. 'Edward…I was a right idiot the other night.' Hurrah! At last, an opportunity for *Gemma* to say sorry.

'What's done is done.' Edward shrugged. 'You made it quite clear what sort of chap you think I am. Just when I thought my…my cousin understood who I was.' He turned and headed back to the house.

'Look, don't go!' With all my strength, I dragged him back to the bench. We sat down.

'Gemma! For God's sake. We've said all that needs to be said.'

'No, we haven't. Look—please, forgive me. Abbey just made a mistake and I should have had more faith. But these things happen—we're only human.'

He sat down. 'I suppose I can see how my cousin might have misconstrued the situation…but it didn't mean you had to believe her with such haste.'

'Look at me, Edward! I'm not your average aristocratic girl. Not the sort of woman someone in your position would take seriously.'

He shook his head.

'Don't pretend it doesn't matter! Abbey's dad goes mad if she dates anyone without an amazin' title or Eton education.'

'He doesn't speak for everyone who lives in a stately home,' said Edward. 'You might be surprised what we're really like—if you got to know us better.'

'Yeah, right… So you think your dad would be chuffed if you brought me home?'

'As long as you were honest and upstanding… As long as you had goals in life and were your own person.'

My heart sank—there was that word, 'honest', again.

Edward took my hand and pulled me nearer to him. 'Grandy—my mother's mother—was a "commoner".' His mouth twitched. 'Not that I've ever liked that word. She grew up in a two-up two-down but married into nobility and never a more intelligent, compassionate woman could you meet. There were no seats left empty at her funeral. So Mother never thought titles were the be-all and end-all. One thing Father always says he loved about her was that she kept him straight, and had a mean left punch if he ever showed signs of being a snob.' He smiled. 'She kept me straight too and regularly told me I was as stubborn as a mule.'

I put my hand against his cheek. 'You're freezing.'

'Well, I am…what was it you called me…a *cold fish*?'

I slipped my arms around his neck. 'Sorry about that. Truth is, you're really, really *hot*.'

He leant forward and our lips touched. Candy popped in my stomach. His arms wrapped around my back—and stayed there, tight and secure, for what seemed like ever. There was no fumbling for my bra—no clumsy attempts to get me in a horizontal position. Instead, he murmured mega poetic stuff, like how my skin was catkin-soft.

'I just felt a spot of rain,' he said gently. 'Let's get inside before it pours.'

'Once…once this whole thing is finished, I won't have an excuse to visit any more…'

He grabbed my hands. 'Of course you will—me! Look, don't go home yet, Gemma. Stay for the rest of the week—I'm sure Abbey would appreciate your support. I don't need to let on that I know you're around, if that's what she still wants. And, as for after the weekend… Surely you don't think I'm going to let you slip through my fingers once again?' Passionately he kissed me once more, on the lips. 'Dear, sweet, straightforward Gemma…' he finally mumbled. 'Where have you been my whole life?'

Wow.

'We'll sort something out. Meet me here, in secret every night, if Abbey still doesn't want your presence to go public—although I'd love to introduce you to Henrietta and Robert.'

'No. Abbey, um, wouldn't want that yet. You know, that old Croxley pride—she'd want people to think she was fine managing on her own, without me.'

'Typical Croxley, indeed.' He grinned. 'It takes a lot for us to admit we need help. How about I take you out to dinner tomorrow evening, then—after I've watched the show with the family? We could grab a late supper somewhere. Take a break from the madness.'

'That sounds epic,' I said. 'I can hide in Abbey's room all day. But just one thing, before we go in,' I said and felt a happy adrenaline rush.

'Yes, Gemma?' he said softly.

With a giggle, I jumped up. 'Let's see who's best at dodging drops of rain. Last one to the woods is a wuss!'

Edward stood up. 'But I'm a mature, responsible thirty-two year old Lord. What on earth makes you think I'd want to play that game?'

'Oh… I…'

'Gotcha!' he said and, with a wink, suddenly charged up the hillside, me following with hoots of laughter, determined to catch up.

LORD EDWARD'S E-DIARY

Monday 10th September

11.30p.m. Welcome to the final week of *Million Dollar Mansion*. After the tremendous success of the evacuee reunion, our chances of winning continue to improve. Fans of the show are now looking forward to Lieutenant Mayhew's engagement party on Wednesday. I have spent a large proportion of today putting together a speech in honour of Henrietta and Robert, my two very good chums.

In fact, recent events have made me realize how very important friends are. Not only those in the real world, who stand by you, but also supportive people in the virtual world.

Drunkwriter and *Cupcakesrock*, I didn't know you lived near each other. How interesting that today you met up for lunch. Jolly glad you both took sensible precautions and met up in public. As we all know, the Internet does have a dark side we should all be aware of. But, on a cheerier note, *Cupcakesrock*, it sounds like you have been a good friend to *Drunkwriter*, offering supportive emails since you first met up on this blog. *Drunkwriter*, thanks to her, you feel your heartbreak is over? Are you both hinting that there is romance in the air?

Here is a poser question for all of you, seeing as we have moved onto the subject of, erm, sentimental stuff... Which of the following romantic things has a Croxley done?

I know—it's hard to believe that I'm talking about such gubbins and perhaps I'll regret this post in the morning. But a wave of emotion came over me this evening, and appears to have no plans to leave. Mother always said this day would come, when I met...Couldn't stop thinking of... Longed to spend every moment with... Erm... Excuse me—I digress.

Let's return immediately to that question... Has a Croxley ever:

Erm, discarded his reserve for a night-time swim in the pond?

Lost his life, fighting for the woman of his dreams?

Abandoned her family at Applebridge Hall to be with her soulmate?

(Admittedly the first option does sound rather weak, in comparison.)

CHAPTER 25

Nick, you f***ing a*****le, smile at me once more and you're dead.

Thoughts are mega, aren't they? You can get a load off your chest and use words you may not want to blurt out. Although, for rude words, my mind now often added in asterisks. Through the dim light of dawn, I smiled back at the gardener before giving a wide yawn. It was Tuesday morning and, as agreed, we'd snuck into the kitchen at seven a.m. I was still gobsmacked at the discovery of cheeky Nick's true character.

He'd tipped off the cameraman so, innocently, I ignored the shuffle of footsteps just outside the half-open window. I gritted my teeth, every ounce of me itching to abandon my manners and punch Nick's smug jaw after his insulting behaviour last night. To hide my face, I adjusted the hood of my dressing gown. Plus, without harsh lighting, it wouldn't be obvious that Nick was with Miss Croxley—or so I hoped. Calling on all my acting skills, I gave Nick a grin. Although, truth be told, it wasn't that hard as my heart still danced because of Edward...me...and our bonkers relationship being on again.

'Remember the film?' Nick asked.

I nodded, having seen *Nine and a Half Weeks* at the insistence of Auntie Jan.

'Open the fridge,' I said. 'The light from that will illuminate our actions just enough.'

'Certainly, Miss.'

As the fridge door opened, we both crouched down in front of it. *Miss*, indeed. He hadn't been quite so courteous last night. As he'd find out, it was a *Mis*take messing with me.

'Do you think the cameraman is ready?' I asked.

Nick bobbed up. 'Yep—but he can't see us on the floor—the window is too high. We'll have to do it standing up.'

I got to my feet. Now, which foods to choose first…? We hadn't got mics on and there was obviously no boom near enough, so it didn't matter too much what we said.

'How about pineapple?' I said. 'Now, remember, even if it's something you don't normally enjoy, you must give the impression that this food is…'

'A real turn-on?' he said. 'If you'll excuse the crude phrase.'

I nodded and reached for a bowl. With my fingers, I took out a chunk of pineapple. Nick opened his mouth and licked his lips. I dropped in the piece of fruit and bit my inside cheeks, so as not to smile. Nick closed his eyes as if in ecstasy, then opened them suddenly and moaned.

'Aarghh, this is—'

'You must act as if you love it,' I hissed, 'if we are to provide a real homage to the film.'

Slowly he chewed, oohing and ahhing, tears running down his cheeks.

'Here, try a strawberry instead, if pineapple isn't your favourite.' I dangled one in the air before lowering it into his mouth. He bit the fruit, leaving the green stalk in my hand. Seconds later, his eyes bulged.

Aw, shame…that I'd accidentally dipped those strawberries in chilli powder before he arrived. And, colour-wise, mustard had merged nicely into the pineapple.

'Oh, dear,' I said. 'Was that strawberry a tad unripe? How about some honey to sweeten it up? Mickey Rourke squeezed that into Kim Basinger's mouth.'

I lifted a bottle into the air. A stream of golden liquid dripped down, in between his lips.

'Goodness me. What a silly billy,' I said as he gagged. 'I picked up the cooking oil by mistake.'

Just like in the film, I poured some milk into a glass and fed it to him. Oops, clumsy me, I tilted the glass too far and it spilt all down his shirt.

'That's enough,' stuttered Nick and gagged. 'I think the cameraman has got all he needs.'

'Do you think it looked sensuous enough?' I asked airily.

Nick gagged again. 'Excuse me, Miss Croxley. I'm going to be sick.'

He charged out of the back door. Vomiting noises carried across the still morning air and, for a very short second, I felt a titchy bit of guilt—it didn't last long. I mopped the kitchen floor and threw out all evidence of the contaminated fruit. Revenge sure was sweet—shame for Nick that the fruit wasn't. I didn't see him for the rest of the day. In fact, according to a cross Mr Thompson, he'd gone AWOL. Jean muttered something about the gardening assistant ringing in sick. Perhaps he would learn a lesson and treat women better in future.

I spent the afternoon with Lady C and Kathleen, practising the canapés I would make in Wednesday's cookery lesson, for the evening do. How posh is this: sun-dried tomato bruschetta, herby cheese puffs and garlic mushroom cups—la-di-da! Three local high school kids, in their last year of studying Food Tech GCSE, were going to star in tomorrow's lesson. Apart from being on the telly, their reward was to serve food at the party and meet Lieutenant Robert Mayhew. Getting school kids involved was my idea, to attract even younger viewers and, hopefully, spread our vote.

As for Edward and Lord Croxley, they spent the afternoon being interviewed by Charlie Chingo. Some of it would be edited into the remaining programmes as snappy soundbites. You know, the kind of *Big Brother* diary room questions like: 'Why should viewers vote for you?' and: 'What would it mean to win the show?' After such a full-on day, it was great to all meet up in the Parlour that evening and chill.

Nick was still missing, which now made me want to bite my thumbnail. What if I'd poisoned him badly? I shook myself. No. It was just chilli powder and mustard. There must have been another reason to explain his disappearance. Trying to relax, I listened to the others' chat and thought about my meal out, later on, with Edward.

'Aren't goldfinches incredibly beautiful?' said Lady C to the Earl as they pored over a birdwatching book.

'The local florist gave me a really good deal on flowers to supplement what I can pick off the estate,' said Jean to Mr Thompson. 'They've even lent me some vases for all the tables tomorrow night.'

'Well done,' he replied gruffly. 'Miss Hamilton-Brown has also approved the jazz band I told her about, so I've booked them.'

'Och, Miss Hamilton-Brown and her mother are so efficient,' said Kathleen. 'They easily found caterers who could help us out at such late notice and have already secured fifty acceptances from the guests they invited. That Lieutenant Mayhew is a popular lad.'

Edward switched on the telly, before pouring out cups of tea. How I longed to give him a hug. Determined to change and make 'Gemma' look amazin', I left before the end of the programme, right after the footage of that morning's fruit frenzy with Nick, which must have been edited mega fast to have been ready for tonight's show. As it turned out, no one in the room paid much attention. The footage was dim and everyone was too excited about the upcoming engagement party to give it too much attention. Although Edward muttered something about Nick taking advantage, bringing girlfriends into the kitchen for an extravagant secret breakfast, and determined to deduct the cost of fruit from his wages. Kathleen paid the most attention and muttered that if raiding her fridge had made Nick ill then he'd got all he deserved.

Still wondering what pineapple and mustard tasted like, I crept out of the house about forty minutes later. In my skin-tight jeans, high shoes and low-cut top, I headed to the bottom of the drive, ignoring the autumn chill. Vanity was far more important than comfort—although I'd not put in the chicken fillets.

I tried to remember when I'd first decided my chest needed a boost. Snarky comments from my brothers probably first knocked my confidence. But then, over the years, none of their girlfriends had looked like Katie Price. As for my fake tan, I was beginning to understand what Lady C meant when she said less was more—with minimum foundation, I was less Tango and more healthy glow.

'Gemma?' Edward strolled out from the orchards. A happy feeling fizzed up and down my insides as I ran up to him and slipped my arms around his neck. For what seemed like forever, we kissed. Eventually he pulled away and led me by the hand.

'The Range Rover is parked at the end of the drive. I've booked a table at the Amethyst Aubergine, a new French restaurant about half an hour away.'

'Oh…'

He stopped for a moment. 'Is that okay? I mean, fussy food isn't really my favourite, but I wanted to treat you—and me. Since Mother died, I've hardly eaten out, our finances being what they are. In any case, Father isn't a fan of what he calls fancy toy food…' Edward grinned '…you know, perfectly piled up high, just waiting to be toppled over like a tower of building blocks.'

After a week without my usual pizzas and burgers, the last thing I wanted was to eat in a place where I'd have to worry which cutlery to use. Aarghh! Just when I wanted a break from all that stuff.

'That's mega thoughtful of you, Edward. I really appreciate it…'

'But?'

I held up my hands. 'You know what I'd really like? A Doner kebab and a Coke.'

'Really?'

'At least I'm a cheap date,' I said with a chuckle.

He grinned again as we walked on. 'Guess we'll have to eat in the car then, if it's takeaway.'

I squeezed his hand. 'I'm sure you can find a scenic view. Turn on the radio, dim the lights… It could be the perfect private restaurant.'

'So tell me—what exactly is in a kebab?'

My mouth fell open. 'You've never had one?'

He shook his head.

'What about chicken nuggets?'

'Aren't they for kids?' he said.

'Please tell me you've been to McDonald's.'

'Never,' he said and opened the passenger door for me. I was still shaking my head when he got into the driver's seat and closed the door.

'What a deprived childhood you've had,' I said. 'All these years and you've never felt a Whopper between your lips or sucked on a thick shake. Never felt the excitement of opening a toy in a Happy Meal.' I shook my head. 'We'd better put that right.'

'Where to, then?' he said.

'Let's just drive and see what takes our fancy. Indian takeaway? How about fish 'n' chips eaten out of newspaper?'

'Ah, now, that I've done,' he said and turned on the ignition. 'Otherwise, I couldn't look any Englishman in the eye.' He switched on the radio. Classical violin music cut through the air. 'Do feel free to retune the music station,' he said as I felt a glassy expression fix itself onto my face.

I turned the dial. Yay! It was a week and a half since I'd been able to sing along to a chart-topping song. 'I love Jessie J.'

'Jessie James? The cowboy?'

'No, she's a pop singer—you know, like Madonna.'

'What, the Virgin Mary?'

I gasped. 'Are you for real?'

He chuckled. 'No, I at least know who Madonna is. But I suspect it's going to be rather a challenge, teaching me about popular culture. I rarely watch television and only listen to symphonies and operas, the news and horticultural shows. Perhaps if I'd grown up with a sister—or brother— things might have been different.'

I glanced sideways at him. Edward clearly regretted being an only child.

And so our chat went on as we left Applebridge and drove along winding country roads to the nearby town. The nearest I'd come to Beethoven was watching a movie about a St Bernard dog. As for *Gardeners' World*, I wondered if *Hollyoaks* counted.

'There's BestBurger,' I said excitedly, and pointed to a shiny glass-fronted shop, done out in orange and beige. 'They do an awesome cheese burger with potato wedges on the side.'

'Why don't we eat in?' he said and parked the car in one of the designated bays behind the building. As we walked around to the front he took my hand. He pushed open the glass door and let me in first.

No more than a few steps in, a young woman in shorts with tights and a leather jacket stared hard at Edward and then blushed. 'You're that Lord Croxley's son off *Million Dollar Mansion*, ain't ya? I love you!' She ran up and gave him a big hug.

'Erm, no… You must be mistaken,' he said and rubbed his neck as he backed away.

She giggled and slapped him on the arm. 'No need to be shy, mate. Hey, Megan, come over here.'

Reluctantly, a pasty-faced girl in a jogging suit abandoned her burger and headed over. As she spied Edward, she stopped chewing and her eyes bulged. She hopped up and down. 'We love you, we do,' she squealed. '*Goss* magazine voted you most eligible bachelor of the month!'

'Prefer that Marwick Castle, meself,' said a man ahead of us in the queue. He wore a tracksuit and silver necklace. 'No offence, mate,' he said to Edward. 'But that Harry Gainsworth bloke and his dad, the Baron, know how to have a good laugh. Birds and booze in a gaff like that—I'd love me a bit of that.'

A smart young man with a badge saying 'Manager' behind the counter nodded.

'Yep, don't take it personal, like, sir, but a weekend at that castle would be the business. All those weapons and armoury…'

Yeah, made of plastic and bought off the Internet, I was dying to add.

'As for those parties and glamorous guests…' he continued.

'But they've got no class,' said the woman in shorts. 'And you don't get more glamorous than Lieutenant Robert Mayhew. I can't wait to see his engagement party on Thursday night's show.' Totally ignoring me, she leant forward to Edward. 'Got any inside gossip? If you want any hot girls to doll up the house, me and my friends are free tomorrow night.'

Edward smiled. 'That won't be necessary, but thank you for the kind offer.'

'Come on,' I hissed as the cashier in the next queue along became available, and dragged him over to the counter.

'Oh my God!' the girl in the beige and orange uniform gasped. 'You're Edward Wotsit from Applebridge! It's a right honour to have you in here, My Lord.' She curtsied, as if he was the heir to the throne. 'My mum thinks your show is the biz and Gran hasn't stopped talking about that reunion dinner. Took her right back, it did, to the time she was evacuated.'

Edward smiled sheepishly around the room.

'This is amazin',' I mumbled, looking around at all the star-struck girls.

'It hadn't sunk in just how popular the programme is, until now,' he said. 'Since we started filming the final I've been so busy I've only gone out to the village, and everyone already knows me there.'

'Here,' said the Megan girl, burger forgotten. She unzipped her jogging suit top to reveal a generous cleavage. She thrust a pen in his hand. 'Please… Sign your name here. I'll get it tattooed on tomorrow.'

'I couldn't possibly,' he said, cheeks purple.

Her mouth drooped.

'I wouldn't want a charming young lady like you to do anything you might later regret,' he said and smiled warmly. 'Although I'd be more than happy to sign, erm, let's see, what about a napkin?' He pulled one out of the dispenser on the counter, put it down on the flat surface and started to write. He handed it to her a minute later, with the pen. She read it out loud.

'"To delightful Megan, with kind regards from Lord Edward".' Eyes watering, she clasped it to her chest.

'Two cheeseburgers with potato wedges, two Cokes and toffee ice cream swirls, please,' I muttered to the transfixed cashier.

While she put together our order, Edward shuffled his feet as everyone in the restaurant stared. I handed over the money.

'Let me,' said Edward and took out his wallet.

I shook my head. 'My treat. Come on, let's eat in the car.'

He grabbed the brown paper bag and, with a small bow to everyone, Edward followed me outside. As soon as we reached the car, I burst out laughing. Edward shook his head as he opened the passenger door for me and then got in the other side.

'Blood and sand!' I said as we shut the doors and put on our safety belts. 'Talk about celebrity status.'

'Jolly hard work it would be, living under the scrutiny of everyone you met.' Edward drove onto the main road and waved to Megan and her friend, who'd just left the restaurant.

'I don't think you'd find it hard,' I said softly, 'because you are such a gent. You could have easily ignored those people or asked to be left alone, but you were great. That Megan girl looked made up.'

Edward shrugged. 'Despite the responsibilities of being a Croxley, I can't complain, in view of the wider scheme of things. Other people don't have such fortunate lives; if anything I can do gives them pleasure, so be it.'

We left the town and headed along a dirt track towards the top of a big hill. There were no street lamps and when we reached the top there was just a small dusty area for a couple of cars to park. Edward stopped the Range Rover.

'Wow. Mega view,' I said as we looked down onto the twinkling lights of the town. I passed him his burger, wedges and Coke. He gazed at his meal, brow furrowed.

'Allow me,' I said and opened up his burger box. I tipped the wedges into the empty lid.

'Knives and forks?' he said.

I caught his eye and chuckled. 'I'll teach you the etiquette.' Well, anything Lady C could do…! I picked up a wedge with my fingers, dipped it in some barbecue sauce and tossed it into my mouth.

Edward's eyes shone as he did the same. Then he took a big bite of burger and I passed him a napkin as cheese dripped onto his chin.

'Good?' I asked ten minutes later.

'Mmm.' He swallowed the last mouthful. 'It was, erm, mega.'

I punched his arm, cheeks hurting, as I'd smiled non-stop since getting in his car—in between yummy mouthfuls, of course.

'Seriously,' he said, 'this takeaway food tastes quite delicious—it lacks a little in texture, but the flavours give instant satisfaction.'

I passed him an ice cream and he prised off the lid.

'What would the Earl say if he could see you right now?'

'"Damn it, boy, what's all this nonsense?" probably. Father is quite particular about eating out. Solid British fare, that's what he likes. As a family, we've never even eaten Indian or Chinese food.'

'Dearie, me, what a lack of education,' I teased. 'At least you've had your first BestBurger.' I took his napkin and wiped some ice cream from around his lips. He caught my hand and pulled me close. Mmm... Nice kiss—hadn't realized I'd be having popping candy with my pud.

Having drained our Coke cups, we headed back to Applebridge Hall. An ABBA song came on the radio and, amazingly, Edward knew the words—apparently, his mum had been a huge fan. At the tops of our voices, we sang along, Edward glancing sideways at me from time to time with a big fat grin on his face.

As we turned into the estate, Edward turned off the radio. A few lights were on in the house and... I squinted through the moonlight. Was that Kathleen, pacing up and down by the fountain?

'Pull up here,' I muttered to Edward as we passed the orchards. 'I'll hide among the apple trees and make my way back in later on.

'Are you sure?' he said. 'You'll get cold.'

I nodded vigorously. Kathleen was heading towards us. I kissed him on the cheek and opened the door.

'Meet me by the pond after the engagement party tomorrow night,' he hissed. 'And Gemma?'

I nodded.

'Thanks—for tonight. For just letting me be me.'

But hadn't he been out of his comfort zone tonight? Sometimes Edward came out with the strangest things!

I gave the thumbs-up and dived into the orchards, just as Katheen reached the car. In the dark, I crouched behind some low branches and listened as Edward wound down his window. Okay, so it was bad manners to eavesdrop, but…urgh, for some reason, I had a bad feeling about Nick.

'Kathleen—is everything all right?' said Edward. 'It's not Father, is it…?'

'Och, no—sorry to worry you, My Lord. It's that Nick.'

Crap. Suddenly my palms felt all sweaty.

'That lad's been away all day, but nipped back this evening to pack up his bags, just after you left. Looking remarkably well recovered from his "illness"—in fact, kind of smug. He handed in his notice.'

'Good riddance. Never trusted the blighter,' said Edward, sounding just like his dad. 'His contract was only temporary anyway, for the show.'

'Aye, but he muttered something cryptic before he left—about us making sure we enjoyed the party because, sooner or later, our good fortune would disappear. And he laughed when he said it would be a shame if something happened to ruin Lieutenant Mayhew's celebrations. Before leaving, he even crept into the kitchen to steal some of my Highland fudge. Lady Constance was there with me, making hot chocolate, and she agreed—he had a reet menacing tone. He insisted we tell Miss Croxley that… What was it?

"Secrets always come out" and…' she shrugged '… that it was "a shame *Basic Instinct* wasn't chosen"—whatever that means.'

Holy fu…dge!

'Och, he's a odd one,' said Kathleen. 'Perhaps we should ring the agency you got him from—see if he's caused any trouble before.'

Edward agreed that was a good idea, and then persuaded the cook to jump in so that he could give her a lift the short way back up to the house.

As the car pulled away, I sank into the soil, that stressed-up, taking GCSEs feeling coming back again. Perhaps Nick had worked out that I'd messed with the fridge food. After seeing his true character…bile rose in my throat.

What if he'd made a deal today with some editor and had already done an interview, revealing Plan Sex-up? The tabloids might be full of it tomorrow. That would ruin the engagement party—and our popularity with the Facebook fans, who wouldn't appreciate discovering that Miss Croxley's fling with Nick was nothing but a cold-hearted, calculated scam to win their votes.

LORD EDWARD'S E-DIARY

Tuesday 11th September

11.55p.m. Apologies, another late evening posting—as the final week progresses, the hours become busier. It is strange to think that on this coming Saturday the winner of *Million Dollar Mansion* will be announced.

What an unforgettable experience this has been. I've discovered new friends—and foes. Today, Charlie Chingo asked me what I'd learnt about life from taking part in the competition. My reply? That one is never too old to be surprised by people, or to surprise oneself…

Now, to yesterday's poser question. Dear blog-readers, I confess I tricked you, as all three suggested answers hold some truth. Congratulations, *Blogger 569*—the first option is true and it, erm, *was* me. A cool night-time swim with someone… jolly special, might not seem revolutionary to everyone, but let's just say if my mother knew, she'd clap her hands that her 'uncompromising' son had finally, and um literally, for want of a better phrase, 'chilled out'.

Historybuff, you were also right to choose the second suggestion and well done, your research was spot on— the very first Earl of Croxley did lose his life fighting for the woman of his dreams. Whilst his relationship with his wife, Margaret, was considered quite happy, his personal journals revealed a secret affection for Elizabeth the First, who awarded him our estate in 1588. In the late 1590s he lost his life when she sent him to Ireland to fight against yet another uprising.

Lovehotnoble, I'm, erm, flattered, you can relate to the third answer and would abandon your family to be with me. A Miss Gracie Croxley did this in the eighteenth century. She ran off one night with a young engineer who believed he could make his fortune in the newly colonized India. Eventually he became a powerful railway magnate. Gracie never returned to Applebridge Hall, but regularly sent long letters to her mother, along with parcels of spices and silk.

Right, tomorrow will be an awfully busy day, and I may not post until the evening again. However, I promise to at least report back here on the engagement party, whilst it is ongoing, so as to give you loyal blog-readers some exclusive bits of news.

Now, on a culinary note, let me finish this evening's post by confessing I've acquired a passionate liking for cheeseburgers, potato wedges and toffee ice cream swirls. Apologies, Father, if this news gets back to you—I expect no approval. But I'm beginning to believe that, once in a while, it's important to let your hair down.

CHAPTER 26

Poo. (Okay, not the coolest word, but better than the unladylike alternative.)Today *it* was going to hit the fan. How did I know? The expression on Gaynor and Roxy's faces.

Right from the off, when I turned up in the kitchens early, to introduce myself to the three very nervous Food Tech GCSE students, it was obvious something was up. Roxy offered me the last of her favourite toffee bonbons and Gaynor clapped me on the back—normally she saved all physical contact for Edward. Both beamed brightly and now and again shook their heads. It was obvious, due to their girlish winks, that Nick had been in contact with them and fully explained our attempts to sex-up Applebridge.

I broke into a sweat, just thinking about who else he could have told that the Facebook excitement wasn't just all down to rumour. My stomach hurt, as if I'd eaten the chilli strawberries instead.

Somehow, I managed to get through the morning's cookery lesson—especially as Jean had been into town early and brought back the papers—they revealed nothing, yet, about my movie exploits. Then, after sandwiches in the Parlour with the Earl and Lady C, I concentrated on helping Henrietta set up in the Drake Diner.

What light relief! She did an awesome imitation of the Queen's voice and told me stories about knowing Edward when he was younger. Mr Thompson and Jean set up the flowers and chairs outside. Annabel worked closely with Henrietta, laying out cutlery to the exact millimetre.

Perhaps Mum and me would have gelled like that. I could have confided in her about this charade and reckon she'd have approved, even given me some tips and thought it a great laugh.

Fifty folded napkins later, that afternoon, the sun shone brightly as if the Indian summer was doing a quick encore.

'You've done a mega job, Kathleen,' I said. We were in the kitchen. She'd spent the afternoon with the students, making even more canapés for tonight. At her request, I passed her a 'wee dram of something strong', to give her a second wind.

'Where are the high school girls now?' I asked.

She took a sip. 'Och, they worked their socks off, so I sent them off to explore, as long as they come back, in their waitressing outfits, by six o'clock sharp.'

'Champagne cocktails to start, this evening?'

Kathleen nodded and looked at her watch. 'Guests will arrive from seven. That gives you two hours to get dressed. The caterers are already setting up. Henrietta and the Viscountess are changing in the guest rooms. The Viscount will arrive before long. Lieutenant Mayhew had a business meeting but promised his fiancée that he'd be here before their friends. The jazz band is already in the dining room, tuning up.'

'Wicked,' I said half-heartedly, and suddenly gave a big sigh.

'Everything okay, lassie?'

'Not really,' I muttered, dreading tomorrow's episode of *Million Dollar Mansion*, when Nick would no doubt reveal all. Today he was probably milking his fifteen minutes of fame, meeting all sorts of hacks and doing everything possible to earn dosh out of his time at Applebridge Hall.

'Och, I can't keep up with you young people,' she said, and smoothed down her curly grey-red hair. 'Take His Lordship, Edward—at the weekend he had the mood of a Loch Ness monster who'd finally been caught on film. Yet now he's strutting around like some caber-tossing champion. I just heard him whistling.' She sucked in her cheeks. 'You'd think it was him getting engaged and not the Lieutenant.'

Ooh, nice mental image—I could just imagine Edward in a kilt.

'Ignore me—just tired… I can hardly think straight.' I gave Kathleen a hug and, before she could tick me off for being a silly lassie, headed for my room. Yet, door closed, I threw myself onto the bed and fought the urge to slip into my Gemma clothes and do a runner. The thought of embarrassing the Croxleys had become torturous. I'd grown to love the sprawling ivy across Applebridge Hall's crumbling walls. The maze and orchards felt like old friends and I felt mega relaxed sitting quietly by the pond. The cosy Parlour reminded me of Dad's house and those portraits in the Long Gallery somehow brought out the best in me, I reckoned, like nothing had before.

An hour later, however, I was still in the building, washed, dressed as a lady. Making sure a few strands hung down in seductive ringlets, I'd pinned up my hair and put on an awesome dress lovely Lady C had bought me. It was bottle-green taffeta with a modest diamanté-edged slit up the side and cinched-in waist. Although still more *Desperate Dan* than *Desperate Housewives*, I'd never looked so slim. The sleeves were short and puffed up just enough to give my shoulders a mega good outline. Lady C also lent me a sparkly choker. Forget *Million Dollar*

Mansion—I felt like a trillion pounds. Hey, I finally owned an outfit that Abbey would want to borrow off me!

'Goodness me, you look quite charming, Abbey,' said Lady C as I walked into the Drake Diner. She and the Earl stood by the long buffet table, admiring the food the caterers had put out. They tapped their feet to the background jazz.

'Decent effort you've made, young lady,' said the Earl gruffly.

'James! You can do better than that,' said Lady C and pushed him gently on the shoulder.

'Yes, well—you're a jolly pretty girl.' He cleared his throat and leant out to pat my arm. 'I don't know what we'd have done without you, to be honest, Abigail. This last week or so, you've brightened up the show and… Applebridge Hall. It's been good for Edward to have some young Croxley blood around. Your father… He must have done something right, to have produced a girl like you. I imagine Dickie is very proud.'

Wow—he almost sounded fond of his brother. Lady C gazed at the floor, while I kissed the Earl on his bristly cheek. He muttered something about checking that Mr Thompson knew where to let the guests park. As the Earl left the room, the Hamilton-Brown women swept in.

'What a super dress,' I said to Henrietta, who wore a crimson one-sleeve floor-length gown and a ruby-red pendant.

'That's sweet of you, Abbey, thank you. Do allow me to return the compliment. Where did you buy that outfit? It's exquisite.'

'Um… how kind. My aunt bought it as a present.' My stomach gurgled as I ogled the food. Wow. 'That nosh is mega amazin',' I muttered.

Henrietta giggled.

'Do, um, excuse my turn of phrase,' I said and cleared my throat. 'Gemma, my flatmate, has more influence on me than I imagined. But seriously—I love your choice of dishes for the buffet.'

'Really? I am pleased. Robert and I thought we'd be traditional and stick to English fare.'

They'd certainly done that and my mouth watered as I studied the bacon and egg tartlets. There were bangers and mash vol-au-vents and mini Yorkshire puds filled with beef and roast spuds. As for the puddings...tiny trifles, Union Jack fruit pastries and mini scones oozing with cream and jam.

'Shh!' Henrietta winked at me and picked up two of the mini scones. She handed one to me and we both turned away from Lady C and the Viscountess while we chomped them down. Who would have thought the Viscount's daughter knew how to be unladylike?

'It's very good of you, Henrietta, to have your engagement party here,' I said in between mouthfuls. 'Robert's support is bound to pull in more voters for us.'

'We both have an enormous amount of respect for Edward and his father—as you clearly do.'

'Of course.'

'You've sacrificed your time to help out,' she said and eyed me closely. 'And I know things between your father and Lord Croxley haven't always...'

'... run smoothly,' I said.

She nodded. 'I'm so glad you are here, Abbey. I have the feeling you and I are going to be such good friends.' She beamed at me and I managed to smile back.

'Since your arrival,' she continued, 'Edward, he's less... contained. Less...'

'Uptight?'

She glanced sideways at me. 'Exactly. You've been a tonic. Clearly, you understand him well. Dear Abbey.' She slipped on arm around my waist and squeezed tight.

'Come along, Henrietta,' said Annabel. 'It's a quarter to seven. Roxy just told me Robert is upstairs changing and your father is helping James sort out the parking. Let us wait at the main entrance, in case some of the guests are early. Constance says some cameras are set up there, to film us greeting any arrivals.'

'Showtime!' I muttered to Henrietta.

Her eyes crinkled before she followed her mother out to the front entrance. My feet itched to dance, even though the music was what Dad would call 'old hat'. Yet it was kind of romantic and I could just picture me and Edward smooching under the stars… Deep sigh. I turned to look at the band, yet was instead met by… Wowsers—an amazin' sexy sight.

'Cousin. You look… delightful,' said Edward.

Blimey—that was quite a compliment from him. And forget popping candy, we were talking firecrackers, as I ogled him in his sharp black tux, pristine white shirt and tailored trousers. Forget Hollywood, Applebridge was home to the lushest hunk in the world.

At that moment, Roxy touched my shoulder and asked for a quick word. Reluctantly, I left Edward, to follow her outside to the patio, as guests started to file into the room. We headed for the tables, which were set up in the sunshine with vases of cream flowers mixed with green leafy stuff. Chatting ten to the dozen, the three GCSE students stood there in uniform.

'You'd better get in,' I said to them. 'Those delicious canapés you made will need serving.'

Roxy glanced around, as if to check that we were quite alone.

'Nick worked hard on this vegetable patch, didn't he?' she said.

I raised my eyebrows. 'You know that he handed in his notice, don't you, Roxy?'

'Yes. Just before he went, we had a chat. Blazing angry he was and called your cousin all sorts. He mumbled something about revenge being sweeter than pineapple... and he was smirking.'

'How odd,' I said, cheeks feeling hot. *Shiiii—sugar*.

'I just wanted to warn you... That angry look of his, I've seen it before. A couple of years ago I worked on a documentary about some art gallery. An artist had his work rejected by the owner. Deluded as hell, he said he was the next Damien Hirst. I caught his face just before he left— the same expression as Nick's. That night the gallery was torched.'

'What are you saying?' I asked, all thought of yummy food and romantic dancing suddenly forgotten.

'Just be careful. And...remember, lots of people, me included, think you're really fab. What with the lawnmower and fountain.... The fridge... Good actress or what. I know you've done everything for the right reasons...'

I stared vacantly, not sure what to say—admitting nothing.

'Right.' Roxy smiled. 'Must go—just heard Lieutenant Mayhew's voice. Charlie Chingo is supposed to kick off the evening with a quick interview with the happy couple.' She squeezed my arm. 'Good luck tonight.'

Mouth dry, I followed her back inside. At least the outfits were a distraction. Henrietta and Lieutenant Mayhew's friends were either in uniform or cocktail dresses that swished and sparkled, with dreamy shoes to match. Slightly out of place, two old ladies sat in a corner, in pastels and pearls. I headed over. The jazz music played just loud enough so that the rhythm got into your feet but you didn't have to shout to make yourself heard.

'Good evening, ladies,' I said. 'May I introduce myself? I am—'

'No need to tell us, dear,' said the shorter one, wearing thick pink rouge. 'Miss Abigail Croxley. Such a lovely young lady, you are. We've thoroughly enjoyed watching your cookery lessons.'

The other woman, in a smart trouser suit (was that a *purple* rinse?) stood up and kind of bowed.

'It's a pleasure to meet you,' she said in a bubbly voice 'I'm Brenda—that's Shirley, my sister—we won the competition to join these celebrations. Out of all the thousands who rang up to answer the million dollar question, our phone number was picked.'

'Congratulations!' I said. 'What was the question about— Applebridge Hall's history or a scene from the show?'

Brenda shook her head. 'Nothing so difficult.'

'It was: which show is the favourite programme of the American businessman putting up the prize money for *Million Dollar Mansion*?' said Shirley. '*Downton Gabby*, *Downton Tabby* or *Downton Abbey*?'

'See, not much skill involved to win,' said Brenda and we all smiled.

'Is someone looking after you both?' I asked as neither of them had a drink.

'Oh, don't worry about us, dear,' said Shirley. 'That nice Gaynor woman said she'd be back in a moment.'

Yeah, right. There she was, black bob girlishly flicking from side to side as she flirted with Edward.

'How about champagne cocktails?' I said and called over one of the GCSE students, who carried a tray bearing full glasses, moonwalker-slow. Clearly, she was terrified of spilling a drop.

'Thank you, dear. It's a wonderful building,' said Shirley and took a sip of her drink.

'Would you like a behind-the-scenes tour?' I asked. If I stayed one minute longer I'd be tempted to throw my cocktail over Gaynor. Ahem. Not that I was the jealous sort, of course.

The old women's eyes widened.

'Follow me,' I said. 'Bring your cocktails. We can start off in the library.'

As it turned out, both sisters were huge fans of countless antiques TV shows. What's more, over the years they'd visited practically all of the National Trust's stately homes. They pointed out a cubbyhole in one of unused bedrooms and informed me it was probably for hanging wigs, centuries ago. Servants would have cleaned them with arsenic powder to kill the nits. *Ick!*

They cooed over ornate door frames and lovingly ran fingers over intricately carved banisters. They explained how bedrooms leading off the Long Gallery wouldn't have been popular due to the noise at night when people exercised up there, or sat and chatted until all hours. In awe, they admired the grandfather clock in the Low Drawing Room and nodded knowingly as I pointed out leaking ceilings and crumbling stonework.

By the time we got back, the guests were eating and I left Brenda and Shirley helping themselves to the bacon and egg tartlets. The Lieutenant and Henrietta were laughing with Edward. Lady C danced with the Viscount while his wife shimmied with the Earl. The students huddled in a corner with mini trifles and I gave them the thumbs-up across the room.

I took a glass of white wine from Mr Thompson who, armed with a tray of drinks, patrolled the party. Then, balancing a plateful of food in the other hand, I headed outside. A ladylike helping, of course—not like the pyramid of salad I would build from Pizza Parlour's free salad bar. As I approached the French windows, a man's voice shouted from behind, 'Get off me!' It must have come from the hallway.

I turned around. *Shit* (forget all earlier comments about not swearing). *It*-hitting-the-fan time was here.

Dressed in designer jeans and a shirt, Nick stumbled into the dining room. He shook off the two men hired to guard the main entrance. Mr Thompson put down his tray, hurried over and grabbed his shoulder.

'Get the fuck off me,' said Nick in a loud voice.

As horrified gasps circled the room, the band stopped playing.

'Watch your manners!' said Lieutenant Mayhew, by Nick's side within seconds. He looked at me. 'Edward nipped to the library, Abbey—please go and fetch him.'

But, for a moment, I stood transfixed, staring at the gardener, wringing my hands.

The Earl shook his head. 'You are no longer employed here, young man, so have no right to attend this party. I'll have you arrested for trespassing.'

'Really?' Nick sniggered. 'You might be interested in what I've got to say, first.'

He didn't sound like Nick the gardener any more. It was the jerk from the other night who'd insulted me, dressed as Gemma.

'For God's sake, man, this is an engagement party,' said the Lieutenant. 'Let's at least take this outside.'

'No. These good people and the viewers at home have a right to hear what I've got to say. All I want is for the truth to come out.' Nick smiled at me. 'Isn't that right, Abbey, mate? May I address you in such a familiar way, because, let's face it, your behaviour over the last week or so hasn't exactly befitted an aristocrat…?'

Henrietta mouthed 'get Edward' and I hurried away to find him, while Nick was dragged from the room.

LORD EDWARD'S E-DIARY

Wednesday 12th September

8.45p.m. As promised, I have slipped out of the Drake Diner to give you an exclusive insight into the engagement party. The band is playing well-known tunes by Frank Sinatra and Father has even taken to the dance floor.

When I mentioned that I was bobbing out to write this e-diary, Roxy instructed me that female blog-readers might be disappointed if I didn't describe at least two outfits. So, if I remember rightly (Roxy kindly summed up for me) Lieutenant Mayhew's sister is wearing a 'burnt orange off-the-shoulder chiffon midi dress'. His dear friend Bombardier Zoe Churchill is in a 'little black cocktail number with diamanté trim'.

Roxy also insisted I provide some 'gossip'. I had to ask what she meant. After a roll of her eyes, she just told me to say, quote... 'Mr Thompson actually blushed and broke into a smile when first introduced to Bombardier Zoe Churchill's widowed mother, and throughout the evening has regularly returned to her side—and even asked her to dance.' In addition...

Erm, excuse me, friends, my cousin has just entered the library and clearly needs to talk...

CHAPTER 27

'Any of you toffs seen the movie *Nine and a Half Weeks*?' said Nick with a smug grin, just as a purple-faced Edward and me entered the Long Gallery. I felt faint. At least Nick had been taken up here, away from the guests. Lady C and the Earl sat on one of the seats at the foot of a large window. Edward and I stopped by the portrait of the Earl's glamorous mum. Mr Thompson and Lieutenant Mayhew had gone back downstairs. The TV crew quickly set up.

'This'd better be good,' snarled Edward and glared at Nick, ignoring his question.

Less familiar than usual, Gaynor reminded him that whatever Nick had to say was part of the reality show we'd all signed up for.

'I doubt anyone has seen that film, Nick,' I said, afraid of throwing up. 'It's, um, a favourite of my flatmate Gemma's, which is the only reason I'm familiar with it.'

'Really? So, what about *Dirty Dancing* or *Ghost*?' He swaggered up and down.

'I've heard of them,' muttered Edward and loosened his collar. 'Look, what's this all about? My best friend's engagement party is underway downstairs. If we're going to play guessing games then I'll leave right now.'

'That's a bit hasty, mate,' said Nick. 'You might be interested in what I've got to say. Abbey—will you tell them about our cinematic antics, or shall I?'

'Abbey? It *was* you?' said Edward, the colour draining from his face.

After a long silence, I blurted out my Plan Sex-up while staring at the floor.

Edward muttered that he'd seen something on the Internet about a movie competition, but had dismissed it as online gossip.

'Huge apologies if I've brought the Croxley name into disrepute.' I lifted my head. 'But, quite simply, I was prepared to do anything to help us win this show. I thought a relationship between, um, the so-called upstairs and downstairs of the house might prompt some interest.' I turned to face the camera. 'I wasn't trying to fool the public in a malicious way—all I wanted was to provide entertainment.'

After a silent minute or two, the Earl eventually spoke.

'Don't be too harsh on yourself,' he muttered, in a gruff voice and scratched his beard. 'No real harm done. Although, young lady, I suspect your father might want a few words.'

'So that's why you and Nick always seemed to be in cahoots?' said Edward, the colour having returned to his cheeks. His gaze shifted down the gallery to the portrait of his grandfather—the serious-looking suited man with the sagging shoulders. 'Over the generations, no doubt many Croxleys have done difficult things for the good of the family.' He thought for a moment. 'The whole plan lacked dignity but…Forget it, cousin. What's done is done. We'll say no more.' His top lip curled. 'In fact it was quite brave of you, agreeing to spend more than a second necessary with this scoundrel.' He turned to Nick. 'What I don't understand, man, is why you decided to tell us all now. From all accounts, you and my cousin got on well. Why would you reveal this secret? Why are you trying to ruin our chances of winning this show?'

He snorted. 'Do you really think this family means anything to me, with your snooty noses and poncey clothes? As for Miss Croxley…' he said. 'Nice try, love, feeding me chilli strawberries. It took me all of yesterday and today to finally work out exactly why that scene was so unpleasurable.'

'What's he going on about now?' muttered the Earl and opened his pocket watch. 'I've had enough of this nonsense.'

Gaynor and Roxy looked at each other and shrugged.

'It was, um, only a joke, Nick,' I said. 'Please forgive me. I thought you'd see the funny side.'

'Oh, it's hilarious, all things considered. You must have felt right at home, feeding me fruit like some little tart— excuse the pun.'

'Take that back!' snapped Edward.

Nick put up his hands. 'Keep your hair on, mate. I just need a few more minutes of your time. Take my word, you'll thank me, soon enough. Now, Abbey…Tell the room—where did you go to finishing school?'

Huh? Lady C and I exchanged looks. She was fiddling with her pearls. A shiver ran down my spine.

'Switzerland.'

'Where exactly?' the slimeball continued.

'Bern,' I mumbled.

'And, as a result of speaking to the locals there, you said your French was "*superbe*".'

'Erm, don't you mean your German, Abigail?' said Lady C to me brightly. 'Everyone who's well travelled knows that's what they speak in the Swiss capital.'

Oh, Highland fudge.

'No—I dug around. Actually, Abigail attended a famous finishing school in the French-speaking Swiss city of Geneva.' Nick crossed his arms. 'I found Miss Croxley's name on their online back register.' He looked straight into the camera. 'Abbey's story about studying catering in Surrey checked out, though. But why would she lie about where she attended finishing school? Unless, erm...' He sniggered. 'She didn't know the precise details of her own history and, on the spot, made something up?'

'You aren't making any sense, man,' said Edward. 'Who exactly are you, anyway? I rang the agency that we employed you from in a hurry, and they could only provide scant details about your gardening experience. I should have questioned them thoroughly before taking you on, instead of being swayed by the fact your hourly rate wasn't much.'

'Me? A gardener?' He shook his head. 'If you'd bothered getting to know your staff any better, you'd realize that was a joke. Jean appreciated my muscle, but she'd be the first to tell you my knowledge of all things horticultural is limited. And didn't you spot my designer T-shirts?'

I did—and his fancy cologne.

'You don't acquire things like that through working for peanuts,' he continued. 'I'm a private investigator, mate—previously a journalist. I've got a degree to my name. The only gardening I do is the metaphorical sort—digging up dirt on people.'

I gasped. How could I have ever been taken in by him?

'This is all very distasteful,' said Lady C quickly and stood up. 'Come on, Abigail. Let's, erm, leave the men to sort this out.'

'Nice try, Lady Constance, but I think the Croxley men will want her here.'

'Who hired you to spy on us?' said Edward in a steely voice.

Gaynor was practically salivating with excitement and looked even more turned on than when she flirted with Edward. 'What a fab coup,' she hissed to Roxy.

'Isn't it obvious? Are you so naïve?' said Nick. 'This is a competition—for a million dollars.'

Of course. The Baron. That's why Harry was in the pub that night. He must have been collecting information from Nick.

'The Baron insisted the Croxleys were too perfect and wanted to know your flaw,' said the smug PI. 'A bit like a diamond—if it looks like there are no imperfections, then it's probably a fake.'

'That family dared investigate us?' Edward's eyes blazed.

'Why not? Reckon they're beneath you because they don't hang portraits of relatives from centuries ago?'

I bit my thumbnail and looked at Lady C, whose eyebrows had almost disappeared into her grey hair. The feeling of sickness had gone now. I just felt numb. Was it possible that this scumbag knew who I really was?

'Would a real Lady suggestively massage the base of a fountain, on film, in front of the general public?' said Nick.

Lady C raised her eyebrows at me, probably wondering why I hadn't told her about the more recent things Nick and I had done.

'Would a successful caterer's daughter burn baked apples and prepare a salad dressing that burns your throat? Would she send onions flying across the table? Would she eat marinated asparagus with her fingers and watch carefully which cutlery other people used? Come on, guys, you've had access to the best education in the country. Surely you must have noticed something strange about Abbey, like…I'm just guessing… a lack of knowledge about Applebridge Hall and its heritage?'

The Earl stared at me. 'I was a tad surprised at how little you knew about the first Earl of Croxley and our history, Abigail. But still…'

'I doubted Abbey from the start,' said Nick. 'I mean, whoever heard of a Lady zooming downhill on a lawnmower or befriending a temporary gardening assistant?'

'You seem to have some antiquated, clichéd view of what it's like to be an aristocrat, young man,' said Lady C. 'The Earl and his son are most fond of their staff, Kathleen, Mr Thompson and Jean.'

'But would they suggestively feed them fruit?'

Lady C's jaw dropped and she turned to me. 'So, that was you?'

'No, of course they wouldn't,' said Nick. 'So, I decided to investigate further and took myself around to Abbey's flat in London. Now, according to a neighbour, Chelsea…'

Oh, crap. Not chatty Chelsea. She talked even quicker—and for much longer—than Roxy ever could.

'… Abigail has indeed been away for the last two weeks—likewise, her flatmate, Gemma.'

Edward rubbed his neck.

'Nice girl, that Chelsea,' said Nick. 'She invited me in for a cocktail; showed me some photos of her house-warming last year.'

I couldn't move.

'Where is this leading?' said Edward.

Nick delved into the back pocket of his jeans and pulled out a photo. He handed it to Edward.

'Abbey and Gemma,' said Nick. 'Just in case you were wondering.'

Edward glanced at me and then back at the shot, which he studied very closely. 'Are you sure? There's a definite likeness, but…' He studied my face, then handed me the photo. 'This Chelsea woman must be mistaken. The well-dressed blonde woman in that picture has definite shades of Abbey, but I don't think she's my cousin.'

'Or perhaps it's this woman, here in the flesh, who isn't related to you. Consider that. Of course, you recognize Gemma, don't you, Lord Edward?' Nick smirked. 'She's the one you were so quick to defend the other night when I found her trespassing on your land. While here, she coloured her hair red—take that away and it's the brunette in the photo.'

'I have no idea what this is all about or… or how you doctored that photo of myself and Gemma,' I said and forced my limbs to move. I headed to the stairwell. 'Edward, Uncle, we have guests to attend to. Nick, you've had your fun, but I suggest you take yourself and your over-active imagination out of this house before we call the police. You, um, need to "get a life"—I believe that's the phrase people use.'

Nick burst out laughing. 'Okay, okay, I get it—you're scared cos your cover is blown. But the least you can do is come clean.'

'That's enough.' Edward lunged forward and grabbed his arm.

'I wouldn't do that if I was you,' said Nick and shook him off. 'The cameras are rolling. I could do you for assault. Okay. You've made me do this, Abbey—or should I say, *Gemma?*'

He held up his phone for Edward to watch and a video started to play. 'That's Chelsea,' he said. 'Listen to what she has to say when I show her some footage of "Abbey" on *Million Dollar Mansion*.'

'Ooh, no,' said a squeaky voice from the phone. 'That's not Abigail. Her nose is slightly too long. The face is a tad rounder and she's not quite so slim. It's a good likeness but... No. Definitely not. The hair's not quite the same shade, either. And Abigail doesn't walk that quickly, her steps are much more measured.' Chelsea giggled. 'If anything, that person looks and acts much more like Gemma, without the dark hair and fake tan. The two of them sometimes get mistaken for each other, you know.'

Silence, apart from jazz music wafting up the stairwell.

'I was as sick as a dog after that mustard pineapple, you little bitch,' said Nick and sneered in my direction. 'It's you, isn't it, Gemma Goodwin—minus the WAG make-up, cheap clothes and home-dyed hair? Are you going to tell us why you've spent two weeks tricking this family and the nation into believing you're a Lady when actually you're a pizza waitress? So much for traditional values—this whole Croxley charade is based on lies.'

Lady C's hand flew up to her face. The Earl's mouth fell open. Only Edward remained statue-still. Despite letting out a mega gasp, Roxy managed to give me a sympathetic glance.

'Sorry, I can't do this,' I said and hurtled downstairs. Heart pounding, I raced past champagne-drinking guests and escaped into the cool evening air. Briefly, I stopped to pull off my shoes and then, as fast as I could, ran around the back of the house and into the maze. After going around in circles I eventually found the grassy bit in the middle and, with noisy breaths, slumped to the ground, evening dew seeping through my dress. My hands shook like my cousin Kevin's whenever he tried to come off the booze. It was too much…the sleepless nights, carrying on the pretence and now these revelations… I gulped. Was this what they called a panic attack?

What were the papers going to say after tomorrow night's show, when that confrontation would be broadcast? I'd be the most hated reality show star in Britain and, as for what Edward must be thinking… My head dropped. I remembered Kathleen's warning of how, above all else, Edward despised lies and deceit.

I sat bolt upright as the bushes rustled and a tall figure appeared by my side, chest heaving up and down.

'Edward…Look. I'm sorry… I never meant to…'

'So it's true? I had to ask you myself.' His voice shook. 'You're not my… my cousin?'

I stood up and took his hand but he yanked it away.

'How could you? My father and I let you into our home. We trusted you. Was it all some kind of joke?' He shook his head. 'Do you know how long I've been waiting to get to know Abigail?'

My throat hurt as I gazed at his face—the drooping mouth, the questioning eyes. 'I hated all the lies, but Abbey, she needed my help, you see—'

'Constance just explained,' he said in a dull voice. 'I can't believe she helped her niece pull off this deceit.' He shook his head. 'Why didn't I see the signs? The unladylike words you played in Scrabble. Calling Henrietta's mum Mrs Viscount…The strange expressions you came out with, only to blame them on the influence of your flatmate, Gemma—who was you all along.'

'Yes. Me. Gemma. Who cares so much…'

He stared at my face. 'Of course… The likeness, I can see it now. You've taken me for a fool.'

'I did it for your family!'

'Ten out of ten for acting—you should go to drama school. How easily you explained your appearances here at night. All those made up stories about your brother dropping you off… How do I know that anything you've said is true? Well, huge congratulations. Thanks to you, we'll lose the show.'

'Please, I—'

'Gaynor wants you to do an interview with Charlie Chingo for tomorrow's programme, so that you can put forward your side of the story,' he snapped. 'You may remain on the estate until the live final on Saturday— Gaynor thinks you should be there—but that's it. You're not welcome any longer than is necessary.'

'Wait a minute…Edward—'

'Father will speak to Richard. I don't know what my cousin was thinking of when she asked you to take her place. It's farcical.'

'Her parents are away on a cruise,' I said.

'The two of you thought of everything,' he said.

'You know what? Yeah, we bloody well did. Abigail was so torn and didn't want to let her father down—I couldn't say no when she asked me to help. Zak—'

'I heard,' he said. 'All of this, so that she could go on holiday with her boyfriend.'

'It *wasn't* a holiday—those war-torn African children are in crisis. Zak and Abbey are probably two of a handful of adults they can trust. But yeah, funny the things people will do for love, isn't it?'

We exchanged looks.

'I think the original Earl of Croxley who fought against the Spanish Armada would be mega proud of Abbey, heading to a war-zone.' I gave a tentative smile. 'Please, Edward… Can't you see that the last thing I wanted was to hurt you? Abbey hoped me taking part—as her—would reconcile the two brothers.'

Edward looked sad. 'If she was that bothered, she should have turned up herself.'

I stared at him for a moment, and then shook my head.

'Have you even thought what it was like for me, facing the cameras for that first cookery lesson, having previously been told I'd just be helping out in a coffee shop? But I stepped up to the mark. God knows how I would have managed without Kathleen's help. It's not all been a bundle of laughs.'

'Kathleen was in on this?'

Oops.

'Were Father and I the only ones not to know?' His face flushed deeper. 'Dennis Smith was right about you and your cookery skills—or lack of. I should have listened to his years of expertise. Instead, I was loyal to my supposed cousin. What a joke.'

'The lies…were for the greater good,' I said, still holding his gaze.

'The words "lies" and "good" don't belong in the same breath. The one thing I love… liked about you, Gemma, was…' his cheeks flushed '…your lack of agenda—you were who you were. But now…' He ran a hand through his honey curls and looked about ten years old.

I took his hand. 'What is it, Edward?' I said softly. 'Someone's lied to you big time before?'

He jerked away once more. 'You don't understand—or know the real me at all.'

'But at least admit…If it wasn't for me, you wouldn't have got this far. Who thought of the evacuee reunion? And my antics with Nick caught the attention of the younger viewers. Does all that count for nothing? We've got this far.'

'What's been the point? We'll have lost the viewers' trust, now.'

'Saving your bloody family, that's what! And how do you think I feel as the new national joke? I've had to transform my appearance and the way I move. I've had to speak posh and constantly worry that I'm letting someone down. Well, stuff you, if you can't see the good in that.' With a stifled sob, I picked up my shoes and raced through the maze, tripping as I went. Edward caught me just as I was about to tumble over and helped me regain my balance.

'Edward… It's me…' I implored. 'It's Gemma, who likes to dip in the pond…play tig in the woods and chase…'

'I… I don't want to see you until the final show on Saturday—when we'll no doubt lose,' he muttered. 'Please, Gemma, understand. The betrayal hurts too much.' He eased his grip on my arm. 'It's not that I'm saying I'm perfect, but lies…No, I can't take any more.'

Biting my cheeks inside, I stared at his expressionless face. How could he dismiss what we had so easily and bring it to an end? Well, there was *no way* I'd allow myself to cry in front of him. With blurred vision, I headed for the house.

LORD EDWARD'S E-DIARY

Wednesday 12th September

'Comments'

10.55p.m. I have just come from… Am about to return to the Drake Diner and our guests after…This library is providing refuge, whilst I recover from an enormous shock. Apologies for my incoherence, blog-readers, but I've just been told what I suspect Roxy might call 'the biggest bit of gossip yet'.

CHAPTER 28

Which would be the quickest way to shut someone up—a stiletto through the eye or death by arsenic-laced chocolate? I smiled sweetly at Charlie Chingo, who'd just sat down to interview me, having paced the Low Drawing Room several times, shaking his head.

Okay. I get it. It's a surprise to see what I really look and sound like, but I'm not part of a freak show. Gemma Goodwin is a human being, even though she doesn't speak as if she's got marbles in her mouth and can't get out of a car without flashing her thong.

Charlie gave a low whistle as he sat down opposite me, underneath the chandelier. 'Damn, girl,' he said finally, 'you've got balls.'

Yeah, and you might lose yours in a minute, I thought. Funny, how, within seconds of meeting me as myself, he'd sworn and burped, showing a total lack of respect. He'd never have done that in front of Abbey.

'Are we ready?' I asked Roxy, stomach cramping now. Urgh. Job interviews were bad enough, let alone ones where I was probably going to be interrogated like some criminal.

She nodded and I smoothed down my blouse. Deciding what to wear had been difficult. In the end I'd worn my shorts and high heels with one of Abbey's silky tops. It was high-necked—an unusual style for me, but I'd come to like it. My false eyelashes were in place and it was great to powder on bronzer. I'd also nipped to the chemist that morning and bought a home-dye kit. Except I couldn't get my head around going back to the chocolate-brown—somehow, it just didn't seem 'me' any more. So I chose one more like my natural colour, called copper blonde. I dissed the chicken fillets, as well. Somehow, they just didn't seem right.

'So, Gemma Goodwin,' said Charlie as the cameras rolled. 'Chat with Chingo—first things first… A stay at Applebridge Hall must be a dream for a girl like you.'

'A girl like me?' I asked innocently.

'No offence, but wasn't your last job at Pizza Parlour?'

'Yeah. So was Miss Croxley's. We were both made redundant.'

From the far side of the room near the fireplace, Roxy grinned and gave me the thumbs-up. Charlie fiddled with his signet ring.

'What I mean is… For anyone, me too, moving to a stately home for two weeks would be super cool! Was this high life one of the reasons you agreed to this charade? Talk about a top-notch holiday, with everything included!'

'It sounded mega exciting, I'll give you that…but no. When Abigail asked me to stand in as her, I thought it was a joke.'

Charlie guffawed. 'Absolutely! I mean, could there be two more opposite characters than an aristocrat and…?'

'A girl like me?' I fixed a smile on my face.

Charlie ran a hand through his slicked back hair. 'So tell me, Gemma, why did you agree to this madcap plan?'

Sorry, Abbey, the time had come to tell the truth. I told Charlie all about Zak and the African orphans.

'I see. And Abigail's trip is very commendable—but the favour she asked of you was huge, no question about that. What has been the most difficult thing about the last fortnight—apart from a, um, few teething problems with the cooking?'

I couldn't help smiling—a few teething problems? Very polite!

'Yeah, the cookery lessons, of course, although I think I did pretty well, considering I arrived believing my two weeks would be spent in a coffee shop.'

'How did you feel when you heard news of the Food Academy?'

'How do you think? Mega terrified. I wanted to do a runner, then and there.'

'Why didn't you?'

'How could I go back on my promise? Guess I was lucky, as it turned out, as I've always been interested in learning about food.' I looked around the room. 'And it didn't take long for me to fall in love with this place. After one night, I was smitten.'

Charlie leant forward. 'With the posh furniture and amazing gardens?'

'More than that. You see, when you're here, as you know, it's the imperfections that are most noticeable. Run your hand over the brickwork and sand will flake away. Stare hard enough at the awesome artwork and faded patches will catch your eye. No doubt, on the telly, Applebridge Hall looks like some grand manor from a film set, but take this room, for example… Look closely at the cracked floor tiles and chipped, um, strapwork, I think it's called, up in that corner…' I pointed in the air '…there are signs of damp. This place has a lived-in feel. You can almost hear past parties and celebrations and family arguments, echoing along the corridors…' I bit my lip. 'A night in this place and I realized, despite its size, Applebridge Hall is basically someone's home.'

'So, it wasn't about being on the telly?'

'No way. Celebrity life—I've always thought that must be a nightmare. But, don't get me wrong, I love reality programmes, watch all the shows. It was one of the happiest days of my life when they brought back *Big Brother*.'

'But you must have enjoyed acting out those movie scenes.'

I reached for my glass of water. Talk about twenty questions.

'To start with, yes—because, as a fan of reality telly, I knew they were exactly the kind of thing I'd like to watch. I wasn't patronising fans of the show, cos I like the same stuff. Although, as time moved on, it became more difficult.'

'Why was that?'

'I guess some of the stuff I'd learnt about ladylike behaviour had really stuck.'

'And I believe you went undercover as Gemma and visited Marwick Castle. Like Nick, were you acting as the Applebridge PI?'

Ah. That cat would be well and truly out of the bag now, of course. The Baron and Harry would have recognized me—plus Roxy, who'd given me a lift home.

'No. It wasn't planned. I just happened to bump into the Baron's son and he invited me over. I thought it would be interesting to have a look at the competition, but that's all. Digging for dirt isn't my style.'

Inwardly, I sighed. Everyone probably thought the worst of me now. There was no sign of Edward. Would he even bother to watch my interview tonight, when it was screened? Would he listen to me explain how Lady C trained me—about my lessons in deportment and etiquette? Would he appreciate just how much work I'd put in?

I cocked my head and nodded and hmmed and answered loads more questions.

'Finally, Gemma…'

Finally? That sure was one great F word.

'Would you like to turn to the camera and give the British public one good reason why they shouldn't feel totally deceived? Remember Patsy, the first person to get knocked out of last year's *Big Brother*?'

'Yeah—everyone hated her because she tried to be "street", when really she was a mega conservative suburban housewife.'

'And Lenny from *Celebrity Spa Weekend*?' said Charlie.

I nodded. He was voted out after the first night for bigging himself up as some kind of stud. When one of the women made a move, he locked himself in his bedroom.

'The British Public are an eccentric lot themselves,' said Charlie, 'and the winners of these shows are as diverse as the birdlife in the Earl's gardens. All they ask is that contestants are true to themselves.' He shrugged. 'Why should they still vote for Applebridge Hall when everything you've done over the last two weeks has been based on lies? When the whole appeal of Applebridge is supposed to be the history and tradition of the Croxley family?'

I gazed into the camera. There were no prepared words. The only thing I could do was talk from the heart. 'Of course, it's mega important to keep Applebridge Hall in good nick, so that all that history is preserved, but, really, there's only one reason I agreed to this farce—to be there for my mate, Abbey.' I gave a wry smile. 'It's a surprise to me, more than anyone, that the plan almost worked. Who am I? My ancestors haven't been friends with a queen or hosted parties attended by Hollywood stars. But what this fortnight has taught me, more than anything else, is that money and status don't change things that are important, like looking after your own and not letting down those you love.'

I took another sip of water, chest aching at no longer being part of the Croxley clan. It'd be great to merge their family with mine and have the Earl as a real uncle and Lady C as my aunt. I reckoned they'd both get on with my dad.

'As for pretending to be an aristocrat,' I continued. 'Well, sorry, but I wouldn't change that for the world. Lady C…I mean Constance, taught me that being a Lady isn't about fancy clothes and houses; it's about having morals and goals; it's about having respect for yourself and nothing to do with some cliché of a woman who dresses like a nun and doesn't say boo to a goose. A Lady is brave in spirit and actions. She is fair, she works hard and treats others like she'd like to be treated herself. In fact… I hope I'm now more ladylike than I was before.'

Wow. Where did that soapbox speech come from? Charlie stared at me intently, along with everyone else in the room.

'That's it,' I said into the camera. 'Vote how you like, but please don't let my actions put you off Applebridge Hall. And…' damn that wobble in my voice '…to their Lordships, I'd just like to say… Don't think too badly of me. I meant well and tried my hardest for your family, for Abbey and this freakin' amazin' house.'

My chair scraped as I stood up, seconds after Gaynor called, 'Cut.' Five minutes later, I sat down again in the kitchen, in front of a mug of tea, along with several cubes of Kathleen's Highland fudge.

'Och, don't fret now,' said Kathleen. 'This will all blow over. A month from now you'll have a new job and no one will remember *Million Dollar Mansion*.' She smoothed down her floral apron and sat down opposite. I gave her a smile.

'You've been brill, Kathleen,' I said, 'and sorry for dropping you in it with Edward. Has he spoken to you yet?'

She shook her head. 'But the Earl came to see me early today. We ate breakfast together. He actually thanked me for helping you out.'

I nodded. 'He and Lady C found me by the pond, just after lunch. The Earl gets it—he understands why I lied. He mumbled something about everything his father did to try and save this place; said, despite the failed business deals, he never gave up. He said needs must and I'd shown myself to be a loyal friend.' I smiled again. 'He and Lady C seem closer than ever. Clearly, he's forgiven her for this stupid charade.'

'Och, aye. They spend as much time together as Mr Thompson and his gun.'

'Perhaps they're loved up?'

Kathleen smiled. 'Aye, perhaps. Despite all the furore, they were out birdwatching again this morning.'

'Whereas Edward…' I said. 'He won't listen to reason. When I tried to chat to him, just before my interview, he held up his hand. Back to his usual mega stubborn, uptight, withdrawn self…just like when I first arrived.'

'I was reet surprised, you know, to find out about you and him. But, after some thought, I reckon you two could be good for each other.' Kathleen patted my arm. 'Give him some time, lassie.'

'Time? He wants me out after the live final. And if we lose the show, there's no way he'll accept an olive stone, let alone a branch.'

'Look… Try once more to talk to him—he just headed for the forest, up by the cemetery, a moment ago.'

I finished my tea. Guess it might be worth one last shot. 'Can I borrow your cardie?' I said. Clouds had gathered and, if I was to catch him, I didn't have time to head upstairs to change.

Wrapped up in the long brown woolly, I battled against the wind and headed up the hill. There was no sign of him by the cemetery. He must have been among the trees, checking out the fence at the back.

'Aarggh!' shouted a voice.

I ran into the woods. 'Is that you, Edward? Everything all right?' My heart raced as I cut among the trees, avoiding knotted roots and patches of tall grass. In the middle it was dark and I tripped over a stump. If only I'd changed into my jeans. I hopped up and down for a second, blood trickling down my shin. A loud grunt came from the back fence and, with a slight limp, I headed that way.

'Edward?' I said, out of breath. A tall figure sat on the ground, brooding face lit up by a chink of sunlight that had broken through the cloud and treetops.

'What are you doing here?' he muttered.

Panting, I came to a standstill by him. 'What's… happened?'

He gazed at my shin. 'I could ask you the same question.'

'It's nothing. I tripped over. You shouted…'

He stared at me for a moment. 'A sprained ankle is the least of my worries.' His sock was pulled down to reveal a large purple-black bruise.

I slipped my hand under his arm. 'Come on, let's get you back to the house.'

He shook me off. 'Don't be ridiculous. I'm twice your size.'

'What's bonkers is you thinking you can get back without me to lean on. I'm not leaving. We can wait here all day if you like.'

He glared at me. I raised my eyebrows and, after a couple of minutes, won the stand-off.

With a big sigh he stood up. I slipped my arm around his waist and his arm rested on my shoulders. I looked up at him.

'Let's get this over with,' he said, expressionless.

It took us twenty minutes to get out of the woods and, back aching, I suggested a sit-down by the cemetery. Collapsed on the grass, Edward tore up a fallen leaf.

'Nice cardigan,' he said.

Hurrah! His anger had mellowed to sarcasm. This was a start.

'Tell Mr Thompson where I am,' he muttered. 'You go, before permanently damaging your back.'

'Perhaps I could get the lawnmower?' I said with a half-smile. Please let him smile back.

Instead, his brow furrowed. 'I guess there are similarities to our situation and *Titanic*, in that the hero and heroine end up apart.' He bit his lip. 'It was one of my mother's favourite films.'

'Edward…We don't need to split.'

'Why? Who knows what secrets are in you, still untold?'

'Everyone has secrets. They don't necessarily have to be bad.' I cleared my throat. 'Look—there's only one other thing I haven't told you, that Charlie just reminded me of.'

He pursed his lips.

'One night I went out to the pub—as myself. I met that Baron's son, Harry. Little did I know, at the time, he must have been there to see Nick. Anyway, he asked me back to a party at the Castle. I thought it would be interesting to see what they were really like, compared to us.'

'Have a good time, did you?'

'Hardly. Parts of that Castle are like a fancy show house on some new estate—everything is recently bought and only there for effect. There's no history, nothing much, ornament or furniture-wise, that dates back further than this Millennium. It's...soulless.' I shrugged. 'Plus the Baron and Harry are right prats.'

'Still, it must have been a fun night out, after experiencing my quiet life.' Edward didn't catch my eye.

'No!'

He snorted.

'Please, Edward, you've got to believe me.'

He shrugged.

'I... I can kind of guess how you feel,' I said. 'Discovering that Nick wasn't the person I thought came as a hell of a shock. And it was never easy for me, not for one second—keeping up the pretence and deceiving you,' I said and felt my chin wobble. 'In fact it was the hardest thing I've ever done.'

His face softened for one second and uh oh, adrenaline rush, here we go... What was the point of more words? The only way forward was, in fact, for me to lean forward and...our lips met. Tingles ran up and down my spine and candy popped faster than any Spacedust as I felt his chest heave against mine.

'Oh, Teddy,' I mumbled, after eventually pulling away for breath.

'The name's Edward!' Cheeks flushed, he wiped his mouth as if my kisses contained poison.

'Is this really it, *Edward*? Doesn't anything that's happened between us count?'

A muscle in his cheek flickered. 'Look, I get it—you're not a monster, Gemma. But... I can't understand how you agreed to this farce. You had the choice not to lie—not to pretend to be someone you weren't. Whereas...' He looked away. 'Take the hint, Gemma—us, it's over—you were... just a bit of fun.'

My voice cracked. 'What about me being the soundtrack to your silent movie?'

'That was just a corny chat-up line I've used before.'

My eyes tingled. Why couldn't he see that my motivations had been well-intended and forgive me?

'How charming—you fed me a line, like some drunken teenager out on the pull.' I scrambled to my feet, a sob rising from my chest. 'Well, fine! Your loss!' Without glancing back, I power-walked down the hill.

LORD EDWARD'S E-DIARY

Thursday 13th September

11.55p.m. The 13th isn't supposed to be the luckiest of days, but it would seem to be fortunate for the interloper that is Gemma Goodwin. Having watched tonight's programme and her interview, more people than ever have commented on this blog. The majority view seems to be that she is some kind of hero. It will be interesting to see what the newspapers say tomorrow.

On balance, I can see how some of her qualities might appeal to the average viewer. She stood by her friend and placed herself in a totally alien environment, in order to help. Yet that does little to dispel the discomfort I now feel when I hear her...her quirky voice, or see her infectious smile...

Knityourownmansion, no doubt Gemma would appreciate the knitted medal you feel she deserves for her efforts over this last fortnight. If you send it here, I suppose Kathleen will forward it to the right address.

Lovehotnoble, that's very generous of you, but I don't erm, think a tantric massage would relieve my stress.

Drunkwriter, no, please don't worry, I won't turn to whisky just yet—which is just as well, as your tinned cat food hangover cure sounds quite disgusting. Honestly.

I'm fine and have bigger things to concern me now than a young girl having her bit of fun by pretending to be my cousin.

In fact, anyone reading this, I implore you more than ever, please vote for Applebridge Hall. Despite this ridiculous charade that has come to light, family values and tradition still mean everything to us.

By the way, *Drunkwriter* and *Cupcakesrock*, I'm glad your relationship is going from strength to strength. And *EtonMess*, sympathies now that you are torn between fantasizing about the pretend Abigail Croxley or real Gemma Goodwin. For your emotional wellbeing, my advice would be to steer clear of both.

CHAPTER 29

Gemma's a Genuine Lady!
  Stately Star
  Dare to Doubt Abbey!
  Posh People's Pin-up!

I gazed out of the limo's window. Saturday the fifteenth, the day of the final, had come around so quickly. I still couldn't believe the newspaper headlines yesterday and today. Roxy reckoned the public really loved me. Apparently, kids thought I was the wackiest reality star yet. Fogies said that in these challenging times how inspiring it was to see a young person put a friend's needs first. Plus, according to…what were they called…? *social commentators*…my close friendship with Abbey proved that, nowadays, accent and birth were irrelevant. Not that any of this made the slightest bit of difference to Edward, who barely spoke to me all day Friday. Not that he went out of his way to be unfriendly either. I even caught him looking at me a couple of times as if he wanted to talk.

Lunch was a couple of hours ago and now we were driving to Watermill Nook, an amazin' hotel, according to Lady C, where, at seven o'clock, the final would take place. It was halfway between Applebridge Hall and Marwick Castle. For the first time, the two competing finalists would meet in person. Gaynor, Charlie and Roxy had left in the early hours to set up.

I looked around the limo. Edward and I sat opposite Lady C, the Earl and Mr Thompson. Jean and Kathleen were in the next row back. Lady C brushed some fluff off her silky peach dress. The Earl wore his trademark tweed suit and grumbled about not being able to smoke his pipe in the car. Edward looked as if he had under-dressed on purpose, in his checked shirt and cords. With serious eyes, he chatted over his shoulder to Mr Thompson about the recent overgrowth of weed in the pond. Jean and Kathleen marvelled at the luxury car and sipped their champagne. The Earl had insisted that the gardener, cook and estate manager accompany him to the live final. He said they'd done as much as anyone to give Applebridge Hall the chance of winning it deserved.

'You look nice, Gemma,' said Lady C softly.

I smiled back. 'Thanks for helping me choose this dress—and doing my hair.'

We'd gone shopping yesterday, in town, and found an outfit more my style—not Abbey's and not quite the old Gemma's any more. The hem hovered just above my knee, instead of halfway up my thigh, and the neckline, whilst low, didn't accentuate my cleavage, if you could call it that without the chicken fillets.

Yet it all felt right. Plus Lady C suggested I tried less outrageous false eyelashes. She also treated me to a subtle air-brush tan, which made me realize how my mahogany bronzer powder was more suited to polishing the Earl's ancient furniture. And this morning she'd pinned up my hair, letting just a few curls dangle down—not that I was remotely, in any way, keen to look sexy for, for *him*.

'Almost there,' Edward muttered and rubbed the back of his neck.

See. I was over him completely. No popping candy at the sound of his voice. I didn't even reply. All I'll admit to was a slight twist in my stomach. Well, okay—maybe it was a titchy fizz.

'So, Gemma,' Edward said quietly, without catching my eye, 'what can we expect from the Baron—seeing as you've already met him?'

'If you're a woman, watch out for octopus hands,' I muttered back.

'Did he…upset you?' said Edward.

Blimey, his fists curled. He really didn't like the opposition.

'Nah. He's pretty harmless.' I pulled a face. 'Not very subtle about going for what he wants. In any case, I can look after myself.'

A smile flickered across his face before he turned away. The limo turned left and passed through cast iron gates leading to Watermill Nook. The car drove along a huge drive, in between two holes of a golf course. It stopped in front of a swanky red-brick hotel with a flag on its roof and shiny swinging doors. To the right was a narrow building with big windows covered in condensation—obviously a swimming pool. Roxy was waiting for us and waved as I stepped out. It reminded me of the first day I arrived at Applebridge Hall.

'Quite the heroine, aren't you?' said Roxy as she led us all inside and past a swanky marble reception desk and plush armchairs. Porters in maroon suits and caps pushed gold luggage trolleys past. A woman on reception whispered something to her colleague and I was sure they both stared at me for a moment. Then one of them gave me the thumbs-up.

'I don't feel like I deserve any cheers,' I muttered.

'Haven't you seen the papers?' said Roxy.

'Not all of them were kind.'

She guided me past the fancy reception and a black marble bar towards the lifts, where we waited for the others to catch up.

'The important ones were,' she said. 'Did you see the *Daily News*?'

'Yeah—the headlines included something about "Stately Shenanigans" and "Gemma's Ghastly Gamble Failed".'

'Well, the Baron's cousin owns that paper, so don't worry too much.' Roxy lowered her voice. 'Just between you and me, voting since Thursday shows that the result is neck and neck—what with the Castle's entertaining X-rated celebrity footage versus your moving confession and emotional evacuee reunion.'

At least we weren't being thrashed. Palms sweaty, I entered the lift with Roxy and everyone else from the limo. It stopped on the fourth floor and Roxy led us along a magnolia corridor and stopped outside a room called The Platinum Suite.

Roxy looked at her watch. 'Five o'clock. Time for make-up and a drink before the Baron arrives.'

We went in and nodded our hellos to the familiar cameramen and sound guys. It was a massive lounge with two sets of chairs, one to the left and one to the right, all facing ahead, where there was one chair—for Charlie, no doubt—and a big TV screen. I peered left, through to another room. Was that a grand piano?

'Come on,' said Roxy and headed that way. The make-up girl stood in there, waiting at a desk littered with eye pencils and foundations. Gaynor chatted to a man with a clipboard, perhaps the director for Marwick

Castle. This room led into others—the bedrooms, I think. The décor was mega luxurious, with velvet curtains and margarine-yellow wallpaper. The floor was laminated with oak and mirrors hung all around. Whilst we each waited for the make-up girl to work her magic, we sat down on a white dimpled sofa and sipped yummy filter coffee out of posh cups. Edward borrowed Roxy's laptop to, no doubt, conscientiously check his blog.

Eventually, we heard loud chat and a voice boom, 'Any proper drink in this place?' Cocky as ever, the Baron had arrived. He sauntered into the room, winked at the make-up girl and told her to make him and Harry look like brothers (no one laughed, except him).

'Hello, mate,' he said to the Earl, and held out his hand. A huge ring was squashed onto his little finger and, as his Italian-cut jacket rose up his arm, a shiny gold chain bracelet came into view. He looked around the room. 'How twee—you've brought the staff.'

The Earl didn't stand up.

'Come on, matey, you're not still sore about that business with Nick? All's fair in love and war.' The Baron gazed around. 'It's great to finally meet the competition. Although I've already had the pleasure of your company,' he said to me and, before I knew it, my hand had received a slimy kiss.

Edward put his laptop to one side for a moment, as if he might punch the competition out.

'Good on you, little lady,' continued the Baron. 'I like a girl with spirit. You ever want a job, just contact me. Once we've won this competition, Harry and I will be recruiting at top speed.' He winked. 'We're going to install some lap-dancing poles in the Nightery.'

'Yeah, babe, knocked out, we were,' said Harry, 'about how you fooled the toffs.'

'I didn't enjoy fooling them,' I said, cheeks burning.

'Course not.' Harry grinned, his highlighted hair blonder than ever.

'Damn pity you weren't confident enough to win, without having to hire a private investigator,' said the Earl in a gruff voice.

The Baron shrugged. 'No offence, mate, but you're clearly no businessman—confidence ain't the only important quality for success. You need nous and an ability to sniff out the opposition's weaknesses.'

'Shot yourself in the foot then, didn't you?' said Edward. 'As, according to the press, Gemma appears to be our strength.'

Wowsers—a compliment. The Baron gave a tight-lipped smile.

'Don't count your chickens yet, Lord Edward. Come on, Harry, let's go schmooze Chingo. See you in front of the cameras, guys,' he boomed, before putting a shoulder around his son and returning to the lounge.

'What an appalling man,' muttered the Earl. Even charitable Lady C failed to come up with anything positive.

'How are the nerves, lassie?' asked Kathleen softly.

I smiled. 'Do you think we stand a chance?'

'Och aye. Surely the public will see that the Baron is nothing but an eejit.'

At that moment Roxy came in. 'Please come through and take your seats, everyone,' she said.

Eek—it was already quarter to seven. Gaynor led Edward into the lounge. Everyone else followed. Charlie Chingo said his hellos. Us Applebridge Hall lot sat on the left, the Baron and his son on the other side. What saddos, just the two of them, sitting there alone with their egos.

'Sure you don't want to sit like a sandwich in between us, little lady?' the Baron shouted over to me.

While I shook my head and cringed, Edward's face kind of scrunched up—a bit like he had the night Nick tried it on with me. Clearly, he didn't like the Baron any more in the flesh.

The sound and camera crew stood at the ready. Nervously, Jean coughed and I told her how fab her hair looked. She'd had it especially styled and I'd done her and Kathleen's nails. The temptation to bejewel them had been strong but, even though I wasn't an aristocrat-in-training any more, I couldn't face one of Lady C's disapproving dinner lady stares.

Three, two, one… Charlie introduced the show. Oh my God—we were *live* on television! This was kind of exciting—or terrifying. I couldn't decide which. Once I'd seen the coverage in the papers yesterday, I'd rung Dad with an explanation. Usually, we spoke at least once a week. He just thought I'd been busy looking for a new job. Proud, he was—said I'd been a good friend to Abbey; said it was nice to see me classily dressed up. Apparently, my brothers had hooted with laughter when they found out and put YouTube clips of my *Titanic* lawnmower antics onto their phones. Yet Dad said they both thought I had *Iron Man* nerves and threatened to duff up 'that tosser, Nick', if he ever crossed their paths.

Smile fixed on my face, I sat on the edge of my seat as Charlie chatted to the Earl and the Baron. Boring! For the hundredth time, he was asking them both what it would mean to win. Cue footage on a TV screen we could see, at the front next to Charlie, of both properties and comments from members of the public. Then various celebrities chipped in with their views.

Just as it was getting more interesting, there was a commotion outside the door. At that moment the programme went to an interval and filming stopped for five minutes. The make-up girl rushed over to Charlie, passed him a comb and powdered his nose. Quickly, Edward typed on the borrowed laptop. The door finally opened.

Uh oh—embarrassing for me or what? Looking mega tanned, it was the Honourable Mr and Mrs Richard Croxley. What the fu...dge were Abbey's mum and dad doing here?

LORD EDWARD'S E-DIARY

Saturday 15th September

7.25p.m. All too quickly, my e-diary is coming to an end. Here I am, writing this post whilst you watch the last show, 'live'. Can I just take this opprot... I mean opp*or*tunity (excuse me for typing fast before the interval ends) to thank you all for your support. It has meant everything. My heartfelt wishes extend to you all. I...

Erm, excuse me, blog-readers, there has been an unexpected turn of events. My cousin's parents...they've... Richard Croxley, he's... Well, I never...

CHAPTER 30

'Well, well, well,' said the Baron, with a smirk. 'Richard Croxley, I presume?'

'Watch it, you troublemaker!' said Abbey's dad and stepped forward. Still in holiday mode, he wore three-quarter length trousers and his balding head shone bright red.

'Richard?' Unsteadily, the Earl got to his feet. 'What's all this about?'

The two brothers looked at each other.

'James…old boy… It's been a long time.'

Richard scowled at the Baron and wow! Talk about a family likeness—for one second he looked just like Edward!

'That rogue contacted me…' continued Abbey's dad '…said he intends to reveal something live on air about… you and me. The whole story.'

The Earl's cheeks flushed purple. Blimey—more revelations? Really?

'We're about to go live on television again in a few minutes,' said Edward, on his feet now, hand on his dad's arm. He, the Earl and Richard stood together on our side of the room. 'Whatever it is, Baron,' hissed Edward, 'is this really necessary? Do the decent thing, man.'

But the Baron was whispering into Gaynor's ear. Like ink drops in water, her pupils spread wide. In turn, she muttered something to Charlie. Less subtle, he gave a long whistle. Like dominoes falling, now it was Lady C's turn— she sucked in her cheeks as her tanned sister, greying hair swept up Princess Anne style, filled her in on the secret. Meanwhile, Gaynor had an excited word with Roxy, whose jaw dropped before she skedaddled out of the room for a moment.

'Ten seconds to go,' said Gaynor.

'Don't do this,' said Richard to the Baron.

Harry sneered. 'What's the matter, buddy? Worried the public might realize your family ain't so picture perfect? We know what you lot think to me and Pops, looking down your noses. But at least we haven't misled our fans. With us, what you see is what you get. It's time you lot dropped this wholesome Walton family charade.'

'Three, two, one, action,' said Gaynor.

'Ladies and gentlemen,' said Charlie to the camera. 'Get dialling those numbers—there's one hour left to get your votes in… And, to help you make up your minds, perhaps, here's something unexpected. Out of the blue, the Earl of Croxley's brother has arrived. The Honourable Richard Croxley and his lovely wife have been away on a cruise and, undoubtedly, knew nothing about their daughter's involvement—or not—in this show.'

One of the cameras zoomed in on Richard's face. His wife was sitting next to Lady C.

'A friend alerted us to this matter when we returned from our trip, two days ago.' Abbey's dad said and sighed. 'I can only apologise for my daughter putting you in this impossible situation, Gemma. And we've had words with Rupert for not giving us the heads-up. We had no idea. But you did a sterling job. Well done. We've watched most the episodes on catch-up. It was quite a marathon.'

'Oh, um… Ta,' I stuttered.

'But, as for Abigail…' said Richard and ran a hand over his bald head. 'We can't understand why she would let us—and the family—down. I suppose the situation in Africa couldn't wait…'

'She wanted to tell you,' I mumbled.

He leant on a nearby chair. 'I've thought it over and…well…since watching the footage of that evacuee reunion—how having somewhere safe to stay with responsible adults changed children's lives… It made me think… Perhaps I misjudged young Zachary. It's shaken us, to be honest, that Abigail would go to such lengths to help him, and I can't say I'm not worried about her safety, but I'm also...immensely proud.'

'Abigail's a good girl, Richard,' said Lady C.

He nodded and glanced sideways at the Earl. 'I reckon Mama would have been proud of her as well.'

'She wanted to do the right thing,' I said. 'It was urgent. She asked if I'd help out. And Lady C… Lady Constance… has been amazin'—really supportive.'

'You knew about this, Connie?' asked her sister.

Oops—foot in mouth again. I'd forgotten that this fact hadn't come to light in my interview with Charlie.

Lady C blushed. 'Yes. I… know what it's like to spend your life as a spinster, dreaming about the past. I wouldn't want that for anyone, least of all my darling niece, Abigail. She's happy with Zak and I'll do everything I can to protect that.'

'This is all very heartening, folks,' said the Baron with a snort. 'But how about we get to the real reason I rang the Earl's brother, to say he should be here.' He stood up. 'Tell us, Richard, mate… You Croxleys are such a proud bunch, mouthing off about the importance of family values.

So how come you ain't seen your brother since you lasted visited the estate, ooh, fourteen years ago?'

'My, my, Nick *has* been busy,' said Edward and his top lip curled. He couldn't take his eyes off Richard, though.

'You two brothers have been estranged for years,' continued the Baron. 'Thirty-two exactly.'

'Since Edward was born,' Harry chipped in and sniggered. 'Funny coincidence, that.'

'Stop filming,' said the Earl.

'You aren't serious?' said Charlie. 'Surely you can see, Lord Croxley, the public would find that highly suspicious. It would leave them feeling you had something to hide.'

'Which you have!' said the Baron and clapped his hands. 'Let's cut to the chase: admit it. Edward is Richard's son—not yours. That's at the root of your fall-out.'

What the…? How…? The Earl sat back down and suddenly looked even older, like a wizened centenarian.

Richard? Edward's dad? Nah, that didn't make sense—yet there was no angry reaction or laughter at such an idea. Edward didn't even flinch.

'Edward is illegitimate,' said Harry. 'He shouldn't even inherit Applebridge Hall. The Earl's younger brother, Richard, is officially the next in line—and then his son Rupert, I presume. The Croxley remit for winning this show is based on nothing but tall stories.'

'How did Nick find out?' said Edward quietly.

'You don't deny it?' said Charlie.

'No. All these years, I've lived with this lie.' Edward's cheeks flushed. 'It's not been easy—don't ever think that, viewers. But I…we—tried to do the best for our ancestors.'

My mouth parched and my heart raced. Really… I mean, *really*? All this time Edward had lied? What a hypocrite! How could he give me such a hard time for my two weeks of pretending I was someone else, when he'd done that all his life?

And yet, thinking back to Edward, head in hands, in the library, and to his reaction to comments about thoroughbred Croxleys and him wishing he could be more forthright… Plus moments when he'd seemed to want to say something important to me—all of this made sense now and pointed to a mega tortured soul. A mega tortured soul who treasured honesty above everything, yet was expected to tell porkies about himself.

I caught Kathleen's concerned eyes. She didn't look surprised. But then the loyal cook had previously hinted that Edward had deception in his life. She must have known.

'Nick got suspicious when looking into Abigail's history,' said Harry. 'People in the village never remembered seeing her here before. And Gemma and Abigail's neighbour, Chelsea, once overheard something about a long-running Croxley feud.'

'So Nick asked around,' said the Baron. 'Eventually, he tracked down a housekeeper who'd worked at Applebridge Hall in the eighties. She spoke of how well the two brothers seemed to get on until Edward was born. Apparently the Countess—'

'Stop,' said the Earl in a croaky voice. 'That's enough. Don't bring my wife into this.'

'Your wife was much younger than you when you got married, wasn't she?' said the Baron. 'Twenty-three to your forty-two. You naughty boy…'

'Don't use that filthy tone with regard to any member of my family,' spat Edward.

'Ooh, I could talk all night about your ma, if you wish.' The Baron's eyes narrowed. 'I don't *do* losing—I do whatever it takes to win. Nick tracked down several more former employees. Like a gardener who once heard the Countess sobbing by the pond, a few weeks after she moved into Applebridge Hall…'

'The Countess was an incredibly special woman,' said the Earl finally, 'and…' he glanced at his brother '…I should have appreciated her more when we first got together. But…'

'This all happened just after Papa died,' murmured Richard and shot the Earl a sympathetic glance. 'Applebridge Hall was in crisis, with major electric and plumbing issues as well as a few surprise debts of our father's to clear. After a few whiskies one night, you let slip that you didn't think we'd make it through the winter, financially. It was all on your shoulders, James. The next day you joked that it was the alcohol exaggerating the situation.' His voice broke. 'I should have been more help.'

'It was my responsibility,' said the Earl. 'And Rosemary bore the brunt of my black moods. Papa's death came just after I'd proposed to her. I…I've thought about it a lot, over the years. How I closed in on myself and hardly spent any time with her, for those few months. She'd moved away from her parents. Richard, you were practically the only friend she had. You were both the same age…'

'I never planned… It was just one night, James. Unforgivable. I… was smitten with Rosemary from the moment you introduced her, however much I tried to fight my feelings and keep my distance, spending time away from Applebridge Hall. But one evening I found her alone and crying. We talked for hours. I tried to cheer her up.' He shrugged. 'One thing led to another and we both hated ourselves, afterwards. We wanted to tell you and I kept away as much as I could.'

'I assumed your absences from our home were because I took everything on and wouldn't let you help,' said the Earl. 'I knew how passionate you were about catering and Dad always wanted you to follow your dream. I just thought it was your business dealings that kept you away so much. It made sense for Edward to inherit—you'd hinted often enough that you wouldn't have wanted to be in my position, as heir.'

'I would have given up all my plans in an instant if I'd really understood what pressure you were under,' said Richard, eyes all shiny. 'I just assumed you were overcome with grief for our father. But you're right—I never felt like you did about Applebridge Hall.' He gave a wry smile. 'The irony is, Rupert is the exact opposite to me and would do anything to run a place like the Hall. Guess genes will out eventually…'

'What happened when you found out the Countess was pregnant?' Charlie asked the Earl, as everyone listened for the reply in absolute silence.

The Earl cleared his throat, stood up and paced the room. 'I was unable to have children. Rosemary knew this before I proposed. It made no difference to her. That's the sort of woman she was, so…' He stared into space for a moment.

'So, we came to an agreement,' said Richard. 'I'd leave once and for all and never return. James would bring the baby up as his own. It… It suited us both, although… It's been more than hard, not knowing Edward—my son.'

'So, Lord Edward,' said Harry sarcastically, 'you're not really an aristocrat with rights to a fancy mansion at all. You're nothing but a bastard.'

I snorted and opened my mouth to hurl insults back, but Edward caught my eye and gave a shake of his head.

'You think titles, big houses mean anything to me?' he then said to Harry. 'I've always known the circumstances of my birth and my parents...' Edward glanced at Richard '... *all* of them, did what they thought was best for me. I'd sacrifice everything to protect the Hall but that's because it's where my ancestors were born, grew up and died. I may not be the direct heir, but I'm still a Croxley.'

'That one last time I visited,' said Richard, 'Rosemary told me how very happy she was with James.' He glanced at his wife. 'The Countess and I both agreed how happy we were, in the end. I thank God daily for the day I met my wonderful wife.'

The Earl cleared his throat. 'I never forgave myself for the way I treated Rosemary in those early months. I made it my life's work to make it up to her.'

'Och, never a day passed without the Countess humming,' said Kathleen, cheeks flushed bright pink.

'She always spoke of you in the highest terms,' said Mr Thompson gruffly.

'Abbey hoped this show might bring you two brothers together,' I said.

'How touching,' said the Baron and sniggered with Harry.

But Richard was looking into the Earl's eyes, then slipped his arm around his older brother's shoulders. A lump swelled in my throat. Finally, Richard pulled away and turned to Edward.

'I'm sorry—about all of this, young man. Maybe now... Perhaps we can... I'd like to be part of your life, Edward.'

'Let's not get carried away with sentimentality,' said the Baron and stared into the nearest camera. 'Despite all that guff on their stupid blog about being honest, remember, you voters, the Croxleys are nothing special—their family history is just as full of secrets and tacky scandal as anyone else's.'

'Absolutely correct,' said Edward. 'That's the point. We're just trying to save our home, like anyone else would. We've never held ourselves up as perfect... Not a day has passed, in my life, without hating the deception—people treating me like someone special as the heir to Applebridge. I guess...' he glanced across at me '...it's made me judge harshly others who lie. I've been forced into deceiving everyone I meet. It's hard to understand why anyone would choose that type of life—even for a short time.'

'I'm sorry to have burdened you with that responsibility,' mumbled the Earl, a tear hanging from the corner of one of his eyes.

'Don't ever apologize to me over this,' said Edward firmly. 'The Croxley family means everything to me. I'd die to protect our name.'

Richard shrugged. 'We're no different from *Million Dollar Mansion*'s viewers. We all have skeletons in our closet...' his eyes twinkled '...apart from the one our grandfather's cousin buried under the maze.'

The Earl's face brightened. 'Bless me, Dickie, I'd forgotten that story.'

Charlie Chingo raised his eyebrows.

'Just before our father died, part of the foliage died in the middle,' the Earl continued. 'The gardeners dug it up and stumbled across human bones. Then Papa recalled a tale from his childhood, about Grandfather's cousin, Ned, accidentally killing a love rival in a fight after a party. Apparently, Ned buried the body in the middle of the maze. Grandfather didn't tell anyone about it until the day he died, and at that point people just thought it was the morphine talking.'

'So, there you have it,' said Charlie, as Gaynor glared at him and made various animated hand movements. 'Viewers—you have a lot to think about as we go to an interval. But, before we do...' He glanced at Gaynor, who was nodding frantically. 'We just have time to screen some rather special footage. No one else has seen it, apart from me and the editing crew... We couldn't manage a live satellite link, but our contacts managed to track Abigail Croxley down in Africa and shoot this earlier today...'

Everyone in the room gasped. I leant forward and stared at the screen. It flickered for a moment, there was some crackling and... I clapped my hands! Perspiration on her brow, yet hair tidily tied back and in smart khaki trousers and matching shirt, there stood Abbey in a barren field, sun beating down.

'Hello, everyone...' she said nervously. 'To my surprise, yesterday, a journalist appeared at the orphanage to fill me in on what's going on.' Her voice wavered. 'First and foremost, I beg of you, British public, don't blame my dear friend Gemma for her deception. She stepped in to help after much persuasion. Her good heart saved the day and meant I could have a shot at saving both the African orphans and my family home. Plus...' her eyes glistened '... have a chance at reuniting my father and uncle...'

'Emotional poppycock!' boomed the Baron.

Oh, Abbey. How I wished she was here. I could hug her tight—tell her that everything between her dad and the Earl had turned out all right.

'And Edward...' she continued; Edward sat more upright '... I know you did try to contact me and Rupert over the years... I'm sorry we weren't in a position to reply. One day getting to know my cousin... It's always been something at the back of my mind and turning down this opportunity wasn't easy.' Her face broke into a smile. 'Just let me say, I am hugely thrilled to have another brother, instead. I can't wait to get to know you now.'

Oh my God. Of course. Abbey was the half-sister he'd hardly ever met, both of them having green specks in their blue eyes. He must have been doubly disappointed when my true identity was revealed. What with Rupe, now Edward was one of three siblings and not on his own.

Edward's face flushed and softened. For one second he looked like a little boy who'd just been handed back a lost toy.

'As for my parents,' continued Abbey, 'I'm told they are back from their cruise and there, at the final. Please, both of you…' she stepped forward to the camera '…try to forgive my lies. But Zak means everything to me. In fact, I think I might stay out here longer than expected. Daily, the number of orphans grows. But I'll be back for Christmas. Why don't we…oh, I don't know…have a big family reunion? Baubels and tinsel, fruitcake and turkey—these are all things the Croxleys can at last enjoy together, in the same room.'

The screen flickered.

'Must dash,' she said. 'Best of British. I miss you all awfully. Gemma, I'll write soon! And stiff upper lip, everyone—even if we don't win the money, we've done our very best. The ancestors couldn't ask for more.'

The screen went blank.

'Sentimental rubbish!' boomed the Baron again. 'Baubels and tinsel?' He shook his head. 'Vote with your heads, viewers,' he yelled at the camera. 'I wouldn't trust these Croxleys with a cent, let alone a million dollars! Don't be swayed by the promise of Christmas sparkle.'

But everyone ignored him and his son. As the interval began, the room was silent for a moment and then filled with chatter. However, Edward sat down quietly to one side while Roxy got us drinks. Much as I wanted to go over, Richard beat me to it. Then the Earl joined them and the three men talked quietly. Eventually, Edward gave them both man-hugs. The Croxley men showing such emotion? My throat ached—by now I understood just how much that meant.

During the forty-five minutes off-screen, I chatted with Abbey's mum. She wanted to know everything about the African trip and couldn't help giggling as Lady C and I described my crash course in how to be a lady.

'It's time for the result, folks,' said Charlie, after what seemed like just a few seconds. 'Everyone into position.'

The make-up girl busied herself with her powder and brushes.

'Three, two, one, action!' said Gaynor, as I crossed my fingers.

'Rightie!' said Charlie, to the camera. 'Here it is—the result of *Million Dollar Mansion*. Viewers, you've been voting in your thousands. The lines closed ten minutes ago. The result has been checked and verified. Please don't ring the numbers any more as your vote won't be counted but you may still be charged.' He grinned around the room and waved a card. 'So—who has the Great British Public voted to be worthy of this enormous amount of money? Baron? You'll spend it on converting Marwick Castle into a top-notch hotel?'

'Yes, siree. Babes, beers and banquets. Marwick Castle will gain a worldwide reputation for twenty-first century fun in a medieval setting.'

'And Applebridge Hall?' said Charlie in a softer voice.

'The Applebridge Food Academy shall be our pride and joy,' said Edward, eyes bright and forehead lines disappeared. 'Once outstanding repairs have been done, the prize money would be invested and give future generations the chance to safeguard everything we cherish about our home—the burial ground of our ancestors; the antiquities paying tribute to everyone who has ever entered its doors— aristocratic or not. People residing with us at the Academy will be given a tour, so that they too can share our history. Plus, ultimately, we'd like to strengthen our links with the village and, as in years gone by, recruit more staff from the local population.'

'Here we go, then,' said Charlie. 'It's been neck and neck since Thursday but, within the last hour, a distinct winner has emerged.'

The Baron and Harry high-fived each other. I was going to be sick. Please, don't let it be Marwick Castle.

'The winner of *Million Dollar Mansion* is…'

Urgh. Trust Charlie to do a long *X-Factor* pause. Come on! Come on! I couldn't wait any longer!

'…Applebridge Hall,' said Charlie and gave a big grin.

Oh my God…I was going to faint!

'There's got to be some sort of mistake,' boomed the Baron, looking as if he'd just eaten one of my chilli strawberries or mustard pineapples. 'Why would anyone vote for some boring old fart and a moronic cookery school?'

'Tell us, Lord Croxley,' said Charlie, 'how are you feeling at this precise moment?'

'I…' His voice cracked. 'Rosemary would have been so very proud.' He turned to the camera. 'Enormous thanks to everyone. Every last penny of this prize will go towards making sure Applebridge Hall remains a going concern and to spreading the wealth into the local community. But, more than that—this programme has brought my family back together and there's no price on that. We are eternally grateful.'

The door slammed. The Baron of Marwick and Harry had gone. So much for their losers' interview. Then Edward stood up and left too.

'Hey, folks, don't anyone else desert us!' Charlie grinned. 'Richard—tell us how you, Abigail and Rupert can help your brother run the Food Academy, now that you are on board.'

Lady C gazed at me whilst the interview continued. Eyes glistening, she nodded. I nodded back. We smiled. Then, subtly, I crept out of the room. Edward had sunk to the floor, back up against the wall.

'You all right?' I said and sniffed, throat still feeling all lumpy. 'What are you doing? Shouldn't you go back in there and celebrate?'

'I…need to clear my head. Look, Gemma…' He stretched out his arm and pulled me down to the floor. 'Can you ever forgive me for chastising your deception when I've had to fool people for years? It was just such a shock. In one fell swoop I lost my sister and the… the beautiful, funny, red-haired, supposedly honest girl I was getting to know.'

'But I am honest, Edward—over feelings and important stuff. Pretending to be someone else was on the surface—it was all for the show.' I sniffed again and he passed me a hanky. 'I'm sorry you were on your own as a kid.'

'Don't be—for the most part, I had a wonderful childhood. I never stopped dreaming about meeting my half-siblings, though.' He smiled. 'Sounds like Rupert will be perfect for eventually looking after Applebridge Hall.'

I nodded.

His voice cracked. 'Living a lie was stressful enough but, you know, there's been something else even more difficult.'

I raised my eyebrows.

'Telling you our relationship was just a bit of fun. I thought it best; was still in shock. But it killed me to hurt you.' He smiled. 'You know, I felt a strong connection with you, right from the start when you were disguised as Abbey. I put it down to a DNA bond with my supposed half-sister…'

I dabbed my eyes. 'So…you really aren't the heir with some fancy title?'

He shook his head. 'No, Richard will inherit and then his legitimate son. But I'll help Father run things as long as I'm needed. Rupert is still young.'

Butterflies stirred in my stomach. 'So, doesn't that make us well-suited? I'm just a waitress although, after the last fortnight, I quite fancy doing a catering course—"chef" might one day be my title.'

He turned to face me. 'You'd be suited to be the Queen of England, Gemma. Please accept my apology for the things I said. I meant every word about you being the soundtrack to my movie… Can you ever forgive me?'

My heart beat quickly and I felt my face crease into a broad grin. I handed back the handkerchief. Then I leant forward and our lips met. Cue popping candy, of course— from my ears to my toes.

'I'm not sure,' I mumbled eventually. 'I was only ever after you for fancy clothes and jewels.'

He took my hands, cheeks flushed, tones gentle. 'Right now, I'm holding the most beautiful, precious "Gem" in the world.' He kissed me again.

We stared at each other and he tucked a ringlet of hair behind my ear. Then he jumped to his feet and pulled me up. 'Come on!' We ran along the corridor.

'What about the show?' I asked.

'There's something very important I've been dying to do for a few days.'

We went downstairs in the lift, passed the swanky marble reception desk and out of the swing doors. Edward called over the limo and we got in the back.

'Edward! Tell me immediately!' I said and giggled. 'Where are we going?'

'It's no good.' He beamed, looking more boyish than ever. 'I've fought it, but ever since you took me to BestBurger, I've been craving another of their cheeseburgers with potato wedges. And don't mention the toffee ice cream swirls.'

'Are you serious?'

'I wouldn't lie to you,' he said softly. 'Never again.'

'Ditto.'

'Perhaps we could serve burgers at this Christmas reunion Abbey mentioned,' he said, eyes twinkling.

'Hmm, sounds perfect—and mistletoe would make the perfect garnish.' I leaned in for another amazin' kiss.

Finally, I drew away for breath and he explained to the chauffeur which route to take.

Uh oh, I spotted a button on the car's ceiling. Adrenaline rush. I pushed it hard.

'Ever stuck your head out of the sun-roof,when the car's at full speed and felt the wind rush through your hair?' I whispered.

Edward grinned and rolled up his sleeves. 'No—but I've a feeling I'm about to.'

EPILOGUE

Close to Abbey, I stood in the Drake Diner as we ogled the towering Christmas tree. Nothing could be more different from the pop-up white one I'd grown up with. A mixture of decorations hung from its branches—new sets of sparkly red baubles and pimped-up pretend robins. Glittery tinsel filled in the gaps, along with twinkling fairy lights.

I pointed to a small wooden Virgin Mary. 'Apparently, that one's been in the Croxley family for almost a hundred years.'

'Uncle James said they've found a lot of old keepsakes since clearing the evacuee dorms out, these last few weeks,' said Abbey. As a new Christmas song sounded out, she swayed from side to side in her floor-length sequinned chocolate gown. 'I do so love the festive season—all that decking the halls with holly and listening to cattle low…'

'Cattle?' I grinned. 'No, that's Charlie Chingo. Mega unenthusiastic, I was, on hearing that his eighties band was reuniting for the party. But Gaynor insisted it would make amazin' footage for this Christmas Special.' I shook my head. 'It was a fab idea of yours to have this festive reunion, but the whole concept's snowballed. The TV company's become obsessed with our viewing figures beating *Downton Abbey*'s one-off Christmas episode.'

Abbey smiled. 'I happen to think Mr Chingo is doing a terrific job.'

We both turned around. At the far side of the Drake Diner, near the kitchens, was a wicked buffet. The Croxleys had hired caterers so that Kathleen could also enjoy the fun. Next to that, near the windows backing onto the garden, stood 'Sheer Velvet' with their guitars and mics. The modern romantic band headed by Charlie had reunited following his success presenting *Million Dollar Mansion*.

'Just look at those tight trousers and that unbuttoned white shirt with its flared cuffs!' I said to Abbey and giggled. Charlie had as much hair on his chest as his head. Clipboard in her hand, Roxy stood not far away from him, speaking to a cameraman. I waved and she gave me the thumbs-up. In front of the band was the dance floor and, nearer to us, tables and chairs.

'At least the band has stuck to covering Christmas songs,' she said and we watched various couples dance. Jean and Mr Thompson, Annabel and Ernest and Reverend White with a woman wearing a multicoloured knitted A-line dress—*Knityourownmansion*, of course! Having had an animated chat with Edward about poetry and booze, *Drunkwriter* and *Cupcakesrock* smooched. Edward was still writing his blog, to keep 'those jolly decent voters' up-to-date with how the prize money was being spent.

I waved to a rosy-cheeked Kathleen, dancing with Dennis Smith. Next to them swayed former evacuees Gerry Green and Linda Sloggit. Since the end of filming in September, I'd helped Kathleen turn all the unused rooms off the Long Gallery into more guest accommodation. They'd be useful tonight and from January, when the Applebridge Food Academy became residential. In just three months the number of bookings had soared. Happy bunnies, the Earl and Edward were becoming, about the possible future for their home. Lady C and 'James' had even decided to start running bird-watching tours, followed by dinner, in the New Year.

'Where's Henrietta?' I asked Abbey.

She pointed to a distant table to the left.

'Ah, yes, talking to *Historybuff*.' I grinned. 'Or, rather, "Colin"—I'll never get used to those bloggers' real names.'

We headed over, just as their converstion finished. Henrietta stood up. Us three girls linked arms and then navigated tables and dancers to finally reach the buffet table. Mmm, turkey tartlets, sage and onion sausages, mini mince pies and sherry trifle... In the old days I would have stuffed myself stupid but, like it or not, I still imagined being monitored by Lady C's fierce dinner lady stare.

'Hey, beautiful,' muttered a voice behind me. 'Have I told you how much I love those leather trousers and that silk halter top?'

I swung around. Mmm, popping candy sensations as Edward's teasing eyes gazed into mine. No one compared to my lovemuffin, with his broad shoulders and honey curls, all wrapped up in a Rat Pack cool tux and dickie bow. It had been fab living at Applebridge Hall since the final to help the Croxleys with the Food Academy.

He bent down and kissed me on the cheek. Ooh, I was honoured—a show of emotion in public!

'Robert and I will commence the charity tombola in a second,' he said.

Shame, I thought, and glanced towards the windows. Flakes of snow now tumbled from the black sky. A romantic stroll under the moonlight would have been well cool—um, probably literally as well. Perhaps tomorrow I'd wake up to a white Christmas Eve.

'Mince pie, Edward?' said Abbey. 'I hear there's a, um, booby prize in the tombola. Are you going to draw the tickets soon?'

With a grin he took a plate. 'Thanks, little sister.'

Their eyes crinkled at each other and, shyly, Abbey punched his arm, 'Don't you start—I've had that from Rupert ever since he grew taller than me when he hit fourteen.'

Edward's eyes shone.

All tanned and smiley, Abbey had only been back from Africa for a fortnight but immediately Edward had invited her to stay. More than once they'd chatted long into the night. Then last week Rupert arrived when his autumn uni term came to an end.

'Right, yes, there, erm, is a booby prize,' said Edward. 'I'll draw that out last. And Richard should pull out the other tickets, seeing as it was his idea to raise money for Zak's African charity. Where is the old boy?'

'By the windows,' said Henrietta, 'with James and Constance. The last time I walked past, Zak was telling them all about Rwandan birdlife.'

If fact I only had time for two small sausages before the tombola got underway. The cameras didn't take long to get into position; Roxy stopped the band and Gaynor cleared the dance floor.

'Thank you, friends—and family,' said Edward, 'for joining us to celebrate a new era for Applebridge Hall. Everyone here played an important part in supporting our quest to win *Million Dollar Mansion*.' His voice wavered. 'I like to think our ancestors are watching over these proceedings and believe we've all done them proud. Remember—you are welcome to return any time...' He smiled. 'But please, give us due warning, as Mr Thompson doesn't take kindly to potential intruders…'

A chuckle reverberated around the room and the estate manager—who'd actually taken off his Sherlock Holmes hat—gave a gruff smile.

Richard patted Edward's arm. 'Shall we get this show on the road, son?'

Edward nodded and glanced at the Earl, who grinned and came forward to roll the tombola barrel.

'Right, third prize…a limited edition set of knitted Croxley family members goes to…' Richard pulled out a ticket.

Blushing, *Knityourownmansion* straightened. Her website had really taken off and Edward and I agreed the set of figures was a brill fun prize.

'Irene Cooper,' said Richard.

Oh my God—the evacuee who used to take the little knitted elephant to bed every night, during the war. She beamed as she collected the figures, holding them tight as if they were made from spun gold.

'Second prize—a popular one with the ladies,' said Richard. 'Lunch out in the company of Lieutenant Robert Mayhew…'

I caught Henrietta's eye and she grinned, having convinced her fiancé to put himself forward.'

'And the winner is… Miss Diamond.'

Oh, dear. Poor Robert! But then, if anyone could bring out the accountant's human side it was a dashing war hero!

'And first prize…' Richard smiled towards the buffet table at Kathleen '… was put together by the wonderful Croxley cook. A hamper of festive Scottish delights— all home-made, of course—plus a bottle of the finest champagne from my brother's wine cellar.'

Everyone held their breath as the ticket was pulled.

'And the winner is…Dennis Smith!'

Applause wafted around the room. Dennis shook hands with Richard, a mega big smile on his face. Only recently we'd found out he was divorced. Lots in common with the Croxley's cook, he had—like yummy nosh, Elvis and being outspoken. Naughty Kathleen—I suspected a wee romance! There were almost ten years between me and Edward, but Dennis Smith was practically old enough to be my Scottish pal's dad!

Charlie's band started up again, the tombola barrel was moved and the lights dimmed. Fairly lights from the tree gave a magical touch to the party. Robert strode onto the dance floor with Henrietta, a scarf of red tinsel around his neck. The smell of mulled wine wafted past.

Suddenly feeling hot in the stuffy room, wearing my leather trousers, I headed away from the cameras, for the patio doors. Thank goodness they were unlocked. A moment under tumbling flakes of ice would soon stop me feeling flushed. Once outside, I stared left at the maze and into the darkness, up the hill.

Playing hide-and-seek with Edward… Drying off up there, after our swim—what mint memories. And nowadays Edward looked truly content. Since no longer being in line to inherit the estate, his commitment somehow appeared stronger than ever—except minus the dull eyes and sagging shoulders. In fact belly laughs and non-stop chat had filled the library yesterday, when he and Rupert mulled over long-term plans for the family pad.

I sighed. The last three months had also been wicked cos I'd learnt loads from Kathleen and Dennis Smith's granddaughter who had, after all, been called in to help.

'Running Granddad's restaurant in the South of France was a dream come true,' she'd recently said. 'Honestly, Gemma—you should go travelling like I did. Taste dishes where they originated from. Learn your cooking skills from locals. Then there's college to train you further, if needs be, when you get home.' She'd shrugged. 'I've loads of contacts abroad who'd be happy to put you up. You could work your way from country to country, washing up in kitchens and serving in bars.'

As the patio doors creaked behind me, I realized more than ever that cookery was my future. Lady C always said goals were important and, thanks to *Million Dollar Mansion*, I'd discovered my aspirations.

I turned around. 'Edward!'

He smiled, leaned forward and kissed me tenderly on the lips. When he stood back, snowflakes glistened in his hair. He pulled a Christmas-wrapped object from his pocket.

'You won the booby prize, Gemma,' he said, mouth upturned, eyes dancing with humour as he put it into my hands.

Just my luck! 'That sounds like a fix to me.' I grinned. 'Is Abbey in on this?'

He smiled and held his breath whilst I tore off the sparkly paper to reveal…a small red box.

Brow furrowed, I prised open the lid. Oh my God—there was the most exquisite diamond ring, even better than the ones on the shopping channel.

'It's been handed down through the generations,' said Edward softly. 'The last Croxley woman to wear it was my mother.'

'Wow.' My heart thumped. 'That's the most mega… awesome gem I've ever seen.'

Edward brushed a snowflake from my nose. 'No—you're the most precious Gem that ever existed.'

Thoughts whizzed around my head, banging into each other like fairground bumper cars. I looked up.

'Marry me, dearest Gemma,' he said. 'Say yes and I'll be the happiest man in the world…'

* * * *

Read on for an exclusive extract from
Samantha Tonge's new novel,

MISTLETOE MANSION.

CHAPTER ONE

Another splat of rain landed on my head and I hurried back to the car and grabbed my pink case and Christmas tree. I'd pull Jess's bike out of the hatchback later. There'd be room for it in the massive double garage. Like an evacuee from a city, I hovered in front of the cylindrically carved white pillars either side of the front door. There was a brass lion's head knocker right in the middle. On the red brick wall to the right was a fancy gold plate, saying 'Mistletoe Mansion'. My eyes ran over the classy Georgian windows and moss-free grey-slated roof.

'Come on,' I called, 'let's get in before this rain does more than spit.' On cue, thunder rolled. The car door creaked as Jess fetched her rucksack. Seconds later she stood beside me and took the keys out of her pocket.

'Maybe we should knock first,' she said and chewed her gum slower for a moment. 'I thought I saw someone at an upstairs window. That Luke might be inside.'

'Hopefully filling the fridge,' I said and realised all

I'd eaten today was that cranberry and orange cupcake. I smoothed down my hair, grasped the knocker and rapped hard. The sky was charcoal-grey now and a shiver ran down my spine. Maybe I should have rapped quietly in case some giant dog really lived here. Yet there was no barking, just the pelting of rain. I reached for the knocker once more.

At that moment, the door swung open, but no one appeared. Prompted by a small yap, Jess and I glanced to our feet.

'Aw, what's your name, buddy?' said Jess and knelt down.

You had to be joking! Who could be afraid of this tiny brown-and-white mutt? With those chocolate button eyes, it wasn't the slightest bit fearsome. In fact, it would have looked well cute in a little tartan jacket.

'Scoot, Groucho,' said a flat voice. From around the side of the door appeared the man from the photo, wearing a lumberjack checked shirt with fawn cords.

I rubbed my ear as my eyes swept over his frame. Cords and a checked shirt? That was the uniform of granddads. Except he somehow made them look fashionable, and as for his chestnut bedroom hair and half-shaven face... A frisson of something stirred in my belly. Huh? That had to be a hunger pang. I'd only just broken up with Adam. It couldn't be anything else.

I hauled my case over the doorstep and he watched me drag it into the ginormous hallway, unlike Adam, who would have insisted on carrying it for me. His almost old-fashioned manners were one of the things that had attracted me in the beginning—the way he'd always be the first to buy a round at the pub; how he'd offer to drive, if he and his workmates went out on the razz. I took in the arrogant stance of this Luke, with his hands shoved in his pockets. Would I ever meet another bloke like Adam?

'Groucho's an unusual name,' I said, as Jess followed me in. At least there wouldn't be any poop-scooping up after a Great Dane. I gazed around. Oh, my God! That staircase was amazing. You'd build up an awesome speed sliding down those banisters.

'Walter Carmichael—Mike Murphy's deceased uncle, the guy who used to own this place—he bought Groucho at the turn of the millennium, the year he gave up the evil weed,' said Luke. 'It was his idea of a joke.'

Groucho…Marx. Of course, that ancient comedian with a bushy moustache and eyebrows, and a fat cigar always between his lips… *Must love G…* So, I was right, those red scrawled notes were about the dog, but the G stood for his name, not his breed. I looked down as he cocked his head sideways. What possible harm could this Groucho cause, especially with those little grey hairs sticking out from his chin?

'Does he, um, behave himself?' I asked, as the white-tipped tail vanished around the side of the staircase.

'He's toilet-trained and doesn't bite, if that's what you mean,' said Luke, staring at the flower in my hair. 'But he's a Jack Russell—nosy, always into everyone's business.'

'You must be Luke?' said Jess and smiled as she

closed the front door. 'I'm Jess and this is Kimmy.'

She held out her hand, but he shoved his hands deeper into his trouser pockets, which irked me, as it made me focus even more on the great things about Adam I was missing.

'There's milk, eggs and bread in the fridge. Help yourselves to anything else you find. The last house-sitter quit this place in a hurry.' He smirked. 'The kitchen cupboards still have some food in them.'

I set my Christmas tree down on the laminated floor, next to a mahogany coatstand, and took a good look around. The winding staircase really was well impressive, with its oak banisters and burgundy carpet. At the top it branched out, to the left and right, past several glossed white doors with gold handles, on both sides leading around to the front of the house. On the cream walls hung brass-framed paintings—I squinted—of foxhunts and deer and fishermen. All this place needed was a tinselled pine tree much bigger than mine—it would be the perfect family home to live in during the festive season.

'Wow! Impressive,' I muttered, head back as I gazed up towards the high ceiling and a waterfall-effect crystal chandelier. Downstairs were more paintings and to the right a watercolour of Mistletoe Mansion, in the far corner, above a door—perhaps that was a loo. On the same side, near the front of the house, was an open door leading to the poshest lounge. I walked over to peek in and admired the sage green armchairs and sofa, the long oak coffee table, matching dresser and mega fireplace.

On the mantelpiece was a photo of a friendly-looking old couple.

'Mr Carmichael liked his paintings,' I said and came back into the hallway. Jess was still gazing at the chandelier.

'Yep. Murphy's already sold some of them off.' Luke stared at a portrait, to the left of the lounge door. It was of an old man, serious looking apart from a twinkle in his eyes—the man from the photo on the mantelpiece.

'That's him? The uncle?' I asked.

He nodded and then pointed to behind the staircase. 'Groucho's gone to the kitchen. The patio doors in there lead on to the back garden and there's access to the dining room, which is at the back of the lounge.'

Not really listening, I looked out of the front windows and the torrents of rain. Wind rocked the honeysuckle and the weeping willow shimmied like…like seaweed caught in a stream. Listen to me—I'd gone all high-falutin', thanks to this place. It was even more impressive than I'd expected and felt homely—kind of lived-in, not grand or imposing. Not what I'd expected for the empty house of a dead man. My chest felt lighter than it had since Adam and I split.

'What's through there?' asked Jess, looking left to a heavy mahogany door, next to a white hallway desk.

Luke consulted his watch. 'See for yourselves. I'm off.' He tugged his thumb towards the desk. 'Murphy's phone number's in an envelope on there, along with other stuff like a daily "to do" list with my phone number on, and things like how to work the boiler. Also there's the remote control to open the garage.' He grabbed a thick jacket from the coatstand and opened the front door. An earthy, musky smell of aftershave wafted my way—so different from Adam's favourite fragrance that smelt like clinical air freshener. 'Just one more thing— a couple of bedrooms are locked. Don't try to force them open.'

'As if we would!' protested Jess.

'They're full of the Carmichaels' personal stuff,' he continued. 'Murphy hasn't sold much of that yet. He won't sort through it until he has to, I reckon, when the house sells. So just keep out.'

No 'Nice to meet you' or 'Good luck, I'll pop in tomorrow to check you're OK.' Adam would have at least told us to lock the windows at night and taken us through a fire drill. Not that I needed a man to look out for me, but his attentive ways made me feel all fuzzy inside. After a childhood spent practically fending for myself, Adam's caring nature had initially dazzled me.

Whereas my initial impression of Luke was the complete opposite of considerate Adam. Whistling, the handyman upturned his collar and slammed the door as he left. Groucho appeared and after several minutes of tickling jumped up as if to say 'I'll show you the place,' but a sharp crack of thunder saw him skedaddle under the white desk. Jess picked him up and he licked her nose.

'Let's take a quick look behind that mahogany door and then find something to eat.' She turned the handle and we went in. Wow! This was the Games Room with… I couldn't believe it! Only what I could describe as a mahogany *throne* in the corner! That was it. From now on, in my head, this room would be named after my favourite show of the moment, *Game of Thrones*! I'd have to plait my hair to enter and create a cocktail called Sex in Westeros!

Polished, rich-brown panels covered the left and far side walls, with the rest painted racing green. In the middle stood a full-size billiards table and on the right was the small, but well stocked, bar. There was lager, and cola, and a professional-looking line of spirit bottles hung in front of mirrored tiles. As the mahogany door creaked shut behind us, I tiptoed across and bent over the bar. This would be perfect for Adam, I thought, gazing at the different-shaped glasses, the small sink and silver ice bucket. After a hard day at work he was often too tired to go to the pub.

Jess pointed to a dartboard at the end of the room, fighting to keep hold of Groucho, whose legs pedalled mid-air. Eventually she put him down and, yapping, he ran back to the door. 'I don't think I'm the only one who's hungry.' Jess threw her gum into a small bin.

I walked over to a window. It was almost dark now and rivers of rain down the glass warped the view. I pulled on a cord which closed the curtains.

'Picture us,' I said, 'sipping fancy drinks, eating Pringles… And getting handyman Luke answering our every beck and call.'

Jess pulled a face. 'He's hardly Lady Chatterley's lover.'

'What, our bit of rough?' I grinned. 'His manners are almost as bad as my brother's.' Tom never ate with his mouth closed and wiped his nose on his sleeve. Mum let him do what he wanted—eat pizza in bed, not tuck his shirt in for school, drink juice straight from the carton.

We went back to the hallway and I stopped by the desk, impressed at how the sound of rain resounded around the big hallway. A dog lead lay curled up, next to a bunch of letters, and I flicked through, looking for the 'to do' list Luke had talked about. A scrap of paper caught my eye and I pulled it from the pile. Scrawled across the front in red it said 'IMPORTANT! NEW HOUSESITTERS READ THIS ASAP!'

Lightning flashed again and Jess pulled the hall blinds shut. I unfolded the piece of paper—the words looked as if they'd been written in a rush. With the chandelier light now flickering, I read the note out loud:

'Leave now. Don't stay a single second. If I told you why, you wouldn't believe a word. Just trust me; this is the worst job I've ever had—especially when it's dark.'

'It's probably a joke,' shrugged Jess.

'Must be,' I said and smiled brightly, the hairs standing up on the back of my neck as I thought of Deborah chasing us, purple in the face. As if on cue, an ear-splitting clap of thunder rang out and all the lights went off. Groucho's claws, on laminate, scratched and skidded to a halt, no doubt under the desk.